MORE THINGS
IN HEAVEN AND EARTH

An author, TEDx speaker, columnist and mentor, **Kiran Manral** in previous avatars, has been a journalist, researcher, festival curator and entrepreneur. She has received multiple awards, such as the Women Achievers Award by Young Environmentalists Association and the International Women's Day Award 2018 from ICUNR and the Ministry of Women and Child Welfare, Government of India, for excellence in the field of writing.

MORE THINGS IN HEAVEN AND EARTH

KIRAN MANRAL

AMARYLLIS

AMARYLLIS

An imprint of Manjul Publishing House Pvt. Ltd.
•C-16, Sector 3, Noida, Uttar Pradesh 201301, India
Website: www.manjulindia.com
Registered Office:
• 10, Nishat Colony, Bhopal 462 003 – India

Copyright © Kiran Manral, 2021

Kiran Manral asserts the moral right to be
identified as the author of this work

ISBN 978-93-90924-08-0

Cover Design: Drawater by Mishta Roy

To Kirit.
For all those infinite road trips to Goa.
You married a writer. Everything becomes material.

'There are more things in Heaven and Earth, Horatio,
than are dreamt of in your philosophy.'

—William Shakespeare, *Hamlet*

CONTENTS

HERE, NOW

When I looked in the mirror today, I saw a stranger. Framed within the mirror's carved ornateness was a soft-faced woman, her eyes mellow and accepting, displaying none of the haunted anxiety that had once settled into them, her lips full and tremulous. Her face was rounded with comfort and eating. This was not the woman who had come here, all those months ago. That woman's face was encrusted over with rage and grief, the planes sharp and angular from an inability to eat more than a few morsels at a time, her movements jerky and disoriented, her mind clouded over. The woman staring back at me was unblinkingly confident, her expression questioning. She had found her centre. Her mid-length hair had now grown out to her waist. It fell unfettered, thick and defiant of all attempts at taming it, the humidity and salt in the air frizzing it into waves she never knew it capable of. Her eyes were calm and did not brim over with the saltiness of the soul that often any more. She was at peace. I was at peace.

Outside the window, the seasons had changed. The blaze of the tropical summer had segued into the tepidness of a late autumn. Though, to be honest, in the tropics, autumn was a wish of tepidity, every season was a variation of blazing to warm. Within the room, I had changed. My steps were heavier, my tread weighted. My body was fuller, my breasts swollen, my hips rounded. The enforced captivity within the house through the months that the monsoon clouds emptied themselves over this speck of an island had made me indolent, softened the leanness of my silhouette, deposited curves where there was lean muscle once. I had stopped resisting the change. There was a lot I had let go of when I came to this house, with its swinging, rusty iron gate, the vines growing wild over it, the moss-kissed boundary walls with the bougainvillea spilling a violent pink over them, the wide balustrades, the sweeping stairways, demanding opulence and show of the kind that I was inadequate to give. The rooms, lined up on either side of the central hallway, some still shut, some now open, contained stories I had yet to acquaint myself with. Letting my body go was the least of my concerns now, I had let my soul go too. When you finally gather the courage to release what you've been hanging on to for a while, you realise it is not just a release, but also a relief. It frees you to find something else to hold on to, something else that was also waiting to be held.

Over the past few months, this little island had been battered by the south-west monsoon, that swept into it from the vast expanses of the Indian Ocean up over the Arabian Sea. Fat raindrops splatted on the leaves in the garden, on the elephant ears fringing the front porch, forming puddles in the red mud of the compound, where the grass and the weeds hadn't taken over. The droplets washed the island in a blaze of green, before graciously giving way to the crisp heat of an indifferent autumn, where a few trees shed their leaves into a damp carpet of mulch on the ground while the rest maintained their foliage. The constant overwhelming damp and mustiness evaporated in the brazier of the sun's heat, leaving the walls stained with Rorschach patches of bottle green, emerald and pale aqua. The moss and the fungus would have to be scraped off the walls, and the latter would need a scraping and plastering, with a slick coat of whitewash until next year's deluge from the skies. I would need to oversee that now, I realised. I was a house owner. Responsibility felt strange, alien. I had always lived in places but never owned them, never put down the roots I should.

On this island, seasons came and went, lives unfurled, ebbing and flowing like the river that rushed past on either side of it and the sea that came in occasionally from the west, when the tides came in. There were the big tide days, the super tide, they called them. I'd learnt to dread these days, like the islanders, even though the house was too high up on the island to be impacted. Those living in the homes touching the water's edge packed their valuables and took themselves and all that they considered precious to the houses of friends and relatives higher up on the island, or to the church that welcomed them all, at a moment's notice. That's what a place of worship should be, I told myself, a place of refuge and shelter from the storms without and the storms within. The warm wood of the pews and the soft, melting eyes of the statue of Mother Mary, high above. I had been looking for refuge all my life, perhaps this house on this island was where I would find mine.

This was also a forgotten island. Only the old or the very young lived here. I was amongst the few stuck in limbo between childhood and death. The younger generation had left the island, going to jobs on the mainland, in other cities, in other countries, emigrating to where they would eternally be the brown-skinned interlopers, in climates so cold that they forgot how the warmth of the tropical sun felt like on skin, or to desert countries where they earned the envied status of being 'Gulfies', a nomenclature that their families back here held aloft like badges of honour, displayed in the gold on their person and the regular whitewashing of their homes. This was an island of the old, the lines on their faces sandpapered by the sun into a coarseness of decay, waiting for life to play out with unfailing regularity every single day. The island was deserted by the young but they visited from time to time. The old waited for them, and for death.

This was also an island of the new people, people who hadn't been born here, who hadn't grown up here, who knew nothing of the rise and the fall of the tides and the sweep of the sun across the sky as the months passed. They brought with them money, they bought up land and crumbling old homes, doing them up with the help of city architects who brought with them city sensibilities, unwarranted noise, fast cars and the decadence of luxury. I was neither. Not the old. Nor the new. I was just here, happenstance. And I had no intention of going anywhere. At least not now, not yet.

The waters were getting higher every year, they told me – global warming, a tilting of the earth's axis. Whales marooned themselves on the Konkan coastline, their internal compasses altered by the full moon. The shift in the gravitational pull and ebb of the tide, the fluctuations in the earth's magnetic field, the ice shelves breaking off into the Antarctic oceans, calving into little cities of ice set adrift to melt into the warmth of the equatorial currents, island nations declaring themselves climate change refugees, it was all crumpling upon us.

The world, beyond this canopy of green, ringed by the incoming sea and the outgoing river, was changing. Perhaps, here I would be safe from the change I didn't want to be part of. Falling off the radar was easy, I just stopped communicating with people from the outside. After a while, they stopped reaching out to me. There was solace in being left alone, a comfort I had been looking forward to for a long while, but never really found.

Here on this island, all we had was the flood line indicator on the old footbridge connecting us to the mainland on the north; it went up a notch every other year. The island was going under, slowly, imperceptibly, like the rest of humanity. But here I was, but one monsoon old, a stranger to myself, in this house with its cool patterned tiles underfoot, and the warm sun filtering through the net covering of the windows, adding a fine opacity between the self and the outdoors from within. I was insulated from the world. Or perhaps, the world was insulated from me.

The island rose resplendent from the fork in the river, between the mainland and the sea, bordered by the blue-grey of the sea in the distance. It was visible only if one strained one's eyes from a vantage point on the western side, a narrow ridge, a high cliff, and a thin stretch of beach that was more gravel than sand. Who was to say where the river ended and the sea began, water flowed into itself and the sweet became the salty, where the brine and the riverine coagulated and became the ocean, primordial churn, from the beginning of time and earth and life.

It was as different from the hill town I had grown up in as I could imagine and as similar and as insulated. You travel around the world only to come home, they say. Stay where you are and make it home. Perhaps this was home to me now. This house, with its strange curving staircases, its rows of rooms, its high ceilings from which hung elegant crystal chandeliers that tinkled gently when the wind blew in through an open window, its brick-lined pathway down an unkempt lawn to the long stairway up to the entrance porch flanked by trees and shrubs that made it seem like it was rising from a bed of green. This was home now. This house with the long cool verandah that circumvented it, held up by pillars shaded by a red-tiled awning, where the dogs lay panting when the noonday sun got too much for them. It creaked and sighed the same way that home back in the hills did, the roof here bore the brunt of rain with the same groaning protest that the roof back home did, braced itself against the drifting down of snow and the occasional pelting of hail. The family of monkeys danced damnation and ruin on the roof here too, like they did back home, bold and raucous.

Home was not in Mumbai where the tiny rented one-bedroom-hall-kitchen apartment had nothing of me, except the few motes of skin I shed while there, and some clothes I hadn't packed in my hurry. They would moulder there until I went back and retrieved them, if I ever did. My lease on the place was almost up; I would have to return, to give up the key in a few months. Delhi was not home either now, not in the high-ceilinged, marble-floored home we'd bought last year just before it all unravelled, the home I'd fled from to Mumbai, escaping memories and the ghosts accompanying them. Nor back in the mountains, where the winds howled through the gaps in the window panes, sneaking in icy tentacles that froze skin where it touched it, where the fireplace burnt with the remembered warmth of a childhood half lived. Home was perhaps just this body I inhabited and this too was alien to me at times, its folds and creases, its pains and needs. Home was everywhere and nowhere. Home, I realised now, was anywhere the heart slept in peace. Home was where one unpacked one's cares and settled them into the wardrobe with one's clothes. It was where one was complete.

Perhaps I was destined to come here, and live these days in this room, my room. Perhaps I would leave this room soon, and go elsewhere, and have it remain a ghost room in my memories. I knew it like the back of my hand, having lived in it for eight months now. This room, with its brown and beige-patterned tiled floor, the balcony with its frosted-glass window panes shuttered to a salty sea breeze that swept through the wooden slats on the top, on a never-ending mission of seeking, finding and abandoning.

I had come here on the wind, flying in on a tiny airplane filled with tourists, honeymooners, and flight attendants with expressions that could curdle milk through the plastic smiles they had slapped on. I had come packed for a couple of weeks, and stayed on in the way that vagrants do, spreading my presence, with more possessions bought, a cupboard filled and a suitcase half emptied, ready to leave at a moment's notice. That was then, this was now. The suitcase had been unpacked and kept carefully wrapped in an old bed sheet in the loft above the bathroom. The tomorrows extended into the day afters and the yesterdays, making time elastic and looped, a groundhog's every day, a newness to them all, a waiting, an anticipation and, now, the countdown. A countdown to what, I did not know yet.

'Come back. Even as a shadow,
even as a dream.'

—Euripides

ONE

HERE, THEN, EIGHT MONTHS AGO

There were eyes in the dark watching me. A mass of faces blurring into an amorphous whole. Indistinct. Fuzzy. A single, slobbering creature that would devour me if given a chance.

I would have my moment of a full-fledged panic attack now, I always did, just before I stepped on to the stage. The nerves would leap and skitter, a fist of iron would clench up my intestines, a cold clammy sweat would break out on my forehead ruining the carefully applied make-up, the breath would bunch up in my throat. And I would wait for it to pass. It would. I dreaded the day when it wouldn't and the eyes became a face and then an open craven maw to devour me. I have an overactive imagination, I've been told, I tame it occasionally. At others times, it runs loose.

The auditorium was dark, the stage lit up so bright it almost hurt the eyes. I would request them to turn the lights on, dimmed a bit if they must. I hated talking to a uniform blackness, it terrified me. Blackness was free-falling, spinning through space and time and not knowing where one would land. Often, I had landed in places where I had not known how to return from, falling through blackness that had a texture as thick as molasses and as bitter as vinegar. Luckily, I had always woken up. I was awake now. I didn't have the luxury of waking up if I fell when I was awake.

Deep breaths, one, two, three. One, two, three. Feel the breath go in and out. Calm down. It is nothing, the blackness. And now, I heard my name called. Kamla Malik. I stood up from my spot in the front row, blinking in confusion. I could hear the voice amplified by the loudspeakers, go over the standard biodata I sent out when they asked me for one. They could have been talking about a stranger.

The voice echoed off the high ceiling. 'Kamla Malik is a gender rights activist, acclaimed freelance journalist and the author of *Daughter of an Arranged Marriage*, which received much recognition for its insightful analysis into how the gender equations in an arranged marriage set the pattern for skewed gender perception amongst girls born from arranged marriages. She will be speaking to you about gender stereotypes at home and how, you, as young girls, must combat them.'

She stopped speaking and turned to look at me. She gestured to the stairs leading up to the stage. I stood up and walked towards them, step by step, disjointed, marionette-like, trying hard to dispel the anxiety from within.

One, two, three, deep breaths. The stomach was, as always, a skittering of a Lepidoptera colony, infested with the nervous ones, fluttering, battering anxiously against the soft tissue and muscle of the abdomen. I had almost reached the podium. The lady who had been speaking put her hand out and shook mine, before graciously stepping aside. As I bent lower to adjust the mike according to my height, a man rushed up to change the alignment. Giraffe, they'd called me all through college. I'd just learnt how to stand with my back straight and shoulders thrown out. A tall drink of Long Island Tea, that's what Nihar called me. There he was in the first row, in fitted jeans and a white t-shirt, his hair cropped close to his head, his eyes brown copper-gold shards in the dark, smiling at me. I blinked. He was gone. A stranger sat in his place, his eyes indecipherable in the dark, his hair a mass of curls.

I had completely forgotten the opening line to the speech I had prepared. I fished the notes out of the pocket of my kurta, having kept them there in a brief moment of uncertainty before stepping out on to the stage. The words I'd printed out blurred and swirled in front of me, my hands began shaking, an involuntary tremor I couldn't stop. Bile rose in my food pipe then subsided. I took another deep breath and began speaking in a tremulous voice.

'Do you know the girl your mother was? Do you know the girl your children will call "mother"? What are the stories from your mother's childhood that you know? What are the stories from your childhood that you will tell? Between what you know and what you tell, is where you are.'

I had rehearsed this so often in my head, yet the words came out like a brook, first hesitant, jagged and uneven and then tumbling and gushing through. I looked around. Nihar had gone. I needed to convince myself that perhaps he was really gone. After all, I had seen his dead body with my own eyes, hadn't I? I had touched his skin, cold and hard, his face devoid of expression, unrelaxed by death the way sleep lends a softness to the expression in repose. I had seen him dead.

Dead. The word had a finality that could never be erased. A heart attack, said the post-mortem report. He would have a post-mortem report; he had died under suspicious circumstances. The report, though, pegged it at something less insidious, a stopping of the heart. There had been no history of heart disease. He was barely thirty-eight, didn't smoke, didn't drink, ran every day, watched his diet, did all he could to help him live a long and healthy life. The universe does not play dice, they said. And here I was still standing, despite my fat-loaded diet, and complete lack of a fitness routine. I'd coasted by on my metabolism and my bone structure, long and lean. All angles and bony edges when I was a child, and long lines of fluidity, and softly flared curves when I'd grown up. I'd lucked out on having a body type that fashion designers designed for. Clothes hung well on me with no effort. I'd never dieted or exercised in my life, until his death. A month after he died, I pulled on a pair of shorts, a t-shirt and a pair of running shoes. I began running, I didn't know why, I didn't know how to, but I ran. I pushed muscle with my mind, exulting in the burn that would come after my body, unused to exercise, would cross a predetermined limit, relishing the tired tremble of the limbs with lactic acid build-up after I pushed too hard. The soreness of the muscles the next day, when they became sodden and unwieldy, made me realise that the body was a creature separate from the mind. I ran down narrow paths, broad avenues, around the neighbourhood park, through the promenade, feeling the sea breeze lift my hair and my spirits. Sometimes, I would feel him running next to me for the briefest of seconds, a fleeting but immediate sensation. A sudden brush of wind against my arm, and there he was, whispering into my ears. We do all sorts of strange things to exorcize our ghosts. This was mine. There was a purgatory on earth that we the living wandered into, clinging on to the memories of the person, breathing in the clothes still hanging in the closet until time gently ameliorates their fragrance, blending it into the sameness of air. Our ghosts resided there, in that closet. Few of us had the courage to shut that door, to lock it, to never peep into it again, to let the ghosts swirl within the closed confines desperate for release. We kept returning to peek into those closets in our heads, we kept letting our ghosts out.

I looked at the faces lined up ahead, as always to find that one face there that seemed to be receptive to what I was saying. If I was lucky, I would find a few scattered at different points in the audience and I would aim my entire talk at them. A young girl in the second row was looking at me and nodding, I looked directly at her and smiled as I spoke. She smiled back. I had one face to look at. I looked towards the other end of the auditorium scanning the faces, hopeful of another person

I could talk to. A young boy was looking on intently, his head a curly mop of hair that spilled to his shoulders. I smiled at him. He was startled for a moment and then he smiled back. I looked at the back, centre. That was all I needed now, one more face in the centre and the talk would go on smoothly as I spoke directly to these three. There were other faces too, faces that were closed, some on their phones, looking at their laps. I looked a little further back. I knew he would be there. He smiled at me. I smiled right back. Nihar. He would be there, he always was. His eyes undimmed from the distance, sparkling and alert, his smile quick and hesitant, lighting up his face better than any spotlight could. I kept smiling, I dared not stop and when I looked again, he was gone. The smile remained on my face. He liked to see me smiling.

I could see myself on the big screen at the other side of the stage at an angle to the podium. Straight brown hair down my back with a centre parting, a style that I'd stuck to for years just because it was convenient and no fuss, given the texture of my hair that wouldn't know the meaning of volume if it was turned up loud. I was dressed, as I always was, in a long burnt ombre silk kurta worn over fitted jeans. This had become my de facto uniform. A silk kurta or a cotton one dependent on the weather. And jeans. High heels for an event. Slippers for every day. T-shirts and jeans for every day. There was comfort in familiarity; it released one from the anxiety of planning what to wear. Nihar liked to see me wearing dresses. 'Show off your lovely long legs,' he would say. He would preen as he introduced me to folks when I wore what he had chosen for me, always slinky and sophisticated. I felt like a gauche pretender in them. He loved me to wear clothes he picked out, they were always not me, too deep at the neck, too short in length, too bright to allow me to blend in like I loved to. He loved me to stand out. I'd spent all my life trying to blend in.

The talk went off well. The questions from the audience were never-ending and there was nothing I wanted to do more than just sink into the back of the cab and get back home, to my cosy little one bedroom tucked away in a leafy by-lane in Bandra. Mumbai was barely a couple of months as a rented home, and it had already become my carapace.

The queue to get copies of the books signed shuffled along slowly, much to the chagrin of the PR manager from the publishing house that had brought out my last book, Mini. Her name suited her, I thought, as she manifested at my elbow, a bustle of furious energy in a short, fitted skirt and murderously high heels that made me wonder how she navigated the insanely uneven streets of Mumbai without breaking an ankle. Mini was always impeccably dressed, and had taken it upon herself to ensure that I stepped out for every public appearance looking impeccable myself. She was also my go-to person when I moved to Mumbai from Delhi after Nihar's death, insisting on taking me out to dinner, for drinks, to see the sights, until I finally managed to convince her that I could now be trusted to navigate the city on my own. Sometimes life gives you angels in power suits and shoulder pads when angels with wings desert you without a by your leave.

'Be quick, Kamie,' she hissed into my ear, 'We have to be at Vikram's launch in an hour.'

Vikram Singh. He was a star author of their stable, just out with a new book. I knew him, although it had been years since I'd met him. An ex-colleague. I'd dropped out of touch with him in the slow, insidious manner I'd lost contact with all the people in my life before I met Nihar. Why did I need anyone else, he said, when I had him? I only spoke to family now, Maa, Roopdi. I'd lost my friends. Perhaps I'd lost myself too and didn't know where to find myself.

I'd messaged Vikram, last, a couple of months before Nihar

died, a totally random moment of wondering what was up with him, loaded with a curious kind of surreptitiousness knowing that there was something unresolved between the two of us that had begun one drunken night after work. We'd been part of a news magazine, loafing around with more weed and alcohol at a house party after an issue had been put to bed. He'd come home with me, ostensibly to drop me home given it was late, too late for a girl to be out on the streets alone. We'd climbed up in a prescient silence to my rented little barsaati. We'd never spoken of it again, that night, where it was all a haze of bodies and sweat and orgasms that never ended. It seemed silly to take it further, after all it was unprofessional and I didn't want one night to derail a promising job by a night of lust. A couple of months later, Nihar had muscled into my life.

Vikram had replied to my message, all those years later, perfectly politely, echoing the tone of my message. Perhaps we could do coffee, he suggested. I hadn't replied. The conversation had been deleted. I wondered if he knew about Nihar's death. I wondered what he would say to that. I wondered if that offer for coffee still stood. I wondered if I would take him up on it, if it was.

It was strange that we'd never met in the years of living in the same city after I was married and would now meet in another city, albeit one that I'd made my home after I was widowed at thirty-three.

I weighed the word, speaking it without sound, feeling the mouth form it, pursing the lips with the w and contracting into a circle with the ow. Constrained into a circle of one. I kept rolling the word around in my head, on my palate, tasting it, straining it for tenacity and give, testing its hold on me. There was a certain bereftness to the word itself. But it contained, within its bereftness, a quiet power. That of survival, of tenacity, of grit. The grit was the residue of generations of hardy women who had outlived their husbands and survived, raised children, lived out their lives. Widowhood now gave women power, where once it had reduced them to outcasts. I was a widow. And widowhood had given me freedom.

How did other women come to terms with losing a husband? Did they pick up the pieces of their shattered selves and glue them back together, sealing the joints with metal to prevent them from falling apart again at the slightest whiff of remembrance, motes of a residual ghost perfume, familiar and overwhelming in a just-vacated elevator, a familiar stretch of shoulder and head in a distance, in a crowd, snatches of a song that had been playing when....

Some nights I missed what we had had, back then. The hand under my neck and the leg over mine as we slept. His weight on my body, our breaths intermingling, me breathing him in, he breathing me in. His absence went through me like a gust of cold air, raising gooseflesh on my arms, putting a dagger of ice into my abdomen. Most nights I didn't. He wasn't there but there he was. Everywhere.

Mini took my elbow when the last book was signed and the last selfie clicked. I would now be steered out politely and put into the waiting cab. I flashed a general smile in every direction and said my goodbyes, the principal of the college pressed a potted plant into my hand and a shawl, which would add to my rapidly increasing collection of shawls, acquired at most such events. I would be thankful for them when I visited home and could distribute them to assorted immediate family. Shawls always came in handy back home. Everyone wrapped themselves in shawls through most of the year, and beneath the shawls were the layers on layers of hand-knitted sweaters, socks, vests, the warmth of the hand that had knitted them seeping through the skin that wore them like a benediction.

It had been a while since I'd been home. I missed Maa. I

missed Roop, my sister, so far away in the land down under, but only a touch away on the phone, her face crackling and freeze-framing mid-sentence. I missed Pappa. I had never loved him, and he had never loved me, but what was love except the recognition that one missed the other. Did I miss Nihar? Miss was a word that couldn't quite express the hollow pit of my stomach filled with nothing but cold gusts of air where the intestines should have been, walking around with a gaping hole in my chest where my heart had been pulled out from, feeling hollow within and without. It was a missing that filled me up, an absence that was a presence, a bereavement that wasn't a release. Grief is grey and damp, a marshland of emotions that suck you in, tendrils of mist that caress you, asphyxiate you. Grieving is the journey you do alone, a penitence, a pilgrimage, an affirmation of being alive in the face of death that shadows us, every waking moment. Grief was the country I was on a pilgrimage within, searching for redemption from my grieving.

We walked towards the exit, escorted by the student volunteers. The cab came up outside the gates beyond the cobble-stoned driveway, a remnant from the days of the Raj which was when the college had been built. Above my head, the stone gargoyles looked on with their sightless eyes, surveying all that was at the distance, preparing to swoop down if required, prepared to become flesh from stone if called upon. The evening sunlight was filtering down in pale patches through the dappled tree cover that spread out magnificently over the porch. The birdsong was hushed; the valiant chirping of a few birds were all but drowned out by the sound of the traffic whizzing past on the road ahead. We reached the gates, said our goodbyes. I exhaled, the pit of panic uncoiling itself from my intestines. The cab door was opened for me, I climbed in, Mini clambered in from the other side.

I shut my eyes, put my head back against the headrest. That

wasn't so bad. Nihar came back to me and smiled at me, the lines around his eyes crumpling like the folds of the mountains when one looked down upon them from the sky. Mini looked at me and squeezed my hand. She didn't understand. It wasn't grief. It was fear.

Thirty-eight was no age to die. Thirty-eight was no age to be found dead far away from home and family, with the do-not-disturb sign hung up on the hotel door, ensuring he was truly and completely dead before they opened the door with the housekeeping key after he hadn't emerged for two days. I hadn't called him for those two days. When the call came, I knew what it would be. I curled up into bed with that guilt every night now.

I had been fast asleep when he'd left the house for his morning flight, not even opening my eyes for a goodbye, festering in anger from a fight half finished. Now I slept the broken, disturbed sleep of one all alone in an apartment, crippled with fear. I had run away to another city. Would he find me, would he come and ring the doorbell here, the flesh rotting off his body, the bones held together by visible tendons, the hair fallen off in clumps from his scalp, the jaw exposed where the skin had peeled off?

The restaurant where Vikram's launch was being held had high walls and impassive guards in black suits manning the gate. No vagrants loitered outside, and a velvet-rope barrier indicated that there was normally a queue to get in. A maelstrom of blended expensive fragrances competed with the lit scented candles as one entered. Expensive clothes and moneyed voices punctuated the air. Mini steered me quickly towards the front, a chair materialized out of thin air and I was pressed down into it. An elderly gentleman was holding forth with a voice as dry as paper and crackling in my ears like static. His hair was white and flowed down to his shoulders, his glasses were perched up on his forehead, his face was crumpled up with age and had the discontented expression of one who earnestly believed the world hadn't given him his due. His voice grated on the ears with its implied whine. He was, by the stench of self-importance that emanated from him, someone whom I should know, but didn't. I pulled out the invite from my bag and pored over it. I finally placed him, an academician who had consistently taken umbrage to my writing. A member of the Group of Small Penises, as Roop called them. 'Their Old Boy's club is what you and other women like you threaten. Allow them their bile, it just shows them for the pricks they are.' He'd had some nasty things to say about my last book, I remembered. I smiled at him when he caught my eye, I felt him startle and fumble mid-sentence.

Vikram caught my eye from the stage and smiled, his expression softening discernibly. Nihar came on silent feet and stood next to me, putting his hand on my shoulder. 'He's making puppy eyes at you,' he said. I turned to look at him and felt the blood freeze in my veins. He lifted his hand off me and disappeared, a slight haziness where he had stood lingering on the retina, like the ghost imprints one sees after staring into a bright light. I smiled back at Vikram. He'd grown into a man, I thought, noticing the years now hung on him with a fair bit of authority. The lankiness had been filled out and the uncertainty that hung over him back then had been traded in for a cloak of nonchalance. I realised, as I looked on at him, that he was that strange thing, a person familiar yet strangely unfamiliar. It unsettled me.

The discussion ended and the panellists rose to their feet. There was some hearty clapping from the audience and everyone began standing up and looking around for the waiters bearing wine and canapés, because that's what the evening had promised and that was what had tempted most of the attendees to be there.

I looked around for Mini; she had ambushed a waiter,

appropriated two glasses of white wine and was carefully making her way back to where I was with the precarious painstaking walk of someone with a track record of spilling things.

'Here,' she plonked the glass into my hand. 'Drink up. And then drink one more. It will be good for you.'

'Babe, I'm just about trusting myself with alcohol again.'

'I'm here. I'll make sure you won't have more than two glasses.'

Sometimes Nihar came to me when I had more alcohol than I could handle. Sometimes I drank too much just to see him walk into the room, sit next to me and have him hold my hand and know he was not real. At others he came to me when I was exhausted, my limbs trembling with lactic acid build-up, the endorphins pounding in my brain. A sudden whisper through my mind. Lotusface, he would whisper, running through the nooks and crannies of the memories we had created together, reliving them, altering some. He would never leave me. I went to the mediums at first, seeking them out through the shady underground of those who dabbled in the occult. The first couple of them were complete frauds, I felt nothing around them. The third woman I met recoiled with a physical shock when she took my hand.

'You were right. He's around you. Why do you need me?' she asked. 'You can talk to him yourself.'

'I don't know how to,' I'd told her. 'I can hear him but he can't hear me.'

'It will come back to you, how to talk to him,' she told me, 'If you want it bad enough. Go to where he was when he crossed over.'

I hadn't dared to. Not yet. What if what I found there scared me? What if here and there merged into a nowhere. Mini slid into the just-vacated chair next to me and elbowed me ungraciously with the firmness of one who had an agenda to complete. 'Come back. You've got a glazed-out expression and there are cameras around.'

'Would it look terribly rude if I left without meeting Vikram?' I asked. 'He's surrounded by too many people. I doubt he's going to surface for air soon.' With his tangle of curls and broad shoulders, he was cutting quite a swathe in the crowd.

'What rubbish, we have to get a picture of the two of you against the promo flex holding the book for the promotions.' All said in a single breath, a rush of words that had no full stop, no comma, no pause. She was a woman who did not need gaps between her words. I needed words between the gaps.

'Let's get it done and then we can leave.'

She took my hand and dragged me across right into the throng of people trying to get their selfies for social media along with their copies signed.

'Hey,' I said.

He looked at me, his expression inscrutable. He rose to his feet and gently pushed through the folks surrounding him and enveloped me in a bear hug. 'I'm so sorry, Kamie. I heard. How are you?' His kurta crinkled as I was squashed against him, I squeezed my eyes shut, willing the tears not to spill. 'I should have come but I didn't know what to say.'

I understood. I wouldn't have known what to say too. I mumbled something incoherently into the fabric of his kurta, silk, caressing my skin. A tear or two escaped my eyes and was quickly soaked up by the fabric. It felt comfortable being held by Vikram but the embrace had extended for far too long now and people were beginning to look on curiously. I pulled myself away slowly. 'I'm messing up your kurta.'

He laughed, a quick burst of a laugh. 'You messed me up a while ago.'

'I'm sorry,' I replied. He smelt different yet the same, it was the familiar odour of him, musky and pure, dressed up with the pretentiousness of an expensive perfume that didn't smell of him. I inhaled him. The new with the old.

I had missed the feel of a man in my arms, of being held by a man for longer than a polite social hug permitted, for when the body began arching into the other, and looking to mould into it. My body pressed into his, I felt his muscles tense up. I stepped back. When you lose a spouse, no one tells you about the other loss, the loss that the body must deal with. That of a body against a body. Of sweat, of scent, of bliss. He put a hand out and caught my wrist, it was a gesture that was involuntary, reflexive, making me catch my breath with its unstated appropriation of my body.

'You're looking thin, too thin,' he said. 'Are you on your own in Mumbai?'

The statement waited to be answered. I nodded.

'Have dinner with me tonight. We'll go someplace quiet after this?' His eyes were shining with a curious mixture of warmth and anticipation.

'It's Nihar's birthday today.'

I don't know why I said that. His face shuttered down. The silence grew uncomfortable between us. He was still holding on to my hand.

'Come home tomorrow for lunch,' I said. It came spontaneously, I couldn't explain why. What do you say to someone you haven't spoken with in years, the conversations that should have been would intrude upon the conversations that should be.

'I don't want to put you through any trouble of cooking,' he replied.

I burst out laughing.

'Vikram, if I cook, you'll probably need to be admitted to hospital for food poisoning. Don't worry, I'll order something in, let me know what you like. I'll message you my address.' He nodded, hugged me briefly and I extricated my wrist from his grasp, as the throng of people pressed into us again, eager for their two minutes with him. Mini cleared space and got her promotional photograph with us against the backdrop with the book in our hands, and I stepped back as the throng closed in again.

'Tomorrow, then, don't order, I'll bring the food,' he called over the heads of the crowd that had thickened around him, almost swallowing him up. He looked cornered, he hated people and crowds, I remembered that about him.

As I walked out, Mini hot on my heels, gulping down the last of the wine in her glass, and mine too, given I'd handed her mine as Vikram had begun to hug me, I found myself ducking down beneath a slew of selfie sticks.

'We didn't get enough pics,' Mini rued as she settled herself into the cab. 'I didn't know you knew him.' She turned to me, a question on her face which I chose to ignore. I would be home soon, and safe.

As I shut the door of the cab, I heard a familiar voice call. 'Lotusface.' Clear as a bell. My head swivelled around but before I could roll the window down and look out, the car had moved off in the early night. 'Stop the car!' I yelled. When I turned back to look there was nothing, not even a disappearing shadow to indicate that someone standing there had just turned the corner.

I thought of that voice as I fell asleep in my bed, unalleviated by the warmth of another body. No arm under my neck to support me through my wanderings in the land of dreams, no leg across my own to keep me moored in this world, to make sure I came right back into this, the land of the living.

'Lotusface.' It echoed in my dreams, that voice.

'Come to me,' he said.

I woke up shivering, dripping with sweat. Next to me, on my solitary bed, was the indent of a body, still warm. And the whispers in my head that wouldn't stop even though I was awake until I fell asleep again.

TWO

HERE, NOW

Back home the birds woke up before the dawn shaming the sun into showing itself, their chatter filtering through the cracks in the windows, down through the chimney, breaking dreams and dragging us into wakefulness. In Mumbai, the chirping birds were barely around, all we had were pigeons with their disgruntling sounds, mournful harbingers of gloom, nesting in crevices between window and wall, laying eggs, hatching them, laying them again after the hatchlings flew off. The alchemy of the sun's rays was already changing the sky from pewter to a hazy tangerine pink. Soon it would be silver white and blue in the blaze of the day. I was Here and he was There.

In my dreams, I had found myself in a cave at the bottom of a cliff face, opening up on a thin beach. I slipped in, walking on the rocky floor of the cave illuminated just that bit by moonlight and, as I went deeper, by the glowing phosphorescence from the walls. I kept walking. Distances had no meaning, the depths I descended had no measure. I descended down to where the air grew sulphurous, the smell of a distant fire burning within the depths of the caverns I was walking into growing stronger, until it became impossible for me to breathe and before me a cavernous portal, a slab of stone that had on the other side the one I wanted to speak with.

A thin, silvery stream of forgetfulness ran by my feet, water I knew I should never dip my feet into, even though they burned from the bleeding cuts I'd received walking barefoot on the sharp-edged rocks on the floor of the caves. This was water that would never let me return to the land of the living. I should have tied grass to my feet to keep them from bleeding. He was on the other side of this portal. He was watching and waiting, I knew. I called his name and waited, sitting on the sands that gleamed silver in the light of a moon that didn't shine in the darkness within the bowels of this earth. I waited for him, until I fell asleep and woke up drenched in a cold sweat. It was a dream that recurred most nights I fell asleep without the pills. I sought these dreams in the faint hope that perhaps some night I would gather the courage to cross the stream, to come face to face with him, talk to him, have him hear my voice. But the night would pass with me waiting by the stream, hearing the growling of the hounds behind the stone portal, tasting the salt of the tears my body was shedding while my soul went into the afterlife. Ghost breaths would kiss my eyelids and I would open them, the eyelashes stiff with the dried tears I had shed in my dreams.

The mirror this morning reflected a woman with haunted eyes. I splashed water on my face, dissolving the brine of the dried tears stuck on my lashes and she morphed into a woman with sad eyes. I went running every morning these days, before dawn broke over the smoggy horizon to the east. I had taken it up after Nihar died. I did absolutely no physical exercise before, content that my genetic leanness would see me through. Nihar was a runner, he ran marathons and his dream was to do the Ironman someday. I ran now, to get away from his memories.

I brushed my teeth, pulled on an old pair of tracks, a comfortable t-shirt, zipped up my hoodie and closed the door behind me. I pulled the hoodie up, hiding my face within. It was my invisibility cloak. I had come to this city because I wanted to disappear into its amorphous multitudes of people who didn't know me. I wanted to be seen only when I chose to be seen. Cities allowed you that, they took you in like quicksand and spat you out if they found you indigestible. I had slipped into my rented home, wearing this tiny one-bedroom dwelling in a tree-lined shady street in Bandra like a carapace. It was where I was hiding out until I could bear to emerge into the world again. This building was one of the few older ones, built before the century turned, home to the aging and the forgotten, their children emigrated to more prosperous countries, resuscitated every year during the Christmas season, when it was too cold to live where they were, when they longed for the warmth of the tropical sun on their skin and the flavours of their childhood on their tongues.

Once upon a time they called Bandra 'Queen of the Suburbs'. The crown was tarnished now and askew much like Bandra itself, florid and flatulent with hard living and grace gone to decay. Perhaps the suburb still was a queen, albeit one who had aged badly, the gentle grace of her youth now degenerating into a florid maelstrom of chaos, honking traffic, dug-up roads, overspilling hawkers. The by-lanes were narrow, made narrower by the parking that spilled out on to the streets and compelled the pedestrians to navigate the constrained spaces cheek by jowl with the cars, the two-wheelers and the auto rickshaws, not to mention the hawkers who encroached on every bit of road. The cafes that sprang up and disappeared in a matter of months, the evenings that converted entire stretches of roads into shopping meccas and the beautiful people who paraded themselves through its twists and turns were a country all their own, separate from the indolence of south Mumbai's old aristocracy and the brash new money that fuelled the suburbs to the north. Bandra was the intersection of both, the class and the crass. The roads had their own beauty, through the potholes, the dug-up bits permanently under repair or line laying, the cracks letting life through, a sudden green burst of grass, or the eye-stopping beauty of an untended periwinkle bursting through.

The suburb began its existence as a fishing village that was burnt down by a Portuguese sea captain, Diego da Silveira, who entered the creek in 1534 and decided that arson was in order to establish supremacy. Over the centuries, the islands would sand and bridge themselves together into what was now the financial capital of India. This would become Bandra, a suburb with a pulse all its own. Back then, it was just Vandre, Bandar, names that would morph themselves through the Shilaharas, the Chalukyas, Portuguese, the British, going back and forth through post-war treaties and being a dowry endowment. Later, it wrested free from the colonizers and wrapped itself around the idea of an independent India, finally emerging as this hybrid of coolth, the crucible of the city, the suburb with the vibe, where superstars lived in mansions they'd declared they would own when they came as strugglers to the city, making the dream of struggle come alive for the seeker, and tourists came in bus loads to wait for a glimpse of these superstars; where street fashion rubbed shoulders with high couture, and the restaurants were to be seen at rather than eaten in. It had always been a port, this suburb, earlier for sailors and fisherfolk, and now, for lost souls like me who chose to settle into its generous all-encompassing embrace and sink into a life that demanded nothing but breath and the ability to pay one's bills. I had both to give, and all I asked of it, was that it left me alone to go about my day. Day after day. Which it did.

The morning on the small lane outside the creaky gate, rusting on its hinges with the salt of the sea breeze, was still tentative and hushed. The sun was hesitant, pale yellow and apologetically watery in the east. The milk delivery boys were going about on their cycles and their two-wheelers, the newspaper delivery boys had piled up their newspapers at the gates of buildings while they went in to deliver the ones for each apartment complex. Children doomed to rise early for sports training made their way riding pillion on two-wheelers or dozing

on the front passenger seats, with sleep-addled parents driving
them to cricket, tennis, badminton or whatever it was that they
did to develop a competitive spirit in them. The walls as I ran
past them, called me with their brightly painted graffiti, unnamed
artists who had spray-painted them, faces, slogans, colours that
slowly clambered out from the greyness of the early dawn into
blazing definition as the sun climbed higher into the sky through
the day. I ran down the lanes and on to Turner Road, turning
towards Carter Road where I could run right to the end where
Khar Danda began, the fishing village with its line of fish strung
up to dry, the stench hitting one before the village did, one of
the few spots where the original Kolis who inhabited this island
still resided. I was one of the many bodies hurtling themselves
over the promenade, a camaraderie in my solitude, a kinship one
did not acknowledge with the others who ran. The body ran in
a rhythm that was all its own. My feet pounded over the paving
blocks, step before the other step, dodging stragglers, running,
running, pushing myself until the muscles began crying out for
relief, and then hit the endorphins pushing themselves through
my blood stream.

I was learning to love my morning run, it began as a
punishment I inflicted upon myself, and now, a few months
later, I was just about beginning to understand the need for
the body to move until the ground moved beneath one's feet
without one thinking about moving one's feet. I pounded away
at a steady pace, waiting. Some days, I would feel him running
next to me, his scent filling my nostrils, his voice in my head,
whispering my name. My heart would begin pounding faster,
my rational mind would tell me it was impossible, I'd seen his
dead body with my own eyes, he couldn't be next to me. I would
turn to look and see nothing beside me.

Today was not one of those days, today I ran alone. I returned
home. Biscuit, the ginger stray who had adopted me like the rest

of the building had adopted her, was mewling outside the door. I opened the door and she slid in through my legs, uncaring of right of entry and permissions to be asked. I set down a bowl of milk for her in the corner of the kitchen, and she got to work diligently while I went in for a shower. When I came out, she was gone. The box grill to the living-room window opened up to a parapet, which led to a branch from a benevolent mango tree that was just inside the compound wall. I guessed the trail of her footprints would lead from the kitchen to the side table just beside the window and, from there, escape to the outside world. How lovely it must be to come and go as one pleased. But then, whom did I have to come and go from now, except myself.

I downed my bowl of muesli and half an orange, which had slowly turned teeth-chillingly acidic from the time it had been bought. My dead phone was still in my handbag since last night. As always, I'd forgotten to charge it. The uncharged mobile was my sole act of rebellion, staying deliberately disconnected from a world that insisted on tying you to it. I would have done away with a phone altogether but there was the guilt of Maa, alone back home, stubbornly clinging on to the house, the silence echoing where once our voices did, insisting on living on her own despite the arthritic knees and the yo-yoing blood-sugar levels that needed insulin to keep her on an even keel. It helped that she had Behra, or Badri Kaka as we were constantly told to call him but never did, still with her, as old and arthritic as she was and considerably more cantankerous. I plugged the phone in and switched it on. Around twenty missed calls from Maa, ten from Roop. A slew of notifications began pinging through fast and furious. All from Maa. Then a last one from Roop, topping them off.

The gist of them all were that Maa was convinced I had now slit my wrists and overdosed on sleeping pills but Roop had tracked me down to my Twitter updates and reassured

Maa that I was alive and well, and had indeed spoken at an event which had been tweeted about so I was alive until the previous night. There was the usual laconic silence from Veer who could be counted to come to the funeral if I had indeed slit my wrists and overdosed on the sleeping pills and perform the requisite last rites. He was a charmer, he was, our adopted little brother, all wrapped in himself and trying to find himself in places so off the beaten track that one couldn't even find potable water there. Right now he was somewhere in South America. Peru, Lima, Brazil, Rio De Janeiro, the names reeled off his Insta stories without me looking them up on the map but noting that he looked happier or frailer in each and wondered about the stories between the stories that had been posted. He called himself a digital nomad, our brother, travelling with a laptop and hunting down wi-fi where he could find it. He made a living from clicking photographs of the places he travelled to, and writing travel stories for the magazines that commissioned him. This was one of the longest stints he'd been away, travelling without an agenda through South America. He hadn't come down for Nihar's funeral or to offer his condolences. Facetime had sufficed. After all the loss was mine to bear, not his.

Kanchi's feet swinging above my head still came to me in my dreams, at others she walked to me, her feet turned backwards, her sloe eyes dark with pain and begging for the redemption of retribution. Sometimes when I looked at Veer, I saw Kanchi in the blacks of his eyes, looking at me like she could read my innermost thoughts. I wondered if he had ever remembered her, the mother who had given birth to him and nursed him for those few months before he became a part of our family. A mother we didn't even have a photograph of to show him, to let him know he was the spitting copy of, in every way, except the soft tread of her feet which defied even wooden-planked floors and creaking stairs.

I gritted my teeth and called Maa. The phone rang interminably before she answered.

'You will kill me with all the tension you give me, and then you will dance on my ashes,' she began, dispensing with all pleasantries. 'Our agreement was that you will call me every night before going to sleep. Are you alright? What happened last night, your phone was switched off....'

Her voice trailed off. It was worry that was corrosive, the fear of the what if. 'I hope you're eating well and taking care of yourself?' Her voice was back to normal again. 'And stay off the alcohol. You know that. I don't need to keep reminding you. You are an adult. I hope you're not drinking again.'

I had been straight and sober for a while, I reminded her. An occasional glass of wine was all I allowed myself. The pills were with me for some nights when sleep didn't come, when I feared what I would find next to me, in my bed if I couldn't fall into a dreamless sleep.

'I wish you would let me come and stay with you for a while till you were better or you could come and stay with me. God knows this house rushes to bite me every single moment, with everyone gone, only ghosts lingering in those rooms we don't open any more, making all sorts of noises to get us to open up to them. You, Roop, Veer, all so far away. Is this why I raised three children to spend my dying days on my own with only this grinning idiot for company....'

'Are you keeping alright, Maa?'

She had shrunk into herself, this time, after Papa's passing away. She was always straight-backed and commanding, all through my childhood. Now she seemed diminished. Her hands and legs had thinned down to the bone, the hair on her head had thinned to show her scalp. She was permanently wrapped in her shawl, the prayer beads in one hand, her lips in perpetual movement in prayers that were audible to no one but her gods.

'I'm fine, what is wrong with me. I miss your father, of course....' Her voice trailed off, suddenly uncomfortable of having said the wrong thing. After all, I, her daughter, was also a new widow. We were bonded under the strangest circumstances, both having lost our husbands suddenly, and under strange circumstances. My father, in an inexplicable hit and run road accident. My husband in a sudden heart attack when he was travelling on work, to a conference in Goa.

'I miss him too. Do you need anything?'

'The only thing I need are my children next to me. I can't understand why you can't live here with me for a few months. You know pain shared is pain halved, don't you?'

I sighed. I couldn't stay with her. I couldn't take my ghosts to her. She probably had her own, the ones she didn't speak about, not when she was younger and could fight them, not now when she was much older and had given up the fight.

'Bye, Maa. I'll call you tonight, I promise.'

She sighed, a gust of wind that travelled through the airwaves of the phone instruments we both were holding, and gently tickled my eardrum. I let out a sigh of my own. All would be well with us, both of us, separated by geography, years and pain.

'Bye, beta.'

The line was disconnected, the silence accusatory. I was not a daughter who appreciated a mother's worry. But I was taking care of myself, as I had assured her. I hadn't been drunk since the last time I went on a bender a week after they'd found Nihar, his body naked in a pristinely white hotel room bed in a resort far away.

It had been a scandal. His nakedness. The hotel room. The whispers about who else could have been in the room, about how they found him. There was always an angle to debauchery that the investigating officers would zoom in on first, it made for good headlines for the newspapers. 'Start-up whiz kid found naked and dead.' He always slept naked in warm weather, I tried telling everyone who would listen, but that was too simple an explanation to be credible. A heart attack didn't warrant as much pity as the whiff of immorality.

It was a heart attack. It was a drug overdose. It was auto erotic asphyxiation. The rumours hit me, brought to me by well-meaning folks with expressions that didn't quite mask how delighted they were to feed off my grief. I listened to them all and nodded.

The day he died, I'd been at home all day waiting for the call that I knew would come. When the phone rang, I knew it would be death, its breath miasmal, heavy on the nape of my neck, its rotting fingers holding my shoulders as I listened to the words coming through the phone. Nihar was gone, the voice said. It was over. It was Mohit, Nihar's partner. He'd received a call from an impersonal police officer investigating the sudden death of a tourist found dead in a hotel room. He broke it gently to me, as gently as he could, given he was the iron-demolition ball of the three partners, sent out to handle difficult tasks because he could say things without hesitation. His voice shook with uncertainty as I remained silent.

'Kamla, are you there, are you listening?'

'I am,' I reassured him. 'I'm listening.'

I was calm, unnaturally so.

'He's dead, completely dead?'

It was a strange question to ask, I would realise later.

'Are you sure?'

'We're getting the body to Chandigarh.'

Nihar was now an 'It'. A body. The rest was a blur. Perhaps I had fainted. I remember only the blackness. Someone from his team came home, opened the door with the spare key the neighbours had when I refused to answer the bell. A doctor had been called for. I was bundled into a car and taken to Chandigarh, where the body would arrive. The drive to Chandigarh was a blackness too, of horns and the headlights of the oncoming vehicles. Stopping by the side of the road to throw up, time and again. And then, the body. It felt strange to see him like that, lying there defenceless, his face waxen and a stranger, clots of purplish bruises dappling one side of his jaw. No one mentioned the bruises. He seemed like he was in a deep sleep, he could spring up anytime, his eyes seeking me out in the crowd.

There was nothing in him. No breath, no life force. The fragrance he carefully sprayed on himself everyday had been replaced by the sharp unfamiliarity of embalming fluids, his skin, always so clear and taut, was mottled virulently purple, red and black. I stood back, stunned by the finality of this, this slab of unresponsive flesh, cold to the touch. The stench of decay enveloping him, a slab of meat on a block of ice. It smelt of release. His. And mine.

When they took him away, I didn't accompany them to the crematorium. Electric it was. He'd insisted on it, all his organs had been donated, they'd found a donor card in his wallet when the body was discovered. The call asking for consent had gone to his parents. We hadn't been married when he'd pledged his organs; it was their name and number on the organ donation card. There were pieces of him around in this part of the world, I didn't want to know who they were. Somewhere, his eyes were seeing the world his body had once existed in, his kidneys filtering waste from someone else's overindulgences.

'Such a good boy, he was always,' his father had said, his voice thick with pain, 'Always thinking of others, always looking to do good, even after he died.'

'Stay back with us for a while,' his mother said, her eyes swollen and her voice rough with the weeping, her demeanour accepting of the loss. She had already buried three of her children before they had reached adulthood. Two just out of the womb, one in his childhood. Nihar was the fourth she had outlived. What calliper can measure pain without pinching the soul?

'There's nothing we have of him anymore but you.'

It had taken me a while and a shifting of cities before they were content to let me move on with my life without them in it. Here I was finally. Alone. Or was I?

The phone pinged. A message from my editor gently enquiring whether I'd been able to get back to work on the manuscript I'd promised them last month way back when I'd signed the contract a lifetime ago, but of course there had been extenuating circumstances. She had been gentle, but she had a production calendar to keep to. I didn't have a writing calendar. I would reply to her later, I told myself. I hadn't opened the file in months, the idea of the manuscript in progress sat on my conscience much like a draug on a grave, guarding it from the danger of being opened, the treasures within pillaged, the words within rendered inadequate. The words had dried up inside me, lodging like a block of concrete in my thorax, in my intestines, blocking everything, air, thought, voice, from emerging. I had no clue when they would dislodge themselves and what I needed to do to dislodge them. Till then all I could do was gasp and hope to breathe.

Widowhood had resulted in an unexpected windfall. Half of Nihar's wealth had come to me, half had gone to his parents. And there was the insurance too as well as the pay out from selling his stake in the start-up. Even when divided equally between his parents and me, I got a hefty bit. Did they resent me taking the wealth their son had set up and earned, I wondered? They had been gracious and more than generous. Their lawyer had helped me invest my money to ensure that enough came into my account to help me with my every day without panic, even if I earned nothing. I was even a house owner now, a small property Nihar had invested in which had been under construction all these years in Noida was finally ready, and the possession handed over to me. I promptly had the lawyers help me put it out on rent.

It was a parachute I had done nothing to earn and nothing to deserve. There was no getting away from it, I was quite comfortably placed even if I didn't earn a living for the rest of my life. Money was liberation and a manacle at the same time. It kept me from worrying when the next cheque would come in and whether I would need to take the begging bowl out at the end of the month in order to survive on more than a hope and a prayer. It also made me complacent and soft. There was no longer that ferocity to push myself and do more with myself now that my basic needs were taken care of. It wasn't something I was accustomed to, the sanguinity of wealth. Wealth. The face of money. I didn't have it yet. The anxiety of not having enough still shadowed me, a ghoul perched on my shoulder, hissing into my ear, making me accept assignments I knew I would hate working on, until I realised I wasn't compelled to say yes any more. I now had the luxury of saying no because I had the money.

I called my in-laws once a week, a tenuous connection, half formed, fed by guilt, which was already fading. I'd barely met them, a few days at a time, always in very formal situations. Family weddings. Festivals. Those conversations had been polite. Now they were raw with grief. My father-in-law was in his eighties. That he was able to wake up everyday was a bonus for him. 'I should have been the one dead,' he said. 'Even in his death, he made sure we would be taken care of.'

I was learning how to take care of myself now. 'Lotusface,' he'd have said. 'You've got to be careful about what you eat, you're eating too much junk.' He'd stand at the kitchen counter and empty the fridge of all that I'd stocked it with, the ice cream, the chocolates, fling them into the dustbin. He ate healthy. He made sure I ate healthy too. The first month after he died, I ate all the junk I wanted. Pizzas. Burgers. Chips. Greasy Chinese takeaway.

Food was comfort. Food was solace. Food kept me calm. I found myself wandering the city, haunting all the spots he frequented, wondering if I would spot him somewhere, a glimpse of a familiar silhouette, a recognisable torso, a way of walking, rush up to a familiar t-shirt that I knew lay ironed and folded in the wardrobe back home, tap the wearer on the shoulder and hold my breath until he turned around to reveal a stranger wearing the outline of the man I'd married.

My eyes opened every morning at 4.30 a.m., followed a gust of cold wind, a whisper in my ear, 'I'm leaving.' The room would be empty, only the ghosts of my memories keeping me company. I kept going over the last day with the fervent detailing of one going through a chain of prayer beads, a mindless repetition guaranteed to bring no further enlightenment. It had been dark and chilly, a November morning. Winter had not yet set in. The alarm had rung at 4.30 in the morning, he'd swiped it shut, jumped up, showered and kissed me goodbye on the forehead. I had just muttered goodbye. I hadn't even opened my eyes for more than a sleepy second to look at him.

'Going,' he'd whispered, kissing my forehead, stroking my hair, like one would stroke a quiescent pet.

'Bye,' I'd mumbled, snuggling back under the covers. And then, as an afterthought I added, 'Close the door quickly, the cat will get out.'

I hadn't got up, made him a cup of tea and seen him off at the door. 'You get dark circles under your eyes when you don't sleep well,' he would say, ordering me to sleep in. It wouldn't do for me to look sleep-deprived.

The cat had got out, I guess. I never did see her again, and didn't miss her. She had adopted us when we'd moved in, and came and went as she pleased, wanting neither affection nor interest. I'd named her Nefertiti for her sinuous imperiousness. Perhaps there was a reason why she had left us the same day when Nihar had on his trip, never to return. The call regarding his death came three days later. Perhaps she'd recognised that I had no affection for her, and that the one who actually cared about her was gone.

I messaged Vikram my address with as many directions as I could put in, including the cobbler at the turn of the lane and the pin for google maps. The doorbell rang at around nine, it was Shantatai, my maid. I had inherited her with the apartment, and it had never occurred to me that I could have looked around for someone else. She served my purpose. She was of indeterminate age, anything between thirty-five and fifty-five, with skin that was leather and a face that was carved in stone, her teeth brown stones in a mooring of a constantly masticating jaw. Wiry and resilient, she had survived one husband's untimely demise to alcohol and the second's hurtling down the same path. She bore it with the stoic resignation of one who expected no better. Women knew what men didn't, that they kept the world turning.

'*Chaa peenar*?' she asked in Marathi, a language I was slowly familiarising myself with. I nodded. She made the tea fierce and sickly sweet which was kind of comforting because it reminded me of the first road trip I did with Nihar and the pit stops for tea en route at dhabas where the tea was so sickeningly sweet it could instantly corrode tooth enamel.

'What do you feel like eating?' I WhatsApped Vikram, thanking the world of quick food delivery that only existed to keep me fed and functional.

His WhatsApp profile picture was the cover of his latest book. It felt strange to be having a conversation with a book. It felt strange to have conversations with anything these days, books and humans. Sometimes I felt it was easier having conversations with oneself, one didn't have to keep having to make the effort to have the conversation flow, and one completed one's own sentences. Most of the times, anyway. At others, the sentences hung incomplete, terrified to come to an end because I'd forgotten how to have conversations. I'd become accustomed to listening and keeping quiet, terrified I would say the wrong thing.

'I'm bringing food along, don't worry,' he messaged back. 'Any preferences?'

'Edible.'

'That's very specific.'

And with that, I went back to my laptop. At around 1.30 p.m., I wondered if he'd forgotten he was supposed to be bringing me lunch and pinged him.

'On the way,' he replied. 'Traffic.'

It was a blue cloudless sky outside, the blue hurting the eyes. It was so bright, the blue was bleached to white where the horizon was, a thin oyster pearl whiteness, translucent and delicate, like an egg white, stretched and taut. The sky in Mumbai was always grey and indefinitely hazy, the pallor of hopelessness hung suspended in it for eternity. I munched on an apple. Nihar walked into the room and perched himself on the kitchen platform. 'You need to eat well, you've become too skinny. I don't like you too skinny.' I threw the half-eaten apple into the bin. He disappeared.

The doorbell rang. At first, one hesitant ring. Then, as I sat glued to the chair, unable to raise myself from it, insistent and loud.

The phone in my hand rang. I swiped across the screen with a quivering finger.

Vikram.

'I'm at the door, doofus, don't tell me you're not at home.'

I threw the door open in the three strides it took me from the couch to the main door.

He was standing outside, a plastic bag in his hand with what seemed like cartons of food. Lots of it. And a bottle of wine in another bag. It looked like a Merlot. Reds made me acidic, but then how was he to know that. I wasn't to drink with the medication I was on, but he had no idea. He was in a fitted t-shirt with some inane slogan on it and slouchy jeans. He looked like he'd uncurled himself from the cover of a romance novel and stepped outside into the real world. When had he become quite so attractive, I wondered, from the earlier version of him that was all tangled hair and limbs? He put his arm out to reach out to me, I flinched and recoiled, a reflex action.

'What's the matter?'

I shook my head, my phone still in my hand.

'Nothing,' I shook my head again, and returned the hug, trying hard to dissipate the knot that the physical contact had brought to my intestines.

He placed the bag containing the takeaway he was carrying, Chinese by the smell of it, on the dining table, which occupied one corner of the small living room. The aroma of the food the bag contained slowly floated through the small living room poking and prodding the corners, bringing warmth and joy and satiety into the air.

Nihar hated Chinese food, or rather the variant we called Indo-Chinese. The seasoning didn't agree with him, he felt dizzy and short of breath every time we ordered in, until we made the connection and had stopped. I only ate Chinese food if I was lunching with friends; with Nihar it was always Mughlai. I'd soon stopped eating out with friends. I hadn't had Chinese for a long while. Nihar was a creature of fixed habits. Biryani. Butter chicken. Naans. Kababs. A mint chutney. Onion rings. And after that, ice cream. Preferably litchi when in season.

'Nihar liked litchi ice cream,' the words came out of my lips without me thinking.

Vikram sighed, one of those long sighs that contain words that one thinks better than to give voice to. So much of what goes on in our heads one filters out, and blocks from escaping into the ethers. Giving voice to words gives them power, makes them real, makes them generate responses. Keeping them within one's head is always safer, allows one to ponder over them, test them on the tip of one's tongue and then swallow them if they don't sound too right.

'Shall we order litchi ice cream?' he said, his voice quiet and lined with just that hint of worry. I shook my head in the negative.

'I hate litchi.'

Vikram sat me down on a chair at the dining table. It creaked a little, the sound adding to the weight of the ambient noises that never quite left the apartment. Outside the window, the afternoon sunlight filtered through the leaves of the mango tree that had spread to form a canopy over the narrow road, leaving the lane I lived in cool and breezy.

I looked ahead at Nihar standing by the fridge and smiling his half smile that twisted his face into a threat. Tears formed in my eyes and began spilling over. Vikram took a hard look at my face and shook his head, before gathering me to him, tenderly, so tenderly, it turned the tears into sobs.

'It will take time. You will miss him until you can't miss him any more. Talk to me about him, get it out.' I didn't know. How many things did one talk about? How could I begin? Vikram sat next to me, putting an arm around me. It felt comfortable, this solid presence next to me. I had missed the comfort of just resting against another body, the crook of the shoulder to nestle into, the dip of the earlobe on my forehead. The warmth from his body flowed into mine.

I eventually withdrew myself and mopped my face and my nose with the back of my sleeve. Grief isn't elegant. It is messy, snot-nosed, feral, aching. It is a beast that slobbers into one's sane moments, and scratches the door of one's composure insistently, demanding to be let out.

'Here, drink some water.' He had somehow managed to locate a glass and a bottle of water and was pouring out some for me. I couldn't help but smile.

'You'd make a lousy parent,' I told him. 'Everything doesn't get cured by a drink of water.'

'Well, it would make you stop sobbing and that makes it work.'

'I'm sorry. I don't normally cry in front of folks. I reserve that for the walls.'

'I'm not folks, I'm an old friend.'

I stood up and looked around for the box of tissues. As always, it was never where it was supposed to be, then I remembered I'd last kept it next to the couch for a marathon binge-watching session which had opened up the lachrymal ducts. Sure enough, there it was, I grabbed it, put it on my lap and honked my nose noisily.

'You're more than a friend.'

I nodded. Perhaps he was. I brought out the wine glasses as an afterthought. The bottle was steadily depleted. The conversation was easy, I didn't have to watch what I said, terrified that it would be filed in some remote corner of the brain to be brought out twisted and mauled into grotesqueness later, and thrown at me. And when lunch was had and the table cleared up, the wine glasses kept aside, I found myself next to him while we watched something, I forget what, *Stranger Things* perhaps, and then in his arms and not resisting. On the television ahead, horror of a different sort played out. I horrified myself with my urgency. The feel of a body, hard, male and demanding, was a need that I could not deny. It was the wine, I told myself. But I knew it wasn't. It was me.

I tried to form the word 'no' on my lips, but that was crushed by his lips on mine. It was a half-hearted 'no' at the best and it was then rendered redundant by the feel of his hands on the bare skin between my t-shirt and the waist band of my jeans. His hands went from the back of my waist, circling my waist and then cupped my breasts gently, almost reverentially. A shudder went through me, beginning where my body could not lie. He nibbled gently on my lips and then kissed my cheeks, my forehead, my nose, my neck, bending lower until his hands guided my breasts to his lips which he nibbled and sucked from like he was dying and my breasts were exuding the elixir to life.

I could smell the scent of the sweat on him mixed with the fading fragrance of whatever perfume he'd doused himself with. It aroused a dry ache within me, drying my lips, making my limbs quiver. My heart began beating faster as he pressed his lips down on me. It felt strange to have to look up while kissing him. When we tumbled on to the couch, the idea of resisting didn't even occur to me. Was I being unfaithful to Nihar? Was he unfaithful to me? Wasn't this what I had expected when I'd invited him home, rather than meeting him out for lunch? And then there were no thoughts, no analysing what I was doing, just bodies moving with each other, and waves on waves that spasmed through my body draining me limp, and gratitude and some tears.

He rolled off and lay back with his arms behind his head. I curled up in foetal position.

'That was long overdue,' he finally said. 'Ten years overdue.'

'You know, I'm not in the market for a relationship right now, this is rather bad timing.'

'Neither am I.'

'You know, this is the first time I've had sex since Nihar died. And perhaps months before he died.'

He was silent.

'I don't know how I'm supposed to react to that.'

'You're not supposed to react at all. It is just something

I'm trying to assimilate. I never thought I would ever have sex again.'

'Why would you think that? You're not the one who died. You're a living breathing woman, and it is only natural for you to want sex.'

'Seriously, I don't think ever... I mean... I never wanted it.'

'Man, your husband was doing something seriously wrong. If there was anyone who wanted it, it was you. You are one dangerous woman.'

Icicles went up my spine, gooseflesh pricked my arms. What did he know. No one knew, or did they?

'Sorry, that was tactless of me. I was just kidding.'

'What's your scene, Vikram, do you have someone in your life?'

He looked up at the ceiling and replied, 'No. Not really.'

'I find that hard to believe.' He didn't deign to reply but pulled out a cigarette from a pack he had in one of the pockets of his jeans and lit it with a lighter he pulled out from another pocket. He offered it graciously to me after one drag.

'I don't smoke any more, Nihar didn't like me smoking,' I replied. 'And you haven't answered my question.'

'I did. I said, no, not really. Because I don't have someone in my life unless you count yourself.'

'I can't be in your life. We've barely interacted for all these years. I don't want to be in anyone's life, not yet.'

He shrugged and drew me to him.

'But that's where you're wrong. You've always been in my life. In my head.'

Nihar perched himself on the shelf, watching us, his face a torment of rage and anger. Perhaps it would make him real. Perhaps it would make him disappear forever. I watched him from over Vikram's shoulder, unblinking, until he faded into translucency. He would be back, I knew. He had followed me across the stretch of the country, to another city.

The fan whirred on relentlessly, vapourizing the sweat off our bodies. I liked his body, I realised, it was very different from Nihar's. Nihar had been compact and ferociously fit, built like a small pugilist. His muscles and his aggression were compressed, he moved so lithely you barely heard him. He wasn't very tall, we were almost the same height, but he had the illusion of filling a space with his presence. Everything about him had been dense, his thoughts, his words which he fit into sentences to ensure economy of speech, his gestures which were always studied and measured. He could own a room by merely stepping into a doorway. Inevitably, a hush would descend as the conversation died down, and all eyes turned to him.

In contrast Vikram was a riot of extravagance, leonine hair that was a mass of curls to his shoulders, a grimy day-old stubble that had sandpapered my face and my inner thighs, a body that had filled out generously while mine had shrunk in. His newfound muscles glistened self-consciously on his torso like newly pinned medals on the uniform of a recently decorated soldier. At that moment, my body craved him. The body did things the mind did not sanction, I understood that. Sometimes we needed to allow the body its cravings in order to keep it obedient to the mind. Once I had allowed the body its cravings, I would be done with it. I would live alone and would be fine, I knew, just as I needed to allow the grief to moult itself from me, to allow myself to emerge ready to take on life as a single woman again.

'Dammit,' I said. 'I should be mourning my husband. I shouldn't be fucking you. What kind of a slut am I? When do you get back to Delhi?'

'Tomorrow.'

I fell silent. He looked at me curiously.

'Why do you ask?'

Words have a way of somehow slipping past the self-imposed barriers one erects between them and articulation.

I was suddenly terrified of being alone again. 'Don't go. Stay the night.'

He put his arms around me, and kissed my forehead. 'I've been waiting for you to say those words for years.'

The sinking feeling in my stomach refused to die down, but escalated into a churning that drowned out the words he was whispering into my hair which percolated through my cranium into my brain where I realised I had heard those words before and I had heard them in a different voice. I didn't want him to go now. But there was no telling what tomorrow would want from me. All I had wanted was not to be alone through the long, long night of darkness, with no one next to me, except my dead husband.

—❦—

THREE

HERE, NOW

I woke in the morning to the feel of a heavy arm across me. I opened my eyes and saw a smiling Nihar. I grabbed at his arm, feeling it dissolve in my grip. The dream slipped away crumbling into motes of a discombobulated consciousness. My eyes felt gritty, the eyelashes glued together. I must have cried again in my sleep. Sitting up with a start, I found Vikram sprawled across the bed, too small to contain both of us, his breath rising and falling evenly. He wasn't snoring. I looked at him with the sudden realisation that he was uncharted country—I had to map the contours, valleys, plains, mountains and plateaus that made him. Perhaps, he was better left unexplored. I gently disengaged his arm from my body, slipped out of bed and got into my tracks and hoodie as quietly as I could. As I was pulling on my running shoes in the living room, I heard him stir in the bedroom.

'Kamie...'

His voice, uncertain and questioning, cut through the silence of the morning, scattering the motes dancing in the beam of sunlight that had found its way in through the small pane of glass which blocked the gap in the wall that was meant to hold the air conditioner.

'Where are you?' he continued. I hated being asked questions, I remembered. I hated this neediness for me in another.

'Just off for a run, I'll be back in an hour. There's juice, milk and eggs in the fridge, coffee and tea in the stand above the microwave.'

He grunted in response. I shut the door behind me. This early in the morning was not a time for conversations. It was not easy to slide back into the regularity of human companionship.

Those who pounded the streets of the suburb every morning took Sunday as their weekly off after the Saturday-night hedonism. The others were the groups who ran long distances on Sundays, a ritual, a bonding, a cult of asphalt worshippers. I hadn't joined any, I preferred to run alone, with my thoughts, waiting for Nihar to fall into step next to me when the endorphins hit.

I slipped my phone into the pocket of my track pants, put in my earphones, swiped till I found my playlist. The starting beats came on, pumping through the buds in my ears, on to my eardrums, then on to the three little bones within. Malleus, incus, stapes, the tiniest bones in the human body. Anvil, hammer, stirrups. Flowing through my inner ear, until they hit my brain and shuddered through my veins. The city had barely any bits of pavements for walkers or joggers, at least this part of the city didn't. The roads were meant for traffic, pedestrians, the occasional animals, and the hawkers. Right now the early morning was unfolding on the roads, the milk men, the newspaper guys, the stray dogs and the morning walkers and runners, a city stretching itself, yawning, shaking the sleep and grit from its eyes to grab another day.

Run, run, run. One foot in front of the other, get into the stride, focus on your breathing, in and out, in and out, slow and easy, let your arms move. The legs pound the concrete, making it yield, giving each step a spring that the knees would accumulate over the years, wearing out bone and stretching tendon.

I passed other runners. The running groups had planned routes and very occasionally ran through these small lanes and by-lanes that I preferred running on. For the most part they stuck to the broad giving expanse of the Carter Road promenade which was a bustle of activity the first thing every

morning. I went there for a couple of days until the sheer human
extravaganza there every morning overwhelmed me, making
me want to get back into the relatively warm cocoon of my
new home. I wanted to stay untrammelled by the weight of
enforced interaction. Everything about Mumbai was cramped,
stifled, pressing in on one.

I'd run a complete circle back to my tiny lane and my new
home. The body moves in the patterns the mind sets. I pushed
the gate open and ran up the stairs. The building was short and
squat with two flats on each floor. It was built in the 1970s,
in the strange functional style that dominated that era with
ugly concrete balconies that everyone who lived within had
long enclosed into an additional room. The flat I rented had
its balcony enclosed as well. I used the repurposed balcony
as a study to write in, a few lackadaisical plants pretended to
make it one of those urban gardens that populated interior
design blogs. I'd even fitted in a makeshift table and a collapsible
chair. Thick curtains blocked out the evening sunlight, which the
tree canopy did a great job of filtering most days. I needed a
cocoon of darkness to write in, me wrestling with the unblinking
brightness of the computer in order to get my thoughts into
place. The rest of the apartment had basic furniture that was
functional and efficient. A couch and a three-seater sofa faced
each other in an unblinking face-off across a wooden block of a
coffee table. A round dining table squashed itself into a corner
of the living room, afraid to be the catalyst to set into motion
a spiral of aggression from the other elements. The furniture
was older than I was, some of it was patched together with
hope, Fevicol and scotch tape. But I could live with it for the
few months I had this place on lease, after that I would need
to think where I wanted to go, back to the hills and live with
Maa or to the house that was now mine in Delhi, chilly in the
winter and a furnace in the summer.

It was rather a pity that Nihar had had the heart attack barely a couple of months after we'd got the wills made. 'Thank goodness you were so in love,' our lawyer told me when I went to sign on the paperwork after Nihar's death. 'And that he died of a heart attack. Else I would have suspected you had plotted to kill him.' He'd punctuated it with a laugh which could have meant anything, that his statement was meant to be a tasteless joke, that he meant every word he said, that he'd been watching too much of bad television crime dramas.

I had looked up in shock, my eyes filling up with tears. 'How could you even suggest that?'

He'd patted my back, his manner paternal but distant. 'These things have happened before. Nothing surprises us anymore.' He had been kind and helpful enough though, taking me through the nitty gritty of investing the money I'd received so that I received enough as interest to take care of my basic living expenses and more. Selling off the car because I didn't need it anymore, I didn't know how to drive, had never learnt how to. Taking possession of the completed flat, and then doing the paper work and the basic woodwork required to put it out on rent. We might have been living here, I thought, in this nice apartment, on the 32nd floor, with its high-speed elevators, swimming pool, club house and manicured gardens. There was to be a gym on the premises that Nihar had looked forward to working out in. He'd convinced me that I should use it too when it was ready and I'd agreed without much enthusiasm. 'We can have our children here, look at the park they can play in right here,' he'd said when we'd last gone to see the progress on the construction.

It would have been a complete change from the house we rented out now, in the hub of Delhi, with its two floors of walk-up stairs, and the narrow, congested lanes that led to it. I rented it out to a nice, young couple in their first year of marriage.

I opened the door to my rented home and let myself in as soundlessly as a cat. It still was alien, a caravanserai for the soul rather than home. The sharp squeak of a hinge needing oiling betrayed me. It was the same hinge that let me sleep securely. If it creaked, I woke up. It never did, despite the indent in my mattress in the mornings.

Vikram wasn't in the bedroom. The bed had been made. He was still around, I could feel him vibrating in the molecules of the air around me, a new presence in the rooms, filling them with an insistent, assertive masculinity. The sound of the shower running trickled from within the bathroom. I stripped off the hoodie and put it out on the clothesline to air. Mumbai was always humid and my vest was soaked.

I couldn't wait to have a shower. What was the etiquette about hitting the shower with someone you had slept with but did not feel intimate with, not yet? How would it be like to shower with Vikrant, would we soap each other up and then would he push me against the wall? I closed my eyes, feeling liquid warmth course through me along with the guilt of being unfaithful to the memory of Nihar. Could you be faithful to the dead while you were still living?

'I'm making breakfast,' I yelled through the door to the bathroom and the sound of the shower stopped.

I got together a quick meal of eggs and sausages, gulping down a mug of hot chocolate. He emerged from the bathroom just as I was setting the plates on the tiny table that was barely enough for two to sit comfortably and a third to be jammed up against the wall.

'I hope this is fine with you?' I asked. There was so much I needed to learn and unlearn about him. All I knew about him was from the distance of youth and a decade. A lot changes in a year. People shed off and replace all the cells in their body every seven years and become completely new organisms. Vikram was a stranger now, but then I was a stranger too to him by the same logic. A stranger who had been married and was now a widow. He had never met me as a married woman. The word widow still sounded strange in my head, I repeated it silently, trying it on for size. Widow. There were stories within stories that the word contained. I would tell myself those stories later. They were stories I spun from the webs of the infinite grief I enmeshed myself in.

'Absolutely perfect.' He sat down at the table, smelling fresh, his hair tousled, a day's additional stubble shadowing his jaw. He would move rapidly from the two-day shadow to the week-long unshaven. Nihar would have never let a stubble grow beyond a couple of days unless he was down with something serious that mandated hospitalization and a saline drip attached to an arm preventing him from doing the shaving. The max I had seen him down and out in the year and a few months that we were married was a flu and even then he'd chugged down mega doses of antibiotics and gone off to work.

'I'm going back tomorrow to Delhi,' Vikram said.

I nodded noncommittally and speared a sausage, transferring it into my mouth so I wouldn't be compelled to reply.

'So,' Vikram asked, 'What next?'

I froze. What next. I didn't know really, and did there really have to be a what next? Could it really not be a what is now, without focussing on the steps any relationship, however fledgling, needs to take from one day into the next?

'Don't look so terrified. All I meant was do you have plans for today or shall we just lounge around, take in a movie and a late lunch?'

That sounded good. A better next, taking it hour by hour, day by day.

'Don't you have someone else you'd rather spend the day with?'

'Are you throwing me out?'

I laughed. It sounded alien to my ears. Sometimes laughter had the ability to rip out shards of sorrow from the deepest crevices of one's mind, rather like a darning needle carefully, painstakingly pulling out bits of glass embedded in skin.

'No, please stay. I have absolutely nothing planned for today.'

So he did. And we spoke. And lounged around. Watched some shows on a binge. Ordered food in. I realised how long it had been since I'd just spent a day with another human being with no professional agenda.

Then when he rose to leave, he pulled me against him. 'What now, what do we do with us?'

'There's no us. There's only us when we meet.'

'So I come to Mumbai and you come to Delhi and we keep meeting.'

'Vikram, this was only sex. I'm not looking for a relationship with you.'

His face crumpled. 'We meet for the sex then, I'm good with that, until you think you could handle more. But I'm going to wear you down, I'm warning you,' he said. 'The last time I let it go, let you go. Not again. Think about coming back to Delhi. This doesn't make sense, you know no one here, and you're not in a job or anything where you need to be here. Come stay with me.'

'That's sweet of you, but I think I need to be alone for a while. Work through things.'

He shrugged, kissing me on the forehead, holding me with a grip that was more than lust and less than love. 'When you don't feel like being alone, call me. I'll come.'

I nodded. He went out the door, his feet clattering heavily down the concrete stairs of the small two-storeyed apartment block. I saw him step towards the gate and pause for the briefest of seconds. The soft wind blowing in from the grey sea put its spectral fingers through his curls, lifting them, teasing them and passing through them without a moment's regret. He turned around and looked up at where he knew my window would be. I stepped back behind the curtain, into the darkness of the room so he wouldn't be able to see me. The Uber he'd called for was waiting just outside.

—◦◦◦—

FOUR

THERE, THEN

A thin, tremulous cry that pierced the cold, dark air. We sprang to our feet in excitement. The parlour was packed with people, friends and acquaintances. The cry heralded the birth of my newest sibling, the third child of my parents Neerja and Chanderprakash Malik. None had survived the hostile environment of my mother's womb after me, I had been the last to emerge alive.

The expression on my father's face when the cry emerged from the dark dank room was eagerness, anticipation, worry, joy and anxiety all rolled into one. Was it the boy he had been longing for? My grandmother came into the little parlour we were huddled in, spattered in blood, wiping her hands on the towel she'd tied around her waist. I couldn't take my eyes off it, wondering what had happened inside that had resulted in so much blood on Daadi's clothes. Had Maa died? I ran to her, stumbling in my tiredness and the sleep dredging my eyes. It was well past midnight, and cold.

'Why is there so much blood, Daadi?'

She shooed me away, 'Let me wash and change, beta.'

'Is Maa alright?'

'For now, she is, but she's very weak,' she replied, her eyes looking tenderly at me, her hand patting my head, reassuring me that no matter what happened she was around to take care of us. Daadi was the spine of the house, she kept us all together. In the grey of her eyes there was steel.

'Go in, Prakash,' she told my father, her eyes cold and hard as the hail stones that sometimes rained down from the sky, battering roofs and unwary heads with no discrimination.

'It's a boy. I hope Neerja survives this one. And if she doesn't, you are to blame, Chander.'

She was very annoyed with him, for what, we didn't understand yet. She was using both his names, his formal work name, the one on his birth certificate and the one he used in all official documentation, as well as his home name, the one on his *janam kundli*, as bestowed upon him by the pandit who made his horoscope. She never called him by his official name unless she was really angry.

He jumped up and strode into the inside room, taller and surer than he had been in all these years. We heard him speaking in low urgent tones with Dr Sharma, who had delivered the baby. Daadi put one hand on my head and called to Roop with the other.

'You have a little brother now. I hope your father is finally happy.' She had been to the fair in April, the Birshu, and the oracle there, the gur, had told her in his state of trance that she had two granddaughters and she would be a grandmother twice over this year, two grandsons awaited her this year.

I'd butted in, 'No,' I'd said, 'You're wrong. She has two granddaughters, and she will have one grandson if Maa has a son this time.' Daadi had tugged at my hand and bid me to hush. Perhaps, I thought, she was scared to contradict the oracle. Bad things happened to those who upset the oracle, I knew, even though I was all of eight. She'd had a grandson. She didn't seem too happy though, she seemed resigned, a little angry, if at all. Sometimes, I realised, what you think you want doesn't give you the joy you thought you would have when you get it. Even if you were someone as strong-willed as Daadi.

'When can we see the baby?' Roop asked, looking back longingly at the book she had been reading. She was always reading books, drawing wonderful things and being relatively well-behaved compared to the rapscallion that I was. I was the one who was destined to doom the family to shame and ignominy, my father always said.

We'd lost count of the number of times Maa had lost a baby. She would get ill and go to the hospital for a couple of days and return home a wraith of her former self. These were things not spoken about, but which lingered on unmentioned... the baby that was lost, how old it would have been today had it been born, what would they have named it. All those unlived babies were quietly disposed of, buried somewhere, unmarked.

But this one was here, alive and wailing in the next room. I couldn't wait to see him. I ran to the door, but was stopped by Daadi with a firm hand on my shoulder. 'Wait,' she said, 'Let your mother rest a bit, we have to tidy up the two of them. She's very weak, she's lost a lot of blood.' She closed her lips tightly together for a long moment, and decided that we were old enough to know at eight and twelve.

'It isn't easy giving birth. We women risk death with every child we bring into this world. But the men will never understand that.'

I already hated this boy child, this baby who had confined my mother to bed for months and, was now the reason I couldn't go near her. Roop, though, had no such misgivings.

'We have a baby brother,' she whispered, her face lighting up with an innocent joy. Even back then Roop was a better person than I was and I still resent her for that. Daadi hugged us, a brief brusque one; she was not very demonstrative. Her tongue scalded more than it soothed, but in the scalding was the care and the realisation that one was worried about, one was important.

'I will take you in to see her and the baby a little later, okay,' she promised. 'Now go to your room and get some sleep. You can see your brother in the morning.'

'What does he look like?' Roop asked.

'He's a little prince, that's what he is, a little prince.' Daadi beamed in the flickering light of the bulb within the lamp that hung in the middle of the room, the shadows making her look otherworldly and evil, far from the rosy-cheeked benevolence she was in the light of day.

'And we,' I asked, feeling the break in my voice, all of eight and already relegated to third place. 'Are we your little princesses?' She laughed and hugged us, before going back into the room.

She hadn't answered us, I realised.

We went to our room, thus summarily dismissed from the grown-up conversations that would now ensue. Shutting the door, we tucked ourselves into the *razais* and huddled up together to stay warm under the huge pile that weighed us down. I wondered if the prince would huddle up with us through the cold dark winters when he grew older. I pinched Roop and she whacked me one.

'Do you think Maa will still love us now that she has a son?' I asked her. She was quiet for a long while before replying. When she spoke her voice had no conviction. 'I'm not sure she loved us very much before she had a son as well. I don't think Maa really loves anyone. She's a little different from other mothers, isn't she?'

I meditated on the truth of this statement for a while, before I moved on to the next concern.

'What about Pappa? Will he love us?'

'He will,' she said confidently, the assurance stemming from being the firstborn, the one pampered for a while until the second one came along. The second one being me. Had she resented my being born the way I was resenting the birth of my brother, the brother I hadn't yet seen. They were kind and loving and indulgent with both of us, but Pappa's face never softened with delight when he looked at me the way it did when he looked at Roop. Maa loved me, fiercely yet reluctantly, the way one might love a stray one had taken in, with a wariness that I sensed even as a child but could never explain.

It was a hushed night, like most nights were here in the mountains. From the window, one could see the distant phosphorescence of the moonlight glinting off the crumpled snow peaks of the mountains in the distance. The arc of the Milky Way crossed over the centre of the sky, an astral carpet with pinpoints of billions of stars, worlds we could not even begin to comprehend, the vastness of beyond the periphery of our galaxy. The only thing punctuating the silence in the room was the sound of the wind hammering at the closed windows, begging to be let in. Scampering feet rustled in the shadows. Rats, perhaps, those creatures of the dark. Tendrils of the wind blew slyly in through the little crevices between window and pane, finding the gaps between slats of wood that hadn't been covered with newspaper or cloth, and crawled into the bed under the razais, insinuating itself between us, cold fingers that touched our skin, froze our bones and petrified us in our dreams. We slept hugging each other, drawing warmth from each other.

The next thing I remembered is waking up, choking and gasping for air. I fumbled and clawed at my throat, trying to call out for help and pushed against Roop lying next to me. The shock of her not responding, not moving, brought the sound back to my throat and I screamed with all the might my eight-year-old lungs could summon. It was still night, the morning star was not yet out in the sky outside my window pane. It was a clear, chilly night. The wind was ice and the wolves were howling over its gusts passing over the towering deciduous forests. Something scampered out of the room, banging the door shut as it left. Was it the wind or something else, I would never know and when I would recount the sequence of events later, I would remember vaguely a shadow with no footsteps exiting the room. Next to me, Roop was not responding to either my screams or my shaking her with all the might of my panicky little-girl strength. Daadi rushed in on hearing my screams, coughed as she entered the room, looked around and exclaimed loudly before throwing the window open. Pappa stomped up with his heavy yet quick footsteps, grumbling about whether a man could get peace to sleep in the night while switching on the light switch and then stopped mid-sentence taking in the scene. The pale gold light from the yellow bulbs inside the awkward lamps flooded the room. The blast of icy wind from the open windows rushed into the room, bringing with it the promise of winter, the winds from Siberia passing over the peaks of the mountains beyond and entering our home with the promise of snow and hail that would be here soon.

'What's happened to Roop? Daadi, Daadi....' I pulled at her voluminous dupatta that I'd never seen off her head ever.

She didn't answer. Her face was set and grim and she was working hard to pump air back into Roop's chest. Roop, in the pale light of the lamps, was even more sallow than she was in the day, almost spectral in her skin.

'Is she unconscious? Is she dead?'

Daadi gulped in fresh air and tried to force it into Roop's lungs via a rudimentary CPR after opening the window.

'Hush,' Daadi muttered, 'stop being underfoot.'

My father asked, his voice strange and choked, 'Is she dead?'

I crawled back into my bed and curled up under the heaped razais, my back against the chilled wall, watching the scene unfold in front of me with double-edged horror. Fear that my sister would die, and I would somehow be blamed for it, as I always was for everything that went wrong in the house jostling with the selfish joy that I would have the room to myself, even if I needed to share it with her ghost.

'Maybe Roop needs fresh air,' I told Daadi, 'Perhaps you should take her to the window.'

She looked at me quizzically and then dragged Roop off the bed and stuck her limp head out of the window, thumping her back forcing her mouth to open and then she was back, gasping in the frigid air that a December night brings, cold enough to freeze the blood in your veins. A gasp of relief escaped Daadi and she hugged Roop to her massive bosom, as she sagged to the ground, breathing raggedly. My father yelled for Behra, our man Friday, named so because of his inability to hear from one ear, to bring the car around quick.

Kanchi, the kitchen girl, helped Daadi. Maa stumbled in, shaky and woozy, rushing to take Roop into her arms, wailing long threads of consonants and vowels strung together that made no sense but were a lament for a daughter she thought was dead.

'Stop howling, Neerja,' Daadi said, her voice dry as a twig and as crisp. 'She's not dead, she was only unconscious, she will be fine. Thank goodness Kamla called out when she did, otherwise...'

She then marched to the other side of the room, next to where Roop had slept and picked up the half-burnt *angeethi* that was still flickering.

'Who left this here when the windows and doors were all closed?' Daadi asked, her voice like crashing waves on jagged rocks.

'Behra,' she called out, the stone more insistent in her voice, the underlying implication now suddenly becoming apparent to all those in the room. Roop began to stir in Maa's lap, coughing and retching on the floor. Maa stroked her hair with trembling hands, pale from blood loss, the cold and the possibility that she would have lost her oldest born on the day she had birthed her youngest.

Poor, confused Behra stood at the doorway, wringing his hands in despair like he always did when he had no words to contribute to the discussion.

'Behra,' Maa asked, 'Did you keep the angeethi in the room? You know this room has no chimney and the windows were shut.'

'I didn't,' he quavered, 'I swear on all that is holy, on all the gods, on my grandson. The angeethi was last outside the kitchen, this small one is never taken out unless we have more guests in the living room and need one more.'

I pulled the blankets around me, the wall behind my back one of ice. Between Behra and Pappa, they carried Roop down the stairs, each step heavy and ominous. Daadi, followed them, wrapping herself in all the shawls she could find. The front door opened and a black blast of chill burst into the room unhindered, making the already chilly passageway an icebox. The sound of the car revving up and driving out, and the gate being clanged shut echoed through the quietude of the night. The night was surprisingly clear and across the centre of the sky, the band of stars that made up the Milky Way carpeted the velvet blackness. It hadn't snowed yet. It would soon. We had been waiting for the snow and the baby, the baby had arrived first, and Roop had almost died.

I trotted out of the room in my socks, wrapping a trailing blanket around me. 'I'm frightened,' I said.

Maa held my hand. 'Come sleep in my room,' she said, looking down at me in the pale silvery light of the moon that was the only thing lighting up the passage we were walking through from the glass panes that punctuated it. Maa was beautiful. I'd always regretted that I hadn't received her finely cut patrician features but instead had a flatter version of her face. My complexion too, while light, was far from the creamy white like Maa's. Mine was freckled and sunburnt, and relatives would sigh when they looked at me, 'At least the elder one looks like Neerja. Make sure you educate the younger one enough.'

I didn't understand it then, but I do now, the only currency a woman had of her own in this world that allowed her to defy the rules that the patriarchy had laid over it was her beauty. In my case, at the age of eight, I showed no promise of it. That would change later, the beauty would become fierce and frighteningly a liability when I hit my mid-teens. I didn't know that then. I was never the beautiful princess in the stories I wrote, I was the one who rode off to tame the dragons.

'Where's the baby?' I asked Maa, looking around the room. The cradle was empty.

She smiled. 'He needed to be fed, so Kanchi will be feeding him for a few days until I can.'

I didn't understand much. I lay down next to my mother and snuggled close to her. I was no longer her baby girl; in a single day the equation had changed irretrievably. I sensed it. She hugged me warmly, smelling as she always did of comfort and love and now mixed with a different smell, the smell of lochia, metallic and sharp in the crisp, chilly air.

'Did Roop die?'

'No beta, she'd just fallen unconscious. You probably saved her life. If you hadn't woken up when you had, god knows what would have happened. She's okay now, they're just going to keep her in the clinic for a day or so to make sure she's okay.'

What she didn't know, and neither did I was that there could have been reprisals from the carbon monoxide poisoning which could have affected Roop all her life. Perhaps it was a good thing not to know, it keeps you from needless worry. I resolved to keep quiet the next time I woke up and found Roop unconscious. I would have the room to myself and none of Roop's supercilious bossing to deal with in school. Then I wondered if God could hear my evil thoughts and would punish me for them and tried to think of other things. Like the baby brother. I wished he was dead too. I was an evil child, I told myself. Perhaps I should be the one who was dead. But then I would be reborn as an earthworm, that's what Daadi had told us. Children who were disobedient were reborn as earthworms and snails, both creatures I completely detested from the bottom of my eight-year-old heart. I wouldn't have minded being reborn as a dog. Street dogs had fun, they roamed about the town without being told to come home at a particular time, they got into fights with each other, they chased strangers in town and nipped ankles. I wished I was a dog, I would bite this new baby too.

Speaking of which, I was curious about this new addition to the family. Most of my friends had younger siblings, but I had been the youngest for too long. I dreaded relinquishing that position especially to a boy, one that my father had been openly hankering for all these years.

'What are we going to call him?'

'I don't know,' she said, softly into my hair. 'I haven't thought of it yet.'

'Why did you name me Kamla? It is such a boring name. You should have named me Katherine.'

Katherine, I knew, had been the empress of Russia. She'd overthrown her husband to grab the throne. Even back then, I admired a woman who went all out to get what she wanted, even if it was something as base as power and pelf.

Kamla, on the other hand, had a layered nuance that I did not understand. To me, starry-eyed with all things western, this was one of the things that kept me gauche. My name. Perhaps I was a lotus who only bloomed when I would become Kamie.

She stroked my hair gently. 'Kamla was my mother's name, your naani's name. I loved her so much, more than anyone. She died too young. I was just a little girl. Kamla is a lotus, you are my lotus girl.' A lotus is a flower that grows from the muck, anchored in slime. It is pale pink. I was pale, yes, but nothing of the beauty that was implicit in my name. Perhaps someday I would be, I told myself. After all, didn't they grow green and then bloom pink? I was yet to bloom, but back then I didn't know that not all buds were destined to bloom, some would wither on the stem.

What I couldn't tell my mother was that Kamla was not cool enough a name for a young girl in a convent school. K for Kamal, that was even part of the Hindi reader in primary school. The kids in class had snickered at me when that came up. Even in first grade, girls could be cruel. Roop and I were day scholars, admitted there only because my father was a government servant and could pull a few favours. A highly respected government official no doubt, but highly respected and well paid did not go hand in hand, not in that era, and Pappa did not have the moral elasticity to augment his income by accepting tokens of appreciation or inducements to curry favour, which was the norm amongst his colleagues, senior and junior.

Sleep wouldn't come to me that night. I curled up like a ball into the warmth of my mother's embrace and slept fitfully. I saw my mother ascend out through the small chimney in the room over the wheezing asthmatic fireplace. She stretched out a long silvery hand and asked me to come with her, and so I did. It didn't feel cold outside in the air, as we floated out of the narrow chimney straight into the sky above the house and all the houses on our street. The moon was full that night, I remember, shining with a pale light that warmed my chilled bones. I was content to follow my mother where she took me, ascending higher and higher up the town, higher to where the town ended and the mountain peaks in the clouds began. It felt completely normal, like we'd always been doing this, every night. Perhaps this was why Maa never slept with us, and why she always looked tired in the mornings. She had been wandering all over the skies through the night.

'Do you do this every night?' I asked her, the wind blew away my words before they could reach her. She smiled at me, a slow, sweet smile.

'Brace yourself,' she said, 'it might feel strange at first.'

'What might feel strange?'

'This,' she said and then we were spiralling through a dark dense hole in the sky through to what was almost a blackness so thick and deep and dark that it felt like we were slamming into a wall. And then, it was gone. There was a light so bright it hurt my eyes. We were in another place, similar to home but different. There was no chill, no dullness of winter.

'Where are we?' I asked her. She smiled at me, her smile liquid gold pouring itself over me, warming me up.

'On the other side,' she said.

We floated past the part of the long ridge most of the town was built around, past where the grand church built many centuries ago stood, amidst the pines guarding the town. We moved past the band stand where the bands no longer played regularly. It was now a restaurant on the ridge, and food had taken away the magic vacuity of nothing that one did there. There were people there, dressed strangely, some in fashions long past, some in fashions yet to come. Purgatory, I was yet to learn, didn't follow linear time.

'Are we dead?' I didn't feel dead, but one never knew with all the strange things that had happened since the morning. Maa's stomach moving ferociously almost like the baby was trying to punch its way through the walls of her abdomen, her screaming in pain till Daadi gave her a wad of cloth to bite on and shooed us out of the room, the announcement that a boy had been born and neither of us allowed in to see it and then Roop going off into a dead faint while we slept, and me realising she wouldn't respond to my elbow jabs with a punch.

'We aren't,' she said, 'We're just here to meet someone.'

'Who is it?' I asked, but she put her finger on her lips and led me further and further into the town which was lit by a light so bright it couldn't be the sun, nor could it be electricity. We moved, not walked through streets that were the lanes of our small hill town, curiously unpopulated by anyone we knew. No women chattering over their porches with each other, no kids marching off to school in line, apple-cheeked and bundled up in layers under their school jackets, no men, wrapped into their mufflers and sweaters that wouldn't leave close contact with their skin until it was officially summer again, and sometimes not even then. We turned into the small lane that led towards our home. I followed my mom quietly. The gate was open, something that struck me as unusual. Normally, Daadi threw a fit if the gate was left unlocked because the cows from the herds shepherded by the nomads came inside and nibbled at the flowers she had carefully planted along the little patch of garden. She had carved it out from the little space just in front of the porch. But the flowers bloomed undisturbed here and the roses were glorious and blood red against the golden glow that seemed to bathe everything.

Maa pushed the door open and stepped in, beckoning me to follow her. I was terrified. The inside of the house was dark and forbidding—it felt like I was entering an open maw that would swallow me up whole and spit me out as bones. The house groaned and seemed to grow as we entered and it was suddenly as huge as the church down by the main Mall Road, with the same high ceilings and rafters across. This was my house and not my house.

'He's waiting for us, come quick.' Maa came up the stairs, light as a dandelion seed floating in a gust of wind, passing the one rogue step that creaked without creaking it. A man met us on the staircase. He reached out a hand to me and caressed my face. His face was sharp carved planes, his hair was cropped close to his head and his body was compact and fit, like a pugilist's. 'Lotusface,' he said. He looked familiar and unfamiliar at the same time.

'Kamli,' he said quite pleasantly, putting out a languid hand and pulling me to sit next to him, with a warm familiarity I should have recognised and remembered, but didn't. His voice was like a blanket of warmth over a cold, shivering body, reassuring, comforting. If there was a voice that one could call home, this was it. If home was a person, he was it. I sat next to him without any hesitation, looking at his face, trying to retrace his features in my memory, coming up against a blank wall. He smiled, a smile that washed over me, molten, liquid joy.

Then I remembered without remembering, through strands of a distant memory that snaked through within me, and recognition flared. And I woke up.

—⚬⚬⚬—

FIVE

HERE, NOW

The bed was cold. The first snowfall of the season had happened when we were asleep. Outside the window, snow covered all that the eye could see into a quilted carpet of white roofs. It felt like waking up inside the paperweight snow dome on my father's desk when the snow within had settled on all the miniature houses and spires of the miniature church, the divinity within as strong as the full-sized one that stood sentinel over the town.

The town stretched out into the distance, dusted with sugar powder, the pines white-tinged where the snow had settled and where it would fall down in clumps as one passed under them or when the wind or an errant bird shook it. The snaking road was white, the compound wall was topped by white, the gate was encrusted with a sprinkling of white. The light was grey and hard, reflecting off the whiteness of the snow, a brightness that was enforced, a morning not quite early, not quite settled into its skin, still stirring and sifting itself around the departing night. Maa was gone. The chill pierced my body as I stirred myself out of the razai. The pale watery light of a feeble morning sun inched its way through the window pane, reaching for me as I reached out to it. I stood at the window hugging myself from the chill. No matter how many times one had seen it, the first snow was always something that took my breath away. The sky was so sharp and blue, the white so bright, the eyes hurt. I unlatched the window and pushed it open, sticking my tongue out to catch the few falling flakes. A clump of fresh snow dislodged itself

from the eaves overhead and fell on my head and the window
ledge. I grabbed a handful and put it into my mouth. It set my
teeth on edge, sweet with the memories of first snows past. It
was a first snow ritual I always did with Roop. She wasn't here
this time. The pine trees in the forest beyond the road going
up were laden with a white frosting, like sugar had been gently
dusted onto them.

I closed the window carefully, making sure it was latched,
else a gust of wind would push it open and the snow would fall
into the room from the ledge. The good thing was that school
would be shut now. The stove would be lit all day in the little
parlour and we would huddle around it. There would be snowball
wars outside and hot stew and lit fireplaces inside.

Maa came back into the room, holding her newborn son in
her arms, my new brother, a smile lighting up her face a way
no lamp could ever have.

'How you sleep, Kamo, like a log,' she said. 'What were you
dreaming about? Who were you talking with?'

'There was a man who called me 'Lotusface.' So strange it
was, Maa....'

She shook her head.

'Roop is fine, Pappa called. She needs to stay in the clinic for
a couple of days, just to make sure she's okay. Pappa will drop
Daadi and Behra home, and then go back to be with her. Now go
out, I need to put your brother to sleep. And be a good girl, okay?
Don't get up to any mischief, I can't be chasing after you now.'

I got up and trailed my blanket out of her room, back to mine.
Pappa, Daadi and Behra were not back yet. Only Kanchi was
bustling about in the kitchen, her gurgling son tied to her side.

∞

Kamo. Lotusface. Kamli. I tripped over the names I had been
called by the ones who loved me like a mantra in my head.

Kamo. Kamli. Lotusface. Kamie. What were we but a patchwork of the names people called us with affection or without!

I peeled my eyes open. The sun was high in the sky. The space next to me on the bed was empty. I had slept alone last night. I had slept the sleep of the chemicals. I was here. Now.

It was well past eight in the morning. Shantatai would arrive soon and I'd missed my morning run. I would run in the evening I told myself; it was too hot to run now and the traffic would have already begun churning up the roads to a miasma of belching fumes and discordant honking. I made myself a quick coffee and sat by the window scrolling through the messages on my phone. Nothing from Vikram. Nothing from Roop. No missed calls from Maa. The world had forgotten me, the small world I had enclosed myself into was moving on without me.

Shantatai rang the doorbell just when I was about to reach for the cornflakes, and quickly made some poha for breakfast. I had got quite addicted to her poha, she threw in roasted peanuts and made it with a bit of a tang that reminded me of home, and *golgappa*s.

'Do you want me to cook lunch or will you be out today?' she asked as I ran in for a shower. 'Cook something and keep it in the fridge. Just some khichdi should be fine.'

I ate light in the nights and khichdi was comfort food. Daadi would make it for us when we were ill, me and Roop and, later, Veer. A mixture of lentils and rice, tempered with ghee and served hot. The blandness soothing the upset stomach or the fevered brow. I missed Daadi, I wondered if she missed us from wherever she was now. I missed her so, I always did. Her warm, soft lap, the chunni always draped carefully around her head, the smell of spices and food emanating in soft waves from her, and that indescribable aroma of comfort that no smell could ever equate with. She smelt like home. Maa had never smelt that way. I had read somewhere that it was the hormones of a post-menopausal woman that made them smell a certain way that was comforting to young children. To my mind, a certain smell would forever be associated with the warmth and security of Daadi and I would never find that again.

The phone pinged. Vikram. 'At the airport. Thinking of you. Call you later.'

I sent back a thumbs up emoticon. What was an appropriate emoji response to declarations of missing one after a night of sex? Why did some men find it so difficult to accept a hook-up as one, how had things changed so drastically between the sexes that women were more accepting of hook-ups and men accepting of them only when they chose to. The phone pinged again. My editor. 'Marketing is asking me for an estimated date of release. What should I tell them?' Was that a passive-aggressive way of checking with me whether I'd managed to get my head out of the sand and back to work again? The book was overdue, long overdue, they'd had to shift schedules, pull other books up and push this down, after doing the announcement in the catalogue and the bookings from the distributors. Dare I be honest and tell her it wasn't going anywhere. I had no courage to be honest. I lied.

'Going good, shall send you first draft by end of month.'

She would now forget about me for a few months by which time I would cobble together a workable first draft. It would come back with comments and edits and so on for another few months until we had something fit to go to print. I knew the routine now. I didn't tell her that where there once had been a reservoir of words, there was now brackish sludge.

The phone pinged yet again. Roop. Perhaps this was a day for people to remember I existed on this planet. I should have been grateful, but all I had wanted was to be allowed to fall off it.

'Are you okay, is it a good time to call?'

I called her. Thank god for Whatsapp and Skype and Facetime

and technology that allowed face to face in this the era of cold text on a screen.

Roop. The sister who was older to me by a year and a half chronologically, and centuries spiritually, was an old soul. She could have been around when the first protozoa was crawling out of the primordial seas. She was the sane voice of reason to my petulant selfishness, and the authoritative 'know-it-all' to my perennially confused 'what-do-I-do-now?' She was also a professor in a university in Australia and had her life sorted. No marriage, only live-in relationships she kept changing every few years. Maa was scandalized initially, but had eventually come to terms with it, as she had come to accept my getting married to a man I barely knew within a few months of knowing him. 'Both my daughters won't give me a grandchild,' Maa would lament to anyone who would listen. 'I will die without one.' Veer, my brother, of course, was never mentioned in these demands for grandchildren.

'What's new?' Roop asked without preamble.

'There's a web series I might be doing. A documentary. Across all states. Ground reports of how women in the hinterland are dismantling the patriarchy. Going to meet them today.'

'Sounds interesting and rather intense. Are you sure you're up to so much travel and work right now?'

'There's only one way to find out, isn't there. For me to jump right in. How long am I going to hide behind this great wall of mourning. It is high time I put myself out there.'

'I might be coming down for a few days during Christmas. Keep yourself free. Steve will be coming too. And then we go to Goa for a week. I've been thinking it's been years since I saw Kamini, might as well see her too. And that fabulous house she has. What do you think she does there, living all alone like a spectre?'

She didn't wait for a reply and continued with the barest of pauses. 'She's probably got a swarm of admirers hanging at the hems of her petticoats, waiting for her attention. And now she's a rich widow, all the local lads must be trying to charm her into holy matrimony.'

I laughed. 'I don't think she's in the market for any male attention, she was quite devoted to Peter.'

She cackled gleefully. 'But anyway, you were always her favourite. Perhaps you could come with us too, unless you don't want to go to Goa after....'

Her voice trailed off. The words hung unspoken.

'I really think your boyfriend won't want me mooning around the place, being a pain in the arse.'

'You can bring a boyfriend of your own. Find one by the time I get there. There's enough time.'

I laughed.

'If only it were that easy.'

'I've told Maa to come with us to Goa. I'll book her flights.'

'Cool,' I replied. Maa and Kamini face to face after years would be interesting. 'Do you think Maa will come to meet Kamini?'

'We will find out, won't we? When are you beginning your shoots?'

'I have a book to finish too, am well past submission deadline. After that let's see what their schedules and deadlines are.'

'Hunker down and finish it. Will ping you in a couple of days. And yes, are you dating yet? Have you gone out with anyone?'

'No.'

'Damn it, Kams, you must start sometime, how long are you going to hole yourself in mourning, it's been what, four months now?'

'Six months and three days.' I paused. 'And I'm having sex, if that is what is worrying you. So that's taken care of.'

There was an awkward silence on the line. 'You do understand, don't you, Kamie, that you have to be immensely careful now.

You are a very rich woman, most people know that. Don't get into something that only sees you as a source of money.'

'I'm not getting into anything right now. And I live in absolute squalor here, no one would even suspect that I am not hand to mouth and likely to spring them for rent money.'

She laughed, a rich throaty laughter that rippled down the airways, bouncing off the satellite and hitting my eardrum. It felt like she was right in the room, next to me, not some ten thousand kilometres away. It was curiously comforting.

'Take care, lil sis.' The screen went blank.

I'd never really thought of it that way. Yes, I was fairly well-to-do now, and as a single woman I was an attractive prospect for gold diggers. Was Vikram a gold digger, I wondered. Did he know just how much money I had tucked away into property and in bank deposits? It was strange how widowhood had elevated me from rank poverty and a hand-to-mouth existence as a content writer to a woman of independent means. The words of the lawyer still came back to sting me.

I stepped out to stock up on my groceries. The day had passed by in a rabbit hole of answering mails and doing research. In Mumbai, dusk just meant that the sun fell quite suddenly into the Arabian Sea in an incandescent blaze of oranges, pinks and reds. Nihar loved sunsets, he photographed them every time we travelled. His mother had shown me paintings he had done when he was a child, sunsets. Sunsets, I realised, were sunrises in reverse. The pictures could have been either, he chose to label them sunset, the ending of a day.

It was against the order of nature to cremate a child. The grief of outliving one's offspring is a different kind of grief, one I didn't know but Maa did. 'You never forget,' she would say, 'Every single day you tell yourself it is unfair that you should be living when your child is dead.'

She'd buried many of her children. Some of them hadn't lived long enough in the womb and tumbled out, tearing it through the veil between life in the womb and life on earth, only to be buried quietly in the garden at the back of the house. Others had been born and not survived the first year.

I decided to call Maa, the phone rang interminably. She would call back, she was probably in another room away from her phone. I kicked off my shoes, switched on the television, poured myself a glass of wine.

When the call finally came, I didn't take it because I was many glasses of wine down, the bottle was lolling indolently on the side table, empty. I was talking to Nihar. He came to me like a gust of wind, brushing the nape of my neck, raising the hair on my arms, wind that was dry and crackling, like the end of autumn before the crisp sting of winter. He sat next to me and looked at me, his eyes pained and searching. I reached out to touch him but my hand passed right through him and fell on to the emptiness of the couch. But he was here, he was listening to me, and his eyes were deep with pain and torment. My words were incoherent sounds to my ears. But he was right there listening, so I didn't stop speaking for fear he would disappear if I did. I fell asleep mid-sentence. He spoke then. He hadn't heard a word of what I'd told him.

'Lotusface,' he said, stroking my face with hands that felt like wisps of cold smoke on my skin, 'Come with me. Do it. It won't take anything, just a cut across your wrists. You won't feel a thing, I promise you.' He handed me a knife. 'You have to do it. Yourself.'

I woke up and found myself with the kitchen knife in my hand and a stinging on my left wrist, where a thin scratch oozed red drops. Blood that I hadn't had the courage to spill, not even in my dreams.

SIX

THERE, THEN

Roop came home after three days in the clinic. Daadi and Pappa had taken turns to be with her. She was put on oxygen the first day. The second day, Dr Sharma ran tests and checked if she needed to be shifted to the hospital. The specialists were called from the hospital to check on her, thanks to Pappa's connections with the administrative heads in the hospital. Maa was not allowed out of the house; she was in a forty-day confinement after the baby.

The morning Roop was to come back, the sun had made a stronger attempt at breaking through the seemingly permanent fog that had, for the past few days, enveloped our small town. The air was crisp with the smell of burning leaves wafting in on the chill wind. I had been waiting at the window since the morning.

Somewhere Whitney Houston was singing '*And I Will Always Love You*' to Kevin Costner, but it was a song I was still to hear in the small town I was in. Macaulay Culkin was home alone, Rahul Roy was making sheep's eyes at Anu Agarwal and Aamir Khan had all of us swooning even though his trousers were hitched up to well under his armpits and his hair had more volume and bounce than a shampoo ad could legally claim to have infused.

I went to the window, staying there with my nose pressed against it. The glass pane was icy, the frost was slick on the lawns and the plants. I blew on the glass and scribbled on the steamed-up surface. Missives to nowhere. We did that to each other, Roop and me—wrote messages on the steamed-up windowpanes that only the other would see.

The house was filled with the smell of sandalwood agarbatti and the acrid smell of puris frying in the kitchen, the two disparate smells blending into what made home. I saw our car climb up the hill, a black speck in the distance at first, an ant slowly turning, slipping out of sight, and then coming back into view, playing hide and seek through the deodars. I heard the car horn piping at the gate and Behra shuffling across to open it. The roads would have been slick and icy uphill, and the car, an old Ambassador, as the Morris Minor was known around here, a car Pappa enjoyed thanks to his designation as a government official, would have sputtered and choked and stalled en route. Pandeyji, Pappa's driver, would have cussed under his breath, Daadi would have grumbled, and Pappa would have clenched his jaw and said nothing. And Roop, she would have been sitting at the back, looking ahead eagerly to enter home. Beyond the town, the roads and the forests, the mountains ahead were pewter and silver in their impassive, crumpled glory.

The car turned in slowly into the small gate that creaked as Behra held it open. I could hear the sound through the closed window. I watched from my window, wondering if I should run down. A raven sat on the branches of the juniper tree just outside the wall and stared down disapprovingly at me. I looked straight in its beady eye stuck my tongue out at it, startling it into flying away to find another bare tree branch to sit on and resume its examination of me. I stuck my tongue out at it again, but this time it stayed put. I ran down, curious to know if Roop was the same Roop as she was before she'd died and come back.

Maa and Pappa had been whispering oxygen deprivation to the brain and possible damage when they thought I hadn't been listening, but Daadi had shushed them up and told them to stop their mournful talk, the child would be fine.

By the time I reached the front door, Daadi was already helping Roop up the stairs of the porch. Maa had reached the door, and gently moved me aside to fling herself at Roop with a ferocity I'd never associated with her before. 'My child,' she said, stroking her hair, raining kisses on her head, making me feel infernally jealous, making me wish for a moment I was the one who had almost died. But I knew now that I could never compete for her affection with the newborn son and the daughter who had come back from the dead. I was the second daughter. It would forever be my cross to grow up with, the one who was meant to be a boy. Roop stuck her tongue out at me. I stuck my tongue out right back and pinched her hard. She yelled. All was well between the two of us, as it should be. Maa slapped my hand back, exhorting me to behave. I never behaved. Well-behaved girls seldom got their way.

'Come, see your brother,' said Maa, leading her by the hand gently to the stairs and I followed, like I always did, regardless of whether I was invited or not. Maa opened the door to her room. Kanchi, her head covered with her chunni, was suckling the baby. Daadi bustled up with a wet cloth insisting we wiped our hands clean before holding her most-anticipated grandson. If Daadi had her way she would scald our hands with a live flame to ensure all the infectious germs were killed before they could dare transmit themselves to the baby. He continued grumbling a bit at being detached from his food source and Kanchi hurriedly put him to her shoulder to burp him, walking him around as she did it. From over her shoulder he opened his button-like eyes in his crumpled-up little day-old face and looked straight at me.

For all that Daadi had waxed eloquent about him being a little prince all I saw was a bundle with a scrunched-up face that squirmed and wailed and created a general fuss until Maa and Kanchi picked him up and pushed me out of the room.

Daadi had made me wash my hands and scrub myself down before she'd let me enter Maa's bedroom which was like a furnace what with all the heaters Daadi could round up placed in the room for her newborn grandson while we shivered in the other rooms.

Pappa entered the room, the door opening with force and bringing a blast of chilly air with it, earning a mouthful of rebukes from Daadi. Pappa had changed since his son was born. No longer was he the apologetic entrant into a room, shoulders curved into a question mark that questioned his existence. He seemed reinvigorated, renewed, the lines had fallen off his face, the shoulders thrown back in new-found machismo. He must have been handsome back then, Pappa, if only I could remember him without being terrified of him. Broad shoulders, a handle-bar moustache, hair that he slicked into place with generous helpings of Brylcream that followed him around, along with the Old Spice he used as an aftershave, and the Four Square cigarettes that never left his fingers, the tip always lit. Kanchi slunk imperceptibly into a corner, looking at him from under her heavy-lidded eyes. Maa moved in front of her, blocking her from view. Pappa stepped out. The baby looked away and began mewling irritably.

'He hasn't finished his feed,' Kanchi whispered to Maa. 'Just let the girls hold him for a minute and then I will feed him again.' I wondered how she had enough milk left over for her own baby who lay on a mat next to her, busy with a rattle. He was chubby and hearty despite being strapped on to his mother for the most part of the day while she went around her chores. Roop and I played with him, tickling him, dangling a rattle over him. He squirmed and gurgled, happy at the attention. He was a happy child, he barely cried. And sturdy too—he took all our curious pokes with good humour. He would be four months now, or was it five, I didn't know.

I barely knew his mother too, she was incidental to my childhood, coming into our lives a couple of years ago. Kanchi was hardy, shy and barely spoke to any of us. She'd come from the villages beyond the horizon, where the Himadri met the Himachal and the people lived like mountain goats, clinging precariously to the steep slopes of the crust of the earth pushed up when the continents collided all those aeons ago, embedding sea creatures within their rocks as the water flowed off over the now raised sea floor. I wondered about her now when I thought back, who had she been, the girl we had never known, barely six years older than Roop.

Roop was made to sit cross-legged on the bed and the baby was placed carefully on her lap wrapped in a blanket. 'Put your hand under the neck,' Kanchi warned, guiding Roop's hand to the right spot. She continued to hold the baby under Roop's hand, just in case. Giggly twelve-year olds, even if they'd just emerged from the hospital and were down to one-tenth their regular energy levels, were not to be trusted with newborns. I myself was terrified to hold the baby. He squirmed and seemed generally disappointed with the lot he'd been sent to live with.

'Be careful,' I piped up, 'he peed on me when I held him.'

She promptly put him back into Kanchi's hands. 'He's cute,' she said, pronouncing her judgement on her latest sibling. 'But quite boring.' We were summarily dispatched to our rooms, and instructed to stay out of trouble. Daadi had no further bandwidth to deal with a new mother, newborn infant and two pre-adolescent girls in the same house as well as deal with house help that was acting up thanks to the constant turf wars between them.

I was at the window, my book on my lap. We were supposed to be studying, but were chatting the kind of aimless chatter that two girls restless to get outdoors have. Aamir Khan stared down at us from a page we'd torn out of a film magazine and pasted on the cupboard. Roop was crazy about him but I found him rather comical, with his pants hitched up too high and a rakish cap placed at an absolutely impractical angle on his head begging for a pebble to knock it off. Roop was painting some flowers in a washed-out palette, sticking her tongue out from between her lips, deep in concentration as she defined a petal with a darker hue of the pink she had used to fill the rest of the flower. She was rather good at painting, much like our maternal aunt Kamini, the renegade of the family, the one who ran away to live the most bohemian life ever imaginable for a girl from a respectable clan that was reported to be linear descendants from the divine themselves, the clan with the jagirs gifted to them by the maharaja, held in high regard among the community. She dropped her surname when she became an artist and was known now as just Kamini. At the time, we had Madonna and Prince who were known just by their first names, and in India, I knew only my aunt, and the heroines of Hindi filmdom. Nargis, Nutan, Madhubala, Sridevi. And Kamini. I admired that about her, that she never needed the additional titular bondage of a family name, nor had she adopted her husband's surname. Perhaps Roop would become a painter like Kamini and run away to marry a man who lived on an island. And we could eat fish every day when we went to visit her.

'So what was it like? Did you die?'

'I don't know if I died or I was dreaming but I was here and not here, I could see all of you and I could hear your thoughts too. You wanted me to die so you could have the room.'

'Yes,' I accepted it happily. 'You kick in the night and don't let me sleep and all your books are always thrown around.'

'If I'd died that night, I would have become a ghost and haunted you. Didn't you think of that?'

I felt sheepish for a moment. 'But you would have been a cool, friendly ghost, like Casper. Because you're my sister, and you would make sure no one troubled me anymore. That would have been cooler.'

The full bladder pressed on me. I wanted to visit the toilet, and dreaded the long way to the outhouse, at the back of the house. We had the Indian style of bathrooms back in those days. Waking up at night in the dead of winter to pee was an exercise in bravery. Maa would be called and she would walk us to the outhouse. Now, we had WCs installed in little cupboard-like bathrooms on every floor. The walls were cold and damp, and moss grew in patches no matter how many times Pappa got the outside re-plastered and painted. The house was old, built when the British still ruled over India and this town had been one of their summer getaways. Old stone, strong, built to last generations, hewed out of the mountains. Our grandfather moved in when he'd been allotted this house post Partition, a bungalow vacated by a family that had moved to Pakistan during Partition, just as my grandfather and grandmother had stayed on in this mountain town, in the hope of finding refuge and safety. They had slowly let go of the hope that flickered faintly of ever going back, letting it float out into the blueness of an indistinct future like a balloon which escapes from one's grasp.

We had heard that story over and over again from my grandmother. Daadi had been educated at Dalhousie and had graduated from one of Lahore's best colleges, one of the earliest batches. She had wanted to be a lawyer, she said, but her brothers had decided to get her married. Luckily, she married Daadaji who allowed her to assist him informally in his cases. But she could never fulfil her wish of becoming a qualified lawyer. And then came Partition, with its blood-thirsty mobs descending down upon all the Punjabi Hindu families in Lahore. Luck had been on my grandparents' side—they had driven east a month or so before the madness of Partition descended, to spend a couple of weeks in the mountains. All they had with them was the car they'd driven down in, a couple of suitcases they'd carried their clothes for a week in and their lives. They would never return to Lahore, not then, not later. My grandfather would die longing to see the house he had been born in.

They were to learn later that my great grandfather, and his wife, along with my grandfather's two younger unmarried sisters, hadn't survived the mobs. The guilt would haunt my grandfather for the rest of his life. It broke him. He blamed Daadi for insisting that they take what was a delayed honeymoon, and causing him to lose his family. It was a splinter between them that would grow to become a pickaxe that would hack the tenuous bond they had forged to bits.

Through plaintive recollections, we heard the stories of the palatial home they left behind, with the many bedrooms and the attached dressing rooms to each, the huge dining room that could seat twenty-four people at the table, the library filled with books that Daadi remembered poring over when she'd just arrived as a new bride. Surely, the rooms got added on by each retelling. Slowly, she had stopped talking about that home. This was home now, it became home to her only when her children were born. She was never going back to the grandeur she had left behind. This was home now, porous and shaky, bolstered by repairs and care into strength.

It also had a reputation for being a jinxed home, which is why no one would claim it and it was available for my grandfather to claim for his own. The first family that had been allotted this house left in a hurry, to humbler tenements down by the bazaar. What made them leave they never did say, and they eventually left town. Daadaji was prosaic. He would ignore the reputation of the house being haunted, and the rumours about the family that fled leaving their youngest daughter behind to die in this house. Her body had been found in the attic, a corpse decomposed and then frozen by the time the authorities took it over. The girl was crippled and used crutches. How she would have climbed into the attic we would never know. Had she been taken there and left to die, for fear she would bog them down in their flight across the border? I'd often wondered with all the curiosity of my eight-year-old self. But as kids, we knew better than to go into the attic alone. Perhaps it was a story created to keep us out of trouble. The little girl with the lame leg never troubled us as long as we lived there.

Sometimes we heard a thumping sound from above which could be the monkeys on the roof or a ghostly presence navigating itself in a dimension it no longer had claim to. Sometimes there was a shimmer of a shadow that fleetingly washed over the stairs making one feel like one had been dragged through an icy waterfall for a moment. We never dared to investigate the attic for fear of death or Daadi's disapproval and the latter was the scarier of the two. Daadi in a rage could have a river in spate retreat in terror. She was a hardy little thing, while little is a word one uses metaphorically with her and all the Malik women. We were all, what is euphemistically known as 'khaatey peetey log', or roughly translated into 'people who had enough to eat'. Although the only drinking the women folk did was that of milk, tea was verboten to us for fear it would ruin our complexion, and hard liquor was only the preserve of the males in the house—Daadaji before us and now his only surviving son, Pappa. The liquor cabinet, locked and accounted for always through small tape indicators at the last consumed level wasn't even in Behra's luck for the occasional purloining.

'What did you do, three days lying down on a bed and being waited on hand and foot?' I asked, slightly envious that she had been the recipient of special treatment while I had been left to fend for myself given the entire household had been taken up with the new baby.

'Got bored. They wouldn't let me sit up. Or walk around.'

'They wouldn't let me come and see you.' I could have just skipped down the lane and visited the small two-storeyed clinic perched on the corner of the road to the market if I'd felt like it but I hadn't. I'd enjoyed being alone. She shrugged. Her shoulders seemed thinner.

'They were scared that I'd experienced brain damage. Doctor uncle kept a continuous check on all my responses.'

'You look alright to me. And you were brain damaged from before you fainted. I'm hungry,' I said, 'Let's go down and get something from the kitchen. And I want to go to the toilet.'

'You go,' she replied uncharacteristically. 'I'm not hungry.'

My jaw fell open. There had never been a time in our entire childhood when Roop was not hungry. She could be found chomping on whatever she could find in the kitchen at any hour of the day. Daadi would call her a plague of locusts, never mind the Biblical reference. Daadi was not your usual pious, Indian mythological-referenced grandmother like the grandmothers our friends had. She drew on a wide range of sources for her jibes. I could be a Kumbhakarna or a Hecate. Roop was a banshee when she cried. Daadi had studied right up to her masters in an era where for a girl to study beyond matriculation was both a privilege and a burden.

I saw Mr Singh stroll in through the gate. 'Maliksaab,' he called from the porch, his voice echoed ominously from the silence all around, only broken by the occasional hesitant birdsong.

Pappa bellowed for some tea to be sent into the parlour, and Daadi yelled back from the inner room that Behra was out to the market and she was up bathing the baby. Tea would have to wait. Everything now centred around the hallowed boy child. Realising the kitchen was clear of supervision, I made a quick dash in for supplies to keep hunger pangs at bay.

I peeped into the parlour on my way up from the kitchen,

having purloined some bread and jam before Daadi could spot me and yell at me for ruining my appetite. I grabbed some apples from a basket in the corner and ran up to my room. Roop was called down to the kitchen to bear the tea tray to Pappa. I didn't feel like studying, I was bored of being stuck at home and, as all children do when bored, I began wandering around the house in search of something to entertain myself with when a thump from the ceiling drew my attention. Outside the windows, a thin fog began curling up, blotting out the pale-yellow sun that had made an abashed appearance in the morning after days of bone-numbing chill.

Again, the thump above my head. I looked up at the ceiling. Was there really a ghost there, one who would drag us into a grey and fearsome afterlife with her, I wondered. Curiosity and idleness always made for a deadly combination. I scooted up the stairs before my courage betrayed me, taking care to tread softly so no creaking betrayed me. I slowly pushed the trap door up and limbered myself into the musty room. The first thing that hit me was the smell. The room smelt of sadness and disuse and dust coagulated in corners, and spiders spinning undisturbed. If you could bottle despair, this would be it. The dust motes shimmered in the faint light coming through a sky light as I stepped through looking around.

The room yawned as I entered, and extended itself, as though shaking off the inertia of disuse. It was, honestly, quite a let-down. Nothing that remotely suggested a ghost within, no shadows, no cold breaths down the nape of my neck whispering sibilant threats, no sudden sounds. It was just another old attic, a place with discarded furniture that had outlived its utility, some boxes which were nailed shut, huge tin trunks, and that dusty old carved wood trunk with its lock imposingly shut. But it was childhood, and locks were no deterrent for curious little hands which always had hope even in the face of obviousness.

All had a layer of dust so thick on it, I could write on it, and with the impunity of childhood I did. 'Roop is a monkey.' Satisfied with my slander, I looked around for what else I could investigate. The air was musty, undisturbed, the faint scent of neglect hanging heavy. The shadows were deeper in the attic, corners were unexpected, the light streamed in faint from a small window set under the eaves, its panes covered with dust and grime of years.

As was expected, I gravitated towards the wooden trunk, pulled towards it like a magnet, unable to resist. Would a genie pop out, would I find documents that proved I was actually born to royalty and given away to this humble family to be brought up for my safety and that I was in troth a princess, or would there be some treasures from a distant era that would make us rich and me special again in the eyes of all the family now that I'd been relegated to a distant also-ran. The trunk, like all mysterious things rightfully should be, was locked. A huge iron lock that was beyond the means of a young child to open. Who might have the key to it? I wondered. Surely the key was one among the many keys that hung from Daadi's waist during the day and I could spirit the bunch away when Daadi slept in the afternoon and check which one worked for the trunk? Or maybe I could just force open the lock, I'd seen it often enough in the movies, hadn't I? And I was strong. Pappa always said I was his strong beti, as strong as a son. I wondered if I would be strong enough now that he had the son he'd always hungered for.

I looked around for something that would break the lock, and found it almost immediately. A small iron crowbar lay along with some logs of wood and sticks in the corner of the attic. Something shifted shape in the corner. In the dimness it was impossible to discern what it was, perhaps it was my shadow. Eight is when one is fearless, when ghosts and demons and unknown things don't scare one because death means nothing yet.

Picking up the crowbar, which could have been a lethal weapon in stronger, more determined hands, I brought it down swiftly on the lock holding the trunk and its secrets together. Nothing happened. I thought I heard a groan, I looked around. There was nothing. A cobweb halfway down from the roof swayed enticingly in front of my eyes, obscuring my view for a long second. I raised my hand again with the crowbar still clutched tightly in it, and felt my hand move of its own volition with a force I knew I didn't have in me. The lock gave way without protest and with a trembling hand I raised the lid up, peering within. I propped the lid up with a stick lying in the corner of the attic. I climbed into the trunk, perhaps there were clothes and hidden treasures. It was huge, one of those monsters that could double as a bed if one put a mattress on it. There were clothes within. Under the blankets, a gleam of burgundy velvet caught my eye; I tried to tug it out. It was a smoking jacket, rich, resplendent, resonant with the smell of mothballs and tobacco, and dissipated perfume, initialled at the pocket. I sat on the blankets in the trunk and put it on. It was huge for me. Stitched for a large man, the sleeves hung off my arms, wraith-like, empty. It was warm and comforting in a way no blanket could be. I curled up in it, and lay down on the blankets and closed my eyes. When I opened them, there was a girl looking down at me. She was transparent, I realised first, then I noticed she was smiling at me and holding a hand out to help me climb out of the trunk. I smiled back and took her hand, it felt like holding smoke.

'Hello,' she said. 'Did they leave you here to die too?'

It was then that I noticed the crutches and began screaming before everything became dark around me.

—⁂—

SEVEN

HERE, NOW

The toughest thing was getting through the evenings and the night. I'd spent the day out, finishing off some long-pending meetings. By the time I'd reached home the previous evening the sun had fallen into the Arabian sea, a ball of flame sending spears of pink and purple through the cloud-dappled sky. I pulled out my phone to order in a pizza and it rang, all of a sudden.

'Kamla, darling,' she said, 'It's Kamini.'

Her voice, raspy with the smoke of a million cigarettes clinging on to the lining of her throat, was the same as I remembered it—imperious, commanding and yet fiercely loving with the kind of unfettered love only an aunt could give. She hadn't called me when Nihar had died. Or had she called when I'd been in the cold grip of sedatives, I didn't know. I could see her in my mind's eye, sitting nonchalantly in her brown Georgian wing-back leather armchair, her feet up on the footstool, her dog dozing at her feet, a lit cigarette in its holder in one hand, the telephone in the other.

Kamini. Maa's youngest sister, maverick, renegade and currently cosily ensconced in a rambling old Portuguese villa on an island in Goa, left to her by her artist husband who had passed away a few years ago. She had been the rebel of the family at a time when rebellion meant more than just shaving off a side of one's hair or colouring it all the colours of a peacock or tattooing every limb on one's body. We grew up with the whispers about her, about her life, her morals and how she had subverted every straitjacket that growing up in a straitlaced conservative family had attempted to pull on to her and lace her into. She had always been my hero.

'Kamini,' I replied. I'd always called her by name, ever since I was a child. No Maasi. She had never dissuaded me.

'Neerja told me you're all alone in Bombay. Why are you living all alone? Come stay with me, I could do with the company. You can work from anywhere, can't you, you don't have a job in Bombay, right?' The city would always be Bombay for her. She'd run away from home here, when it was Bombay, studied at the JJ School of Fine Art, kept herself afloat doing illustrations and freelance work for advertising agencies while she honed her art, remained on the fringes of the art world, which was more welcoming of the men who dominated the conversations and the circuit. What I loved about her was her matter-of-factness. She spoke without the preamble of niceties and the 'how are yous' that were the bane of polite conversation, dragging it into the drudge of the perfunctory. 'I don't know why Neerja lets you stay alone. Catch the next flight and come here and stay with me.'

'That's really sweet of you, Kamini, but I've just taken this house on rent and I have almost ten months left on the lease.'

'Cancel the lease, you don't need it. I have a huge house, with only me living in it, rattling around like a stone in a can. I will give you a nice, big sunlit room to yourself, ensure you eat well and have all the peace and quiet you need to do your work. And Goa is just a short flight away whenever you want to get back to Bombay or Delhi. Or just come for a couple of weeks to see how you feel about staying here, get a feel of the place. Bring your laptop along, stay in your room the entire day and write, you don't even have to come out to see me. I'll even get the internet installed in your room for you, I've been resisting it for years. But come.'

Kamini had been known to have her way, always.

'Kamini, I have work here....' I protested, half-heartedly. She could sense the vacillation in my voice, she had always been very perceptive.

'I'm not going to take no for an answer,' she said. She would get her way, I knew. Staying alone was for the brave and I was not brave right now. Then, unbidden, the thought came to me that this was Goa, this was where Nihar had been found dead in a room. Perhaps this was where I would exorcise my ghosts or resign myself to being haunted by them for the rest of my life.

'I will,' I told her. 'I will come tomorrow on the first flight I can find a seat on. Let me go book my tickets.'

I could tell her face had broken into a smile at the other end of the line, the warmth of it flooded through the ethers of the airwaves and entered straight into my soul.

'Message me the details. Da Costa will come and get you from the airport. Don't book a return ticket,' she said, the patchy line and her discombobulated voice echoing the fragility of my mind.

'I won't.' It was a strange finality of a promise.

I switched the laptop on and booked myself a ticket for the next morning. It took barely five minutes to change the course of my life. It had taken five minutes some months earlier to do the same. It was the decisions one deferred taking that changed everything.

It took me five minutes to pack. I didn't have much. I'd Kon-Mari-ed my wardrobe when I'd decided to move to Bombay from Delhi after Nihar's death. It had been a purge of sorts. I'd cleaned out all the clothes that he'd loved seeing me in and got myself an entire new capsule wardrobe. It was a relief to have just enough possessions I could fit into a single suitcase.

Baggage slows you down, things you own bind you down to the earth and a place. You need a place to keep your things. You need people to keep your heart. People one binds oneself to. These bonds didn't allow an easy freedom, nor was it easily taken. These bonds are cut and then the soul bleeds, the bonds between parents and child, between siblings, or that rare beast, the bond between souls.

Maa and Kamini had lived out their lives being competitive as siblings, and then Kamini had upped the bar so terribly high, that Maa with her three children, conservative husband and rambling old house in a one-horse hill station town, could never ever hope to compete with. She made up though by constantly trying to keep me and Roop away from the evil influence of our bacchanalian aunt, who fascinated us with her bright lipstick, so loud it was unseemly in a world of soft frosted pinks Maa and the other moms we knew wore, when they did deign to apply lipstick. Kamini was the exotic one, her cigarettes smoked through an elegant ivory and ebony cigarette holder, long strings of pearls knotted carelessly around her neck, jackets and chiffons, printed silks and muslin nightwear. She was everything our mother was not and it fascinated us. She gave us a glimpse into a world where women had agency and the currency to live their lives in a manner of their choosing. We had grown up seeing both Daadi and Maa, despite their degrees and education being reduced to progenitors of the next generation and caretakers of a home. Kamini lived a life of pure hedonism, and was completely unapologetic about it. It was even rumoured, in the family circuit, that she had openly taken in a lover when her husband passed away and was living with him. None of my business, I told myself.

Sadly, when I visited her last year without warning, just on an impulse because we were visiting Goa, the phantom lover was nowhere in evidence. She was surrounded by a handful of fiercely loyal house help, and her major domo Da Costa. The house she lived in was much like her, past its prime but so magnificent that one forgot it was bearing the weight of years and the ache of the lives lived out within on its timbers. Built in the Goan Portuguese style, with a red-tiled roof, long rafters holding the ceiling up, elegantly curved balustrade staircases that wound upwards from either side of a small lobby area and a front porch that looked out across an elegantly unkempt and almost overgrown garden, the house was slowly crumbling from lack of maintenance. But she refused to move out from it or to sell it off and settle in something convenient, like a city apartment with all the required amenities down the road. Going to the house was like stepping back in time, located as it was on a small island that needed a ferry in order to get to it or from it to anywhere on the mainland. She was inaccessible in the monsoon sometimes. She preferred it that way, I suspected. She liked being disconnected. I would like it too, I realised. I had contemplated falling off the face of the earth often enough to not resist the temptation to try it when the opportunity thus arose.

I set the alarm for 4 a.m. the next day and drifted off to a deep disturbed sleep which would have been easily assuaged by one of the sleeping pills the good doctor back in Delhi had thoughtfully prescribed for me after Nihar's death. I resisted the urge to take one. I loved the sleep brought on by the pills. Swift. Instant. A blow to the back of the head. And then the darkness. Warm enveloping blackness one fell through that only ended when the alarm burred itself into one's ear, throwing consciousness and memory into the mind.

Kamini's trusted old driver would be there to receive me at the airport, she'd said, when I'd called to tell her I was landing there the first thing in the morning. I'd never felt so eager to rid myself of a city, to shrug it off and drape myself in the indolence of a new place. The morning was sunny in Goa, the heat enveloped me in warm welcoming waves. Goa was a cornucopia of humidity, I was oozing perspiration from every pore as I scanned the faces outside the arrival, some holding placards of various hotels, some with names scribbled on them with an indifferent hand.

Just when I'd given up on spotting Da Costa, he came charging around the corner. Kamini's Man Friday, handyman, errand boy, butler, driver, gardener and all-round in-charge of the premises, from the time she entered Kirov House as a new bride, Da Costa handled everything she needed handling, from dealing with tenants, getting legalities done, to grocery shopping. Kirov House had had another name before Kamini's husband had purchased it off an old established Portuguese family that had chosen to immigrate to Portugal when the Indian republic annexed Goa. It was a handsome house, built in the late eighteenth century, withstanding rain, storms, sea breezes, changes of regimes, liberalization. One could be forgiven for thinking that Da Costa came with the house, and was as old.

Kamini's husband, Pyotr, or Peter as was easier to spell and say, had been a Russian who came to India long before the current lot of the Russians invaded this small home state with their chartered flights, drug and arms mafia and all the ugliness that came with it. He'd come to India with his parents as an infant and had never returned, taking up citizenship of this country. His father, a journalist behind the Iron Curtain, had slipped off the radar never returning to his homeland. To all purposes, Pyotr or simply Peter Mausaji as we called him, was an Indian, if one went beyond his corn straw hair and blue eyes, which always twinkled like there was a secret he was dying to tell us all about. He had been a nice man, the little I saw of him. I liked him more than I liked my father, and that was damning an indictment as ever of my father.

'Good of you to come,' Da Costa said, with a familiarity that was unfamiliar. 'Madam has not been keeping too well, it will be good for her to have some company.'

'What has happened to her?'

He paused delicately, looking indistinctly into the distance as we marched towards where the car was parked, he insisting on dragging the sole stroller bag I'd packed and me struggling to keep pace with him. 'She'll tell you. I think she's lost the will to live. Perhaps what she needed was someone she loved to be around. No company she has except for us, and she never gets out now that she....' his voice trailed away.

'You didn't complete your sentence.'

He smiled and shrugged. He was a canny old man, Da Costa. 'You'll see when you reach.'

I was curious. Kamini's voice on the phone was crackling sharp as it had always been ever since I'd remembered it from the time she'd reduced Maa to tears and stomped out of our home leaving behind the unbearably intoxicating fragrance of French perfume in the air and the fleeting memory of an uncontainable force that had just spent itself. I had always wondered what that argument had been about. Kamini had never visited us after that, but she kept sending us things, and called to speak to us, the children, never Maa.

Why would she never get out now? Had something happened to her, something she hadn't shared with us? An accident, immobility? Perhaps it was age, but not the age of the body wearing her down to limited functionality but the age of appearance limiting her to shadowy interiors and lamplight. She had always been fiercely beautiful and unabashedly vain. I'd admired that about her. And then she had started withdrawing from the world first, and then the family, even though the family had withdrawn from her first. She had withdrawn slowly and steadily from public appearances, stopped having any shows. She worked in isolation, no one saw what she did, until she sent them out into the world through her dealer.

Her stepson from her husband's first marriage lived in the

UK and barely had any contact with her. He'd been content to let her live on in the old home she'd shared with his father and not staked any claim to it. He'd inherited, of course, the other estates around the country and quite a few of his father's paintings which were worth a fortune each by themselves. I'd found them to be atrocious to be honest, all distorted human shapes and violent colour palettes that assaulted the eye. But he painted the human experience and the brilliant colours of his adopted land and, to the art connoisseur in the international markets, they were exotic. Kamini had never cared for the money, all she'd wanted was enough to let her live in the comfort she was accustomed to. His son had got a good enough bargain from the arrangement. It was unfair, I'd told her when I'd met her last, and she'd laughed, the lovely low-rolling laugh that must have been fatal to her admirers when she was still young and unwrinkled.

'That's his father's work. What will I do with the money, I have enough and more to see me through!' She was a generous spirit, she gave of herself unstintingly, until the world began taking more than she was willing to give.

We drove out from the teeming airport, with its wide approach road segueing off into a highway that then went into roads fringed with red soil, waving coconut trees standing at the edges of narrow winding roads, their leaves spreading like ceremonial umbrellas. The landscape was peppered with paddy fields at the distance and quaint colonial era homes, with their red-tiled roofs, porches and cement benches that looked like they had been built for a gentler era when people stopped by to have a chat or two before they went on their way. These homes cohabited cheek by jowl with the brasher apartment blocks built for the newcomers who wanted to sink their claws into a slice of the Goan life. The road skirted gently by the side of the Arabian Sea. We crossed bridges and rivers and, finally, went through the outskirts of Panjim and pulled up by the jetty, waiting for the ferry to arrive from the island.

Da Costa turned the radio on—Arijit Singh came on, singing of love and heartache, his voice velvet and chocolate and all that was heart-breaking blended into one aural orgasm. The longing in his voice filled the small boxy vehicle with a yearning it could not contain. Da Costa switched stations to where a slick-voiced DJ was speaking in Konkani, a language I was yet to understand, its cadences and inflections musical noise to my ears. I looked out of the window, the sun glinted off the water in brilliant reflects and hit the retina, harsh and blinding, for a moment reducing everything one looked at to a white haze. I blinked and put on my sunglasses. Too much light was as blinding as too much darkness. All that was visible to us lay in the median of the spectrum.

Across the narrow strip of water, I could see the island sparkling in a blaze of emerald, a canopy of trees, dotted with the occasional red roofs of homes sprinkled around, with a hill topped by a white painted church overlooking it all. This was an estuarine island, connected to the mainland by ferry services that ran through the day and into the night, and began back again in the wee hours of the morning. A bridge had never been built, the islanders had always fiercely resisted it, the ferry was enough of a connection. There were ferries on both sides of the island, from the north and the south. What if there was a medical emergency, I asked Da Costa. He furrowed his brow. 'Dere's boats.' What if there was a storm, I asked and the ferries couldn't cross.

'Dere's God.'

If a place was a language, Goa was one with a slow, rolling cadence, deep-voiced, indolent and seductive, musical with the wash of the waves against the land and the caress of the sea breeze.

'Cannot walk, she's become too weak and she gets angry

all the time because she's so weak. She can't paint anymore.' Da Costa was filling me in on my aunt's health. This would be devastating for someone who lived with the brush in her hand from the time she woke to the time she went to bed on the days she painted.

I could see the ferry across the narrow strip of water that separated the island from the mainland. It was painted a particularly virulent shade of blue that made the unwary retina wince when it caught one unguarded in the flash of the noonday sun. The sun was so bright it had bleached the blue of the sky into a uniform yellow blaze. Around me were people in various poses of resignation waiting for the ferry to arrive, some clutching on to the shopping baskets filled with fresh vegetables and produce procured from the mainland, yet others with no discernible business except perhaps visiting relatives who lived on the island. Women in dresses or a skirt that ended at their knees paired with a collared short-sleeved blouse, their hair cut short hugging their scalps, or tied in a no-nonsense ponytail at the nape of their necks, gold hoops in their ears, a cross hanging on a gold chain from their necks, two gold bangles on their right wrists, a watch on the left, a flash of gold tooth from an occasional smile from a matronly sort. The men sat on their bikes with the impatience of the ones who had too much time and not much to do with it.

I had forgotten to apply sunscreen and could feel the sun raising blisters on my skin already from the few minutes I'd stepped out of the car. Worship the sun, the primordial source of energy and light, feel its warmth coursing through the layers of your skin. Epidermis, dermis, hypodermis. The rays penetrating through the fat layer, then the muscle until it hit bone, warming up the bone marrow, pouring its energy into blood cells being produced within. After all, when you distilled us down to the atom, weren't we all just fragments leftover from the big bang, within us the hydrogen and helium that had been spat out from our sun, coalescing into carbon atoms and life.

I was no sun worshipper. This was skin inherited from a tribe that had wandered down from the Caucasian mountains, their skin thin and pale, accustomed to the oblique rays of the sun that barely thawed the snows on the mountain tops come summer. It was so pale that at times I was a white blotch with my eyes copper flashes within. This was skin meant to stay under the earth, where the sun didn't reach, where the darkness converged to a point where the eyes open and shut, saw the same.

Some eyes were turned curiously towards me, but not too many. They were used to people coming from the cities to stay a while in the many homestays on the island. There were a few high-end luxury spas as well. Some homes were owned by the wealthy that chose the inaccessibility for a reason. A few men waited on motorcycles and scooters, tanned brown by days spent riding through the open roads with the sun beating hard on them, their hands lean and muscled, their faces leathery and wary. A tourist, straggly in his string vest, tattoos and hair tied back in a stringy ponytail, sat on a rented Enfield bike, his skin burnt red by the sun, his face crumpled into lines carved out by the sun, the wind and laughter. A family of tourists from north India, judging from their clothes which threw every brand label into your line of vision, some of them visible till a mile up, bickered about things so inconsequential that I felt I was listening in to a pastiche act. Another couple, newlyweds going by the *chura*s the girl flaunted on her wrists and the mehndi going up to her elbow, was standing hand in hand by the edge of the water speaking in soft hushed tones to each other, managing to find within the chaos of the many a bubble that enclosed them alone.

The ferry arrived and discharged its noisy cargo of humans, animals and vehicles, a cacophony that was testament to the human effort to fill space and airwaves with its presence. We embarked. Da Costa spoke to the chap manning the ropes in Konkani, a language that was musical in its cadences but completely unfamiliar to me, and so I smiled politely as they cast swift looks at me while they spoke, so I assumed the conversation was about me. We chugged along across the narrow strip of water, blue green and rippling with reflects of the sun directly overhead now. The island upfront was a green slab of trees and green cover, with a white-washed church rising gracefully from what seemed a sea of green. A house with the traditional red tiles, painted a virulent shade of purple, skirted the edge of the water. Pink bougainvillea spilled over a crumbling wall. The marshlands stretched to as far as the eye could see. Children waited friskily at the edge of the ramp for the ferry to land, hoping for a joyride to and fro. There were a couple of villages scattered on the small island, the remains of a fort, a church and an ayurvedic spa resort which was so exclusive that bookings there were available only through personal recommendation.

Da Costa manoeuvred the van off the ferry with the ease of much practice and on to the narrow, asphalted road which was the single road to everywhere on the island. The road was a lesson in sharing in Goa—every now and then we needed to slow down and pull back to let another pass, at times, it was prolonged and painful politeness, insisting the other pass first. The road, lined with coconut trees, looking out at first on to the swampy marshlands and then segueing into an expanse of paddy fields, dotted with low red-roofed homes in the distance, brick walls where the plaster had fallen off, exposed and naked to the elements. At seemingly regular intervals, we passed patches where small bonfires dotted the sides of the road. The locals I learnt, had to burn their garbage every day because there was no garbage collection.

After a couple of minutes Da Costa turned off into a narrow pathway almost obscured by the tangle of shrubbery. As the van moved slowly down the uneven, unpaved path, it bumped around unsettling what I had eaten on the flight: the pitiful sandwich that was now threatening to hurl itself back up through my oesophagus. I looked back, it seemed like the dense tree cover was closing ranks behind us and parting gently to allow us through. And then, out of nowhere, there it was, sprawling out in front of us, through a rusted iron gate hanging tenaciously to a moss-covered wall, Casa de Braganza. The original name was hand-painted with blue glaze on a white tile set into the wall by the gate. Kirov House was written on a board down on the wall below it, apologetically. It bore the weight of both names with grace. It was an old imposing house, built by the Portuguese occupants of Goa before it was liberated. It must have seen the turn of at least two centuries, the rooster on the top of the house still standing proud, though the original inhabitants had long since moved away. Painted blue and white, the detailing of the windows and the doors in relief picked out in white, with red-tiled roofs emerging from the froth of a green foliage that was the riot of a garden below the house, was welcoming and yet intimidating.

A rooster clucked around importantly, followed by a trail of fat hens who fluttered behind him obsequiously. A black cat sat on the cemented stoop, looking at me for a long moment with piercing grey eyes, until she lost interest and curled back to whatever dream our arrival had interrupted. Cats were like that, they deigned to pay you attention at their convenience. Dogs made your convenience theirs. I loved dogs. Cats intimidated me. Nihar loved cats. We had been adopted by a cat, who had unadopted us when Nihar died. It was symbolic, perhaps, of how I was now abandoned by my husband in death and the cat in life. A couple of dogs ran towards the van, barking their heads off. I froze and clutched my bag closer to myself.

'Nothing dey'll do, don't worry,' Da Costa reassured me. 'Only barking dogs. Not biting dogs. Even a robber comes, dey will play with him. Useless fellas.'

The dogs threw themselves at me in welcome, licking my face and limbs, a welcome that dissolved the residual fear I had of them. They were of an indeterminate breed, strays whom Kamini had adopted. They had been vaccinated and were now the designated guard dogs of the house.

They bounded off ahead of me to the steps leading up to the porch. Kamini's husband had bought this house when he'd decided to settle in Goa, when he was in his thirties and newly married the first time around. He lived here all his life, albeit with the complexion and the pale blue eyes that behoved his Slavic ancestry. It came as quite a shock to most people when he broke into fluent Hindi. He'd been brought up across India, with his parents settling in the foothills of the Himachal, a climate that felt most like home and when he'd grown up, he'd made his way to Bombay and then to Goa where he'd finally grown roots.

He'd fascinated me whenever he visited. His blue eyes, curious questions and gentle attention made me, a shy young girl in a hill station, feel like I had something of importance to say to the world. And Kamini would always send me books, and knick-knacks from around the world. Packages of books would arrive from wherever around the world she was travelling, subscriptions to magazines that were beyond my reach, but gave me glimpses into the world beyond the deodars and pines that cocooned me in my stone and wood home, high above the town. I owed her the window to the world before I escaped life in my small town. Books with fine print that covered them from cover to cover, books with illustrations, books with photographs, books with smells of the different lands they came from, some with the smell of ink still fresh on them, the smell of 'foreign' bursting out when one opened the envelope they were packaged in, the stamp cut out carefully and stuck into the stamp album for posterity. The regal profile of Queen Elizabeth when she was in London. The Liberté de Gandon lady from France, in red and green. The satellite dish stamp from the US when we had just got satellite television ourselves in India. The Madonna and Child Christmas stamp from the year she was spending a white Christmas in New York—the parcel came with a hastily enclosed photograph of her in a fur coat over her saree at Times Square. It contained books. Books she thought I should be reading. *To Kill a Mockingbird.* I read it over and over again. She would call me, suddenly out of the blue, I knew, to discuss the book with me. For Roop there were comic books and painting stuff. Watercolour sets, brushes with sable bristles so soft one could have them caress one's face all day. Books on art galleries and works of the masters. Roop had the gift, she had said, when she'd visited, of seeing the world in images. I saw the world in words. Roop would shutter down the images in her head and move into academia. I would continue to ferret through words and narratives, some my own, some disparate, trying to make sense of things.

I stepped out on to the ground, and felt gooseflesh creep up my arms. A sudden dread gripped my intestines. There was something here, in this house. My face must have blanched. The house was marked, I could feel it. There were others here. Watching. I looked up at the rows of windows that looked out blankly upon us. Da Costa noticed it.

'You'll get used to it,' he said quietly. 'Some people died on that side of the house. But that was a long time ago, before your aunt and Peter sir came to live here. Now, Missy baba, give me your bag. If your aunt sees you carrying your bags when I am around, she will make strips of my flesh and feed them to the dogs.'

'Don't be silly,' I told him firmly, 'I can definitely carry this

small bag on my own, and I will ensure that you aren't fed to
the dogs. And what will I get used to?'

'The house....'

It looked down at us as we stepped out of the car, imposing,
welcoming, yet a little wary. The compound walls had perhaps
been painted white once upon a time, but were now covered
with a slowly encroaching green of moss that speckled it into
a design that was a tale of its own telling. The plastering had
fallen off in some patches, exposing the red bricks within, like
gaping wounds. The house itself was a picture in a faded royal
blue with white accents where the architectural details were,
the mouldings, the cornices, the window arches, the pillars.
The porch, reached by stairs from both sides, was large and
welcoming and, at the head of it, where the house began, Kamini
sat in her wheelchair looking down imperiously at us, her hair
sharply cut as usual, now camouflaged beneath a skull-hugging
cap, wispy ends growing out from within. There was a frizziness
in her hair that I had never seen before. The new style was part
of her newly acquired stylistic eccentricities, I presumed. She
still had her lipstick in place, carmine, and fiercely applied, and
the perennial cigarette, with its end lit and glowing, still in its
holder, as she held it away from her face. She narrowed her
eyes to look at me through the plumes of smoke she exhaled. I
wondered how I looked wreathed in smoke. My eyes took in the
wheelchair. Perhaps this was what Da Costa meant. There were
questions that needed to be asked, and answers that needed to
be heard, and I wondered if there was time enough for both.

I climbed up the few stairs as swiftly as I could, lifting my
tiny stroller now that the wheels had been rendered out of
service, and bent down to hug her. She was soft and warm, and
slight, tinier than I remembered her or had I grown larger. Time
changes us all, and memories are the most resistant to change.
A fragility I had never associated with her before had now taken

over her completely. She seemed brittle, porous, chalk-like. Hug her trifle too hard and she would crumble into granules into my arms, granules that would swirl into ash and blow away with the wind. She put her arm around me, the one holding the cigarette stretched away, far away, keeping me safe from accidental contact with its glowing tip, and patted my back. She smelt of smoke, roses, musk and vanilla and something acrid, the smell of medication.

Her eyes, now that I could see them up close, were kohl-lined like I remembered them and moist like I had never seen them before. Were those tears or a moistness from the smoke getting into them, I didn't know. She smelt of all things comforting and seductive, a fragrance I had always associated with her and childhood.

'You haven't been eating,' she said. 'You're all bones.'

'And so are you! Why are you in a wheelchair? And what is this new turbanator style?'

She smiled and fluttered her hand, a gesture that was both residual vanity and dismissive together, the gesture of a very beautiful woman reconciling herself to losing her beauty.

'Isn't it so convenient, no need to keep up with the colouring if the roots show. Psst,' she whispered, gesturing for me to bend down, 'not that I have much hair left anyway. Don't tell anyone. Going to shave it all off soon, save on the shampoo and conditioner and the salon visits.'

I smiled, the vanity was perhaps something that would go with her to the grave. The wheelchair was not explained, the questions I wanted to ask her trembling on my tongue but not daring to escape. She took my hand, patted it.

'You always had such lovely hands, an artist's hands. I thought you would take after me, but you became a writer. What's this lovely ring, I didn't see you wear it the last time?'

It was an antique ring she had spotted. Nihar had bought it

for me as a joke. A cameo on the top carved in coral, it opened to reveal a small space inside. The antique dealer who sold it to us said it was meant for secret missives, locks of hair, lover's trivia. Nihar had snipped off a bit of his hair and made me put it within. 'I just like to think of a bit of me being with you even when I'm not around.'

I, thankfully, had no such sentimentality. I had discarded the hair a few weeks after he died, when I'd given away most of his clothes to charity. Some I kept. I would go to his cupboard in a madness of missing him and bury my nose in his clothes to smell him. And he would be there, next to me, the slight musky smell of him, the perfume he always loved. I had taken to spraying myself with it. It made me feel his arm was around me, we were walking together, he was right next to me, he'd never really gone away. Smell is escape. Smell is a lasso to yank you back in time. I smelt his old t-shirts in the cupboard until they stopped smelling of him and began smelling of me. Smell deserts you too, and memory is unreliable. How soon would it be before I closed my eyes and be unable to recall his face at all, before all that was left of him in my mind was a name that lingered and whispered in my darkest moments?

'It's a ring Nihar had gifted me. He would say the profile reminded him of me.' She smiled and pressed my hand against her face.

'And now it reminds you of him.' Her eyes were sad. I did not reply. There was nothing to say. It was just a ring, I had no reason to need to be reminded of Nihar. He had never really left me, there was no forgetting someone who was still with you, day and night, even from beyond the grave.

EIGHT

HERE, NOW

My sleep was disturbed that night. A celebration somewhere had the tinny sounds of drums floating in through the windows, their immediacy hushed by the distance they would have travelled on the salty breeze. I hadn't taken a sleeping pill the previous night, I'd assumed I'd be tired enough to be able to sleep like the dead. I had, and then I had awakened all of a sudden, my heart slamming in my chest, an uneasiness spreading through me.

I wasn't used to the humidity which, strangely, was much heavier on the body than it seemed in Mumbai, weighing one down, sitting on one's chest like a Khapasa, a night hag from my childhood. They sat on sleeping people's chests and tried to choke the breath out of them with thumbless hands, Daadi had told us, and also that they were especially fond of naughty children. I'd fallen asleep most nights telling the gods that I hadn't been a naughty girl that day, but the Khapasas visited regularly. Much later, when I visited a therapist, she'd told me about sleep paralysis, but she couldn't quite explain the marks around my neck when I woke up. Perhaps I had gripped my own throat in fear, she'd concluded.

Every culture knew them. They just came with different names in each. Digeuton, Bszorkany-nyomas, Karabasan, Phi Am or just simple, night witches. We called them the Khapasas, the red-eyed ones lurking in the toilets, in the rooms of young girls, trying to steal their souls while they slept. The Khapasa who had sat on my chest tonight had flames for eyes, and a voice that slithered into my cranium and sifted things around, making it difficult for me to chase a single thought or an action. I lay paralysed with fear until she tired of me and vanished.

What were Khapasas called in Goa, I wondered? They lurked in the shadows of darkened rooms, clambering down from the roofs, reaching out from the branches of the trees in the courtyard and sliding into bedrooms, through a crack in the window pane. I woke up drenched in an unholy sweat that seemed to pour off every inch of me, drenching the mattress of the huge four-poster bed I was in. It was the heavy dinner causing the unease, I'd told myself, and the sleep paralysis. I'd taken to crediting science over superstition these days. It had been a hedonistic Goan spread at the dinner table, wasted on me given my appetite. Lucenzia, or Lucy as she was called, Kamini's wizened old cook, had outdone herself and pulled out all the stops. From the spicy pork vindaloo, to the chicken xacuti, to the pomfret recheado, topped by the soft yet firm give of the layered Bebinca. I'd eaten with reluctance, my stomach unaccustomed to such richness of flavour and taste. I realised I'd never really thought about what I was eating for the past few months. It had been food to keep body and soul together, and that too, not too much of it because the body was weighing the soul down. We'd sat down for the meal opposite each other at the long, carved rosewood dining table and Kamini smoked her cigarette with quick, guilty puffs and barely nibbled at the extravagant meal laid out before us.

'Eat,' she said, with all the benevolence of one who could not eat much herself. 'You look like you could do with some food in you. Your face has become all skeletal from the last time I saw you.'

Perhaps I had become skeletal. I'd been kicked about reducing body fat levels, but was it down to unhealthy levels, I wondered. I hadn't even been looking at myself in the mirror too carefully these days. I ate last night with the careful delight of one who has finally managed to cross an unspecified threshold in the pathway of mourning and is now prepared to leave the dead behind and start walking with the living. But were the dead prepared to leave the living behind and walk on with the dead? I didn't know.

The ceiling fan, hanging low on an elongated rod from its perch from a high rafter, whirred noisily overhead. Lamps lit in the corners of the room threw strange flickering shadows as the wind moved them, and the buzzing of insects throwing themselves against the netted windows created a discordant beat, the evening insects outside in the grounds created their own background score. All the years of living in a city had me forget what nature sounded like when humans didn't interrupt.

Kamini barely ate, toying with her food like a petulant child. 'My digestion is not what it used to be,' she said wryly, sipping from a glass of Port wine that Da Costa kept refilling as she drained it. My glass was untouched. I had never liked the overwhelming sweetness of the Port wine that was locally produced here. Peter had always kept a good cellar, I remembered. Perhaps I would request another wine, a Merlot, if they had one. Perhaps I would do better to stay away from the wine. The chemicals in my bloodstream were unreliable. I had carried my medication along. Now if only I could be trusted to take it at the right time, in the right doses.

'Why the wheelchair?' I asked finally. I had been itching to ask her since the moment I'd arrived.

She held out her hands for my inspection, they were trembling incessantly. A tremor that was beyond her control.

'I can't paint anymore.' The grief in her voice was heart-breaking. 'The same is with my legs. It makes for lousy balance. Rather than stumble, fall and break a hip and be stuck in a bed till I die, I prefer this. I can get around the house and I'm safe.

If I need to get down the stairs I can still manage with some help and a walking stick.' She smiled, the impish smile that made admirers swoon when she was younger, and pledge to cut out their hearts and present it to her on a plate, with dressing on the side. 'It is nicer to be in a wheel chair than struggle with a walking stick. A wheel chair has pathos. A walking stick has the indignity of ageing.'

'What does the doctor say?'

'He says I'm going to die,' she said, her face grim. Then she burst into laughter looking at the horrified expression on my face. 'Oh, Kamla. We all are going to die at some time, some of us earlier than we'd expected, it's okay, I've made my peace with it.' I had still to make peace with Nihar's death. He still had to make peace with his death. It was a death that would not see peace soon, it seemed.

There was an awkward silence filled by Da Costa and Lucenzia bustling around, bringing in some more dishes and insisting on serving me more than my stomach was accustomed to at a single meal. The long wooden table gleamed with a fresh coat of polish, the high-backed carved chairs we sat on made the meal ceremonial. It was a table that could easily seat sixteen. We sat opposite each other in the centre, where the places had been set for us. Damask napkins, with hand-tatted lace edging them, silver flatware, plates of the finest porcelain edged with gold and patterned with flowers that had escaped a blue meadow. Between us, a bowl of fruit and a vase of gladioli, bursting red and orange, punctuated the space, the words and the silences.

'Take no more,' Lucenzia exhorted, an antipodal statement if any. I would have to get used to these interjections of 'no' where it was not needed. 'Not nice, you don't like?'

I hastened to reassure her that my frugal intake was in no way a reflection on my part of not appreciating her culinary skills. 'Eat, no? Little vindaloo? Fish curry? Don't feel shy.' She paused with a ladle full of the stuff poised over my plate. I waved her away, apologetically. She had outdone herself with this meal, I was sure.

'I will burst,' I pleaded. 'I don't eat so much in an entire year.'

'After long time I cooked so much. Madam not eating only. And why to cook for this rascal,' she threw a disparagingly antagonistic look at Da Costa, who stood next to Kamini to assist her. 'But why you not eating? Dat's why so thin, no? Even my niece, sister's daughter, so thin. Like a stick. Always dieting. I tell her, put on some weight. Men like women with flesh on their bones. When I was young...' she put her hand out to indicate a massive bosom where now only shrivelled dugs remained. Da Costa snorted. She threw him a glance which could have impaled him to the wall. He was made of stronger stuff. It deflected off him, leaving him unscathed. There seemed to exist some curious antagonism between the two of them that only unfinished business between a man and a woman would allow.

'Missy not interested in lissening to your fairy tales. Give her food,' he hissed.

She shot him a repeat of the earlier withering look. 'You keep quiet,' she barked at him and ladled generous helpings of gravy over the rice on my plate. I looked at it with trepidation.

'I seriously can't eat so much...' I began.

'Eat,' my aunt said. 'You have wasted away since I last saw you. This isn't healthy.'

'I've been running and keeping my weight down.'

'You didn't have any excess weight to begin with, Kamla.'

I laughed. 'You're sounding like Maa now. She's also constantly making me eat. What's with all of you trying to make me eat?'

'That's the only way we can show you our love.'

That was it. Love that translated itself into food, flavour, the pleasure of seeing a loved one eat. The kheer Daadi made, stirring in so much more than sugar and the blanched almonds, the poori aloo mom cooked when she felt like and then monitored every morsel that went into one's mouth. I had forgotten what food mingled with love could do to the soul; it had been erased by food mingled with control. Food was an affirmation of life. Eating was an affirmation to go on living.

Lucenzia, in her mid-forties, had already been working in the house when Kamini entered it. She was sent out to work in the big house, then a young girl, barely seventeen at the time. She never left. I would learn about this side of Lucenzia later, but now she was standing just behind me, insisting that I eat more.

Kamini whispered to me, 'She'll be upset if you don't eat. She really doesn't get anyone to cook for, I barely eat, and we have no guests. Let her have the happiness of knowing her cooking is being appreciated by someone.'

I pushed the food down my throat wondering whether the stomach would burst with the unaccustomed gluttony. Dinner was done. Dessert was brought in ceremonially. Bebinca, in all its succulent layers of egg and jaggery and coconut milk. A generous slice was cut and placed on my plate. I stared at it in dread and wondered how many extra kilometres I would have to run to get rid of all I had ingested in the course of a single meal. I worked up the nerve to take a spoon to the slice. I finally did. The taste was an acquired one, I concluded, and laboured through the rest of it.

The table was cleared of the remnants of the meal. I went around to Kamini to hug her and go to bed. It had been a long day. Kamini took out her cigarette case, polished to a sparkle, and put yet another cigarette into the holder that never left her side. She handed me her lighter, her action the gesture of someone who always had someone around to click the lighter for her, an entitlement that she took for granted. I felt the familiar yearning for nicotine flood my bloodstream. It would be so easy to bum a cigarette off Kamini and to drag it in deep into my lungs, to feel the hit of the calm flood me. The tip of the cigarette came alive, embers glowing which suddenly disoriented me, a burning red eye. The room swam into darkness in front of my eyes, speckled with a million unblinking red eyes. I closed my eyes for a second. When I opened them again, it was just me in this dimly lit room with Kamini studying me, her head cocked at an angle. She dragged deeply from the holder and blew a plume of smoke in the direction of the door with the studied elegance of one who had done this a million times.

'How did your husband die?' she asked, a vertical crease between her eyebrows.

'It was a heart attack, they said,' I replied. 'He was here in Goa for a conference. They found him dead in the hotel room when he didn't turn up to give the talk he was supposed to give.'

She blew out a perfect smoke circle, and then another into the rapidly expanding first one, smiling delightedly at her handiwork.

'That's all you know?'

I nodded. That's what I had been told.

'I'll tell you how he died. He was found naked. The room had traces of recreational drugs, he had an overdose in his system. Was it an overdose? Was it suicide? Or...' she paused, cocking her head to one side and looking at me intently, perhaps to gauge whether I knew the information she was imparting already. '... was it murder?'

The blood froze in my veins, a stone dropped into the pit of my stomach and bile rose to my throat.

'How do you know this?'

'I have my sources.'

She misted over and shimmered as the tears flooded my eyes. I blinked hard. I dare not spill them. Not one. I was done with my tears.

'I'm sure there has been a mistake.'

She smiled, her expression gentle. 'You know what I think?

I think whether it was suicide, drug overdose or, perhaps, even murder, you need closure on him. The dead move on, it is we the living who get stuck with their memories and refuse to do so. I've heard you've turned into a recluse, you refuse to meet anyone, you came away to Bombay so you don't have to meet anyone from the family. You have to get closure. You have to come out of the grief.'

I shook my head slowly from side to side, 'Suicide? Drug overdose? That's impossible. He wasn't that kind of a person, he kept a clean body, never even ate anything unhealthy, he was so into keeping himself clear of toxins, never drank alcohol, not even the occasional wine or beer. And suicide, he had no reason whatsoever. He was happy, on top of his game. It doesn't make sense. What makes you think it could be either suicide or drug overdose? And why would you think it could be murder?'

'I got all the post-mortem reports changed to heart attack from drug overdose. I also got them not to mention the bruises on his body.' She looked at me again, her expression inscrutable. 'There were bruises on his body, yes. Did you see them when you saw his body? He had been beaten up, rather badly at that. There were probably some bones broken. And yes, he had been injected with heroin, enough to cause an overdose. But he wasn't a user. That much was obvious from his body. No needle marks.'

I looked at her in shock. She smiled again. 'Yes, I saw his corpse at the hospital. I have friends in high places who can help me with all this. Now would you like to tell me what you know about his death. Or what you think could be behind the murder.'

I remembered them, mottled purple on his face. Bruises his mother had commented on, but had been told they'd been caused by falling down when he'd had his attack. Grief doesn't allow you to question too much. I didn't want to question. There were answers I didn't want to hear. From the velvety darkness outside the window, I could hear the soft hooting of an owl, settling on the branches of the banyan tree that unfurled itself along the western wall that the dining room opened out on to.

'I don't know,' I said in a soft voice. 'I really have no idea why someone would want to kill him.' I only knew that he wasn't quite dead yet, but that wasn't something I wanted to share with Kamini. That was something I would have to deal with on my own.

'Lucy's nephew now works in the hotel where your husband was found. He was here, fixing the switches when you had visited us last year. He had seen him. You might not remember, he was the one on the step ladder, changing the bulbs and had to move the ladder when you both came into the parlour. He remembered your husband. He alerted me. Before you got the call, I knew.'

'He never did drugs,' I said vehemently, 'he was so particular about fitness, about what he put into his body.'

'It wasn't him perhaps. It could have been someone else who put them in his body. There was enough in him to kill an elephant, Dr Mhapankar tells me, he's the one who was called by the hotel when they discovered him. He's the one who was easily persuaded to change the death certificate for the promise of a pay out,' she sighed, her voice deep and scratchy from all those years of dragging on her cigarettes no matter that she used her filter.

'What do you know?' I asked, wary, terrified of what I might hear.

'Not much, except for what I told you.'

'It has to be a mistake. I knew him. It had to be a heart attack.'

I couldn't deal with the narrative shifting again, just as I had made my peace with it.

She smiled gently, shaking her head in reproach. 'You know I never liked him, there was something about him I couldn't quite put my finger on, but then I thought if you were happy who was I to interfere. He was probably involved with dangerous people. So much money in such a short time.'

'That was the start-up, they'd received funding, and they were doing pretty well....'

'Is that what you want to believe? Do you think that fancy home you bought came from your start-up funding? Especially when the business had to be run and there were three partners and operational costs to be dealt with. He was probably involved in something else, something dangerous.' She paused, and cocked her head again as she looked at me. 'Something most probably illegal.'

I put both my hands on the table and closed my eyes for a long while, trying to assimilate what she had told me.

'Why would anyone want to murder him, if it was murder?'

She nodded, stretched out and patted my hand with hers. Her hand was dry and soft, the skin crinkled with age, liver spots sprinkled liberally across them.

'I don't know. You need to think hard and tell me what you know....' She paused. The universe stopped for the briefest of microseconds. The night was balmy but a soft breeze came through the netted windows, and let the soft murmurings of the river meeting the sea drift into the house. I broke into a cold sweat and felt my hands and feet go chilly.

Da Costa came in on soft footsteps to check if we had everything we needed. We were alone in the room now. Kamini wheeled herself away from the dining table and came next to me and took both my hands in hers. My palms dwarfed her tiny, delicate hands. But delicate as they were, there was a reedy strength to them, strength that flowed from her to me, strength I soaked in because I needed it.

She paused, looking again into my eyes, searching them for expression, reaction. I looked back at her, uncaring what my eyes revealed. There was too much despair racking my soul for me to bother about camouflage. The dim flickering light of the yellow bulbs in the Belgian crystal chandelier tinkling gently in the soft breeze cast uncertain shadows on her face, making her expression shift from concerned to calculative to concerned again.

'I made sure nothing about the case came in the newspapers. There would have been the money, I thought, insurance. You could have done with it. Murder, suicide or overdose would not just have been a scandal but also financially inconvenient.' She looked at me straight in the eye, I looked back holding her gaze steadily. What did she know, what was she not letting on?

It had come in handy, the money I received upon his death. I had become quite a wealthy widow. Who was it who had said that men should be careful about making widowhood the only path to power for a woman? Gloria Steinem perhaps. It was a wise statement, one that I realised had truth beyond what the words infused it.

She paused, her hands within my grasp were shaky, an involuntary tremor making them quiver. A bruise had blossomed on her cheek the size and colour of a cherry. Her skin looked like it would start bleeding any moment, she was teetering on an edge of fragility which was about to implode. She was ill.

'There was someone in the room, who left before they found him. No one knows who the person was. I couldn't find out, despite all my efforts. Which is why we suspected it could be murder, a deliberate overdose. His body was roughed up, as you must have seen. But there were powerful people who stopped all investigations. People who even I, with all my contacts, could not circumvent, dangerous people. Now it is for you to decide. Do you want to dig deeper and find out if it was murder or death by suicide? Or do you want to let it rest? Is there something you need to tell me?'

I felt the blood drain from my face and my toes begin to tingle with the stopping of the blood circulating within. The food

I'd just eaten rose to my throat. I rushed to the door and stepped out on the porch just in time to hurl everything up into a rose bush that grew by the stairs. Kamini wheeled herself out behind me, stopping where the slab of the stair made it impossible for her to go further. When I was done, I stood shuddering against the pillar that flanked the stairs going down into the overgrown patch of garden. The crescent moon was still in the sky, its half smile mocking me, the blaze of the Milky Way which spread so graciously across the velvety blackness back home was reduced to a mere hazy shimmering in the darkness above. Da Costa was standing quietly by the side, with a bottle of water which I used to rinse my mouth and wiped my face with a table napkin he had carried with him.

'I'm not feeling too well,' I said, stating the obvious, 'I think I will go to my room and rest a bit.'

'Yes,' she said, 'Go to sleep now, we'll speak about this tomorrow. Da Costa will take you up to your room. I've asked Cajetan to come here tomorrow when he gets off duty to speak to you. Now, go rest. We can start finding out what happened to your husband. That is if you want to find out at all. If not, let it go, stay here for a few months with me, let me pamper you like I always wanted to when you were a child. Start rebuilding your life.'

'I'll see you in the morning,' I said.

Kamini nodded and moved her wheelchair back to allow me to pass into the waiting area from where the stairs led off in all different areas to rooms and rooms and more rooms. The house followed the template that most Indo-Portuguese houses did, based on homes in north Portugal which were built to withstand harsh winters. But ironically, these were located on a land which never had a winter. The summer dipped and rose, the monsoon took over, a dip for a month or two in a matter of a couple of degrees on the thermometer and then it was summer again.

The house was linear from the foyer, leading off to rooms on either side from the large central hall the foyer opened out to.

I followed Da Costa up to my room, which was up a long curving stairway that went up from the left flank that began off the waiting room area. What was on the other side of the right flank of stairs, I did not know. It looked disused and grimy, and disappeared into darkness. 'Don't go thasside, Kamie madam,' Da Costa said rather hastily when I looked curiously at the stairs that seemed to cry out for feet to tread them.

'What is there?' I asked, wondering if I'd heard right.

'They,' he replied, cryptically, refusing to elaborate further. 'You saw when you came. You don't trouble them, they don't trouble you.' I looked down the length of the corridor opposite where the darkness shifted and changed shape as the light filtered through the moving leaves of the banyan tree outside.

A sigh drifted over the rippling shadows and reached my ears. Was someone whispering my name or was that just the wind whistling through the gaps in the window panes?

My luggage had already been unpacked for me, and my clothes arranged neatly in the carved wood cupboard that was many times my age, the wood smooth to the touch. The room gleamed gently in the soft yellow light of the bulbs in the lamps on the sides of the wall. No white light here, except for the lamps outside in the garden lighting up the boundary wall. It took some getting used to, having the evenings tinged with the soft gold of yellow bulb light. I kicked off my shoes and fell on the bed, uncaring about changing my clothes, brushing my teeth, applying the standard moisturiser and anti-wrinkle cream. Sleep, when it came, was swift, dark and a fall into a swirling vortex of nothingness that sucked me into it, swallowing me whole, flashing hallucinogenic sparks of light and colour that soon faded into a velvety, rhythmic blackness. And there were the caves again, lit with neon flashes of phosphorescence that sparkled enough to let one see where one was headed, the fluttering of softly whooshing bats around one, their frantic wings, hitting one as they passed, the dank wetness of a trickle of water somewhere, wetting the soles of my feet as I walked barefoot over the sharp rocks, the sting of the blood the edges demanded as offering for entry into this realm. And then the yawning opening, light filtering in from an opening high above me, a place that I would never be able to reach should I want to climb out, and a huge maw of rocks shifting and opening, a trickle of a narrow river, gleaming silver in the sifting moonlight, running right into the gap in the rocks. I stepped into it, feeling the water, forgetting the stinging it caused to my cut and bleeding feet. 'Lotusface....' he whispered into my ears, 'I'm waiting....'

It was a sound that broke my sleep. A scratching. When I opened my eyes, something large and swift was fluttering outside the window, silent and insistent. The mosquito net the bed was encased in shimmered in the moonlight, a submerged wonderland, where reflections were not to be trusted and light and shade dappled and merged, creating a world which was real and unreal. I sat up with a start, terrified. Bats. On my clothes, there was the faint dampness of having been in a wet space. I put my feet down on the floor to recoil with the sharpness of the pain. I looked at my soles, they were bleeding, wounds that had appeared from nowhere. Then it came again, the sound from the passage outside.

A thump and a drag, then again. And then silence. I moved towards the door. My feet stung as I took every step. I felt like I was trudging through knee-deep sludge, that's how thick the air was with the humidity. The heat swirled around one like a being—warm, breathing, pulsing, enveloping one, weighing one down, grappling one down to the floor with its weight. Was I awake or was I dreaming, I didn't know. I was drenched with sweat, my clothes were sticking to me. Outside the window, a tepid gibbous moon shone in a black velvet sky sprinkled liberally with stars one never saw in the cities. It reminded me of home, on a clear day, when the Milky Way was a semi-circular dappling of stars down the centre of the sky, inviting us to step off the edge of a mountain and climb its bedazzled pathway into other worlds.

Then again, the thump and the drag. I had reached the door, I threw it open and looked down the landing to the stairs, there was no one. It was cold outside, so chilly I felt the hair on my arms rise. I wrapped my arms around myself. I'd stepped into another climate from the heat and humidity in my room, this was Siberia. Frosty winds freezing my eyelashes, fogging the breath emerging from my nostrils. I looked around. A dim light from the sole lamp at the foot of the stairs flickered for a moment and then went out. It was completely dark now. The faint moonlight filtering through the glass panes tinged the edges of everything pewter. From an open window somewhere a breeze blew in, sneaking around my legs like a furry cat, cold, unnerving in its chilly restlessness.

The sound, again. The thump. The drag. Something made me cast my eyes to the flight of stairs opposite, going up into a neverland of darkness so deep that nothing except a solar flare could pierce it. A shadow moved there, crawling up the stairs. A thump. A drag. Another thump, another drag. And then it stopped. I moved down my side of the stairs and looked up at it. A woman, slightly built, dragging herself up, a lame leg slowing her movement up the stairs. I began climbing, the edges of the scene beginning to dim in my vision, shimmer and blur. I reeled, holding on to the banister. Slowly, imperceptibly, the house began to swirl around me, slowly at first and then faster until I felt I was in the centre of a vortex with that figure just ahead of me, now waiting for me to follow it. My legs moved involuntarily, upwards, on floorboards that did not creak.

'Who is it?' I asked.

She swivelled around in the dimness, looking at me, unblinking, from a face with features I couldn't decipher, a blankness of black, the eyes were sockets of nothingness. I could hear her voice in my head, warning me, telling me to go away, berating me for having brought more of the dead into the house.

The passageway swirled away into darkness, the room opened like a maw, swallowing her up, moving swiftly towards me, a tsunami of blackness with red sparkling dots inside swirling closer and closer to me, with millions of eyes within, creatures waiting for me to enter their darkness. I could hear the snarling of dogs from outside within. The gatekeepers, it came unbidden to my mind. Cerberus in the Greek. Bargest to the English. Dip to the Catalans. Yama's four-eyed hell hounds, with their wide nostrils, sniffing amongst the living for the stench of death. The zone they guarded, a grey of an interminable purgatory. Behind the veil of the existence we knew where all our individual hells merged into one.

My feet were rooted to the spot, my body paralysed. The swirling began to slow down and the door receded back to the end of the corridor. My knees buckled under me. I heard a scream, it was my own voice, high-pitched and alien. As I slumped to the floor, I realised what the smell that had disturbed me when I'd first stepped into the house was. The smell of the caves I'd once got lost in during a school picnic, the smell of decay and neglect. Bats fluttering around, navigating their sightless worlds with sounds that screeched into our ear tunnels and impacted them, faint clicks and ominous whirring. The house smelt of bats, guano, caves. And the dead.

NINE

THEN, THERE

When I woke up that morning, I wondered where I was. To my consternation, I was on my own bed and it was the sharp light of a wintry morning that made me realise it was a new day. The journey through the night was over.

I was woken up quite ingloriously by a clout on the ear from Roop. For one who looked so demure and delicate she packed quite a punch in that little fist of hers. 'Wake up, sleepy bones,' she yelled into my ear, almost puncturing my ear drum. 'It's morning, you've been sleeping since yesterday.'

An older sister was a mother and a grandmother in their absentia with all the authority they invested in her. She was also, at the same time, the repository of all one's childhood insecurities and questions because she knew all the answers to questions you didn't even know you had. For instance, that one should never kiss a boy on the mouth and let him stick his tongue into yours because that was the quickest way to get pregnant and then you had to go away for many months to a distant relative's home like Sarla, Balwant the mithaiwala's daughter, who came back looking changed in a way we couldn't quite put our fingers on and was then quickly married off to a man twenty years her senior with four children from two previous wives who had had the bad taste to die on him. Whatever had happened to Sarla, I wondered, we never saw her again, not even on an occasional visit to her father's shop. She had dropped out of existence, simply by being married. I never would kiss a boy, I swore.

Boys were idiots. The years hadn't changed my opinion much.

Roop dragged the quilt off me, and the chill of the morning hit me, dissipated quickly by the momentary warmth from the stray straggly rays of the wintry morning sun that managed to sneak their way into the room just through the clear glass panes. Roop's face was washed and her hair tied, she'd been awake a while. Outside the window, the dense Deodar trees that framed the road down to the marketplace bristled irritably at the slight wind that blew through their leaves, the murmuring of discontent carrying to us over the air. The road snaked down silver, down, down, peeking through gaps in walls, hedges, trees, until it disappeared from sight. There was no fog this morning, nor snow, but there was the deathly caress of frost. In the distance, snow-capped peaks waited majestically for the gaze to drift towards them and settle on them, and then pass them without the wonder of the moment in the earth's history when land collided against land and raised the oceans up in folds that would serrate across the surface of the continent for the coming aeons, the sea creatures, the shells, the molluscs, fossilized for eternity on the highest points the earth possessed.

'There's pooris for breakfast and halwa.' That was incentive enough to emerge from the razai.

I scrambled up and rushed to the little bathroom down the passage, built as an afterthought, an awkward extension to the house, the plumbing put in now wheezing and asthmatic. My footsteps thundered on the wooden planks of the flooring. We had our room on the top floor of the house, above us was the attic where no one went, at least not in our presence. Daadi went there sometimes to pack away the heavy woollens and the razais when summer arrived or to take them down when winter did, along with Behra and Kanchi. We were absolutely forbidden to go there, with the threat of no sweets for the rest of our lives. 'Wait a minute,' I remembered the previous afternoon, stopped in my tracks, and turned around. 'Where did they find me? Did I come back to our room?'

Roop glanced around with a conspiratorial air to ensure that no one was around within earshot and whispered into the very eardrum she had almost pierced by shrieking into it a little while ago. 'They found you in the attic. I thought you were unconscious, but Maa said you were in a deep sleep and to let you be. You would wake up soon enough. You slept all day yesterday and it's almost nine this morning. How much can you sleep, dopey head?'

She added for good measure, 'You're going to get into solid trouble with Daadi. You know we are not supposed to climb up into the attic without a grown-up to accompany, don't you? She's going to bite your ear off and eat it with pickle and salt.'

I shuddered. Daadi's anger was the stuff of legend. Grown men trembled before her wrath. It would blow over soon though, that was the good thing about it. It always did. But while it held sway, the rafters would shake, the glass panes would vibrate and people would swiftly move out of the way from hurling missiles or a slipper wielded indiscriminately.

'You know there was that girl there, in the attic. She's real. I saw her.'

Roop laughed, disbelieving.

'You're just saying this to scare me, or to get off from getting yelled at. If there was a girl in the attic why has no one seen her all these years?'

Daadi yelled from the kitchen, her voice reverberating on the rafters holding the roof up. 'Are you girls planning to come down yet, or should I feed your share to Moti?' Moti being the local stray who had adopted us. He came and went as he pleased but made sure he curled up on our porch in a spot right next to where the sun hit Pappa's armchair every afternoon for his nap.

Pappa was reading the newspaper when we reached the

dining table, breakfast was still not on the table thankfully. Maa was nowhere to be seen, perhaps she was with the baby. The baby took up the most space in the house these days. Everything centred around him, his feeding, his burping, keeping him warm, the washing and drying of his perennially soiled nappies in the feeble winter sun.

'What's the delay, why is breakfast not ready yet?' Pappa bellowed, raising his head from the newspaper like a lion surveying the Savannah for possible stray gazelles floating around to be nipped at. Roop and I shrank into our chairs, examining every knot and grain on the highly polished surface of the wooden table we sat at. After I'd done imprinting every little detail on to memory, I moved on to staring at the bare stone flooring, unalleviated by rugs and carpets I could see in the living room area and in the passageway. The kitchen and dining area stayed carpet free. Daadi didn't trust Behra and his balancing skills.

'Come and make it yourself,' Daadi bellowed back from the kitchen, from which the aromas of deep frying emerged enticingly. Pappa harrumphed and went back to the newspaper. The wail of the baby broke the silence, drawing us to Maa's room to take a peek at it, this squiggly little creature with the crumpled monkey face and old eyes, who had lungs that could give any self-respecting iron smith's bellows a run for their money. Maa wasn't around, the room dark and dank thanks to all the curtains being drawn to stop any errant draughts from wandering in and chilling the baby. In a crib adjoining Maa's bed, the originator of those loud wails was now strangely quiet. He lay still in his crib, his squashed tomato face benign in repose. He was wrapped cosily in layers and layers of cloth through which his face peeped out, wizened and crumpled like he had been folded many times over in the womb and needed to be ironed out.

'Should I poke it?' I whispered to Roop.

'It's a him, not an it,' she giggled.

I took her giggle to mean acquiescence and extended my hand forward nervously to do the deed before any figure of parental authority entered the room. Just then the baby opened his eyes and looked straight into mine, totally disconcerting me. Babies barely out of the womb were not supposed to have killer stare-back abilities. And I didn't know then about babies being severely myopic. I was probably a giant fuzzy round thing hovering above in the immediate vicinity for him. At the point I just thought that the new baby brother, for all that he looked like a red vegetable, was doing a stare dare. I stared right back at him, bringing my face closer and closer to his, until he began squalling again and Maa bustled in and picked him up casually, like she would pick up a toy, and shunted us out of the room.

'Kamo,' she said, in an odd voice when I was almost out of the room. 'Don't go up there on your own again. You might not be able to get back.'

I turned around in shock. Did she know what I had seen up there? Did the adults know? Was that why we had been kept off limits from the attic all these years?

'Maa,' I began. Roop was already on the landing down the stairs and stopped, realising I'd not followed her. She turned back, looking on curiously at me. I gestured that she was to go ahead. Naturally she turned and came right back up in case she was missing out on something. Always the curious cat.

'I was just telling Kamla she has to stay out of the attic, if it wasn't for the fact that she'd left the door open we would have never realised she'd climbed up there and would never have found her inside the trunk until...'

I understood then that they had found me inside the trunk, with the lid closed. And me asleep inside, or had I passed out? The thought sent a cold finger of dread down my spine. Perhaps that wouldn't have been a bad thing. She caught my train of thought, my mother, and shot me a look which had a harpoon attached to it, bringing me back to the here and now, in this small room. Mother, who was sitting with a squalling baby in her lap, shooed us out with one hand, while releasing with another a pendulous breast from the layers of clothes she had on and stuffing it into the baby's mouth. He settled down to a steady suckling, a look of nirvana on his face. I hoped I hadn't been as stupid as this baby.

'Girls', thundered Daadi from downstairs, 'five minutes more and no breakfast for the two of you, I will feed it to Moti and you can stay hungry till lunch.'

We clattered down like a stampede of wild horses making the most infernal racket on the wooden planked stairway. We gulped down the poori aloo with the hunger that childhood brings, uncaring of the consequences, no concerns about body fat percentages. Pappa was reading the newspaper and chomping through his breakfast. On regular days he liked an English breakfast, eggs and bread, toast and marmalade, some oats if he felt like it. On Sundays though, it was parathas dripping with ghee, eaten with pickle or curd, or poori bhaji.

Breakfast done, we skipped out to the garden. It was a day that hung dull upon us. There was nothing to be done but wait for it to pass, like all interminable winter days would be, closeting us in the house, barricaded from the never-ending chill and the thump and whoosh of the snow when it fell. We went back in, to our room, and occupied ourselves with a snakes and ladders game. I saw Maa go out of her room down to the kitchen. I went to her room and looked at the baby sleeping in his crib. He looked peaceful and it annoyed me. I went back to our room after a while, where Roop was reading a comic book and stuffing herself with some cream biscuits she refused to share.

And then it happened. There was a stifled wail from upstairs, followed by a scream. The scream was so sharp it curdled the blood in our veins. I jumped up and ran to Maa's room the same time as Behra managed to reach it. Maa was standing over the baby's crib with a look of utter anguish on her face. She looked up at us. Her face crumbled to one million pieces and fell to the floor.

'The baby, he isn't breathing,' she whispered in a voice so low, I could barely hear her. 'I just went down for a moment to get some water, and now he isn't breathing. I don't know what happened, he was fine, he was sleeping....'

Daadi marched up, her footsteps echoing on the wooden plank staircase, heavy, insistent. She went straight to the crib and picked up the now still infant, pinched its nose, shook it, blew into its mouth. There was no response, just an expression of calm serenity that nothing would displace, not hunger, not the need to be changed, nor the discomfort of an overfull stomach on a delicate new-found digestive system. His skin, though, was mottled, angry and red. Daadi gasped and yelled for Pappa.

Behra quietly steered the two of us back into our room and commanded us to wait there until called for. He went down and called Pappa who clambered up yelling at Maa. And Maa's sobbing, anguished wails pierced the soul and went straight to the heavens where the soul of her child had departed to. If there was a heaven that is.

We came out of our rooms despite the warnings and hugged Maa who held on to us like we were ballasts in a storm and sobbed, deep shuddering sobs at first and then a slow mewling sobbing that disconcerted us. How were we to console our mother? It was against nature's order to have a child die before one and she had seen so many of hers die before her, some in the womb itself, and now this one, outside of it. Daadi carefully placed the now-still baby back in its crib and turned to Maa. 'Wipe your tears,' she said. 'He wasn't destined to live, there is nothing we could have done.'

Neonatal death, I would learn later, could be caused by many factors. It could be a pre-existing heart condition present at birth, a problem with the lungs, pre-eclampsia, respiratory distress syndrome. We would never know why our brother without a name had died. There was no autopsy, of course; the idea of an autopsy would never have crossed Maa and Pappa's minds, nor would Pappa have allowed it. The baby had died in the crib, after having been fed and burped. Perhaps he had choked on his feed, perhaps he had not been burped properly, Daadi said in a hushed voice to Pappa in the other room. When they took the baby away, Maa was inconsolable. Daadi held her with a steely force that would not allow her to disintegrate.

Maa wailed all day in her room. Daadi cradled her gently for as long as she could, and then the neighbours, Maa's friends, came in and sat with her for a while. But there was life to be lived after a death and they went back to their homes. Maa sat alone, wailing like her soul was being ripped out of her body, and I didn't dare go to her. What consolation was I, the second girl, when the boy had died?

The house was teeming with people who had come to offer their condolences, the faces wreathed with sympathy for the woman who had lost the baby she had just birthed, and the father who had, yet again, lost the son he had been longing for. There would just be one day of mourning for the baby, no more. How did one mourn a life which was yet to be lived? The baby had left no imprint on the world yet. When the menfolk had gone off with the baby to bury it, and the womenfolk from the families we knew remained with Maa and Daadi to console them, we were left alone. Roop and me. There would be no cooking in the house, food was brought in for us. Mrs Singh had thoughtfully brought across some cake as well, and surreptitiously handed it over to the two of us and packed us off to our room. Behra was instructed to serve us food in our room, and we were to remain there until called for. Mrs Chauhan who ran the sole bookstore in town, with her husband, handed us a pile of comic books and Enid Blytons to keep us occupied. Rana Aunty, and Bina, my best friend from school, told us we were welcome to come across to their home if we wanted to watch television there.

'What is happening to this house?' Roop said, the moment we were alone, creases of worry crumpling her delicate face. I was flipping through the stash of books and comics we'd received, rather unaffected by the demise of what was to me, only a little ball of flesh with a rather strong sound box attached.

'What is happening to this house?' I repeated after her, wondering what she meant.

'I mean, first I almost died that night when the baby was born and we still don't know who came into this room and put the angeethi in. Daadi never allows it in a completely closed room. Everyone knows that in this house.' I nodded. Yes. That had never been explained. Daadi had been convinced that someone had wanted both of us dead, but hadn't gone beyond mumbling her suspicions about who the possible culprit could be.

'Don't tell anyone, okay?'

I pinched my throat and said 'Mother promise' and swore to die if I revealed what she was to tell me to anyone. We were sitting on the seat by the window. Outside we could see the mist and fog begin to roll in with the evening. Soon the lights in the house would go on, but no one would light the lamp today. The lamp would not be lit for a few days.

'Then somebody pushed you into the trunk and you would have suffocated and died if I hadn't gone searching for you and climbed up. And now the baby. I think someone killed the baby. The same person who tried to kill both of us.'

'Who do you think it could be?'

Footsteps sounded on the landing outside and Kanchi came into the room, switching the lamps on. The light, normally warm and comforting, was dull and cold today. Her expression was strange, she didn't look at us as she spoke. 'Do you want me to get you anything from the food the neighbours have left for you all?' Her little boy, tied in a sling around her waist, mewled, and she looked down at him, her face softening into liquid love.

'Why is he crying?'

'He's hungry,' she replied.

'Why don't you feed him?' I asked.

'It will do him good to learn to wait a bit. We must all learn to wait for what we really want.'

I didn't realise it then, but I do now. Learning to wait is a life skill we are never taught. I still hadn't learnt how to. Kanchi was waiting too, she had been waiting for years since she'd been married to Behra's son, her husband, to come back from Delhi and take her with him.

Strangely enough, despite the chill and the bed that felt like a slab of ice, we weren't hungry or even sleepy.

We waited for her to leave before we continued the conversation. 'Someone from within the house? It can't be Maa, Pappa or Daadi. You think its Behra?' I asked. 'Why would he want us dead?'

'I don't know, it's just a theory I have,' she continued, 'I could be wrong.'

'You are,' I replied. 'No one in this house will kill us. Everyone loves us.'

'That's what you think. But what we see is not always the truth.'

'You're reading too many detective novels, Roo. That angeethi in the room was a mistake. Probably Behra forgot to take it out with all the excitement in the house that day. And the lid might have fallen on me when I climbed into the trunk, and I told you what I saw in the attic. Please believe me, no one else will. Maa doesn't. She thinks I'm making up stories. And the baby died because he stopped breathing. Why would anyone want to kill him? What enmity could anyone have with us?'

'Did you see his face, he was suffocated to death I'm sure. I'll find out,' she said, her eyes fixed on the door where Kanchi had just exited.

She caught me by the shoulders and looked at me.

'There was a pillow in the crib, did you notice? There was no pillow in the crib earlier. Where did the pillow come from?'

Roop was two years older than me chronologically but behaved like she was decades older. She came closer to me as we sat at the window seat, we were already talking in whispers. Outside, the mist was coming in, curling in tendrils over the tops of the trees, slithering around the hedges, blurring the edges of the glass of the windows. The bright pink rhododendron bushes along the sides of the garden were suddenly terrifying, masses of a diffused pink that seemed to take on a life of their own. Many years later, I would stand with my eyes tearing up and see a bright pink amorphous spread of foliage against a wall, and feel the same prickle of dread. It would be a wall spilling over with bougainvillea, thousands of miles down south, in Goa.

'It's nobody, you're just imagining things.'

'I'm not lying. Someone is trying to kill us, and we need to be careful.'

Gooseflesh ran up my arms under the layers of rough wool hand-knitted sweaters I had piled on. I blew on the glass pane, the mist outside that had fogged it up slowly condensed into tears that ran down. In the distance I thought I saw a golden cloud hovering over a mountain top. And a voice long heard, much loved, echoed in my ears. Kamli, I thought I heard it say, I opened by eyes and heard another voice say 'Lotusface'.

TEN

HERE, NOW

It was the dim glow of the sun from beneath the horizon coming through the windows that woke me up. I looked around, I was in that old four-poster bed I'd tucked myself into the previous night. It was still draped with the mosquito nets that had swayed and shimmered in the light of the moon, making me feel as if I was floating in a tank of water, dappled with light reflecting off the darting fish moving in shoals within, when I'd woken in the night.

How had I reached back to my bed? Had I really woken up and gone outside the door and seen what I had seen? Or had that been just another dream? I looked down on the floor, there were red stains on the tiles, dried now, which could only have been the blood on my feet that had been cut on those rocks, the cuts that had stung while I walked out of my room in the middle of the night to investigate the sounds. I looked down at my feet. There were no cuts on my soles. I touched them, nothing hurt, they were as they always were.

The house was silent, the pre-dawn hushed with anticipation. The silence was suddenly broken by a rooster in the distance, sounding his infuriating alarm, confident that the sun was awaiting his cackle in order to get moving with the day. I splashed some water on my face and pulled on my shorts and vest, tying my laces with the slow reluctance that waking early always brought me. I strapped on a small bottle of water to my waist, and stretched a bit. I stepped out of the room and closed the door behind me as softly as I could. I could hear sounds from the kitchen. The house was awake, or at least some of its denizens were. I could hear the dogs barking in the grounds, as I opened the front door. They came bounding up to me and licked me with joy, with all the accepting love of souls who accept another generously. I played with them for a few minutes, before adjusting my eyes to the dimness of the morning sky. The patrician rooster emerged from the back of the house to investigate the proceedings, cocked one curious eye at the two dogs and then went off in search of some fresh worms in the garden, followed by his devout gathering of hens and chicks. The grass was damp, sodden with some dew or perhaps it had rained in the night, it had been muggy enough. The promise of a hot day loomed ahead in the sudden pall of humidity that hung over the pre-dawn. I'd been here a day and the island was already growing on me, staking its claim on me, tendrils of it snaking around my soul and anchoring me to its fecund red earth.

Outside the gate, the road passed through paddy fields and grounds, leading down to the ferry and then up to the church on the hill. A lone cyclist passed, ringing his bell to alert people that he was coming around a bend. In the distance, the church bells chimed for the morning prayers. One of my aunt's dogs, Buddy, decided to accompany me on my run, the other, Devil, went sniffing around the garden for rats he could chase. I was glad for the company, for it was unfamiliar territory, albeit completely safe. Buddy was a mottled specimen, one ear chewed off in an erstwhile fight, a sense of cockiness to him that came from knowing the landscape, and an acceptance that was overwhelming and complete. Would humans ever have the same generosity of soul that dogs did?

The ferry drew up as I ran down to the edge of the road. People waited, restless to get on and begin their day. Standing on the deck was a Norse god, dressed in cargo shorts and a t-shirt. Thor, descended on earth minus his war hammer. Instead, he had a duffel bag and a backpack. In the pale light of the early morning, he was overwhelming. Blonde hair spilling till his shoulders, lit by the morning sun behind him like a nimbus, easily a head taller than everyone else around him. I stopped midstride and looked at him, unabashed. How freeing it was to stare unhindered at a beautiful man. I didn't realise I had been observed until he looked right back at me and inclined his head in a gesture of acknowledgement. My heart caught in my chest and expanded to constrict my throat. The ferry docked. I broke eye contact, confused and embarrassed, turned around and ran off. He was familiar and unfamiliar and I would probably never see him again. Just another tourist here to soak up the sun, have his few days of fun.

The road undulated, went up the hill where the house was perched, gently curving past open fields, occasional houses, ramshackle corner stores, still shut at the moment, motorcycle repair garages. The island was hushed, still asleep at this hour. Only the birds stirred, flying off to find nutrition in sweeping formations that dappled the skies. The morning rays glinted off the red-tiled roofs of the houses that still slumbered, faint noises of early stirring emanating from the few that I passed. Buddy bounded beside me, panting happily, running ahead and then running back when I couldn't keep pace with him. A cyclist passed me, waving cheerfully, the baskets by the sides of his cycle laden with freshly baked bread. Poee, slathered with butter, dipped in tea. I had been introduced to it here and now I would vouch that there were few pleasures of life that could beat it. The baker's boy would deliver to every home on the island, tooting the horn on his cycle as he approached so the residents could come to the door and collect their bread. Most houses had a standing order with the bakery, bread was baked accordingly. The islanders had learnt over the centuries to be as self-sufficient as they could, although the mainland was just a ten-minute ride across a stretch of water in case of an emergency.

The road, sloping gently, now climbed higher as I went past the house on the turn, barely visible from the road, camouflaged in the thickness of the green shrubs and trees that fringed the undulating path that led to it, through the gates, and ran onwards towards where the big white church stood sentinel over the island.

I could see the church from the window of my room, in fact, most of the west wing of the house had a clear view of it, prescient and foreboding, as it stood in the distance, emerging from the green canopy of trees that carpeted the hill all the way to the top. It was an imposing structure, emerging from the foliage like a mountain top breaking through the ring of clouds, its bell tower rising ominously from the turrets that made the rest of it. The road in front of me was a strip of sleek pewter that glinted golden where the first feeble rays of the morning hit it, filtered through the canopy of the trees fringing the road. Buddy bounded up ahead, the church would be around the corner, the climb was making me pant. I wondered how many rounds of the island I would need to do to have myself a decent run, it was barely a couple of kilometres across. I'd already worked up a good sweat, the vest stuck to me in patches on my back, the sweat dripped down my arms.

The cemetery loomed up ahead, the rise of the hill behind me. The headstones of the graves towards the sea, the morning rays hitting them, curious and probing, lighting up the inscriptions on them, lives I would never know. I could see them as I rounded the turn, the crosses, the angel sculptures, the urns, the marble vaults where remains remained undisturbed until another died within the family and the old dead would be dug up to make space for the newly dead. I would go in and read the names, see the dates of birth and death, read the cause of death build up a picture in my mind of the occupant of the grave. I would note the graves lying dusty and neglected, and the fresh ones, with the new tombstones, the marble still glistening white, the bevelled edges of the letters engraved on them yet to be encrusted with dust and yellowed by the rain. They would be faceless forms in my head, sinking into the earth, their unlived years falling into the grave with them.

There was a small culvert beyond the road, under which a brackish stream flowed downhill. I sat on it and looked at the view. There was the sharp dip of the hill beyond the graveyard, into an almost vertical descent to the edge of the island. The blue grey of the river to the left, snaking its way laboriously to the Arabian Sea to the front and across the river, the green of the tree canopy on the mainland sparkled at me. The haze of the morning was forgiving, even to the sweat trickling down my back and glistening on my forehead.

There was a collapsed brick wall with red roses growing up the side and spilling over fringing the cemetery, a curious choice to border a graveyard. Most walls here were a burst of pink bougainvillea cascading over the sides, bracts, not flowers as I remembered from some residual memory of botany in school. The air was heavy with the humidity and the fragrance of the roses slowly opening up, drops of violent red in the green. Blood spilt, heavy, metallic in its tang. In the distance, a hazy plume of smoke rose up into the sky from an unseen fire, dispersing indolently with the soft breeze. Somewhere, piles of rubbish were being burnt, somewhere the day had begun with destruction.

Buddy raced ahead of me and turned the corner, and then barked wildly. I ran to him, we were at the wall of the churchyard, the part that bordered the cemetery. The morning dew was still damp on the graves, and to my shock, the gravestones were pulled right off, broken. I went in through a gap where the compound wall had crumbled to the elements, and tiptoed around. The grass was damp, it grew in unkempt patches. The graves lay sodden, the damp fetid earth within giving off a miasmal stink, the crosses guarding the graves broken, toppled over. I gasped. Something or someone moved in the corner of the graveyard and disappeared into the thick cover of trees that skidded down the hill. Buddy backed away, whimpering. 'What is it, boy, what is it?' He stood staring into the thicket, continuing to whimper most piteously, and then backed into me, rubbing against my legs.

I rubbed him, 'What happened, Buddy, why you scared, boy?' He whimpered and backed away even further, freeing himself from my grasp, barking incessantly. I stood, perplexed, in the midst of the graveyard which had all its graves dug up. Grave thieves? What could the reason be behind this desecration? I looked around for some sign of people, there was no one. In the distance I could hear the ring of a cycle bell, perhaps it was the man delivering bread passing by. I ran out on to the road and waited, breathing heavily. Despite the heat, a chill ran down my spine. I could sense someone, something watching me. I turned around, something moved in the trees. Was it the breeze or was it a shadow, I didn't know. The sun wasn't out yet, the light was the indistinctness of the pre-dawn, the sun would burst out gloriously in the matter of a few minutes. Buddy came back, barking his head off, nipping at the hem of my shorts and pulling me away from the wall, whining. I moved, looking back, a sense of something breathing down the nape of my neck, something I couldn't see.

The cycle bell came to me from around the bend before the cycle came into view, I waved the baker's delivery boy down. He stopped, his sun-browned face breaking into a polite smile, his eyes black pebbles of unfiltered happiness in a world of multiple filters one posted one's life through.

'Good morning, miss. You are visiting the big house?' He was young, barely sixteen, his eyes curious and probing, his skin clear and bronzed, his smile open and generous. How long would it be before his face shuttered down to the world, and he would peel off the faces he put on, the first when he entered his home, the second when he entered his bedroom and, finally, when he gave up peeling them off at all, when the masks he put on finally petrified to become his face. When had my masks welded themselves to my skin? What did I really look like beneath them all?

Everyone here seemed to know who I was. Word travelled on the small island.

I nodded. 'Something has happened here,' I told him, pointing to the graves. He took in the sight with a single sweeping glance and crossed himself repeatedly.

'I'll go tell Father Dominic,' he said hurriedly, turning the cycle back towards the church that was a bend in the road away. A chilly breath blew on the nape of my neck, raising gooseflesh on my arms. Buddy whimpered again, pulling me away. The sun's rays, struggling over the dispassionate clouds scattered over the sky, finally broke through in a heroic burst, flooding the side of the hill with light. As I ran back to the big house with Buddy leaping ahead of me, I had the relentless urge to look over my shoulder, like something was following me, something had stuck to me, like chewing gum stuck to the sole of a shoe. It was an irritating feeling, but something I couldn't quite pinpoint or shake off.

The heat was wet and clingy; it was barely eight in the morning. As I decided about going in for a bucket bath, switching the geyser on, the water supply too feeble for a good shower, Lucenzia appeared, almost soundlessly at the doorway.

'Got up,' she said, more a statement than a question. I nodded.

'Went out.' It was more an accusation I needed to defend myself against than a statement this time. I nodded again. 'Dongo widout telling. I saw dat Buddy went with you running. He's a good dog. He will bite anyone who acts smart.'

Thankfully no one had attempted to act smart, I told her, but there was the strangest thing that I'd seen. She was too pre-occupied with the duties of the morning to pay attention. I decided to keep the news about the graveyard to myself, and what I'd seen the previous night on the opposite side of the house. The news about the graves would spread quickly enough on this, a small island, and what I'd seen had most probably been one of my lucid dreams.

'Not nice peepul. All russhyans. House down road, they doing not nice things. Be careful. Don talk to dem without Da Costa or me. Breakfuss is in the dining room. Aunty already had. Come have when you get ready.' She spoke in staccato style. I nodded. There seemed to be no gap between the words to edge in my replies.

I had seen the house down the road, with a white-skinned couple in the gardens as I ran; one was watering the plants, the other was peaceably doing yoga on the porch. The one watering the plants had raised a comradely hand in salutation as I passed. I wondered what nefarious activities they were engaged in to merit Lucy's censure.

'Had bath now not in the night?'

'I'd prefer to have a bath in the mornings.'

Lucenzia was in a hurry to end the conversation. She drew a deep breath, probably to gather enough oxygen in her blood cells to fuel her next burst of speech. I admired her ability to speak without a pause.

'Come down for brekfass after you finish your bath. Now go switch off the geyser and turn water on, or it will burst on your face.'

I looked warily in the direction of the bathroom. Of all the non-adventures I'd been in through my life, perhaps it would be fitting to die by an exploding geyser. My fears aside, the geyser was well behaved. I had myself a quick hot bath and scampered down to grab some breakfast. In the day, the house took on a different personality. The sun invaded every corner like a determined lover, insistent, prodding, the dust motes dancing their dance of infinity in the filtered rays. A gentle wind blew in from over the river, bringing occasionally the faint salty tang of the sea on it, or the swampy skank of the river bank and the marshlands that surrounded a fair bit of the island. The greenery outside the bungalow, the swaying palm trees, the old spreading banyan tree that stood a little distance away from the left side of the house, shading it from the harsher noon-day sun, all made the place a play of light and shadow. The small breakfast room, just off the main parlour area boasted a table set for two. Kamini was nowhere to be seen.

Da Costa entered, wiping his hands on a dirty rag.

'Good morning, Madam. Madam is in her painting room.'

It took me a long minute to decipher that he was addressing me and speaking of Kamini as well. He continued with the message he had apparently been sent to deliver. 'She told me to tell you to have your breakfast and tea and come to the painting room.'

I did as instructed. Breakfast was bhaji pao, the bhaji not what I was familiar with as a boiled potato-based bhaji, mildly tempered with chillies and curry leaves. It was, instead, a spicy curry with potatoes, ground coconut, roasted whole spices and dry white peas giving it a flavour all its own. I ate it with the pao, a hard-crusted bread that was to be broken and dipped into the gravy. It was fresh from the bakers, tough on the outside, soft as butter on the inside as I bit into it. Sourdough bread came to India through the voyager Vasco Da Gama who introduced oven-baked bread to the subcontinent. One was now left in the bread bag hung on the gate every morning by the same cyclist from the bakers I had stopped in the morning and pointed out the desecrated graves.

I wondered what was happening there. Had the police been informed, had they found an explanation for the many graves, dug up, empty of the cadavers and remains they contained, the dead disrespected in a world where the living had to contend with no respect as well? The island moved slowly, the calls would have been made, the law enforcement if they had been alerted, would reach the scene of the crime once they were done with their morning tea and breakfast. Nothing could hurry the pace of life here, not death, not the desecration of the dead.

In the kitchen, a radio or a music player played local Konkani folk songs, their tunes joyous and foot-tapping, the songs filtered themselves through the rooms, distant indistinct ghostly strains of celebrations in another place and time. When I'd finished, I took myself under the direction of Da Costa who marched before me like a banner man bearing, alas, only a grimy rag that had evidently been employed in car maintenance, to the studio where my aunt awaited me. We arrived at the painting room as the sun climbed higher into the sky. It was a huge room, and had probably at one point been a dining room or a ball room. The house seemed to be never ending, rooms opening up into rooms, leading into other rooms, wings facing each other as adversaries.

Kamini was sitting in her wheelchair, going through what looked like a photo album. 'Come,' she beckoned, her face breaking into a broad smile. Her skin was still amazingly clear, with none of the age damage that one would expect from living in such a sunny place all through the year. It was probably genetic. I had skin that was similar as did Maa. I noticed a bruise along her cheek, or was it some kind of discolouration?

It hadn't been there the previous evening, had she hurt herself? This morning she was dressed in a long gown in a rich fuchsia silk that was cinched at the waist. I had never seen Kamini dressed in colours that did not shout her presence out loud to the world. Coupled with her incredible beauty, she was a woman who people always noticed no matter where she went. She gestured to me to sit on the couch that was next to where she was seated.

'An old lady's nostalgia,' she said, pressing the album into my hands. 'He did love clicking pictures of me, and I loved getting clicked. It seems like such a long, long time ago. Another lifetime ago.'

It was full of pictures of herself clicked in various costumes and various poses. She laughed as I flicked through them. 'You were quite the piece,' I said, amused by the careful detailing that had gone into the photographs and the posing.

'It was a work of art for him, but only for our eyes. Never for the public. He had painted me too, and I never liked the paintings. He was too loud for me. There are quite a few of our paintings lying around here,' she waved her hand vaguely, a generous gesture that could indicate the room we were in, the rest of the house, the expanse of the island, the universe. I looked around, there were huge canvases propped against the walls. An easel stood desolate, divested of the canvas, the colours, the movement and the energy that would give it purpose and reason. The painted works stood against walls, shrouded in sheets that reined in their vibrance, their forms, their energy.

She gestured at them, her hand moving in measured elegance that was almost a dance mudra. 'They're all over. They need to be catalogued. And sent out into the galleries. But only after I'm gone. One of the reasons I've called you here.'

I looked at her, I had wondered why she'd called me. It couldn't have been from pure altruism of spirit. She was a practical soul, there had to be a more prosaic reason behind her summons than merely the need to be a do-gooder for her not-so-recently bereaved niece.

She put the album down and looked at me. Her gaze was steady enough to crack an oyster but her hands shook of their own accord in her lap, the veins raised and gnarled, the liver spots creeping all around with their careless intimation of mortality. 'I wanted to meet you before I died. I want you to take charge of my estate. My paintings. I also needed a favour from you.'

'Don't be silly, Kamini. You aren't dying. You will put all of us into the grave before you do.'

'I am being silly. I'm not dying. Not right now though. But I will. Soon enough. I'm ill, and I am dying. Sooner or later, I don't know. And that's why I called you here.'

'What is it, what are you ill with?'

'What else, the most clichéd disease one could have. Something I always hoped I'd never get after I saw what it reduced Peter to in his last days, but what is to be will be.' She raised her chin high, an impetuousness that even death would tremble to intrude upon. 'Leukaemia. My own blood has turned against me.'

'Surely there is treatment, radiation, chemo, I don't know, I'll find out. Come with me to Mumbai, I'll take you to the best oncologists, we'll find the right treatment, you'll live to be a hundred.'

'I did the first round of chemo. It was hell. They want to do a stem cell transplant. The only person I could think of was you,' she paused. 'A close relative, they said. Neerja wouldn't come. I asked her. And there's no one else.'

'You should have called me sooner.'

She smiled, her eyes unsmiling.

'When I saw you here, I changed my mind. Why should I put you through that when there seems to be no valid reason for me to extend my life. I have lived it out and it has been a good life. I don't want to live to be a hundred, I don't want the best treatment. I just want the best way to go peacefully and in as less pain as I can. I am not as brave as Peter was. I don't have the courage to suffer as he did in the final days. I have nothing to live on for too, and now I want to go.' Here was one of the most courageous women I'd ever known telling me she had no courage left. But then, what one often terms as courage in another is always just no choice but to keep going.

'How long do you have?' I asked. It seemed unreal, hearing her talk about her death, she who had always been so larger than life.

'I don't know. I've issued instructions to my attorneys on how all my estate is to be disposed of on my death. And between you and me, Dr Gomes has been issued instructions to up my pain relief to the point of permanence in case it gets unbearable. I have no intentions of suffering with no end in sight. I have no patience for that. It just...' she paused and sighed deeply, '... seems such a waste of time to be suffering here when I could be with Peter there.'

Words failed me. Silence seemed to be the only response appropriate. But silence was inadequate, unsustainable. Words would intrude and try to make light of the emotion, of the revelation. I waited for them, but they built themselves into a dam in my throat and blocked all sound. I was not ready to deal with yet another death in my life. 'So anyway,' she fumbled around on the table by the side of the couch and managed to locate her cigarettes and the holder, and held out the lighter for me to light it for her. I did, even though rationally I knew that she needed to stop smoking immediately. 'This is it. Here I am and here you are and this is what it is.'

Trust her to be puffing on the nicotine stick even as death tap-danced on her front porch. She must have read my mind because she laughed, throwing her head back, revealing a condition called 'turkey neck', her neck all sinews, bone and stringy veins now. 'Stop looking disapprovingly at my cigarette like a mother hen, it isn't my lungs that have packed up on me, it's my blood, and there's nothing they can do about it. My blood is poisoning me.'

'What can I do, how can I help you? Are you sure you don't want to try the stem cell transplant? I think we should.'

She shook her head firmly. 'No. I'm done with all treatment.'

'What do we do?'

'Just wait till I die. And keep me on enough painkillers to make it easy.'

I reached out and took her hand, it was soft and powdery dry, and delicate. A hand that had never known manual labour, but had only worked with brushes and paint. Her hands were tiny, they circled mine with the undecided pressure of a soft sigh.

'Will you stay here with me till I go?'

'You're not going anywhere, Kamini, so let's get the treatment back on schedule. And there's hell awaiting you if you just go without putting up a fight.'

'Given the life I've lived,' she chortled, 'I'm definitely not going to be allowed into heaven. But then Peter will be waiting for me in hell.' Then, as abruptly as she had begun laughing, her mood changed to sombre. 'I have no one else to be with me, and I don't want to die alone. You don't mind giving me these few days, do you?'

I looked down at the floor. It was a question that had no right answer. But then, what did I have to go back to Mumbai or Delhi for? Who did I have, who was waiting for me? Maa was home, snug as the proverbial bug in the house I was born in. Veer was travelling in the Amazonian jungle, with no way to reach him until he decided to reach us. We lived in anticipation of receiving news about him, unwelcome news, this adopted little brother who was so much that both us sisters weren't. Roop was in Melbourne, living out her life with her current man and cats.

'Kamini,' she interrupted my thoughts. 'I need you with me when I die.'

'You're not going to die. There is treatment and you will get well.'

'I don't want to. I've lived my life.'

In a flash nothing seemed to matter. The world would go on without me if I chose to drop off it this very second. It was a stunning but humbling realisation. No one really needed me, but my aunt, she did. It was a strange feeling to know that someone needed me. I had been loved, but I had never been needed. It was a delicate line that separated the two.

It must have been difficult for her to ask for help. She had always been a fiercely independent soul, ever since she walked out of the parental home at eighteen determined to be a painter, scrimped and scrounged her way through art school and then through the precarious rungs of the art circuit where she broke in with her beauty and charm which only made her prodigious talent even more visible. She'd hung out with the artists of the time, moving from man to man, surviving with her art and her ability to move to where the spotlight swung until she tired of it. That's when she met Peter. He had settled in Goa, after a brief flirtation with life in Mumbai's heady art world. The Progressive Artists Movement had crossed its peak, the artists who would be the canons of the movement were becoming internationally known. Peter was dispirited by the art world and preferred to live away from it all, showing when he chose to. He also was newly divorced. She was tiring of the constant uncertainty of the unsettled life she was leading, with no roof over her head, unsettled relationships that unmoored her. She moved in with him. His wife had taken their young son and moved back to

England where she came from, she was a Londoner, and could only take so much of the laid-back life that Goa offered. The divorce, when it came through, was amicable and with shared custody of their son, Victor, who must have been barely ten at the time.

'I will,' I said. 'I will stay with you for as long as it takes.'

Her face lit up. She gave me a hug that was strong yet fragile, the sense of something crumbling to pieces beneath the steely carapace was evident in the measured movements. The body conserving its strength consciously or unconsciously for a final leap of the soul.

'You're being absolutely silly though. You must listen to the doctors and begin the treatments, I'm sure it will go away and never ever come back. There have been so many cases of people being completely cured of cancer and never going into remission until they die.'

'And then are the cases that never recover. What then? And even if I am cured, then what? To live alone and unwanted until I cry for death to come and take me? No, Kamla, I want to go. I've lived quite enough and lived a full life. I called you here because I wanted you to help me.'

'Help you? In what way?'

'I want you to help me die.'

I sighed. She tightened the grip of her hand on mine.

'How can I do that, it isn't right,' I replied.

She laughed a full-throated laugh. 'I'm not asking you to kill me, silly goose. I'm asking you to stay with me till I go. I don't want to be alone when I die, with no family around. But before the pain makes me go out of my head, I need to tell you a few things.' She gripped my hand tighter. I noticed how the movement seemed to be a strain for her.

'You have always been rather special to me, rather unfairly for Roop. I think you know that. It's always been clear.'

I nodded. It had always been obvious on the rare occasions she visited us. Though the packages she sent us at regular intervals through the year were firmly equal for both, dresses in frothy confections of pale pinks in ribbons and laces with the sizes based on when she last saw us, and which we would inevitably be much larger to fit into, toys that were completely not what we would want—our imaginations running riot with blonde-haired blue-eyed dolls while she sent us blocks and puppets made by artisans from the villages she travelled through, rare flowers pressed between pages of books she sent us to read. The books were boring tomes to young girls growing up in a one-horse hill station for whom the only excitement was tourist season when they got a chance to see what the latest fashion was based on what the folks from Delhi came wearing. My aunt loved me perhaps more than my own father did.

'I plan to give you part of this house. And all my unsold paintings, not that there are many left. But there is a clause.' I drew a sharp breath. This was not something I had anticipated, though Maa had often hinted at Roop and me being named in Kamini's will.

'Roop and me?' I asked.

She shook her head in the negative. 'Not Roop. Only you. Never much liked her. And she's never bothered to keep in touch. There's someone you have to share ownership of the house with. Let me tell you about that clause though. It might not seem so tempting when you hear it.'

The sun was high up and the rays had now stopped entering the window. The light outside was bright and hard and filtered through the thin curtains. The heat, despite the whirring fans overhead, crawled all over one's skin, opening each individual pore and prodding the sweat gland within into activation. My dress stuck to my back. I moved the chair so I was directly under the fan. The change in position also brought me in line with some breeze that blew in from the open netted window and played around with my hair, which I then lifted and tied into a top knot, revelling in the cool wind on the nape of my neck.

'What clause?' I asked.

'So here it is, the clause contingent upon the fulfilment of, you will inherit half this house. Not a physical half, mind you, but joint ownership. I want you to live here, in this house. Not sell it, not give it out on rent, the moment I die. You both live here for twelve months, six months at a stretch each time, the claim on half the house is yours for life. You don't have to answer right now. Think about it. Take your time. Stay with me for a couple of months, I don't know how long I have. That should be enough time for you to decide whether you want to take it up.'

'And whom do I have joint ownership of the house with if not Roop?' I asked.

There was a knock at the door, and we both turned towards it. A giant stood there, blonde hair tumbling to his shoulders and silhouetted against the bright light outdoors so we could see nothing of his face. It was the Norse God from the ferry. Did he recognise me, I wondered, my face flaming into what I knew would be an unbecoming red. Where had he been since he got off the ferry a couple of hours ago, I wondered, and then I didn't because he smiled and my heart exploded like a bomb, blasting all coherent thought and word out of me.

He was a blast of déjà vu. I had never met him before, but I had. He filled the door, the room, the house by just standing there. His huge hands meant to throw war hammers held on to a duffel bag, and a suitcase he was wheeling behind him. The only hammering that was happening was the sudden incessant pounding of my heart in my chest, threatening to crack a rib in its sudden uncontained, inexplicable excitement. Kamini's face crumpled into a smile of sheer delight. She put out a trembling hand, beckoning him to her. He stepped in through the door, his shoulders almost blocking out everything behind him, bathing him in a nimbus of light. An archangel. I expected to see his wings unfurling behind him, knocking down the pillars that held up the balustrade.

'Let me take a good look at you, how long has it been now, four years since you found the time to come visit me?' she said, fumbling around for her glasses and finding them the table, jamming them on swiftly on to her nose with hands that were now trembling even more than they normally did. He moved into clear sight, his eyes blue and warm, his hair blonde and floppy to his shoulders, his body, under the pale linen shirt and light-blue denim jeans, solid, yet well-defined with none of the stringy leanness that seemed to affect most of the current generation. A soft stubble hugged his jaw, begging for me to run my fingers over it. His eyes hit mine. I felt the stubble scratching my cheeks, grazing my thighs, in that moment, that glance, there was an acknowledgement so real, it was almost palpably physical a contact.

He came forward with quick strides, strangely nimble for a man so tall and broad, bending down to envelope Kamini in a quick warm hug. I rose to my feet, awkward, uncertain of myself, moving aside, once again doused in all the awkwardness I thought I'd left behind with adolescence.

His eyes caught mine from over Kamini's frail shoulder. They were the sky and the sea and the wind and sun rays. I was dunked into the warm, salty ocean and floated in it, uncaring, the sun on my face and salt on my lips. When he broke eye contact, I felt a slight jerk as though a physical connection had been broken. He pulled away from her, raising himself up to his full height as he stood a few feet away from me. I felt tiny, inconsequential, an inexplicable need to be engulfed by him and crushed against him. I closed my eyes for a second. This was not me. I had never reacted so viscerally to anyone. Man.

Woman. He wasn't looking at me again when I opened them again, he was on his haunches next to Kamini, his hands holding both of hers with a tenderness that made me ache, for what I did not know.

'Why didn't you tell me?' His accent was clipped British, but not quite. But I knew him. When he spoke, his voice was home.

'What was there to tell?' she replied, delighting in his presence. She then turned to me, half remembering that I was present in the room as well. 'But now that you're here, I want you to meet Kamla, my niece. You've heard about her, of course.' Our eyes met again, his were curious, probing, polite. I smiled, acutely conscious of every nerve in my body knotting up in a vague kind of tension that began in the pit of my stomach and gushed through where my body pulsed with an unspeakable longing. This was ridiculous. This was overwhelming. This was stretching my longing so much it became inelastic with the pull.

I composed myself and smiled politely, putting my hand out. He put his out, a moment of hesitation, a firm grip and a shake, a connection that was forged between the two of us, tenuous, silvery, stronger than Kevlar, insubstantial but permanent. Our hands were welded together, a handshake that was unending, and already, in that one moment I knew this was something stronger than me, something I could not fight, even pretend to. This moment was the beginning of my undoing. His eyes softened, his face softened into a smile that told me I'd come straight home. This was where I was meant to be, this was why I hadn't put the knife to my wrists, why I'd stopped pouring all the contents of the bottle of sleeping pills down my throat when the loneliness felt so overwhelming, when the absence of Nihar was filled by his presence that would not leave. From somewhere in the distance, Kamini's voice came into my ears, whispery, faint, prescient, filled with knowledge of something I was to learn yet.

'Kamla, meet Victor. My step son. You will be the joint owner of this house with him when I die.'

—☙—

ELEVEN

HERE, NOW

The house changed with the arrival of Victor. Everything was brighter, the sun, the sky, the staff. Kamini was more animated. He was the golden child, the one who had lived here for the first ten years of his life before he'd been shipped out to the grey dreariness of London in winter with his mother who had never liked life on an island where it was always summer. He spoke to Da Costa and Lucenzia in their native Konkani, with the smoothness that came from learning the language as he grew up, faltering occasionally for a word, which they would helpfully fill in with a strange pride. They had seen him grow, over the years, over scattered visits, from a strapling of a boy to a man. They knew him in a way I didn't, they had a history with him. And they adored him. Everyone adored him, Kamini, the staff, the dogs. Buddy and Devil would trail behind him, panting happily, snuggling up at his feet wherever he sat. Dogs could sense the goodness in people, I knew. I adored him. I didn't even know him. He was a tabula rasa to me, as I was to him.

Victor went out in the day after a hearty lunch, where he ate through everything served by a beaming Lucenzia. He stepped out to his hired motorcycle and roared off down the pewter and yellow dappled lane like a knight of yore on his steed, only to return just before dinner, his face grim and set. I saw him pass on the landing, walking down the common passageway to his room, two rooms away from mine, his footsteps muted on the tiled passage. I had been working on my laptop, wrestling with the miserable signal on the island that made all communication with the outside world luck by chance.

All through dinner, Kamini had pushed the food around on her plate, not eaten anything at all, and then visibly sank back into her chair, exhausted by the effort of sitting. The conversation was strained, each of us had too much to say but not in the presence of the other. We took her to her room and tucked her in. She held on to our hands as she sank into a disturbed sleep, assuaged by painkillers. Lucy hushed us out of the room as Kamini's eyes closed and her breathing became regular. Asleep, her face was ashen, skeletal. A death's head stretched over bone, her skin pale, speckled with virulent red blotches.

'Will call Dr Gomes tomorrow,' Da Costa muttered. 'Madam will get angry, but I'll call him like that only to come to visit. And he can check Madam properly.'

It was barely ten in the night, too early to go to bed. The owls were winging past the trees outside, making soft hooting sounds. Bats fluttered around the fruit trees. The front door was open, the porch beckoned, the two cemented benches on either side seemed immensely inviting. It was a warm, balmy night. A soft breeze was blowing in from the sea, salty, tinged with the dirges from mermaids speaking of sunk treasure, galleons buried in island caves, lives ended in despair seeking the amnesia of an afterlife with no grief and only redemption. The moon shone above in a navy-blue sky, waning, mournful, the rabbit within obscured by the clouds scurrying across its surface, dimming and intensifying the light in the sky with their journey.

Victor had carried along a red from the wine cellar, one of those full-bodied reds that needed no occasion but a conversation to merit being opened. I didn't know much about wines, but I read the labels diligently. I held two wine glasses in my hand and had stars in my eyes, as I followed him out.

'Shall we sit here?' he asked. He was so polite and proper he made me quiver.

'I'm good anywhere.'

I would have followed him to the ends of the earth, I knew that without hesitation, barefoot and bleeding, should he only ask me.

'So much changes every single time I visit Goa, even here on the island. It seems the same, but there are little changes. A signboard. A house rented out to people one is unfamiliar with, the original family all emigrated or dead. The villa down the lane, for instance, I grew up with the kids, the Baptistas. Tony, Adrian, Janine. Now they've gone away to different countries, and the house is let out to a strange group of Russians who are using it as some sort of commune. My father would have had a right fit. Even though he himself was an outsider.'

'Why did your parents get a divorce?' It didn't feel out of place asking him questions that were no business of mine.

'Mum was not an easy person to love or live with,' he said. His voice was foam-speckled waves breaking over rocks, crashing against my heart. Was it possible for a person one had never met ever to feel like home? Was it possible to feel this intensely about someone one barely knew? Was it proper to feel this way barely a few months after Nihar's death? With Vikram, it had been different, it had just been a coming together of bodies, of convenience. What I was feeling now was different, a crazed infatuation that was roiling my stomach and making me smile too much, and linger where I should have been gone to my room and the ghost of my dead husband, awaiting me, in my dreams.

I sat on one of the benches, tucking my feet under me, he sat opposite. It was too far. And too close. 'It's been a few years since I came home. I last came for Pa's funeral,' he said, 'God, how I miss this place.' Da Costa had called to tell him about Kamini's illness, though he'd been warned not to by Kamini.

'How did you get to know?' Victor asked me, as we stepped out on the porch. The moon was a crescent, hanging like a crooked smile in the sky, mocking us mortals as we went about our daily miseries.

'I learnt about it when I reached here,' I replied. 'I had no clue, else I would have come earlier, taken her with me to Mumbai for better treatment. She insists she doesn't want to be treated, she insists she wants to go as quickly as she can.'

'She's a stubborn little thing,' he said, his face stern, his eyes soft. 'I spoke with Dr Gomes before I took the ferry out here. He's our family physician in Panjim. She doesn't have much time left, he says. A few months at the max, but there's no telling, and she's been steadily refusing all treatment. I met up with the local doctor, Dr Pinto, who's been overseeing her day to day this morning when I landed here, to get an idea of what the further course of treatment is. This afternoon, I went into town to check about room availability should we want to begin treatment immediately. Now to convince her.'

I kept silent. I had done nothing to find out how I could make Kamini better, and he'd already done the groundwork on the first day that he'd landed here. There was too much death, I felt ill-equipped to deal with more. It was the first thing I'd smelt when I entered the house. Miasmal. Circling. Waiting. I didn't know then what it was, fetid and foul, hanging in the air, the anticipation, the helpless waiting, the stench just barely there. Death.

'She doesn't want to do it. The transplant. She's refusing to go in for any further treatment.'

'What made her change her mind? Dr Gomes told me she called you here to check if you would agree to be a donor?'

'That's what she told me, and then she changed her mind.'

'I'll change it back for her,' he replied, with a quiet confidence. I envied him. I felt unsettled, incapable of handling this, illness, treatment, decisions, life, death.

'Are you okay about it, do you have any reservations? We

could put out an ad or something to find a match if you are, I don't know how it works, but we could always find out.'

'I'm absolutely fine with being a donor. She's the one who has changed her mind.'

'I hadn't bargained for this when I got on that flight, honestly.'

I laughed, a short angry laugh.

'What had you bargained for?' The words came out unthinkingly. I looked at him, perhaps there was a question in my eyes he chose not to answer.

'I definitely hadn't bargained on you.' I had no clue what he meant, or perhaps I did. His voice was suddenly heavy. The atmosphere shifted subtly and the dynamics of what was between the two of us changed. I felt, rather than saw, his eyes crinkle around the corners and sensed the smile in his voice washing over me like a caress. The moonlight fell upon his face, making his skin look like it was lit by a pale fire. The hair on his head and his hands glowed silver. Carved from platinum he was. All sharp planes and angles, and a smile that slashed its way straight through my sternum right to my heart. I wanted to raise my hand to his lips and touch that smile. He smiled again. A warmth flooded through my body, a hot need taking over all coherent thought, everything a throb, my veins, my heart, my cunt.

When he spoke again, he was proper.

'I'm so sorry about your husband. He died here in Goa, I believe.'

I nodded. He didn't ask for details. I didn't feel like supplying him any. I did not want to speak about my dead husband. It seemed irrelevant. He didn't speak about himself, his life back in London. I didn't ask him. We sat chatting as the moon moved from the mainland in the east towards the sea on the west, and the bottle of wine was emptied, another called for. A surly Da Costa trudged up with it and with the insolence of someone who had seen Victor grow up from short pants to full-length trousers, asked whether we planned to sit the entire night in the balcony and, if yes, could he go to sleep because he was tired and had had a busy day, and Victor Baba's bedroom was aired and ready properly. Properly was one of Da Costa's favourite words. He enunciated it with the requisite emphasis giving the word the gravitas it demanded.

'Don't you worry, Uncle Dom,' Victor said, 'I'll go to sleep soon and properly.'

Da Costa muttered something not very flattering under his breath and turned back to the passageway leading way back to where the house-help lived and slept. 'Lock the door,' he called back as a parting shot. 'The dogs will come in and whole mess they will make in the house till morning!'

Victor assured him that the door indeed would be locked to keep the canines out where they were supposed to be, prowling the ground, keeping unwanted intruders at bay. Buddy sprawled near my feet, thumped his tail in acquiescence. Perhaps we were the intruders, the unknowns. There would be no thieves torn from ear to ear should they dare plot a heist in the watch of these dogs. The dogs would probably go to them wagging their tails, expecting a good rub down as they had grown to expect as their right from any person friend or foe who entered the premises.

We laughed softly as he marched off, solemn in his dignity as caretaker of the house. We sat for a while. And then he stood up to point out the stars in the sky to me, telling me their names, the ones his father had taught him, tracing with the finger of his right hand the constellations. I stood up too, a step ahead of him, to see better what he was pointing out, unblocked by the roof and the scattered clouds. My head, loosened by the wine and his proximity, rested itself against his chest, strong, unyielding, the broad face of a mountain behind me. It was the wine, I told myself. I knew it was not. So did he.

I stumbled, in a bid to get back to a non-contact position, and turned around, awkward. My heart thudding so loud, it was surely audible across the entire island. He put a hand under my elbow to steady me. 'Whoa there, careful,' he said, his other hand caressing my cheek, tucking an errant lock of hair behind my ear, staying there for a second longer than should have been, the fingertips trailing behind my ear, setting me quivering with the softness and urgency of that single touch. The body was a demon. It wanted. I was powerless to stop it, to stop myself from reaching out and taking what I wanted.

I shivered, my body turning against me, making me act without my mind intervening, stopping me, talking sense into me. I put my arms up to his face, cradling it, stood up on my toes and drew his face down to mine. He drew back, hesitant. I pulled him back to me, feeling his lips come settle on mine, searching for succour. His body was different from what I was used to, taller, more stolid; he smelt different, faded deodorant mingled with unfamiliar sweat. I arched my body into his, confident of not being rejected, feeling the responsive swell against my belly. Then we were kissing each other, with huge gulping gasps, sucking the oxygen out from the air. He steered me quickly into the house, closing and locking the ponderous wooden door from the inside. Our feet skimmed up the staircase, we were in my room, the clothes fell off and our bodies moved against each other with a yearning that was unspeakable. And then again, and again as the stars exploded through my limbs and the waves tossed me on to beaches I'd never landed on before. I knew why he had felt like home. He was what my body had been searching for all those years. And I'd come home.

We fell off to sleep as naturally as we were meant to sleep together. There would be no wandering in the caves tonight, no unseen body leaving an indent in the bed next to me when I woke. I slept deeply after a long, long while, without pills, without needing the lights to be on, without drinking myself into a complete stupor. Perhaps this was what I had needed and never realised it. Sometimes strangers, or almost strangers were all one needed to patch up one's crumpled and torn heart.

A tapping on the door woke me up in the middle of the night. I tried to get up, but there was an unfamiliar weight across my torso and my legs. The Fitbit on my wrist lit up to tell me it was 3.14 a.m. Victor lying next to me, across me. His hair, shone silver in the faint light from the outside, his skin, pale and translucent, deep crescents beneath his eyes where the shadows fell.

Who was at the door? I extricated myself from under him, limb by limb. The room was dark, hushed, perhaps I had imagined it. And then I heard it again, the sound I'd heard the previous night, coming from the passage way outside. A thump, a drag, again, all over again. Outside, the dogs were howling mournfully, their howls swirling into the room with the soft breeze and into my ears. I eased myself out from under him. He stirred, murmured something, and then continued to sleep with gentle snores. There was barely any light in the room. There was no moonlight tonight. The crescent moon that had stood sentinel over our conversations was not in evidence outside the windows that lined one entire side of the room. I was naked. Naked felt vulnerable. I slid my feet into my flip flops, pulled on the hastily discarded sundress which had been lying on the floor and moved cautiously towards the door of the room, dreading what I would see on the opposite side. Then thump, drag, right outside my door. I opened it with a trembling hand. There was nothing outside. I fumbled around for the light switch so I could see clearly. The lights wouldn't go on, perhaps there was a power outage. Then, the sound again, a thump, a drag and a low wail. One that pierced into my mind and drilled into it, speaking sibilantly of terrible things that I could not bear to hear. I put

my hands over my ears trying to shut it out, squeezing my
eyes shut. The wail stopped and there was a heavy silence that
hung over the air. I opened my eyes. There was still nothing to
be seen except darkness and the long passage in front of me,
but I realised the banister was on the other side from where
it was when I had shut my eyes. And I could see across the
divide that overlooked the receiving room, to the row of rooms
on the opposite side, where my room was, and where Victor
was probably still asleep within. Gooseflesh pricked my arms,
a cold chill enveloped me, an unearthly cold that drilled into
my bones. And just then, ahead of me, a drag and a thump, a
shadow of a woman moving slowly deliberately through this
part of the house, waiting to see if I had noticed it, if I was
following it. Which I was, unknownst to me. The shadow moved
towards the boarded-up door, reaching out a shadowy arm and
beckoning me inside. I moved unwittingly, my feet being pulled
towards it not of their own accord. I tried to scream but nothing
emerged from my throat. Sleep paralysis, that was what the
doctor Pappa had taken me to in Delhi had called it. Why did
I think of that now, was it a trigger for me to wake myself up?
The planks at the door began melting away as they had done
the previous night, and the door became a passageway, a portal
to something so dark and fetid that I couldn't even begin to
comprehend what might lie within. And the eyes, glowing red
in the dark, hands reaching out from the dark to grab me, pull
me within, whispering their sibilant tales of loss and mourning,
and malevolence. The woman in front of me, leading the way,
stopped and turned around. She had a black veil on her head,
covering her face and empty sockets where her eyes should
have been. And then there was blackness, deep, dark velvety
blackness. She was leading me somewhere that I knew. I heard
a voice behind me. 'Where are you going?'

Victor, awake, standing in the doorway, looking at me in

sleep-addled confusion. I was on the passageway just outside the door of my room. There was nothing in front of me, except the stillness of a house at rest, the darkness of the night and the shadows that shifted as the wind moved the leaves on the mango tree outside.

'Nowhere,' I replied. 'I thought I heard a sound.'

He put a hand out. 'Come back to bed.' I didn't sleep for the rest of the night, and when I finally drifted off, the morning was low lit at the horizon to the east. The dogs woke me up, barking their heads off. The baker's boy was here, his bell ringing, announcing his arrival. The thin curtains could not keep out the rays of the morning sun. The clock on the wall read 7 a.m. Victor stirred and opened his eyes.

'Good morning,' I whispered. He jumped up, unabashed about his nakedness, hunting around for his clothes which he had discarded carelessly on the floor the previous night.

'A lovely morning, but I need to be back in my room before the staff discovers we've been bonking each other. My reputation will be in tatters.'

'Did you hear a knock on the door in the middle of the night? Just before I went out of the room?' He shook his head.

'Not that I remember. But then I normally sleep like a log.'

I shook my head. There was too much fogginess within to remember clearly. All I could remember was the face with no eyes and the blackness with millions of red eyes looking out on me.

'When you lived here, did you experience any strange things?' I asked him. He looked perplexed, albeit a fully dressed perplexed. He came to me and ruffled my hair gently, his own hair a shoulder-length mess of dirty blonde waves that any fashion model worth their pigeon-toed walk would kill to channel as bed head.

'The strangest thing that I remember is that my parents got divorced, and I went away. What's bugging you, beautiful?' He sat down on the edge of the bed next to me, his eyes a deep cerulean blue, bluer than the sky outside, the sea far beyond. These were eyes one could throw oneself into and not want to be reeled out of to safety. I shook my head and drew his face to mine, it was inexplicable, this constant yearning I had for him. He kissed me deeply, tenderly. I pulled him down to me again, he pulled away.

'I must go now, catch you at breakfast.'

I nodded. This was hopeless. A wild fling that would burn itself out in a supernova of a conflagration. It couldn't be helped, I had to submit to this craving, and burn through it. Perhaps this would help me emerge on the other side, done with the grief and self-loathing that had filled me all of these months. Revisiting the past over and over again was only making me a resident of it.

He shut the door behind him, with hushed prescience of one who knew exactly how the doors creaked. I was alone, again. The raucous noise of children playing football in the ground from across the road carried over with the wind. Somewhere temple bells clanged the morning aarti, just as a little while earlier the church bell had rung out for the morning Angelus. I bathed quickly, a bucket bath with water that had only managed to get lukewarm with the cranky geyser, watched a lizard take a leisurely trip across the bathroom and make it out through the window slats. Pulling on a pair of shorts and a shirt that I knotted around the waist, I ran down to the dining room. Breakfast was laid out, Kamini was seated at the head of the table, two places on either side of her were set and waiting. It was 8.30 a.m. She was a creature of habit. The aroma of bacon and eggs came wafting through the door before I entered it, punctuated by the harsher one of cigarettes.

I frowned. 'Smoking again?'

'I'm going to die anyway, so I might as well hasten the

process,' she replied, her voice even more raspy if that were possible. I bent down to hug her.

She had a boiled egg in an egg cup in front of her, and it was half eaten. A slice of toast, buttered and golden, lay neglected on her table. She had barely eaten anything in the past couple of days that I was here. I could already see her shrivelling into herself, her shoulders rounding into a parabola that accentuated the frailness I hadn't noticed on my first day. It seemed to be intensifying by the day.

'Sit here,' she indicated the chair to her right. 'Pour me a cup of tea, please?' The tea was on the sideboard. I turned and did so, refilling her cup, taking it to her. Her hands were beset with tremors that made her economise her gestures to that of minimal grace. She rang for the staff with the little bell that was kept beside her at the table. The same hands that used to sweep the canvas with broad, determined strokes of the brush, sharp daubs of paint with a knife, creating wild beauty and deathly chaos all at once. She couldn't cut her pieces of bacon, so I sat where she asked me to, right next to her, and did it for her. She reached out and took my hand, drawing me closer to her.

She took a long sip of her tea and winced. 'Trust her to overboil it, after telling her countless times to let it brew lightly. It has turned bitter.' She drained her cup with one quick gulp.

'Now, where was I? Be careful...' her voice dropped to a whisper.

'Of what?' I asked, perplexed.

'Of him...' she whispered, stopping mid-sentence, raising her head and smiling at the door as a shadow fell across it, and Victor entered with quick firm strides. It was not the moment to tell her I had already flung my heart out of my ribcage to him, a token of my surrender, unasked for, given freely and wantonly. Was it love, was it lust, was it the undefined territory that skirted both and had no name, I didn't know.

He moved to her, hugged her briefly and kissed her hand in a quaintly old-fashioned manner, the chivalry of antiquity that we have all but given up in these times when wooing is done with right swipes on a touch screen.

'Good morning,' he said to me, with the strange distance of the morning that had cropped between the two of us. I smiled back politely and wished him a good morning in return. There seemed to be nothing left to do but to ask each other if we had slept well, and then make a comment about how wonderfully bright a day it seemed to be and if we had plans as to how we planned to spend our day. The eggs and bacon were downed. Kamini ate nothing that I saw despite me coercing her to eat. Her hand, as she held mine, was unnaturally warm.

'Why aren't you eating anything?' I asked her, 'You must keep up your strength, you barely ate last night too.'

'I've already eaten a fair bit before you came down to breakfast, you don't worry about me,' she said, a rasp to her voice, a smile that morphed into an unwitting wince as a lashing of something that could only be pain cut through her.

Da Costa marched into the dining room, unbidden, his face the mask of doom. 'Doctor is come,' he announced gravely and stood to a side, to allow a huge round man with a bald head and a goatee beard to enter behind him. He was carrying a valise, such that doctors carried in worn brown leather, and the skin on his face had the same worn brown-leathered constituency. 'Madame Kirov,' he said, with a loud booming voice. 'And how are we today?'

Kamini raised an eyebrow, arched and questioning, at his query. 'Alive,' she replied wryly. 'Though not kicking. Come, Dr Gomes, I suspect this rascal Da Costa insisted on dragging you from your busy practice all the way out on a weekday morning to waste time on an old lady. Do join us for breakfast, please.'

She hadn't applied her lipstick, I realised, all of a sudden, nor was there the usual kohl in her eyes. Her face was clear of all make-up, it was a statement by itself. She was not a person who was seen in public without her war paint. Lipstick, a bright pink she had preferred from the years when it echoed the pink in her cheeks, a thick line of kohl on her lower inner eye rim making her look quite the dancer. She was wan.

'Don't blame him, he was worried, and I was in the area anyway to check the Fonseca's daughter-in-law,' he lowered his voice, shaking his head. 'She's doing badly, might not make it.'

'Might be a good thing for her too,' Kamini replied, without a trace of apology in her voice. I wondered who this hapless Fonseca's daughter-in-law was that they were discussing the impending demise of over breakfast with absolutely no token words of 'How sad!', 'Such a young thing, entire life ahead of her,' etc., that one normally associated with deaths before a ripe old age.

Dr Gomes pulled out a chair for himself and sat down with the ease of one who is familiar with both the house and its inhabitants. 'Lucy,' he called, 'one cup of tea, please.' Lucenzia emerged from the kitchen mopping her hands on an apron which could have done with strong detergent and a stronger hand scrubbing it.

'Tea's there,' she gestured at the sideboard.

'It's gone cold now,' I interjected. 'A fresh pot would be good.' She took the pot and went away after enquiring kindly about the health of Dr Gomes, his wife, his son and of any impending good news from his daughter-in-law.

'Vick,' he boomed, apparently familiar with Victor and most probably had been the one under whose care Victor had dealt with his childhood ailments, 'Have you convinced Madame Kirov to now get admitted to the hospital in Panjim? She needs proper treatment, aggressive. If I could I would have taken her to the hospital without her consent, but you are family, you can give consent.'

'I sure will. We will tie her down to the stretcher and take her to the hospital whether she likes it or not,' Victor promised, his voice grim, his eyes twinkling.

The doctor's eyes came to rest on me. 'And this is Kamla?' There was a question in his voice that he'd answered. I wondered how he knew me. 'Good to finally meet you. Your aunt told me you would be visiting to stay a while. I hope you do, she could do with the company.'

'Yes, I plan to stay a while, hopefully till she recovers.'

Kamini gripped my hand tighter. Her grasp was dry and soft, and the bones felt like rubber within. 'Yes, Dr Gomes, Kamla will be with me. You can discuss everything with her.' She stopped and took a long deep breath, almost as if recharging her voice box with enough energy to speak. 'Victor, I don't know how long he plans to stay here.' She tilted her head and looked at him hard, her head angled to one side like a sparrow, watching, assessing.

'I don't know how long I'm here, have to get a few things settled. Need to discuss stuff with you,' Victor nodded in agreement.

Dr Gomes took a long drag from the cup of tea Lucenzia had placed in front of him without ceremony and then rose to his feet rather like a colossus emerging from the sea. He moved next to Kamini and after asking her if she was quite done with her breakfast, began wheeling her out of the dining room and towards her bedroom. I rose to accompany them, she waved me off. Victor had disappeared again, with a roar of the motorcycle announcing his departure.

'Finish your breakfast in peace, Lucy will come with me.' And Lucy did so, her wizened face tightening in anxiety to make it even more simian than it had been to begin with. She untied her apron and handed it over to Jacinta who was hovering behind. Jacinta was her niece and her sous chef cum general housemaid who did all the dusting and cleaning, and could be found at all odd hours perched precariously on tall ladders trying to get cobwebs out of the high ceilings and cornices. Jacinta was here, working in the big house thanks to the fact that she hadn't got married while the rest of the girls her age were either strategizing how to get a job in the Gulf or get married to a 'boy' who worked in the Gulf with ambitions to emigrate to New Zealand or Canada.

Jacinta cleared the table briskly, with the efficiency that comes from knowing there are other tasks waiting completion. She decided to speak to me one on one as I ate, something she hadn't done yet.

'Cajetan in hotel where he died,' she informed me with her staccato speech I struggled to decode most of the time. Cajetan, I understood, nephew to Lucenzia and Jacinta's brother, had found gainful employment in the five-star resort where Nihar had passed away.

'You want to meet him?' she asked, a statement that was more a demand than a query. I did, I replied. 'Ask him to come here after duty?' she asked again in the strange manner that made every sentence a question. I nodded, then changed my mind. Perhaps, I thought I should go to the room where Nihar had died. Perhaps I could convince myself that he was truly gone when I went there, and couldn't reach him. Or perhaps he would still be there, lurking in the grey zone between here and there, where souls lingered, stuck and desperate to gain our attention.

I was here. Barely an hour or two away from where he had passed away. Was he still there, lurking, waiting for me, dare I go there and set myself free?

'Could you tell Cajetan I'm coming to the hotel?' I told her. She nodded. 'Could you ask him to check and let me know if room number 304 is available?'

She nodded again and bounded off to make a call. When she returned, her expression was that of someone who had managed something stupendous. 'It's available.'

I thanked her for her initiative and called for Da Costa to take me to the ferry. Surely, I would find myself a taxi to the hotel.

I rushed up to my room and picked up my cavernous handbag, shoving in an additional sundress, a change of undergarments and a night dress, just in case. I planned to stay the night, I did. Da Costa agreed to drop me across the ferry and even haggled with a cab driver he knew across the ferry for a reasonable fare to take me to south Goa, reasonable being a misnomer given the exorbitant amounts taxis charged in this state. 'I'll be back tomorrow,' I told him. 'Tell my aunt that.'

'Don't go to beach alone,' he warned. 'All not nice people nowadays. Is dangerous for ladeez.'

I assured him I wouldn't and clambered into the taxi, which was a new one with its plastic still intact over the new seats. As the taxi began its trip, I turned around to see him standing outlined against the white church that rose sentinel over the island across the river. I'd never been a person for faith and religion, but sometimes the strangest coincidences give one comfort. The dashboard of the taxi had a makeshift altar, a Virgin Mary and Jesus on the cross, two pictures framed side by side, garlanded with a rosary. The presence of divinity was soothing, a benediction of sorts on my journey to find closure.

We drove quickly through the winding roads past football fields and churches, past little houses with lives being played out on the porches, through asphalted roads with neat edges fringed by strips of red earth, through lush green paddy fields fringed with coconut trees, passed churches and schools and football grounds and all that went into making the day to day of a place that survived primarily on strangers making it their someday, sometime. There was a turn-off down an unmarked road, the discrete signs telling us that the resort we sought was some kilometres away. And then we past some more fields, and winding roads, before the resort was upon us. We drove in, the gates opened, I went to the lobby and then paused, wondering what was I to ask, how was I to even begin my enquiries, and how could I see the room where Nihar had died. How does one grab one's grief by the collar and look it in the eye? One goes back to where it all ended, or where it all began. This was my pilgrimage to exorcise my grief.

A receptionist looked at me curiously and rearranged her expression into a neutral smile of welcome. I realised it was unexpected, a woman in a sundress and slippers, with no luggage, landing up at the reception desk of a hotel set so far in the interior that only determined effort would take one there. The lobby gleamed of soft lights, strategically placed plants, polished to gleaming bronze sculptures and wall art, water bodies that tinkled graciously into lotus ponds. A huge Buddha sat peaceably in the midst of it all, his expression beatific and amused. I felt unkempt, unworthy of being there, in the glistening manicured setting of it all.

'Can I help you, Ma'am?' she asked, with a smile that began and ended at her lips and did not even bother a perfunctory infiltration of the zone that should have crinkled around her eyes.

'I want a room, for just a day. But I want to make sure it is just this specific room. Room 304.'

She looked at me strangely. 'Of course, Ma'am,' she repeated like an automaton, her eyes darting to the computer in front of her on her desk, 'It is available. May I have your name and identification.'

I gave her what she asked for. I looked at the array of clocks behind her head, giving us the time in all the major cities of the world. In the state I was in right now, the time was just about noon. Ronella, as the badge on her jacket stated, looked up from the computer she had been checking, and conferred quickly and silently with the man standing next to her.

'Ma'am, how long do you plan to stay?'

'Just for the day, I will check out by noon tomorrow.'

'Sure, may I have your card?'

I handed across the piece of plastic.

A signature later, I was being escorted to my room in a little buggy cart, the little duffel bag I had carried seemed sadly inadequate for the immense space that luggage was meant to be placed in at the back. We went down a long path, lined with trees, peppered with lotus ponds in Zen gardens crossed by little bridges which made me stop and look at my reflection in the water below. The villa when we arrived at it, was slightly apart from the others in the line, brooding and wary, two rooms next to each other, the doors separated by a wall that allowed you to not see the occupants of the neighbouring room. The bellboy opened the door for me, led me in and explained the features of some controls, waiting around needlessly until I realised what he was waiting for, and fished out the mandatory tip. He pocketed it with the swiftness of experience.

I took out another note and held it in my hand. 'I need some information,' I said.

His eyes fixed themselves on the note in my hand.

'Sure, Ma'am.' He was young, a local lad, his Adam's apple bobbing in his neck, his voice quavering from anticipation.

'How long have you been working here?'

'Three years, Madam.'

'Were you on duty when they found this man dead in this room?'

I showed him Nihar's picture on my phone.

He looked at it strangely and gulped. For a moment his face looked fishlike.

'I was on duty when we found him dead in this room.'

'Do you remember anything about that day, anything about who else could have been in the room with him?'

'All I know is that when the body was found, there was a lot of pressure from someone very influential. The next day a man came to the hotel and spoke with all of us, warning us all that we had heard nothing, seen nothing. He was bad news.'

Something hit me hard in the solar plexus, knocking all the air out of my lungs. They deflated quickly, my knees buckled. I sat down hard on the chair that was conveniently next to the desk. He looked at me with concern, but was unequal to the task of volunteering assistance when not asked for it. I picked up a bottle of unopened mineral water kept on the desk, broke it open after much effort and took a long sip.

'Could you describe this man to me?'

He shook his head to indicate a negative. 'I didn't meet him.'

I handed the note he had been eyeing for so very long across to him. He took it with a smooth practised gesture and slid it into his pocket with such ease it could have been sleight of hand.

'I'm his wife. His widow, rather, the man whose picture I showed you. I'm trying to find out how he died.'

He shook his head disbelievingly.

'I'm sorry, Madam, I didn't realise. I think you should talk to the housekeeping manager. I wasn't there when they opened the door, it was the second day, I think, when they realised something was wrong.'

'Could you please have the manager speak with me whenever he is free?'

'Yes, Madam,' he replied, and moved out of the room, his feet soundless on the carpeted floor.

I sat down on the bed and looked around the room I was in. It was a well-appointed room, in the manner that rooms in five-star hotels are. Decor inspired from the location. Some shell elements in the decor. Mother of pearl scattered around generously in the wood work, on the coffee table, patterned in the veneer of the wardrobes. Shell and star fish motifs embossed on the dado. Muted tones of sea and sand. Polished wood, deep and carved. A sit-out with an all-weather lounger, small table and two chairs for a breakfast sit-out or an evening pre-dinner drink. I threw myself on the bed, wondering which side of the bed Nihar was found dead on. Was he here now? Was he here? Or was he, as Dr Gulabchand, my psychiatrist had declared, nowhere but in my head?

TWELVE

HERE, NOW

The sudden chill woke me. It was dark outside. The moon, if it was somewhere in the sky, had not made its way to outside my room. I was in the room Nihar had died in, the thought hit me after the chill did. The room had been cleansed of his presence. All that remained was the impersonal sterility of the hotel room, sanitized and impersonal. There were many who would have stayed in this room since the time he had been found in it. It had been months since the day.

Last evening, I had spent wandering around the property, revelling in my aloneness. I wondered what was happening back at the villa. Da Costa would have told them where I had gone. There had been no calls from Kamini. Maa had called, and then was rather upset when I told her I was in Goa with Kamini.

'Why would you go and stay with Kamini and not come home to me?'

'It was a shorter journey, Maa,' I explained. 'And it was a complete impulse decision.'

'Are you sure you will be alright?'

'I am alright, Maa, but Kamini isn't. Did you know she has leukaemia?'

The brief silence at the end of the line told me she did.

'And you didn't think it important to tell me?'

'She was okay, she said, she was getting treatment for it.' Her voice was sulky, resentful. 'And Pappa had just died and then your husband after him. I was in no state to deal with her illness.'

I fell quiet. It had been a difficult time. Perhaps she had

blocked Kamini's illness from her mind, perhaps it was a non-priority for her. At times, self-preservation is greater that compassion for another, at times to be selfish with one's grief is the only way to hold oneself together.

'Well, she's rather serious now. She's refused to continue with treatment. She doesn't look too good, Maa. I think you should come see her.'

'You know I can't travel all that way. I'll die before her.'

'You'll regret it.'

'I know I will. But I haven't had anything to say to her in years. I don't think her dying would change anything.'

'She's your sister, Maa.'

'I know that, you don't need to keep reminding me. Which reminds me, what news from Roop? She hasn't bothered to call for the past so many days. Why will either of you bother about your old, ill mother...'

I cut her off before the speech denigrated into how we had both abdicated all our responsibilities and wouldn't bother to even come to her funeral, and for this she had carried us in utero for nine months and suffered forty-eight hours of labour for me, who was now a right ingrate and I would know when I had kids of my own.

'I'll call you later... bye.'

Conversations with Maa always set me on edge. It would take me a while to recover. Why was it always so with the ones we were the closest to. The most mundane of conversations with them would be an exercise in sparring and jabbing quick and deep enough to draw blood.

The evening faded into night yesterday, a swift descent into blackness from the orange-dappled sky of sunset that spread out before me, right to where the resort went to the stretch of the private beach. The hushed evening sounds of crickets and the birds whirring back to their nests were tempered with the faint sounds of the band at the main restaurant striking up a tune after a few stray discordant chords of tuning. What were Nihar's last minutes like, I wondered. Had he suffered? Had it been peaceful? I would never know. Had he heard the hotel live singer plodding through off-key versions of hits from the 1970s? Had he seen the birds flying back to their nests and the fruit bats emerging from theirs? I sat on the sit-out, staring down the path that connected the villa to the main pathway leading to the reception and the main hotel, nursing a glass of wine for the longest time before I went to bed, feeling the loneliness overwhelm me.

I'd ordered in a chicken biryani, which I'd barely picked through, and then lay down in the bed waiting for sleep, unmedicated sleep. It would be a long time coming, I knew, and when it did come, I never knew where I would be. This was the bed Nihar last slept in, this was where he last drew breath. Some part of him would be lurking around here, struggling to find an explanation for what had happened with him, struggling to find closure. What had his last day been like? Why had he chosen to stay here, rather than closer to the venue of the conference? What had it been like, knowing he was going to die? How had each of the bruises on his body come about, how had he been overpowered, how had he struggled, when had the fight sagged out of him, when had the breath left his body, when had his body become flesh?

Dark shadows flitted in the dim light that lit the pathways, the bats of the night flying through the fruit trees, navigating their way with the sounds they sent out, the darkness no deterrent to them. The sub-aural screeches they used scratching against the inner ear, a faint sense of dissonance. I went back into the room and locked the door. Sleep would be a long time coming, I didn't want the luxury of a quick slide into medicated blackness tonight. I wanted to have my brain with me, not trussed up with the bonds of the chemicals racing through my bloodstream.

The room was cold when I woke. Ice trickled down my cheeks as the tears dripped out from the sides of my eyes. I could feel gooseflesh all over my body. I got up and went to the air-conditioning control panel. It was set to 23 degrees Celsius. It felt sub-zero. Surely my skin was freezing and cracking up with the chill? I switched the air conditioning off and opened the window leading out to the balcony, stepping out into the warmth of the tropical night, feeling the heat seep through the layers of my dermis and epidermis through the fatty layer, the muscle, and hitting the bone. In my chest, thumping behind the sternum, cosseted by the lungs, my heart was still an icicle lodged in my chest, impervious to all that was going on around me. The wind was balmy and gentle and teased me, the tang of the sea in it, and the dirge of the sea sirens riding on it. From the villa next door, I could hear laughter, a female voice. Then the deep tones of a man saying something, followed by more female laughter. The world was created for couples and families. Those who chose to stay alone in it had no place, they were the unwelcome abominations of social constructs. I was one now. I went back into the room, closing and fastening the locks on the full windows, shutting out the laughter.

I lay down on the bed waiting for sleep to come. When it did, I fell straight through into the void. I was running through the forests back home in winter, and the snow was pelting down, dragging my feet into the ground, holding my feet, pulling me into the earth, frozen, cold, dark, where the roots of the tired trees snaked themselves around my feet, tripping me over, grabbing my ankle. A desire to sink into the coldness and end it all overwhelmed me. Voices whispering in my ears, Kamli, Kamli, don't do it, said one. Lotusface, come to me, said another. I opened my eyes to a dark room, the moonlight trickling inside from a gibbous moon outside, ragged at the edges, as though torn from a child's picture book and pasted haphazardly on to the black screen of the sky. I was frozen to the bed, my body stuck in that limbo land where it couldn't move an inch, while my eyes were wide open, taking in everything around me. Sleep paralysis it was, a part of me knew, as the doctor had said, nothing but sleep paralysis and hallucinations.

'It isn't real, my dear, your brain is acting up, imagining things.' I could still see his face as he said it, head cocked to one side, the thin moustache that inspired no trust over a thinner pinched pair of lips.

'They will stop when she comes of age,' Daadi had told Maa, whenever I told them about my travels to different places in my sleep. 'All this travelling in the sky to different worlds, she will forget about it. Just a few years more.'

This was real. I could smell a sharp pungent odour, feel the heat coming through a phosphorescent glow from the ceiling that slowly transformed into a reflective surface like that of a still pond, reflecting the bed I lay on. I could see myself lying in it, the planes of my face angular and hollow, the expression in them haunted. And lying next to me, Nihar. He smiled, a smile that was agony and heartbreak all rolled into one. I turned my head to look beside me. Nothing, just empty bed. I reached out a hand to touch him. The gesture took a great deal of effort, the air felt thick and sticky, I had to push through it to move my hand forward, like swimming through molasses.

I could hear his voice in my head. 'Kamie,' he said. 'Come with me.' The bed felt like a block of ice. The room was freezing, I could see my breath mist up as I exhaled. The French windows were fogged up, droplets of condensed water trickling down like tears from so many unseen eyes. I sat up and reached out to him. He put a hand downwards from the ceiling, reaching out to me, trying to grasp me. Behind him, a chasm opening wider, the bed suspended above in the reflection moving closer towards me, lower and lower, the foul sulphurous stench from it pushing its way into my nose, filling my lungs with its fumes, choking me. I could see a chaos of red-hot lava deep within it, the heat from it searing the room, singeing the hair off my skin from the hand that was reaching upwards. I fell back on the bed with a shock. A spark fell down from the hellish domain above mine, on to the sheets, setting it ablaze. I crawled desperately away from the bed, watching the flames rise in what seemed like a second, hearing from a distance, the sound of the fire alarm and the cold wetness of the sprinklers getting set off, and me waking up, drenched and shivering. The bed was now wet, charred and acrid. To my side, the table lamp had toppled over, the bulb broken.

There was urgent knocking at the door, then it swung open; a master key had probably been used. I hadn't locked the door, I realised. The room was dark, smoke-filled, musty with the smell of a doused fire. The hotel staff rushed into the room, two bearing fire extinguishers that they put down when they saw that the fire had been extinguished. One carefully helped me up to my feet and then led me outside to a traditional balcony seat. The rest of the staff surveyed the damage caused. 'Are you alright, madam?' he asked, perhaps slightly discomfited that he had no dead body to discuss over drinks with his mates when he went off duty.

'Yes, I'm fine,' I replied.

I began shivering uncontrollably.

'Are you okay, madam? Are you alone? Should we call the doctor?'

They handed me a bottle of water from the sideboard. I held it with trembling hands and took huge swallows, too grateful to even mumble a coherent thank you until my thirst was sated. I was still shivering. Someone wrapped a blanket around me.

Another retrieved my handbag and duffel bag; they would move me to another room, they said.

'More likely a short circuit of the bedside lamp,' said another man in a suit, who looked like he could be a lobby manager, judging by the polished accent and the self-important manner in which he carried himself. He looked at me warily as I sat there, just trying to get air back into my lungs in huge greedy gulps. The acridity would not go, it tinged my throat, my tongue—the taste of rotting flesh, the smell of sulphur and hellfire and all that was a world I did not want to see again.

'Anything else of yours in the room, ma'am?'

'My phone,' I replied, 'on the table next to the bed.'

They retrieved it, I was escorted to another room, a humbler one, part of the hotel proper, not a detached villa, decorated in the cookie-cutter manner of the luxury resort chain hotel. It was still dark outside, the day was a long way from breaking.

I changed into the dressing gown in the closet and hung out the drenched sundress to dry. I curled up on the bed, and let the tears flow. Catharsis and closure were what I longed for, perhaps I would find it here. Nihar had been here a few months ago. He had died. I was being a fool, hanging on to the ridiculous hope that I would find him here. He was gone. I would leave Goa tomorrow and go back to Mumbai and my work, and tell Kamini I could not accept her offer and she should give the villa to Victor who truly deserved it. And then the sleeping pill I had downed took hold of me and thrust me down into a vortex of blackness where there was nothing, no thought, no memory, no dream, no here and no there.

THIRTEEN

THEN, THERE

It was cold. The snow settled itself like a fluffy blanket all over town, the rooftops, the trees, the roads. The house was hushed, the snow smothered our words, if we had any. It held us in and kept the world out. It floated down over the house, over the school, over the market, over the desolate forests that fringed our small town, in the little valley where the villagers shivered next to their tiny stoves, drawing the little heat that emanated from them to keep the blood in their veins running. It fell on that little mound of earth that marked where a baby, not yet a week old, had been hastily buried, his presence on this earth, a momentary aberration, a karmic debt that was repaid by a few days of human existence.

We were housebound by snow and death. After all death had visited our home and we would be home for a day or so in mourning. Infants were not mourned. They had left no memories to warrant the mourning, they were but a visit from the divine, affirmation that while life goes on, death has dominion. Was there a format of grief one needed to express and what was the template of appropriate behaviour? We didn't know. After all, we were but eight and twelve, and all we knew was to keep quiet and to go to our rooms when asked to, and refrain from upsetting our mother. This comprised primarily of staying out of her way, and not asking uncomfortable questions. When I think of it, a major part of my childhood comprised staying out of the way of the adults. One stayed out of their way and didn't get to ask too many questions, that was the way it was.

We received information on an as-is-required basis and to get the rest we kept our eyes and ears open for, and pieced together in a sodden tapestry of half-gleaned snippets that we filled in with the febrile creations of our imagination.

We were not allowed to go out of the house. Into the garden, yes, but beyond it and the swinging gate was the entire universe that beckoned to me. The garden was Daadi's pride and joy. In spring, it was a riot of colour—dahlias, hydrangeas, marigold, chrysanthemums, lilies—all jostling for place in the sun. Now in winter, the bulbs were dormant on the hard, icy ground, waiting for spring and the thaw. Side paths ran off the steep road to homes of friends, to playgrounds that were now hard and icy but still places where we could congregate before rushing off to some warmer refuge to play our games. The best time for us to do things the adults wouldn't rebuke us for was when they were distracted. For me, it was time to play unhindered.

It was blindingly white all around because of the snow, and the complete opposite of the grey and foreboding at night. I pressed my nose against the window and watched the snow float down. I couldn't wait to go outside and play in the snow. I would go down into the backyard where no one would bother me, where the compound wall had fallen out, and slip out through the gap into the thick of the trees which led to the old pastures. I was just about one foot out of the back door, when Behra spotted me and called me back in.

I waited for him to get distracted so I could slip out again, but he asked me if I had seen Kanchi anywhere in the upper rooms. Daadi ambled to the back door and began grumbling too. The kitchen duties had begun getting too much for her to handle on her own. She was wondering where the wretch was when there was so much work to be done, calling out her name so the house reverberated. Maa had taken to her bed in a deep sadness. She would not speak, she would not eat, she would not bathe. It would be a few days before she emerged, we knew. Perhaps more. She would mourn a few days for those who were not born. For this one, who she had fed and held, we didn't know how long it would take for her to emerge. I didn't realise it then, but now I did. Daadi was unlike other mothers-in-law of the time, she allowed my mother time to grieve. The others insisted that the housework could not be stayed for grieving, even if you had held the corpse of your newborn.

I took myself and my comic books to the window seat which looked out towards the tree-lined approach to our gate.

Roop was sitting on the floor, her sheets of paper spread out in front of her. She drew all the time, filling pages after pages with pictures of flowers and meadows and smiling faces and all the things that had gone with the summer, and which to us, two girls, shivering in an unheated room right under the attic, seemed a lifetime away. Suddenly, we heard a roaring on the road—a police jeep, followed by an ambulance, and its tinny siren. I sprang up and ran down the stairs. After a moment's hesitation Roop followed too.

Daadi, hearing the sounds of feet pattering down the stairs yelled after us, 'Where are you girls running off to, don't open the front door, there's a terrible wind outside...' the rest of her words were drowned by the said terrible wind as we opened the door. Pappa followed us outside, looking to all purposes like a turtle given the number of sweaters he had put on.

He stared at the disappearing police jeep followed by the ambulance and looked thoughtful for a while, and then unable to resist the call of some excitement happening in the small hill town we lived in, went out to the gate, peering down the road for someone, anyone to give him the lowdown on what had caused the hullaballoo. Finally, after struggling with the imposed need to stay in seclusion, and the need to find out what had made the somnambulant constabulary move themselves with such unaccustomed efficiency, he pulled on his overcoat and began the long march down the steps that led to the sit-out, and the path through it to the main gate. Daadi stood up from her perch on the low stool before the kitchen platform, straightening her arthritic legs. She spotted me as I returned through the passage hoping to run up to our room, unspotted. 'Why are you down? And now that you're here, go find that useless Kanchi. I've been calling for her since the morning. Behra says she went out in the morning to the market and hasn't yet come back. How am I supposed to get lunch ready for all of you alone, and your mother in the state she is...' Her voice trailed off. We'd always known that Maa was fragile, she was not like other mothers. Right now, to the eight-year-old me, Maa was sad and she was asleep and not to be disturbed and that was all there was to it.

I grabbed the opportunity to skip out to the marketplace, my hand in my pocket holding on to the coins that I picked up from the side table as I went out, enough to buy myself a handful of boiled sweets, with some left over for Roop if she would be nice to me. 'Put on one more sweater and wear your boots, and are you covered enough for outside?' Daadi bellowed loud enough for Roop to scamper down with the intention of accompanying me, if at all I was going anywhere.

'Am going to find Kanchi,' I answered her squawks of protest at being left out of this escapade.

'I'm coming,' she announced dryly. We ran out of the door before Daadi could change her mind. We scrambled down the steps and were out of the gate, the chill wind outside hitting our faces relentlessly with angry slaps that froze us to the marrow.

We ran down the sugar-kissed streets, passing the homes of folks we knew, before they stopped us and asked us what we were doing out of the house and if all was well. We stopped panting at the store at the corner of the market. Kanchi would invariably stop here to get some groceries if required. 'Bhaiyya, did Kanchi come here this morning?' Roop asked the greengrocer outside the store, her attention already fixed on the glass jars full of peppermint-striped candies lined up like sentinels in the store behind him. I went up to the store and bought two dozens of the dental enamel-rotting agents, dividing them between me and Roop, storing them, as we did, in different pockets of the layers we had on, to be discovered much later, and to eardrum-shattering rage from Daadi, as melted sticky indeterminate masses that no detergent could eliminate successfully.

'Nath chacha,' Roop asked the shopkeeper of the grocery store, after he'd enquired politely about our parents and grandmother and consoled us about the loss of our brother and assured us that our parents would soon have another, much like brothers came off an assembly rack made to order, 'have you seen Kanchi?'

He hadn't, he said. In fact, he hadn't seen her for a couple of days but he'd assumed it was because of the events at home. It was quite strange. She was always in the market every morning to pick up fresh vegetables and provisions, but no, he had not seen her. Nor had the tailor. Nor had the medical store assistant who knew her because she was the one who was trusted to get refills on Daadi's prescriptions and Maa's sleeping pills. Kanchi had disappeared. Kanchi of the flat feet, flat features, sloe eyes, permanently chapped cheeks, the reticent voice, and the even more reticent self, was nowhere to be found.

Badri Kaka spotted us from his perch up at the counter of the sweetmeat shop. The aroma of the jalebis coming sizzling hot out of the oil from the huge *degchi* right up front, to be ferried quickly to paying customers waiting for their morning fix of jalebis with milk, called out to us. We stopped and peered in with the hunger of children towards sweets. He called us in and offered us two steel tumblers of hot sweet milk and some jalebis while enquiring after everyone at home. The wall behind

Badri Kaka was covered with posters and framed pictures of every god in the pantheon. On a rickety shelf below them was a flickering lamp with a sooty flame.

'Now, go home quick, there seems to be trouble up ahead, up on the road towards the ridge, ahead of your home. Kanchi will be back, don't worry, she's probably gone to the Bholenath temple.'

Our curiosity was piqued, now wild horses couldn't make us go back. We scampered off towards the ridge, two girls out from home on an errand they had all but forgotten about in the thrill of finding out what had happened to merit a police van and an ambulance to rush past their house in the morning. While we walked we discussed where Kanchi could be and listed out all the people we'd asked if they'd seen her in order to recount the list to Daadi.

The morning sifted into noon, the fog became denser, as we walked back home. Perhaps she had returned home, we told each other. Kanchi was like one of those soundless ghost people in the house, one who never spoke, but listened to all that was being said, a shadow that moved around efficiently, getting things done. She had been married to Behra's only son when she was barely fifteen and come to her in-laws' home when she was eighteen. Her in-laws' home was the outhouse behind our house, where Behra had lived with his bed-ridden wife who had died a couple of months ago.

Behra's son, a strapping, handsome young lad with the typical broad features of the hill people and the sharp piercing eyes that went with it, had ambitions of owning his own tourist taxi in town. He had shifted his attentions to the smog and grind of Delhi, moving there to make his fortune as a private driver for a family in Vasant Vihar and returned home once every few years. The last time he returned was when they got him married. One fine day Kanchi's belly began swelling and she delivered a bonny boy a few months ago. She would be seen everywhere with the infant tied to her back as she went about her chores outdoors, and would place him in the carton the television came in, when she needed to work in the kitchen. We played with the baby warily, from a distance, a fragile toy we had been warned not to touch unless under supervision and neither of us had the gene that made babies fascinating to us. Babies pooped and pissed and howled loudly and generally were no fun because all that one could do with them was marvel at their expressions. We didn't understand the censorious way people looked at her as she passed. Behra's son hadn't visited home in years. But these were calculations beyond our years, insinuations beyond our ken.

As we neared the ridge, a friend of our father's spotted us and shooed us back home. 'What are you girls doing here? There's nothing for you to watch.' Disappointed, we went back home, skipping past the stores, the stalls, past the chaos of the bus and taxi stand at the edge of the lower market, then climbing up the steep road leading off the marketplace through to where the houses hugged the edges of the roads, in hope and desperation, higher to where the houses thinned out from being packed together cheek by jowl to where they lay, scattered, in regal semi-isolation, with patches of garden and stretches of road defining boundaries where lives ended and began. At the end of one such little path off the main road, was our home. A home that had been ours for decades now, and hopefully would be a home our children knew as well. But back then, we weren't thinking about children, and the future or the past of how the bungalow came into the family, all we were wondering about was the mysterious disappearance of Kanchi.

'Where could she have gone?' I asked Roop.

'She's probably back home by now, she must have gone off to the mandir. It is Monday, right?'

Kanchi went to the temple every Monday, the ancient Shiv

mandir just a sharp hair-pin bend and a steep climb up a flight of stairs off the road a good distance away from town. It was part of her penance, the walk, she didn't speak about it, but we knew, she would go there to get away from the house. It was the only sanctioned time she had to herself, the rest of the time, she was on 24-hour fetch-and-carry duty in our home. How entitled were we, I thought now, red with shame, and how like a serf we treated her, us still in pig-tails.

The god of the hills, the ash-smeared, trishul-wielding ascetic with the snake coiled around his neck, draped in animal skin, the destroyer of the triumvirate. A god with the feared third eye that brought destruction, the fini of the cycle of creation, preservation and destruction. A god to be appeased, quick to anger, generous to giving, and indulgent. I liked Shivji. Maa liked her Krishna Murari, but I was always drawn to Shivshankar. Daadi liked her satsang. We were a family of eclectic religious affiliations.

Perched up high, hidden from sight from the road, with nothing to mark its presence except an indifferent faded road sign, long battered into unreadability by the elements, this temple was thronged on Mondays by young women seeking appropriate life partners who fitted in with caste, religion and gotra (mandatory bucket lists) as well as channelled a bit of Aamir Khan or whoever was their current cinematic crush du jour. Kanchi went there as a good wife. It was a tough thing, I realised, to be a good wife. My mother had given up trying, she didn't even pretend to be a good wife or a good mother anymore. But she loved us all, in her own vague, distracted way. When we reached home, Pappa was at the gate, leaning against it, chatting with Sub-inspector Jung, who was looking to all purposes, even more imposing than he normally did with his handlebar moustache and broad shoulders. He had a strapping personality but a voice that was as pip-squeakily non-threatening as a teen's before it broke into manliness. Now he was saying to Pappa in that pipsqueak voice of his that there had been a double murder in the night in one of the summer houses on the ridge. He noticed us listening, ears agog, and shooed us into the house.

'What are you doing rambling around all over town, I thought I'd told you both not to step out?'

'Daadi told us to go find Kanchi,' I replied, ever defiant, wiping any tell-tale fleeting remnant of the milk moustache with the sleeve of my sweater and my sticky fingers on my trousers, and pulling my snow boots off on the porch.

'Did you find her?'

'Nope. No one has seen her,' I replied, thrilled to be the bearer of bad news. 'Perhaps she was murdered too?'

Pappa looked at me searchingly, a scathingly dismissive gaze that completely eviscerated the momentary flippancy with which I'd said that. I felt a chill run down my back. Pappa's unblinking gaze did that to me.

'Don't joke about death,' he said.

Perhaps he was thinking about his son, I thought, mourning the child he never knew and we, his two daughters were painful reminders of what he now no longer had. Suitably chastized, we scampered into the house, sought Daadi out in the upper floor where she was instructing Behra on the weekly cleaning which he had conveniently junked in the assurance that a house in mourning did not clean, a theory that Daadi did not hold true because mourning for a newborn according to her did not come with the same set of rules and regulations that mourning for an adult did. Ask a mother how old her dead child would have been, the one who left behind nothing but the empty grasp of a life unlived, anytime years later and she would tell you exactly the years, the months. A bereaved mother walks out her years with the ghosts of her dead offspring keeping step with her, while the rest of the world spins on, unconcerned.

Behra took the news that Kanchi was nowhere to be found with complete lack of expression, perhaps not realising that he was the sole person responsible for his daughter-in-law and grandson ever since his wife passed away and that they hadn't been seen since the morning.

'Where could she have gone with the child?' Daadi wondered aloud, grumbling about young girls who shirked work. Sensing a lecture coming on, we quickly skipped up to our rooms, the pieces of barfi we had been handed already ingested, and the peppermints still sticky in our clenched fists. We clambered up to our room, wondering how to spend the long cold day ahead of us. There was no more going out allowed for the day that we knew. Kanchi would come back, that we knew too, and Maa would emerge from her dark room, and hopefully be better today. The mourning for this child would be longer than for those who had died in the womb. She had held this one in her arms. Those had been phantoms, this one had been flesh and blood.

And there would be lunch soon, it was almost 1.30, unless, an awful thought struck me. 'What if Daadi hasn't made lunch?' There had been food coming in the previous day. It was what one did in recognition of a house in mourning—one sent food over as a neighbourly gesture. But we didn't know if the neighbours had been as generous today. And Daadi wasn't quite a stickler for rituals, it came from being an iconoclast of her generation, part of the territory of being among the few well-educated girls from amongst her peers.

'Of course she would have made lunch, you ninny,' Roop declared. 'You think she would take the risk of getting Pappa annoyed. Of all things Pappa can't bear is having his lunch delayed. He will start bellowing like a bull and then all of them will start scurrying from the kitchen to the dining room, bringing plates and food until he settles down.'

Just for once I would like to see someone tell Pappa that lunch was not ready, I would like to see him work himself into a screaming froth of anger and implode. I quickly squashed down the thought. Roop picked up the Archie's comic books she'd borrowed from the only lending library we had in town. It was three days overdue and she'd already read them thrice over, and would read them a couple of times more before returning them and picking up some others. Maa was in one of her phases which meant we would be more laxly supervised and Roop would pick up a romance novel or one of those photo-romance books which we would giggle over. I decided to go down to the kitchen to investigate what was available for lunch.

I stepped cautiously past the room Behra was cleaning up. My grandmother had sallied forth downstairs, resolutely holding the crumbling universe around her together with yellow dal and paneer mattar. If all of life were falling apart, there would always be food that would hold bits and pieces of us together, I knew. Pappa had begun moving towards the dining table, calling out to us. It was then that I heard it, the unmistakable cry of a baby. It came from up above, far above. I stood on the landing between the ground and the first floor and looked up. Roop emerged from our room and looked up too, Daadi ambled out the kitchen, her massive frame thumping on the wooden flooring with a definite smack with every step. She looked up. We all looked at each other. I was the first to react, and sped up the stairs as quick as my feet could take me. Roop hesitated for a moment and then charged behind me, the wailing increased as we went higher and then we were at the door of the source of the wailing. The attic. My body began shivering involuntarily. The door was, as always, closed. Ghosts lived behind that door I knew, ghosts who had lived here before us and never ventured out, because they could not navigate the stairs down on ghostly feet that hadn't yet accepted that they didn't need the support of crutches.

'You go first,' Roop pushed me, with the surety of being obeyed always.

I did, clambering up as fast as my feet could take me and opened the latch, pushing it open gently despite the protesting creak it made. These joints had not seen oil for a while. The baby was wailing in the middle of the floor, lying on a soft mattress of hay and old rags. And hanging above him, from the beams, was his mother, Kanchi. Her head at an awkward angle, her tongue protruding, her eyes glassy and staring. The smell of urine in the air, a smell that hit the nose strong and hard. I called out loudly, and Roop who had followed me up added her voice to my cries, scampering down to find Daadi.

When they cut her down and prised her fist open, there was an inland letter in it, one she waited for anxiously every month from her husband. In it he had told her he would not be coming to take her to the big city ever. That she and her son could live their lives without him. She was swinging from the rope she'd managed to tie to the beam which spanned across the not-so-high attic. It was high enough for her to be successful in her attempt to die by suicide, I realised. The box she must have climbed on and kicked off from under her feet was askew, next to the same trunk I had opened when I'd last come here, the trunk I'd climbed into, filled with warm clothes and mothballs, and memories that weren't mine to peruse.

'Daadi, Daadi,' Roop yelled, 'Kanchi's here, she's dead.'

Daadi limbered herself up into the attic nimbly for her size and stood for a moment staring at the body hanging in the centre, the eyes unresponsive glassiness, the limbs limp and lifeless. She yelled for Behra. Pappa came up, pulled the footstool and took the body down, checking the vitals.

'She's dead,' he said, his expression strange in a manner I

couldn't comprehend.

The baby, hungry and cold, continued to cry unheeded on the floor, until Daadi picked him up and looked Pappa in the eye, her expression inscrutable. The command in them was undeniable. Pappa took the baby from her and held it, looking into his face. The baby gurgled, his arms stretching out to our father. Roop clutched my hand and we knew, at that moment, even if it would take us decades to acknowledge what we knew then to each other in actual words. Some things are never spoken of within families, they just exist. It was at this moment that Maa climbed into the attic, her face like stone and with leaden steps, looking at Kanchi lying limp on the floor and the infant in Pappa's arms. She extended her arms towards the baby, Pappa placed him in her arms. No words were said. No words were needed. Outside, the snow continued to drift down gently on a sugar-dusted grieving world that was drowning in its melancholy.

FOURTEEN

NOW, HERE

The car was waiting outside the gate of the resort when I emerged wearing the shorts and t-shirt I'd had the foresight to pack in the little duffel bag. The sundress was still fairly damp from the sprinklers. On it I could still smell the acridity of smoke. I was grateful Da Costa and Victor had arrived to take me back, Cajetan had made the call informing them about the fire in the room, making it out to be a blazing inferno which needed to be doused by the collective efforts of the staff making a line and ferrying water from the pool. I gently dissuaded him of the notion. 'It was a freak accident, my hand hit the bedside lamp in my sleep, it probably sparked and lit the bedsheet. The sprinklers were on before I knew it though. Nothing happened to me.' Except for some of the hair on my arms getting singed.

The drive back was in relative silence, with only Da Costa admonishing me good-naturedly about deciding to stay back at the hotel instead of returning home in the evening as I had promised him.

'Herself was worried. All dangerous peepul. Kilt your husband. You know.'

I shook my head in the negative. 'Tell me.'

He looked warily to his side where Victor sat, in the front with him. Victor nodded his head. 'Tell her. I think she deserves to know.'

Da Costa stuck his head outside the open window of the car and spat theatrically to indicate his disgust at a porcine chap astride a motorbike who almost made us land in a ditch by refusing to give way.

'Them Russian fellows. I beg your pardon, Victor baba, your father was not like them.'

Victor laughed and patted him on the back. 'No, he wasn't, but he loved Goa too like they do.'

Every few days during peak tourist season, the cheap chartered flights arrived from the cold north, circling the tropical state like vultures disgorging their entrails, filled with pale-skinned hard-faced tourists. Thousands of them. Some stayed back for months on end, shop signboards now read both in English and Russian. They were a different kind of tourists, the Russians. Further north, a town was now called Little Russia thanks to the Russians taking it over completely. They ran the drug trade in these parts, prostitution rackets, child prostitution and bought over land by coercion and threat. Insidiously, they'd taken over all the nefarious activities that plagued the coastal state and created their own dominion.

'They're like the plagues of Egypt,' he muttered, putting his head out of the car and spitting again to reiterate his disgust. Victor yelled at him to put his head back in as a bus roared past, uncaring of the possibility that it might detach his head from the torso. 'First it was the Israelis, now it is the Russians. Children. Drugs. They will burn in hell.'

'What did Nihar have to do with any of this?'

Victor took a deep breath. 'Cajetan thinks your husband called in the cops on a child prostitution and drugs orgy happening in a room next to his. Important people were involved. Highly placed. People whose names could not be in the newspapers in these circumstances. He was found dead the next day. Too much of a coincidence.'

My stomach knotted and unknotted itself. Da Costa filled me in with details he'd gleaned off Cajetan. Apparently, the supplier had brought the kids to the wrong room, with the drugs. Then he'd rung the doorbell of the next room. Nihar had called the authorities in, spoken to a few friends he had in the media. Banged on the door and had the children taken out, and created a scene. Nihar was scheduled to leave the next day for the other hotel where the conference was being held. He never got to check out. What happened between the time the police took his statement and the time he put the Do Not Disturb sign out and closed the door no one knows.

Da Costa's theory was one that Cajetan had carefully explained to him, whether from empirical evidence or the flights of his fevered fantasy, I did not know. The door had been opened by a masterkey, a man or two had entered and injected him with more heroin than his system could take. They had roughed him up too, tied him and held him down. He died of an overdose. The syringe was placed carefully into his hand, all fingerprints were erased. It was an open and shut case of an overdose, except it was not. It was murder.

Kamini had taken a turn for the worse; they were shifting her to the hospital. She was insistent on waiting for me to return. My plans to book the first flight out were put on infinite hold for the moment. 'She is ready to go,' Da Costa said.

'Go where?' I asked. He didn't reply. Perhaps some questions were not meant to be answered.

My flip flops clattered awkwardly on the smooth tiled flooring as I rushed through the passages, following Da Costa as he led the way, imperious in his unhurried languidness. Kamini didn't stir as we walked in. She was lying on her bed in a foetal position, her face devoid of the pink carmine lipstick that I so inextricably associated with her. I wondered if she would wake again. Victor looked at her, his expression curiously tender. 'Such a tiny little thing she is, isn't she? So different from Mother.

I could never reconcile how my father could have loved two such vastly different women, but then that's the heart, I guess, it has its reasons.'

I nodded. We could discuss the heart and its reasons later, right now I wanted to speak to the doctor. I called up Dr Gomes from Da Costa's phone from outside the room, pacing the balcony with the restlessness I'd always marvelled in caged animals. I felt that now in me. I felt if I sit, I would burst, there was too much churning in my chest to be confined by the lack of motion.

'We have to be practical, she has to be admitted,' he said bluntly. 'Now that you and Victor are here, I think we need to take a call. She is sinking, it cannot be managed from home anymore. I will have the ambulance sent tomorrow morning for her. See you at the hospital tomorrow at 9 a.m. and we can speak to the oncologist together. Today is Sunday, no point getting her here today.' I felt my heart sink at these words. I was not ready yet to be an adult and take adult decisions about the medical treatment of a loved one. I went back into the room, having ended the conversation, suddenly overwhelmed and exhausted. I couldn't deal with it. Nihar's death. Kamini needing treatment, Maa's precarious state back home. It wasn't fair. I shouldn't have to deal with it all alone.

I needed Roop. I needed Veer. Our little brother of the heart, if not of the blood, not completely. His eyes, pebbled dark and sloe-eyed, reminded me of his mother. And occasionally, the flashes of sadness in them, so much like hers.

Lucenzia had come into the room while I was out, bringing with her the overwhelming aroma of garlic. She had changed out of her white blouse with a lace collar and black skirt that she had been wearing when we entered the house. That was probably her Sunday best, worn to go to church that morning.

'What to do?' she asked.

I had no clue. In fact, I was even more clueless than she was.
'I don't know, just do as the doctor says, I suppose,' I replied.

'No,' she replied with the scathing dismissal of one who had
more pressing concerns than what imminent death from a life-
threatening disease and a doctor's instructions mandated. 'What
to cook for dinner? Herself is sleeping and sleeping.'

I had never given a thought to how this massive house
ran itself; somehow, I assumed it functioned on autopilot. But
Kamini, frail and dying, had been holding the reins firmly until
this point when she couldn't gather the strength to even hold
on to them.

I realised I was the one in charge of domestic arrangements
now. It wasn't something I wanted to take charge of, all I wanted
to be in charge of was myself, but imperceptibly things and
people were getting added onto my gambit of responsibility.

'Have lunch? Is made now.'

I nodded, some food would be welcome. I was starving.

'Tell what to do for dinner.' I assured her I would do so a
little later, and decided to get to a daily routine of planning the
menu with her soon for as long as I was here. I wasn't going
back to Mumbai for a while, that was now certain.

On the bed, Kamini mewled in pain, still deep in sleep. She
turned around slowly, the skin on her face was mottled. She was
in a sedated sleep after, in probability, being administered pain
relief and sleep medication.

Lucenzia spoke to Da Costa in rapid-fire Konkani, of which
I understood nothing. Da Costa said something to which
she reacted with dramatic horror, clasping her hand to her
mouth, untying her apron and putting it down on a side table
unthinkingly. She scurried out of the room, followed by Da Costa.

'What is it? What has happened?' Victor asked her, having
entered the room and then following them out. Jacinta, who had
come into the room, broke out, in her excitement, in English,

talking about the church and then lapsing into Konkani. He seemed to understand what she was saying and a frown creased his brow. Was it possible to love a man and not want him physically and want a man and not love him at all? I knew it was. I had now experienced both of these extremes, and knew it was possible. At the moment I was insanely jealous of Jacinta, who had his attention. I wanted him, but it was a want that did not think of him as a person, but just rather a body that could deliver pleasure.

He turned to me, explaining briefly what had happened, while Jacinta crossed and re-crossed herself hurriedly.

'There were some desecrations in the grave yards some days ago. Family graves had been dug up, bones missing, crosses broken. At first they thought it was the work of vandals, you know, grave robbers. Today in church, Lucy heard it was the work of devil worshippers. There were more desecrations this morning, bones gone from graves. Every family from the village has loved ones buried in this grave yard. Apparently, a tantric has just been arrested on suspicions of doing black magic with the remains.'

'I saw it when I was out on a run a few days ago. Did they just call in the police this morning?'

It suddenly struck me. 'What about your father? Was he buried there?'

'I think Sunday mass is what spread the word, with everyone in church this morning. About my father, he was a non-believer. He chose to be burnt in the electric crematorium and had his ashes scattered in the sea. Most sensible of him.'

'Did he really do that, the tantric, what do you think?'

He shook his head. 'You never know, the outsiders are the ones who cause all the trouble....'

The sun was moving towards the west already, the light outside getting softer, the wind blowing in from the sea cool.

The curtains, tied with their sashes to the sides of the window billowed gently. On the bed, Kamini shifted herself slowly, and mewled again. I could see deep pain that even the strong sedatives weren't blocking.

'What do we do, how can we make it easier for her?'

'There's nothing we can do except persuade her to not resist treatment when we take her to the hospital tomorrow. She's being a pest about it. Saying no way is she going to go bald and have chemicals put into her again.'

Perhaps, I thought, she had the right to decide how much pain she wished to take, and if she wanted to end it all by refusing treatment, who were we to prolong her misery?

The fan whirred overhead, doing little to dissipate the humid heat that clung to us. I sat down next to Kamini, taking her hand in mine. She tightened her grip on my hand and smiled in her sleep.

'I'm here, Kamini,' I said softly. 'Victor's here. We're all here.'

She squeezed my hand, the eyes moving rapidly under her eyelids. Her lips parted, then closed, a pitiful sound escaping from them. There was so much pain that she could not bear. Her breathing got more ragged. Her lips began moving but no sound emerged from them. Then, 'Don't leave me alone, I'm scared of the dark,' she whispered, the words forming slowly and thickly on her tongue so I had to bend to catch them. Her skin was blotching, flaring into red sunspots in places, the clear pearly luminescence of the past now an angry mottled pelt. She looked beyond my shoulder, her eyes unfocused. 'Why did you bring him with you?'

'Who? Victor?'

I turned around to look at him, standing a step away from us.

'No, him. Your husband. Why did you bring him?'

I looked around, there was no one.

'Her husband is dead, Maa,' Victor said softly, sinking down to his haunches next to her. She shook her head slowly, side to side, her eyes never leaving a point near the window.

'No. He's here. There he is, at the window.' She got restless, sat up in her bed, her terrified eyes looking, at a point behind my shoulder. I turned around, looking at the window she pointed at, there was nothing there, just the shimmer of the heat beyond the trees and the dappling of the shadows of leaves rustling in the wind.

'You're imagining things, Maa,' Victor replied, stroking her hand like one might soothe a child.

She sighed and closed her eyes. 'I'm not. Call Da Costa. He knows someone who can help.' Lucy came into the room like a gust of worry and began settling Kamini back into the pillows, muttering at us for having agitated her.

Victor rose to his feet and left the room. The room shrunk a bit with his exit, like he'd vacuumed out some of its width and the air it contained with the withdrawal of his presence. The grip on my hand tightened, the hand gripping mine frail, skeletal, the veins pulsing feebly in my hand, the blood fighting itself. It was burning hot, she was running a fever. I had never experienced this kind of overwhelming helplessness in my life.

'You must tell him to go away. Why is it so dark, is it night already?'

'There's no one here, Kamini, except the two of us and Lucy. It's three in the afternoon, Kamini, it is bright and sunny outside. Close your eyes, Kamini, go to sleep.'

'He's here. Send him away. It's paining me, my back,' she said, her voice terrified, 'Give me something for the pain. Give me something to make me sleep.'

I looked around helplessly. Lucy fished out a pill from a strip lying on a side table, poured out a glass of water, propped Kamini up on the bed and made her swallow it. Kamini sighed, the effort had been too much for her. I could see the will leaching out of her with every breath she took, ragged, rattling her chest, the peremptory assumption that the next would follow challenged with each.

'You go,' she said to me. 'Lucy is here. I'm okay. Keep Victor or Jacinta with you. Don't be alone.'

She rang the bell for Jacinta. Her grip on my hand tightened, her eyes were shut. She took deep gulping breaths of the air almost like they were going to snatch the air away from her anytime now. Perhaps they were.

Victor re-entered the room. She turned her head to the side and smiled at him. It was a smile that was wrung from her with effort, pain was written all over her body. 'Ready to go to the hospital tomorrow?' he asked, sitting down on the other side of the bed. Jacinta moved to the side, almost imperceptibly as he neared her. I could see her holding her breath, her eyes on him, with the kind of expression I couldn't ever misinterpret.

Kamini winced. 'What are they planning?'

'You have to begin treatment, you've been putting it off for far too long and you might as well get it done while I'm here. And Kamla.'

'How long are you here for, Victor?' Kamini asked, the sharpness suddenly coming back into her voice, the tone imperious. She drew the strength back into herself and pulled herself up, ramrod straight, into a seated position.

'I haven't really thought about it, I'd thought a couple of weeks at the max, so let's see.'

'That would be quite enough I think, a couple of weeks. Could you do me a favour and call Bhandarkar across tomorrow in the morning.'

'You need to go to the hospital tomorrow morning,' I said.

'Nothing at the hospital that can't wait another day,' she said, turning back to Victor. 'Call Bhandarkar tomorrow. I have things to take care of before I go into hospital.' Her voice brooked no disagreement, despite the barely discernible shake in it.

He nodded. 'I will.'

'And,' she continued, barely registering his words like his acceptance was a given, 'I would like you as well as Kamla to be there while I discuss matters with him. And on Tuesday you can take me into the hospital and pump me with all the chemicals you wish and make arrangements for my funeral.'

'Stop talking rot, Kamini,' I said, 'You will be fine once you begin treatment.'

She shook her head slowly, the effort of moving it from side to side too much for her to sustain.

'I won't. I'm dying and I know it. Don't try to pep me up with your talk, missy. I'm okay with dying. I've lived my life. What I won't have is you living your life with the dead perched on your shoulder even while you're alive.'

Did Kamini know how long she had? How did one face the body slowly turning traitor and the mind following, with spaces and gaps between thoughts that stretched until they joined and became stretches of emptiness punctuated by pain, pain so relentless that it made death seem like a release. What was this about Nihar being there with me, could she see something I could not? Surely, I would sense him if he was around me. I sensed nothing. I went to my room to change and keep my bag.

Being a Sunday, the village was even more languid than it normally was. The village folks would have gone to the white-painted church that stood on the hillside for morning mass, dressed in their Sunday best. And returning through the winding roads, stopped a bit and chatted about this and that, and everything else. I wondered sometimes, how lovely it would be to have a God to turn over one's dilemmas to, and to rest knowing that it would all be taken care of by a higher power. All that was needed was to offer candles, a mass, a puja, a havan, donate something to charity.

The quid pro quo of religion was something I couldn't wrap my head around. It helped that Pappa was never deeply religious. In fact, he did most rituals rather unwillingly. Religion was never imposed upon us and Maa couldn't care about anything except getting from day to day. I wished I believed in a god to pray to, perhaps I would have prayed for Kamini. But within me, the belief had taken root and was unfurling its little plumule out from the mulch of my heart, she would die. She was already fading away. She would die, and it wasn't because medical science couldn't cure her of the rogue cells trampling through her blood stream. She would die because she wanted to. Was it right on our part to delay the inevitable? Wouldn't it be a kindness to let her go, as she wished, with her dignity and without her suffering?

When I reached the dining room, Victor was already seated at the table, a place was set opposite him, I supposed it was for me. I had no appetite, the spread in front of me nauseated me.

'Are you alright?' he asked me.

'Why shouldn't I be?' I replied, 'I'm not the one who is ill.'

'No, it has been quite a difficult couple of days for you.'

The table was dwarfed by his presence at the other side opposite me.

I put my hand across but the table was too wide, I couldn't reach his. A shadow moved at the back of the room, a finger of ice brushed down the length of my spine.

The words I was beginning to speak held themselves back. These were not conversations to be had in the presence of the staff, that much I had learnt in all the years of growing up, even staff that one considered family members because they had been with you for years and years, perhaps all your life and theirs. Jacinta noted the silence in the room and put it down to

Kamini's health. Lucenzia came into the room, her face so long her chin almost tripping her up.

'Is badly now, I told her to go doctor long back. Not listening only. Now what to do? Why you din't come before? You din't know she was so sick?'

I shook my head to indicate a negative. I had no idea. Words seemed to be failing me all the time now, I hadn't written for a while, I could barely hold a long conversation anymore. Lucenzia, having absolved all responsibility for Kamini's ill health from herself, now proceeded to squarely lay the blame upon us, which in hindsight, we probably did deserve.

I had come to Goa, expecting the same Kamini maasi I'd grown up seeing, resplendent in her bright sarees, smoking her cigarettes in her elegant holders, each one with a history behind them. The ivory, which she had given up using because she couldn't bear to think of the elephant slaughtered to have it made, another of ebony inlaid with delicate mother-of-pearl work. That I would be confronted with this shell of a woman, so fragile it seemed she would etherize into dust if one touched her was a shock to me.

'She din't tell you? But she told her sister, your mother, she din't tell you?'

Maa knew. Maa didn't tell me. I shook my head again. Lucenzia clucked her tongue disapprovingly.

'She's dying, she is. She needs family around. She's not going to go into that hospital you listen to me. She's....' Footsteps at the door interrupted her, Da Costa stood there, framed against the bright sunlight outside looking to all purposes more imposing than he should rightfully be.

'Madam is calling you,' he informed Lucenzia who scurried off in the direction of Kamini's room, after instructing them to bring more food from the kitchen if needed. Victor and I ate in silence.

'How long does she have?' I asked Victor. 'What do you think?'

'I really don't know either, all I know is that Da Costa told me to come down immediately, and the doctor said she needed to get into hospital immediately.'

Later, as the afternoon segued into the coolness of the evening, when he moved over me and within me, I knew that to want someone was more than to lust for someone. It was more feral than that, it was a want that devoured everything, body, mind, soul. I wanted Victor. I wanted all of him. I could not have all of him. He wasn't mine for the taking. He would leave, back to the life he had in London, his girlfriend and the life he lived before he had come into mine. And I would let him go and let him return. Over and over again, until there were no spaces between him going and returning and the rhythm of our coming together and separating made a music all its own that would fill through my days of waiting. And I would wait for him right here, in this house he had grown up in because this was where I belonged now. Until I couldn't bear his leaving. It was an acceptance of the inevitable. Or had we lived out this dance before, and did I already know the rhythm to it, the steps I must take?

FIFTEEN

THERE, THEN

The police took the body, asked us questions, and went away. Kanchi was dead. I couldn't remember her as she had been, swift-footed and soft-voiced, her presence had barely registered in the house. When I thought of her, all I could think was that of her swinging above me, her neck at that awkward angle. I had never really thought about her as a person, with desires and aspirations. With all the arrogance of youth, I assumed that she was here purely to make our lives easier. Had she hated it, living here, working all day for a family that barely appreciated her? Had she hoped of escape, of going to the big city and living life as a regular family with her husband and son? She, who was to me just someone around the house, with her sloe eyes, and light footsteps, her voice muffled to the point of erasing itself. As she had. Who had she really been, and why had she died by suicide? It haunted me, that question, over and over, for days. I had no answers.

'Why did she kill herself?' I asked Daadi after it was all over, the hullaballoo had died down and the house had returned to its regularity of three meals a day and early winter days to be spent at home huddled under the razai or running around the garden slowly getting frosted up or snowed in. Maa was back to functionality, the baby kept her busy, she took perfect care of him but without the smothering of love she had showered on the one who had died. I felt sorry for the poor baby who would grow without his mother and father, with a surrogate family to take care of him. I would love him like I would have my real brother, I swore, and made Roop swear the same. At least Pappa was not smarmily chuffed about this one, which made it easier to like him.

'When you grow up, you will understand,' Daadi had replied cryptically, as she always did whenever the question was about something she had no answer to. There were very few questions Daadi had no answers to, and the few that she didn't, I wrote down in my book hoping to ask them when I grew up.

I had a lot of time to myself to assimilate all that had happened over the past few days in our home. Death surefooted, twice over. His first visit had been tentative, his plans foiled. He'd worked harder the second time around. And then the third. His footsteps soft and steady, sneaking up on us, sniffing out life, for one unwittingly, not of his choosing, he had barely figured out how to work his lungs out of the amniotic fluid, for the other, she'd chosen to stop breathing.

Winter had gripped us, sharp and sure, with its ice and sleet and snow, and the never-ending fogs wrapping around the house. Kanchi's son was now sleeping in the crib our brother had barely slept in for a couple of days. He was hardy, he hardly wailed. Perhaps he had sensed that he would get his mother's attention when she had the inclination to give it to him, his was not the luxury to be fussed over at a whimper. He was our brother now. Pappa would adopt him, we were told, after a decent interval. It was luck beyond what Behra could have ever imagined.

'But what about the girls?' I heard Daadi arguing in a low tone with Pappa, one evening, as I stood on the landing outside the room, trying to scoot past the room without them noticing. 'What about their rights?' No good came from eavesdropping, Daadi had drilled in us, and which we always disregarded because we only got our juiciest information about what was happening in the adult world around us through eavesdropping.

'Roop and Kamla will get what is rightfully theirs...' his voice trailed away at that point.

Daadi got up with a sigh, 'What strange things fate does. You must make right what you did wrong.'

Pappa must have nodded at this. I didn't see it. I only heard his voice. 'Anyhow how does it matter now.'

We had a brother in place of the son my mother lost. He gurgled happily in the bassinet, a square squat face, with sloe eyes and a shock of hair that fell straight across his forehead like a recalcitrant juvenile attempt at style.

Children cooped up inside a cold house have a way of making their own adventures. The long afternoons when Daadi napped was my chosen time. And only because it was too cold to step outside, and Roop was being such lousy company, I decided to go up again to the attic. I wanted to see if the girl with the crutches was really there or if I had imagined her. They should have locked it. They had said it was to be locked. But nobody had really checked if it really had been locked as it was meant to be. The house was dark, the day was dull and gloomy, hanging over us purposeless and chilly. The sky was sulky, demanding obeisance to lighten its mood. Somewhere behind the clouds that covered us was a sun that shone brightly over other parts of the world but you wouldn't believe it right now. The chill was all-pervasive, one that no number of heaters and razais would dissipate come night, I knew. I tiptoed up the stairs, past Daadi's room where I could hear her snore loud enough to trick an unwary listener into believing a rumbling landslide was in the making. She wouldn't wake for a couple of hours at least. Mom was asleep in her room, her arm around the baby boy she had now taken for her own. I was curious to see what name my mother would bestow upon him. She had picked out Shamsher for my brother who had died. Shamsher. The name of her father. My father had disagreed. He had wanted to name his son after his own father and Daadi's husband, Pushpesh. Both were soppy names according to me. My humble suggestion, which no one had quite paid heed to, was Rahul, after Rahul Roy in *Aashiqui*. Eventually, Pappa got his birth certificate made and it had the name Veer on it, as decided by Jung chacha. And that was that.

I climbed the stairs that led to the attic, they weren't dusty this time. There had been plenty of footsteps going up and down that had scattered all the dust motes away. And there had been the body that had been lowered down, undignified in death, bundled into a sack, taken away for the mandatory postmortem. Pappa and Behra had cremated the body this morning. Behra had been uncharacteristically jolly on his return. Daadi sniffed hard and berated him for having stopped off at the local liquor store and ordered him to sleep it off. Pappa had bathed and gone off to the office. Maa was busy with the baby.

The attic was untouched from the previous day. The trunk, which had been in the middle of the room was pushed to one side. I was drawn to it by something inexplicable. Would Kanchi be there too now, another ghost? There are no ghosts, Pappa said. But Maa always smiled softly when he said so. There were ghosts, she knew, amongst the living and the dead, ghosts of the living and the dead, and often one couldn't tell the two apart. I opened the trunk, the smell of mothballs hit me first, then the sudden smell of fresh grass and spring that hadn't come here yet.

I should have known by the footsteps. Soft, yet definite. I turned around. She was standing behind me. Kanchi. I turned around. Her face was soft and clear, not mottled as I remembered it. She was standing right below the beam she had hung herself from. Her eyes were sad. She shimmered like the image on a screen with poor reception, just before Pappa cursed and got up to shake the twin antennae on top of the television. In the distance, in a corner of the room was another person, a little girl, sitting on the broken armchair, her crutches resting against the side. The little girl was looking on at both of us with great interest.

'Don't be afraid,' she said.

'I'm not,' I replied, more bravely than I felt.

'I need your help,' she said. I noticed her lips weren't moving. I could see the window through her, frosted up and sparkling hard with the greyness of the winter light.

'How can I help you?' I asked, perplexed. Help was not something I had to give I thought, I was only a child.

'Help me get my revenge.'

I shook my head. 'For what?'

'You will know. You will grow up and you will know.'

There were footsteps below, approaching the ladder. My absence had been noticed, if it was Daadi I would be scalped. I had been expressly forbidden to clamber up here again. Roop called out my name. I turned around to look. I had shut the door behind me, no one would guess I was up here, I hoped. She wouldn't look here, we had been warned to never come up here alone. When I turned back, Kanchi was gone. And so was the girl with the crutches. Had I been imagining her too?

And then I heard her voice in my ear.

'Kamli, you know what you have to do. I will wait.' From the window, I could see the smoke uncoiling from other chimneys in the land of the beyond, reaching up, up, up, far into the many other heavens that I did not know.

———◦◦◦———

SIXTEEN

HERE, NOW

Mr Bhandarkar arrived at around ten in the morning and was shown into the parlour. He settled himself on the sofa and made himself comfortable. From my position at the banister on the stairway, I could see him as he sat unperturbed, with the air of one who knows he is welcome and awaited. I walked down the stairs and took over Kamini's wheelchair from Jacinta, who had been wheeling her into the parlour just as I reached the landing. She'd been unhooked from the drip that the doctor had put her on yesterday.

I'd gone for a run and had an early breakfast. Victor hadn't knocked at the door of my room. I'd spent half the night up waiting before allowing myself to slide into sleep. Kamini hadn't been keeping well all night. She'd been throwing up, crying from the pain. I'd spent a couple of hours with her, until Lucy shooed me off, asking me to get some sleep. Victor had stepped out in the evening, and hadn't returned for dinner. Kamini had smiled softly when I'd asked where he was, and shaken her head ruefully.

'He comes and goes as he pleases. Don't wait for him ever.'

She was sitting erect now, a twinkle in her eyes, staring imperiously at Bhandarkar who shook her hand with more vigour than mandated given she was so fragile. A pink and purple patterned scarf was tied to her head, covering up all her little dandelion fuzz of hair growth. She had defiantly slashed on her lipstick. Her face was deathly pale. For all her bravery, she was a shell of her previous self. This is what illness did to one, broke one down into a shadow of oneself, until the shadows overtook the substance, turning one into a living ghost. I poured her a cup of tea from the fresh pot Jacinta had brought in, adding milk and sugar to her preference. Mr Bhandarkar declined the offer of another cup; he'd already had his.

She made the introductions with an elegance that belied the pain she must have been in. 'This is Kamla, my niece.' Mr Bhandarkar, a tiny sparrow-like man with gestures as quick and furtive as the species of bird he resembled, nodded at me and acknowledged Victor who had just made a soundless entry into the room. He seemed to walk on air, so quiet were his footsteps. He stood silently behind me, filling the room with his presence. I turned around and smiled at him, he smiled back, his eyes the warm liquid caress of sky and the sea rolled into one, an endless all-encompassing horizon where his gaze led me, the tang of sea breeze in my nostrils, the whisper of the breeze tickling my ear. I sighed, a deep long sigh. This wasn't just lust or infatuation, this was intoxication, a craven's craving I could not explain. But then, what was love but a want of the flesh, or a want of the soul. I wanted this man. I couldn't not want him. I couldn't not breathe. I wanted him in a way that was so absolute I couldn't care if he didn't want me back the same way.

'And this is Victor, of course you know Victor, you've met before.'

Mr Bhandarkar extended his little hand courteously to Victor for a quick handshake. I couldn't take my eyes off that handshake, a monkey's paw engulfed in a bear's. I looked up to see a wry smile on Victor's face. 'Why don't you sit?' he said, gently indicating the chaise lounge behind me. I sank down gratefully. Victor perched himself casually on the arm of the chaise lounge, positioning himself next to me. It was a curious, unseemly, rushed intimacy he declared simply by his choice of position. I felt Kamini's eyes go from him to me, and understanding dawn in them. The heat from his thigh was searing my arm. Kamini looked again at the two of us, and then her expression became inscrutable again, the pain that she was undoubtedly going through clouding her face.

'You have my will ready and sealed with you, Mr Bhandarkar?' she asked. 'Will you explain the basic premises of the will to my niece Kamla and to Victor, my stepson?'

'Yes, madam,' he scuttled to her so swiftly, I half expected to see to his tail swishing and his whiskers bristling.

'Madam Kamla Malik,' he said, addressing me first, 'I would like to inform you that your aunt has willed to you the joint ownership of this house, Casa de Braganza, all the furniture it contains as well as the works of art by Madam Kamini that remain within it upon her death. We only have a current valuation of the land it stands on, the acreage surrounding it, and the house itself being a heritage property. We have yet to evaluate the contents of the house, including the present and incomplete works of art in the studio and on the walls. All that is in process and we should have a figure within a couple of weeks for you.'

He handed over a sheet of paper to me with the valuations of everything the house contained, the grounds and the house itself. My eyes glazed over at the numbers.

'Who am I a joint owner with?'

'Master Victor.'

My heart skipped a beat. I turned to look at Kamini who was breathing heavily now, her breath ragged with pain, each being torn from her with visible effort.

'What about Roop?' I asked, unsure as to why I had been singled out to benefit from this largesse from Kamini. Why had my sister been left out of this will?

Kamini shook her head to indicate a no and gestured to Mr Bhandarkar that he should continue. He picked up the sheet of paper in his hand and perused it again, his brow knitting into a frown and then looking questioningly at Kamini. Victor shifted on the arm of the sofa next to me, the restlessness within him unable to make him stay still for a moment.

'Why don't you sit on the sofa proper, Victor?' Kamini said all of a sudden, her voice crisp and crackling. 'I'm afraid that armrest might not be able to take your weight and you would have ruined a perfectly good colonial antique.'

He laughed and shifted smoothly into the space next to me. Only now it was even more unbearable because the heat his body gave off was all along the length of mine, making it difficult for me to concentrate on what was being read out. All I had assimilated was that this property was worth a king's ransom, just the house and the land it stood on. What the contents of the house were worth, I didn't know yet. And I owned it jointly with a man who I didn't know at all, except for the fact that I'd slept with him, a relationship that was built firmly on the foundation of honest lust. The house was a windfall I hadn't factored into my plans for my life.

'The conditions are that you cannot sell off your share to anyone, you have to live here for six months continuously at the very least every year, and you have to maintain it in its original condition, no additions or modifications to the structure, except for repairs. And if you want to sell off your share you can only sell it after ten years, and that too only to each other.' Ten years was a lifetime, a heartbreak, a death, a birth away.

I shook my head. I had doubts, plenty of them, they were swarming in my head like locusts. Was this what I wanted, the rest of my days being laid out for me? A life not of my choosing. Would I be able to live it out here, in this isolation, six months on an island, the days unfolding one into another, a series of Russian dolls, diminishing in their intensity and diminishing me as well. Would I be diminished? Or was this what I needed, to live here undisturbed for the rest of my life and never have to interact with the fractiousness of city living ever again? It would be ideal for my work, I knew. There was nothing I needed more than the absolute sanguinity that living here offered. But how long would I be able to live like this? How long would Kamini be alive before the rogue cells running helter-skelter through her blood stream claimed her, all of her, for their own? And why did I always come into largesse riding on the corpses of the ones I love?

'Any questions?' Mr Bhandarkar asked, his voice faint in the distance. I came back to the here and now. Victor put his hand gently on mine, a tenderness I had never hitherto felt from him. It had all been unbridled unapologetic lust, hard, demanding, unslakeable.

'Of course, Kamini ma'am realises you are still very young, with your entire life in front of you. And she has made concessions for that.'

Kamini coughed. 'I will speak to her about those in private.'

'I'd like to know about my father's paintings which are still here in the store room,' Victor asked. 'Are those also jointly owned with Kamla?'

'They're all yours,' Kamini said blithely. 'And you know they're worth a lot more than this house.'

'I grew up here.'

'I've lived here for decades,' Kamini replied. 'I've only been fair.'

'Is this fair, willing half the house to someone my father never had any connection with just because she's your niece?' He was looking at Kamini as he said that, I could see his jaw line tense up into angular planes and his nostrils flare. His skin, the smooth pale skin that had deepened to a molten gold over the past couple of days, now had colour up high in his cheeks. His voice was soft, almost a whisper, a threat that suddenly chilled me to the bone even as his hand tightened around mine with a grasp that staked claim on territory I hadn't realised I'd conceded to him.

The blinding sun outside was filtering into the room through the thin billowing curtains which did nothing for either privacy or to block the brightness. Birds chirped on the trees in the wide grounds outside, all was right with this world. Or was it?

'She's a lot more than my niece, Victor. She's the daughter I never had. And I am being fair, I'm willing half of the property to her. Given it is completely my right now, I could have left her everything, but I didn't. You have received your share or at least your mother has, and it was a fair arrangement. She gave up all claim to the house when Peter paid her the settlement.'

'She received it. I didn't. As his only legal child and heir I have a full right to his house, especially since he died intestate.'

His only legal child. The odd choice of words stuck with me. Were there other children that would spring up to stake a claim to this house. Kamini sat up straight in her chair. 'He transferred the house to me, sole ownership, while he was alive. I own the house. You should have contested his will back then.'

Her voice, so fierce and firm, had begun to quiver a bit. I could see stubborn tears begin to fill in her eyes, she jutted out her chin in a manner that seemed strangely familiar until I suddenly realised I did the very same thing when I was cornered.

'It didn't seem right given you had lived here with him for years. But now, I have right over it as his sole legal heir.' His voice was soft yet definite. 'This was my home before my father met you, Kamini. I was okay with you living here for the rest of your days, but you cannot deny me what is rightfully mine.'

I felt obliged to interrupt. It was a generous gift, but one that I did not want. 'I'm so honoured that you thought of me to take on the responsibility of this lovely house, but honestly I can't see myself living here. And it doesn't seem fair to take half of it, after all it was Victor's father's home. I have no claim or connection to it.' I felt his hand tighten upon mine slightly.

'No, Kamla,' he said, without turning his head to look at me,

'This is not your battle. Nor would I like to fight this with you.'

At that moment I didn't care about the house, about the will, about the money. I had enough and more.

'It's yours,' I told him. 'I have a home of my own and enough. I need nothing more.'

'If you both don't take it, or if you don't fulfil the conditions of living here for a minimum of six months of the year every year,' said Bhandarkar, inserting his squeaking words into a conversation that was not his to intrude upon, 'the house will go to charity.'

I turned to look at Kamini. Surely my aunt was not so determined to not let Victor have the house, the kind of virulence was not something I associated with her.

'Let it,' I replied. This was not a battle I wanted to be drawn into. There were other battles. In other worlds.

'Think about it,' Kamini said, her voice weakened by the spasms that were racking her body. 'Stay here for a while. Let it grow on you. Both of you have to decide how you plan to run it, six months each. Divide the time you spend. Convert it into a guest house, if you please. But you can't sell it. Else it goes to charity and I will have a trust for abandoned children that will take it.'

'Perhaps that would be a good thing,' I replied. Victor disengaged his hand from mine, the release of pressure of his hand, a dismissal, for the moment I could not fathom nor did I care to.

'I have memories attached to this house, I don't want to give it away, this is my childhood, I'd want my children to come here, live here.' I wrapped my arms around myself, a chill infusing me that defied the warmth of the tropical summer day. He would have children with Leah, his girlfriend. He would bring them here. We were but a momentary dalliance, one that would blow over before the summer was over, and the thick blackness of the pelting monsoon arrived on the coast. Victor stood up, and paced the room, managing to shift the air in his wake into little draughts that blew gently around my bare legs as he passed me.

'Kamla...' Kamini began softly and her voice trailed off, the disappointment hanging at the edge of the sentence like a semi-colon. Despite the sun shining so brightly outside, the room was cool thanks to a soft sea breeze that blew in gently. It stirred the thin muslin curtains that billowed into the room like lost souls searching for a body to inhabit. 'There are more things in heaven and earth....'

She looked straight at me.

'He's still here.' She pointed up, her expression was terrified. 'Be careful. Mathew will help you. I've told Da Costa.'

I shuddered involuntarily. Kamini reached a hand out for me, the once limber-fingered and elegant hand now a chicken's claw, veined and scrawny. I took her hand in both of mine and knelt down beside her, putting my head in her lap. It felt like home in a way my own mother's lap never had.

She stroked my head with her other hand, soft, gentle strokes. She whispered into my ear, 'Don't be afraid. He can't do anything to you unless you allow it. Don't let him into your head. Crowd thoughts of him out of your head. Fill them with other thoughts. Once he realises he's not needed he'll go back to his side.' I looked up at her. 'And going away won't rid you of him. They're like chewing gum, these spirits, they stick with you wherever you go.'

She was right, I knew. I had to listen.

'Stay here,' she said. 'I want you to stay here. Victor can stay here too. There's enough room for the two of you. I don't have much time, you know, I want the two of you to have this house, god knows I've loved it far too much to see it go to a stranger,' she said with a wry half laugh and then fell silent. The words struggled to emerge. She sat, still, waiting, looking towards the window, her eyes fixated on something, someone, none of us could see. They softened and she broke into a smile so glorious her face lit up into a blaze of happiness.

I turned again to look at the window. There was nothing there, only the light streaming in through dappled rays, their beams broken by the mango tree right outside the porch, which spread its canopy, along with the others on the grounds, over much of the garden the boundary wall enclosed. I got to my feet, following her gaze. She looked back at me, her expression was beatific.

'I'm ready to go now,' she said, a soft smile on her, all the pain that had been twisting it a few minutes earlier seemingly disappearing.

She sagged softly and sank into the chair. Her hand went to her throat and pulled at it convulsively, her chest heaving. Breath deserted her, the traitor we all cling to. Her breathing became shallow, she was drawing air in huge desperate gasps. Her hand which was stroking my head barely a second ago had gone slack and limp, her face was slowly turning a mottled shade of virulence that did not augur well. Her eyes were open but stared into the dark.

Breathe, breathe, breathe. Breathe, damn it. I was yelling. Breathing, I realise now, wasn't a given. It had to be forced on you. From the first smack on the behind one got as one was pulled out of the uterus, slithering through warm, moist canals that closed onto one into the shock of a dry open nothingness, one had to be shocked into drawing breath in.

'Lucy,' Bhandarkar called, his voice sharp and urgent, the panic cutting through the sanguinity of the air. Da Costa stumbled into the room. Perhaps he was just outside, listening in, waiting to be summoned. 'Oxygen,' Bhandarkar threw at him, a word that was a command and a plea. Da Costa rushed out and rushed back in with an oxygen cylinder on a wheel-like contraption, something I had seen lying in the passageway but never wondered what it was for. He, with the ease of practice, fitted the tubes under her nose, and turned the cylinder on and waited for the gas to work its miracle. It did, she slowly settled down, the crazed wide-eyed look morphed into one of acute suffering, but a look that was buffered by regular breathing.

'Call Dr Gomes immediately,' Bhandarkar ordered. Da Costa ran off to do his bidding.

Da Costa scurried out of the room and a few minutes later the car was brought to the front of the porch. I wheeled Kamini to the door, and Victor carried her in a swift swoop down the stairs to the car. She was light now, a feather, barely any weight to him. They settled her into the back seat, I sat next to her, only running up to grab my handbag. Lucenzia stood at the door as we drove off, wringing her hands into her apron, crossing herself repeatedly, fervently muttering a prayer. 'Hail Mary full of grace, the Lord is with thee,' snatches came to my ears over the wind, words I had heard in my childhood of morning assemblies in a convent but had now forgotten, prayers that were alien yet comforting.

We went through the narrow road straight to the jetty where the ferry had been informed and was waiting, to take us to the other side. Da Costa did not drive at his usual pace, and was scattering any itinerants who happened to be in his path. Kamini was breathing heavily, her eyes closed and dark with pain whenever she opened them for a quick check of the surroundings.

She drew my head to hers and indicated I should align my ear to her lips. 'Stay here. This is your home. Don't leave. Don't sell. Promise me.' I nodded.

'Victor,' she said, her voice hoarse and raspy, 'Take this damn thing off of me. I'm feeling choked.' They stopped the car and took off the tube. She smiled and closed her eyes. We drove on, into Panjim. I could feel it ebb out of her, life. It went with a quietude that was dignified and hushed. There was a smile playing on her lips, soft, contemplative, mischievous.

I raised her hand to my lips and kissed it gently. It was still warm. It would be a while before it would get cold and stiff and rigor mortis stepped in, making an inanimate block of a living person. One breath in and none out, and she had morphed into it. That was it, the end of life, quite underwhelming in its suddenness.

'She's gone,' I said. Da Costa stopped the car with a suddenness that almost caused an accordion crash, came to the back and collapsed into tears. Victor took over the wheel and drove us to the hospital. Dr Gomes checked her and wrote out a death certificate. His florid face was drained of colour. 'She left it too late, always stubborn that woman. In life, in death.'

I called Maa when we reached the house. She answered after an interminably long time. Her mood swings I could measure by how long she took to answer the phone, given she always ensured the mobile was on her person, or at least a hand stretch away.

'Maa,' I said, 'Kamini's dead.'

Maa was in one of her moods. I could make out from the hello when she answered her phone, a hello that was flat in a manner that indicated anything you told her would be inconsequential. 'Dead.'

It wasn't a question, it was a repetition of the word, not to test it on her tongue to savour it for the finality it brought, it was a statement that was stripped of all the emotion the word evoked.

'Now what?' she said, wondering as she inevitably did when she was in those phases, to be told what she needed to do.

'Would you like to come for the funeral? I can check flights

and book one out for you right away. I can have it delayed if
you want to be there.'

'No. I'm not coming all the way for her funeral. I'm not
travelling all that way to be at her beck and call even when she's
dead. I've done enough while she was alive, but did she ever
appreciate it? Good she died. Good riddance. Always causing
trouble, that one. Running away from home. But she was my
sister, my blood. I kept taking her back, giving her shelter. What
could I do? I was all she had. But did she appreciate it? I'm not
coming. Too beautiful for her own good, with all sorts of silly
notions about being an artist. Women didn't become artists, we
became wives. She didn't even want to become a wife. Sleeping
around. I forced her. Marry him, I told her, make him divorce
his wife. Give him an ultimatum. And when she became the
wife of a rich man, did she think about her poor sister, stuck in
this crumbling house in the mountains, shivering to death every
winter. No. Selfish creature. Burn her. Bury her. Do whatever you
want with her. How does it matter? Give her body to science. Give
her body to the animals. I don't care. She won't care. Nobody
cares. Did she leave the house to you, she told me she would?'
The line went dead on me. I sank to the floor, sobbing deep
hacking sobs that came up dry with no tears.

Outside, the sun was shining on determinedly. Inside, the
darkness swarmed over us like angry bees, buzzing in our ears,
our heads, buzzing in our brains, stinging, stinging, painful
stings, deep. Things happened without me knowing they were
happening. Victor holding my hand, telling me Kamini had not
specified what was to be done with her ashes. I knew, I told him,
and my voice trailed off as I looked down at her, on the bed.
The sudden stripping of dignity that death brings to a person,
her body stiff and unresponsive, her lips still and cottonwool
stuffed into her nose and ears. Wrapped in red, laid out like she
had just drifted off to sleep. She was still now, even her eyes...

she who was in motion even when she was still, her eyes, her expressions, her hands all a chaos of movement and beauty defying being confined to a wheelchair. She loved the ocean, she would swim out in it like a fish, even though she was born and raised in the mountains. And now the ocean filled my eyes and spilled over, salty, stinging, unforgiving. I sat at the head of the body, feeling the tears course down my face and the grief slam my diaphragm as I struggled to keep the sobs down.

'Let it be done with,' I told him.

The house was lit up and yet dark, a paradox I couldn't explain. The parlour was overflowing with people. Strangers lifted her up and bore her off to a place I could not follow her to. Her ashes, she'd told me, were to be scattered on the sea. And she wanted me to do it. I'd laughed when she said that. 'Don't be silly, you're going to be fine. We'll start on the chemo and you'll lick this damn thing.'

'I don't want to. I'm ready to go,' she'd replied. Those had been her last words too. 'I'm ready to go.' Were we ever ready to go? Had Nihar been ready to go? What had his last words been? Who had been the last person to see him, had it been the room-service person, waiting obsequiously as he signed the slip? Had it been the housekeeping staff? Whom had he spoken to last? Had he told them he was ready to go? Had he known he was ready to go?

I was suddenly bereft, in a strange gut-wrenching way which made me nauseous. I ran to the bathroom just off the room. Breakfast came out in long glutinous strands of the digested and undigested, yellow and brown and transparent, and then when it was all out, the bile, corrosive and burning the lining of my oesophagus as it hurtled up. I was vaguely aware of a person behind me, a hand stroking my back, another steadying me, holding my hair off my face and I threw up over and over again. When I was done I rinsed out my mouth and splashed water on my face, standing up and looking at my reflection in the mirror in front, the edges blackened with time, framing me unevenly. Behind me, barely a footstep away, was Victor, filling up the frame with his shoulders, saying nothing, just there, solid, unyielding. I sank back against his chest and closed my eyes, my head still spinning. He lay me down gently on the bed.

'Sleep,' he said, handing me a pill and a glass of water. 'Close your eyes for a while.' And so I did. The thoughts jostled with each other for a long moment. Then deep, velvet, sparkling blackness.

Pappa walked into the room. He was wearing the faded sweater he had on when I last saw him. There was a bump on his head. I knew it was from where the fatal truck had hit him. He cleared his throat and sat down on the rattan chair by the window, looking out. I found myself telling him all that had happened since he had been gone. Nihar dying. Moving to Mumbai. Mom sinking into depression. Kamini. Her illness, her dying. I know, he said. I met her. She's given me the house, I told him. She would, wouldn't she, he answered cryptically. I didn't know why, it didn't occur to me to ask why. Will you stay here? he asked. I don't know, I replied, I don't know, I can't make up my mind, there's nothing I would rather do than stay here, away from everything, but I would die of boredom from the sameness every single day. And I've been sleeping around. There have been five men since Nihar died. I can't seem to help it. He nodded. You didn't bring me up to be a slut, Pappa. My lips weren't moving. The dad I knew would have yelled and screamed at the information about my sexual incontinence. This dad, sitting in the arm chair, with the bump on his head, the muddied sweater and the cracked spectacles on his nose, was understanding and forgiving. Or perhaps from where he was, the needs of the body didn't matter much. You couldn't feel any desire for that man, he said. Make the best of your body, you will miss it once it is gone. I've made my own mistakes. You know I regretted it. But that's what happens in marriages. You know. Your mother never forgave me. His lips didn't move as he spoke. How is your mother, being as pig-headed as usual about her medication? I nodded. I miss her, you know. She was a reason I kept going. Neerja and her moods. Good, bad and ugly. Here there's nothing to look forward to.

The wound on his head was deepening in colour even as he spoke. It sat there on his forehead, a big blooming red flower, blooming larger by the minute, swelling until it held my eye there, fixing my gaze on it as it burst open and spilled out, blood and brain and bits of bone, spattering all over me. I flinched and recoiled. I wondered how it must have felt like to die from a head-on collision, a truck turning a corner at a speed unwise for the narrow mountain road, Pappa on his morning walk distracted as usual by all the thoughts that consumed his mind. Maa told me when I reached that his skull had cracked open like a nut. 'They had to scoop his brains up and put it into a container,' she'd said, her eyes dry and her voice unshaking. 'The truck driver said he just stepped in front of the truck, he had no time to brake. It was deliberate.'

Don't go, Pappa, I pleaded. He smiled and patted my hand. The bits from his brain came slithering out, and I held onto his hand for just a moment longer, feeling it dry and bleached from the sun, the phosphorescent sun in the place where the dead go and the rays blaze onto spectral bones melting the flesh off them into vapour.

When I woke up, I was in my room. The curtains were drawn and the night had taken over the evening. An owl hooted in the distance, the fireflies were hitting the lone bulb someone had left on in the room. The sun had plonked into the sea, going beyond the garden and the wall, and the road and the football field, and the small path, to below the sea to the other side of

the earth where lives stirred and stretched and woke to the
newness of another day. If I listened hard, I could hear the sea
whisper and roar alternately, sending whispers of sirens into my
ears, and dirges of seaweed and white gnawed on bones. The
sea shadowed everything that happened here, in this tiny state.
It was the boundary of everything, the beginning and the end.
This is where Kamini had chosen to live, with the sea a short
walk down a straggly path over a cliff, a path she would take
when she was young, and throw herself into the welcoming,
warm saltiness. The sea on one side, a river on the other, the
road which ended where the ferry met it. I fell asleep again, the
sleep of the dead, and nothing woke me up again, not even the
dream where Nihar was talking to me, trying to convince me
to come join him.

I leapt up from the bed, my head suddenly heavy and
daggers within stabbing at the soft mass of pink and white,
soft and squishy within the cranium. The door to my room
was open.

'You're awake,' said Victor, standing against the door jamb,
a dark silhouette that felt like a watcher over me. He stepped
into the room, drawing in all the air within, leaving me gasping
for breath, filling it with him so I felt pushed to the wall. Was
there a space he went into that he did not fill? Perhaps if he
stood on the shore of the ocean, infinity would be the only thing
that dared hold out against his taking over of all the space he
occupied. He brought gold into the grey of the darkening room.
The fan whirred on stoically overhead, it's repetitive creaking
the only sign that time was passing in that long moment when
it was us looking at each other.

'Is it done? Is she cremated?'

'Yes, it's done.'

'Where are the ashes?'

'We'll get them tomorrow evening.' He closed the door

behind him carefully.

'She wanted them scattered in the sea.'

'We'll go scatter them together.'

That she would be reduced to one small urn, she who filled up every room she occupied. My knees buckled and I sank to the bed again. He moved swiftly to the bed and sat next to me, taking my hand. 'Are you alright?'

'I'm fine,' I replied. 'Just another fainting spell, I must get myself checked. I'm having them too often.'

He nodded. And then leaned in to kiss me, a long, lingering kiss that had me pull his head down closer and arch my body into his. I opened myself to him, giving in to the need that had been consuming me ever since I met him, a need I could not explain but only succumb to over and over again. And in the dimness of the rising moonlight, we moved against each other like I knew we would, our bodies doing their cosmic dance of destruction and creation that peaked and ebbed and peaked and ebbed until I was spent and drained and quivering with the waves of ecstasy that had racked my body over and over. Victor drew himself out of me, pulling off the condom and knotting it up with the practised ease of one who had done this many times. I opened my eyes. From over his shoulder, in the dimness of the room, I saw Nihar above us, his hand reaching down inches from us when my eyes met his. And before I could say a word he dissolved right back into the shadows on the ceiling. The last thing to fade were his eyes, the expression in them would haunt me for all the days to come.

SEVENTEEN

HERE, NOW

Victor was standing beside me on the boat as I overturned the urn of ashes into the water, his expression inscrutable. This was as much as I was prepared to concede to the formality of ritual.

Kamini was in the sea now. I stood on the deck of the boat we'd taken to go right out deep to where the humans practising their clumsy crawls didn't disturb the waves, and poured out her ashes into a sea. The ashes swirled on the surface, the late morning sun reflecting back from the surface of the dappling sea, and swiftly became the form of a woman, slight and lithe, draped in sea weed and froth. She turned around for a moment, looked me in the eye and then dived right into the depths of grey-green waters. Perhaps it was fitting that we should throw ourselves back into the ocean. We were the ocean, the ocean was us. And now Kamini was the ocean. All of her, one tiny urn, upturned in one smooth gesture, some of her blown away with the wind, some floating on the surface.

The boat was a hired one from the many which took tourists on the nearest beach for joyrides out to where the ocean sloped towards the unfathomable depths, far enough to feel the panic of not being able to see the bottom, near enough to not lose sight of the shore. Some boats offered dolphin sightings. Out there in the middle of the ocean, there was a sudden awareness of how remarkably still everything around me was. There was only the rippling of the sun off the surface of the water, the screeching of the gulls overhead hopeful of this being a fishing trawler, the phut-phutting of the motor of the boat, regular and reassuring, the lapping of the waves against the side of the boat, the gentle rocking of the boat that made it impossible for me to stand without feeling my head spin.

The man at the prow of the boat manning it was waiting for us to tell him when to begin taking it back to the beach. I stood in silence watching the water, thinking of all that I had lost and how I could find myself again. Voices around me echoed as though they were coming to me from a barrier, or through water. Da Costa was somewhere at the back of the boat. I heard my name being called, I leaned over and looked down into the water, grey-green ripples laced with froth foamed and slapped salaciously against the sides of the boat. Hands reached out to me from within the water. Nihar. 'Lotusface...' I leaned towards the voice. The next moment I was falling through air through water, through thickness that squeezed me tight and bound me, lungs choking, gasping, as hands reached out through the murkiness of the water, grabbing me, drawing me deeper within. There was comfort in floating in the warm salty water—the sea cradled one gently, in a manner the air never did. I saw the bubbles coming from me where water forced the air out of my lungs floating upwards towards the surface, felt the diffusion of the light on my skin, mottled and purple green from the shifting surface above me. I stopped resisting and let myself go. I sank and sank towards the hands reaching out to me, rocked in an embrace that was primordial and unrelenting.

'Lotusface,' he said, 'come to me.' I let myself sink, into the warmth of the water, pulling me down, until there was blackness swirling around me, entering my chest and exploding. All was black, all was warm and wet and comforting. And I wasn't here anymore.

Then a wrench, a pumping of my chest and emptying my lungs of all the water I'd ingested, retching and retching, until it all came out of me, opening my eyes to the blinding sun overhead. Light, so much light, I raised a feeble hand to block out the sun. Another surge of salt water heaved itself out of my lungs and spilled on to the floor of the boat I was lying on. Some of the morning's breakfast emerged too, scalding my oesophagus as it backtracked. The sky above me whirled, the clouds making shapes not completely amorphic.

Victor was kneeling next to me, as drenched as I was. Two men from the boat's crew were also drenched. Had we all fallen into the water together, I wondered? But the hands had been reaching out to me, I thought. Had they all seen hands from their own loved ones emerging from the murkiness of the brine too?

'Why did you jump too?'

'She's okay, she's okay now,' Victor said, 'thanks guys.' The men around looked at me curiously, as I lay, their expression a mixture of wariness and pity.

Victor sat down next to me cross-legged as I struggled to sit up. The boat continued to rock gently, its motion indifferent to my confusion. 'What made you do that? Jump off into the water all of a sudden. The next time you decide to do something as silly as that, give me some advance warning, please? I've lost my mobile, my wallet and all my identification cards in the water now. You're going to be stuck with me longer than you'd expected.'

His eyes were smiling, pools of sunlit sapphires, his expression stern. Why had I jumped off? There had been times in the past I admit when I'd willingly have jumped off a boat, a balcony, a bridge. These were things that begged to be jumped off, and then the moment of free fall before the splat of making contact with water, concrete, rocks. And then oblivion. Instant, painless. Could I be as silly to jump with an audience watching, comprised of all sturdy men, who knew the sea like the back of their hands, its ebb, its flow, who had grown up transferring out of amniotic fluid into the salty spray of the waves. Had I reached out to touch those hands reaching out for me from within their shadowy depths? Or had those hands, green with slime and decay, reached out too swiftly for the human hand to see and pulled me in?

Victor helped me up to my feet, seating me on the bench on the boat, where the sun warmed me while the chill within me made me shiver unwittingly. He rubbed my hands in an ineffective bid to warm me up. My chest hurt, I threw up more bile over the side of the boat. Someone handed me a bottle of water. I rinsed out my mouth, washed my face, felt human. I rested my head on his chest, he smelt of sea and salt. I probably did too.

'Kamla,' he said now, his voice molten honey, warm, soothing, 'Why did you jump? Do you even know how to swim?'

'I don't know,' I replied as honestly as I could. 'I can't swim.'

The boat had reached the little jetty, we stepped over. They rushed me to a little polyclinic, just off the main market. The waiting patients stared at me resentfully as I was led in first after the situation was explained to the compounder, then taken to a room to lie down for a bit. I felt fine, if a little woozy. I closed my eyes and drifted off into the blackness that was waiting for me.

A few hours of observation, that was what the doctor said was needed after he had finished checking me. All those years ago, Roop had been under 24-hour observation when she'd almost suffocated to death thanks to that angeethi left in our closed room. 'Her vitals are all okay,' I heard the doctor telling Victor, as they stood beside my bed, the sterile ungiving of hard foam bound by synthetic leather, covered by a thin white bedsheet which had seen more bleach, detergent and disinfectant than its threads could withstand. The smell of rubber and phenyl amalgamated into something that bore within it death and dread.

'She could have aspirated some water into her lungs, thankfully, not too much.'

'Does she really need to be under observation?' Victor asked.

'I would prefer it at least for a few hours,' said the doctor, whose voice faded as they receded down the long passageway leading to the main part of the clinic.

Being left alone in a hospital room for hours gives one time to think. There's something about whitewashed walls covered up midway with the sterility of white tiles and the inescapable odour of floors swabbed with a strong disinfectant that gets into one's brain and clears out all the fogginess and the salt that had entered it through the days here. The day had morphed from bright and incandescent into the blurry, grey indistinctness of the southwest monsoon rolling in. It would hit any moment, I knew. It would have dashed against the Malabar coast already, the blurriness of white that swirled over the Indian ocean from the southwest, and moved upwards, bringing with it the moisture-laden clouds that would open up over the lush-green coasts, and then thin out as they moved over the plateau, into the rain shadow zone. For now, for here, this was green that sparkled in the dullness of a grey sky that blocked out the sun.

The window framing one wall of the dismal room I was in looked out to what was an expanse of a red-soiled sports ground fringed by trees. Shapes moved in them, kicking a ball about. A soft wind blew gently through the trees, swaying them about in a polite dance, where one moved and bent and acknowledged the presence of the other, but never reached the zone of complete abandonment which is where movement actually becomes dance. It was the only movement I could see from the room. The fan overhead whirred spasmodically, barely shifting the humid air that settled on one like a wet sheet, making the perspiration coagulate in the armpits, in the folds of one's body, sticky, uncomfortable, like a lover who would not leave even after the love was gone.

Outside in the passage, I could see shadows in white, the

occasional flash of colour when a relative came in to see a patient. Low hushed conversations, urgent and filled with anxiety filtered through from a distance. There was life somewhere, the demanding surprised wails of a newborn that pierced the air every now and then. And there was the stench of death as well, stalking the corridors. I could sense it, feral and determined.

My phone was lying next to me on the table beside the bed; it shared space with a steel jug and glass. The jug was covered with a lace doily, probably crocheted by ageing hands in an old-age home. It was strange to see this sudden evidence of human effort at beauty in a space that existed to worship efficiency. I picked up my phone and dialled Roop's number. The phone rang for a while. I disconnected. Perhaps she was at work. I'd wanted to be left alone, but now being alone was strangely suffocating. I called Maa. She hadn't bothered to call since I'd called her informing her of Kamini's death. The phone rang interminably. I called the landline, knowing Behra would reach it and answer it. He did.

'Where is Maa?' I asked, dispensing with the preliminaries.

'Sleeping,' he replied. 'With the pills. She took two in the morning after breakfast, told me I was not to wake her up, she hadn't slept all night. She had had very disturbing dreams of you drowning.'

I gasped and then brought my voice back to a normal keel.

'When she wakes up will you make sure she calls me?'

'Yes, beta, I will. Are you alright? Is the cremation done?'

'Yes, it was done that very day,' I replied, 'I scattered her ashes in the sea this morning, that's what she would have wanted.'

'She was quite like the sea,' Behra said, wisdom that suddenly sprouted from him in moments he came unguarded, 'She came and went as per her will, couldn't confine her, couldn't restrain her, could never ignore her. Even when she came to take you and had that huge fight with Bibijee....'

'When was this?'

There was a long pause on the other end of the line.

'You were very young, four or five, I think, she had just got married. Bibijee wouldn't let her take you. And you refused to go. I think someone is at the door, I have to go,' he said hurriedly, putting the receiver down. It was one of those old telephones with the handset and the buttons in a square to punch in the numbers.

I wondered what arrangement Maa had violated when she'd refused to let Kamini take me. How my life might have turned out had I gone with Kamini.

A nurse in a stiff bleached uniform and a face to match walked into the room and took my pulse. She went about her task with such detached efficiency that it made me realise that I was just another casualty in the jetsam flotsam of life and death she dealt with on a daily basis.

'Normal,' she announced when she was done. Then she deigned to look into my face. 'Fell into the sea?' she asked. I nodded. 'Jumped?' she continued without a pause, her eyes slowly morphing from the disconnected to the salaciously intrusive. Her eyes knew. 'Did they call you, the dead you saw inside the waters? Did they pull you in?'

I nodded. Her face swirled into blackness until there were only two black holes where the eye sockets were. 'He will come again for you. And again. Until he takes you with him. Did you think you could get away?'

I shrank back under the sheet. Outside, the sky was grey black, and thunder and lightning had begun piercing the humid air, crackling and rolling into the sterility of the room. There were no lips anymore in the black mask that was her face but I could hear her voice in my head. I drew the thin cotton sheet up to my chin and stared into her black holes of eyes, unseeing and all seeing and they looked into me and scooped out chunks of my soul and scattered them into the ether. I was imagining her, I told myself, squeezing my eyes shut. I could see her with my eyes shut.

'There's nothing you can do,' the voice came through in my cranium, thin and spidery skeins of a voice on a single note, piercing and insistent. Footsteps echoed down the corridor outside, firm, definite, heading this way. The wraith turned her head and looked down the blankness outside. It was post lunch. I knew her. I had seen her before. In the house, on the stairway.

Goa had its siesta now; even the dying would not die at this hour. The footsteps in the corridor intensified. A shadow fell across the threshold of the room, Victor entered, bringing with him sunshine and the blue of the sky in his eyes, lighting up the room even without the light bulbs being switched on. He glowed this man, he radiated a warmth that was visible to the naked eye, leavening the overhanging pall of the grey with a faint golden luminosity.

'Are you feeling better now?'

'I'm fine,' I answered.

'You are white. You look like you've seen a ghost.' I laughed at that, a short quick bark of a laugh. If only he knew. Perhaps I could tell him, perhaps he would understand.

'Maybe I have,' I replied, looking into his eyes warily, to judge his reaction. Victor's eyes crinkled in curiosity and he cocked his head to one side, intent on listening to what I had to say. The willingness to be heard was perhaps what I had been searching for all my life, and now that I had found it, I didn't want to stop speaking. I didn't even know what I was speaking, the words tumbled and spilled out, a brook of thoughts running over the jagged edges of my words.

I didn't even realise when they came in with the hypodermic and gently eased me back into the blackness where all I had was myself wandering around in caves that opened into other caves, and then some more, and where the only light was the glimpse of an opening far above my head, a climb I couldn't manage because the only way I could climb out again was by falling through.

—◦◦◦—

EIGHTEEN

HERE, NOW

When I opened my eyes, I was in my bed in the villa. The clock on the wall far ahead had its hands at a quarter to six. It felt like morning. It smelt like morning. It even sounded like an early morning. Somewhere in the distance, a rooster was making the most infernal racket, confident that the sun was awaiting its summons to rise. There was the soft fragrance of wet soil that floated in through the open windows, it must have rained last night, I'd slept through it all, the sleep of the chemicals, black and stygian.

I had slept the sleep of the dead, but then how would I know how the dead slept. A shadow shifted in the armchair opposite the bed towards the open door. Bare feet placed up in the armchair which allowed its arms to be extended so that the person within could put their feet up. The person within, head lolling back in deep sleep, the faintest snores emanating from him. Victor. How long had he been sleeping here, I wondered? I picked up the water bottle kept on the side table and drank deeply, gently rinsing my mouth of the staleness as I drank. I needed to brush my teeth, wash my face, void my bladder. Hunger. A fire in my insides. The body will not be denied. Even the leaves on the trees swaying outside the window seemed edible right now. I stepped off the bed, parting the thin net canopy that was meant to keep the mosquitoes at bay and which I never ended up drawing around me and tucking in. My slippers were nowhere to be seen, the tiles were cool to my feet, the coolness of the night breeze still to dissipate by the warmth of the sun that would settle over the day. If it did, indeed, shine today. The air outside was heavy, laden with the damp of a rainy spell done with. The monsoon was here, and it had arrived hesitantly as if unsure of its welcome, without the son et lumiere one was promised on its arrival in this part of the country.

I went into the bathroom and splashed water on my face, brushed my teeth, peed a never-ending accumulation of fluid that I had not ingested. I looked tired, there were faint smudges of purple under my eyes, standing out against the paleness of my skin. My eyes looked haunted, the sunflower print on the dress I had was more alive than my face. I walked noiselessly, barefoot on the tiles, passing the sleeping giant curled up on the armchair towards the door. As I crossed him, he put out a hand and caught my wrist. 'Good morning,' he muttered, the sleep still heavy in his eyes, pulling me onto his lap. His lips settled on mine and all was well with the world again.

Had I met Victor elsewhere, at another time, I probably would have had a second thought about him. But now, in this moment, I nestled my face into the crook between his neck and shoulder and stayed there awhile, breathing in the muskiness of a long-faded aftershave and sweat, a fragrance that was uniquely him.

'Why did the doctor inject me with a sedative?' I mumbled into his neck. I trusted him, strangely enough, to tell me the truth, despite barely knowing him.

'You were in a state of shock, you were talking strange things. In fact the doctor recommended psychiatric observation. Anyway, I got you discharged and brought you home. I knew you would be fine once you were home.'

Brought you home. There was a comfort in those words, a comfort that was warm baked buns fresh from the oven, sliced into halves, slathered with butter and dunked inelegantly into steaming hot mugs of sweet tea, of jalebis brought out sizzling from the hot oil before being immersed into the sugar syrup to infuse them with the sweetness that would define them, of the final touch of home-made ghee being dolloped onto freshly made khichdi, releasing its aroma as it melted. Victor was bread and butter, and jam and sponge cake topped with icing and dotted with Cadbury gems around the edge. He was the first leaf to poke out of the hard ground after winter, the birdsong that heralded the morning, the smell of logs burning in winter, the warmth of a fireplace with the snow outside. He was home, I realised. He was home in a way Nihar had always been a transit house. It was a realisation that made me gasp and raise my head to look up into his face. It was crumpled with sleep and magnificent in its weariness.

'What do you mean by talking strange things?' I asked, bracing myself for what was to come.

He laughed and shook his head. 'You have some unresolved issues, man. It was probably just the shock from your aunt's death and falling into the water playing out, you had begun talking nonsense and you just wouldn't stop. About ghosts and how your dead husband pulled you into the sea and that a ghost nurse had just checked your blood pressure. They injected you with a sedative. I decided to get you home, you are my responsibility I told the doctor, I would look after you.'

'And will you?'

'Will I what?'

'Look after me? Am I your responsibility?'

He tightened his arms around me, I breathed him in, unwilling to exhale.

'While I'm here, yes.'

'And when you're not?' My question hung in the air, a terrible silence weighing down its aftermath.

He sighed. Then he spoke. 'You're on your own then. I have to go back to Leah. I love her very much. I barely know you. I like you, I like you very much but I barely know you. What I have with Leah is love, we've been together since we were kids in school. I'm not about to end what I have with her for you. Let me be honest.'

Words can sometimes cut straight to the bone. I drew in a sharp breath, it was true. He barely knew me, I barely knew him. All we knew were each other's bodies. Bodies were not souls. I knew his body. I had thought I knew his soul too. But souls aren't creatures to know, souls are experiences, either as disparate from one, or as part of one.

He hadn't hidden his girlfriend from me. In fact, the night we met he had fished out his phone and shown me a photograph of her and him together. They were laughing, a common joke I would never know, a comfort in his arm around her like it belonged there, her head resting in the crook of his shoulder with the arrogance of ownership. She could have been pretty. It was difficult to tell from the photograph. Her features were strong, square and determined, her hair brown and contrasted with his dirty blonde. They were a couple. They looked a couple. I was an interloper, a fling, a momentary distraction while he was here. That hadn't mattered to me. It terrified me, the realisation that my moral compass had gone so awry that I would willingly become the other woman in someone's relationship.

'I'm not asking for love. I'm not asking anything of you.'

'I have nothing to give you, except me when I'm here.'

'I'll take that,' I replied. It would be enough for me. I would stay here, waiting, Penelope to his Ulysses, working on my word tapestries, weaving them and unravelling them as I waited for him to return.

He sighed and shifted. I sensed the shift in the mood and stepped off his lap, disentangling our limbs which had automatically interlaced themselves in the manner bodies do when the mind does not intervene. I went to the bathroom and splashed water on my face to wash away the tears that had come unbidden. When I came out of the bathroom, he was gone.

He turned up in the dining room when I was almost done with breakfast.

'Have you seen the entire house and the grounds yet?' he asked, wolfing down the pao and sausages along with the fried eggs sunny side up that Jacinta had placed before him, the yellow of their yolks the one bright spot in a room dimmed with thin muslin curtains that kept out the faint greyness of the monsoon day outside.

'I haven't,' I confessed.

'Well, since we own it now, you really should know what you have been given charge of. Let's do a short tour of the entire property after breakfast?'

'I'd love that,' I replied, genuinely interested in seeing the house from the inside apart from the few rooms I'd been to during my time here. This was home now, as different a home from the stone and wood home up in the hills, the walls ice blocks in winter, the hail clattering a rhythm of its own on the roof, the frost icing up with roads, the roof shuddering as the snow fell off it when it got too much, the windows hissing dirges of woe when the wind whistled through it, the melted snow dripping from the gutters as the sun emerged.

The meal was over. He wiped his mouth on the napkin and stood up, extending a hand to me. I took it. It seemed the most natural thing to do.

'Here then,' he said, 'is your first detailed look at what you will own if you choose to stay on. It is a lot to take on, and not all of it is pleasant, so that's a choice I leave to you. We need to find a way to make this strange will work and own this house together, without being at loggerheads with each other.'

We stepped out of the dining hall into the passage leading to the main parlour from which the house branched off like a spider's web. The front door, accessed by a few steps going up from the central hall, was open and a soft diffused light from outside poured in, golden and reassuring.

We stepped onto the porch where Buddy lay disinterestedly on the landing. He raised a lackadaisical nose to sniff us and woof out a greeting, thumping his tail on the cemented floor, before snuggling off to his mid-morning snooze again. Devil was nowhere to be seen. True to his name, he would be stalking the premises, scaring off vagrants and chasing rats. Outside, the flight of stairs went down steeply into the grounds, which stretched around for a couple of acres of lushness. The compound wall at the distance which led out through the thickness of the vegetation to the main road was fringed with coconut trees. In the centre of the ground, to the extreme left of the house, was a banyan tree with its aerial roots reaching down, probing the air for moisture. It spread out like a canopy over the driveway, dappling it with light and shadow as the sun trickled through the leaves to the ground. To the back of the house and to the right were the fruit trees, mango, chickoo, pineapple, jamun, papaya, kokum and more. Lucenzia had pointed them out to me one morning as I strolled around the house. The trees had their denizens, the birds, the fruit bats and the langurs who had made these their home. The langurs and the dogs lived in a state of permanent face-off, with spats happening through the day at times, and at others, a tenuous truce reigned. The sun shone dappled on the ground, through the canopy of the trees, the yellow and brown patches a mottled map of a mythical realm of islands. On the pillar holding the porch and the roof together, and keeping the sky from falling on us, a nervous lizard skittered off as we approached. The rose bushes planted along the periphery of the approach stairs and the porch bloomed in variegated hues of pink, red, yellow, planted with no thought to the symmetry of hue and shade. Their fragrance wafted towards us as the wind blew, soft, pleasant, riding over the faint distant skank of the river bank.

'As you might know, my father bought this house in a distress sale. It was being auctioned off by a bank that held the mortgage to it. The original owners had died or emigrated, the family had thinned out to none. It was quite dilapidated when we moved in. My father restored it bit by bit. My mother had no love for it, she missed home. The heat got to her, the mosquitoes got to her, and she hated not being able to pop to the pub around the corner for a pint when she pleased. She was a city girl, who fell in love with my father when she was down on a holiday. I don't blame her for not being able to adjust to a life on an island.'

He took my hand. I let him. Whatever it was between us, that delicate connection of the body, it fluttered within me. It was comfortable, this equation. This here and now. The tomorrow could wait.

We went through the rooms on the ground floor. The living room. Lofty ceilings. Elegant mouldings painted gold framing the edges. White-washed walls. Beams high above where the occasional lizard darted. Ceiling fans that hung low. Floor fans that stood obsequiously in the corner. The furniture, old, burnished teak. Mahogany. Carved intricately. The sofas upholstered in brocade from another lifetime, a pattern that was out of favour in today's aesthetic sensibilities. Gold-stitched tapestries hung from the walls, depicting scenes from a life alien to us today, of ships in the sea, of armies in battle. On the floor, the pretty mosaic tiles were occasionally interrupted by rugs and carpets. Framed portraits of people I didn't know adorned the walls. Strangely, for a home that was owned by painters, their work was not on any of the walls. The only place you could see their paintings were in Kamini's studio, where they waited, wreathed beneath draped cloth, for a hand to lift the cover, an eye to see them, for them to serve their purpose of creation, that of being seen.

The rooms led off from a central atrium and lined two opposite wings that ran parallel to each other. The upper floor was reached by a long curving balustrade of a stairway which was burnished mahogany wood that felt warm to the touch, the polish had worn thin, the knots and the grain were showing through. Built over a century ago, the house was constructed of the locally plentiful red laterite stones, and set with lime mortar as was the norm when it was built. The thick walls not just keep the outside where it belonged, outside, but also blocked out the heat, of the languorous Goan sun in summer, keeping the interiors cool and dim. In winter, the thick walls trapped in the little heat making the homes cosy. Every room had big windows lining them from end to end, windows which had thin curtains meant only to be drawn if one wanted to cut out the light from outside and, yet, needed to keep them open for the breeze. The roof was slanted, tiled with red Mangalorean tiles supported on what he called pattyos, huge wooden beams which one could only imagine a wealthy person being able to hire enough labour in order to transport them. These beams were then bolstered by the smaller beams, called *vashe* in local Konkani.

The roofs needed to be slanted to drain off the rainwater, as we needed them slanted up back home to have the snow fall off, or drain off as it melted when the sun came out. The rooms upstairs were simple yet elegantly done, rectangular, facing north and south so that any point in the day there was enough sunlight, not too much coming straight in. The full-length windows opened up to small balconies, the smaller ones supported on corbels, oyster shell in their panes that glistened in the light outside and tempered down the brightness of the sun. The doorway, the balcao, had seats on either side of the porch, constructed with cement, meant for an age when neighbours had conversations as they passed and the world stopped and chatted on the balcaos of every home; receiving areas for vendors and others whose business it wasn't to enter the house. The porch ran around the front of the house and was fringed by an awning supported by white painted pillars. And there was the private chapel, with the altar in place, the candles burning, the pews knelt at diligently every morning by Lucenzia, Jacinta and Da Costa. The eastern section of the house, built as an addendum after the main house was constructed, had a ballroom when lavish banquets would be hosted, with a minstrel's gallery attached to it in order to provide the music for the evening. If I closed my eyes, I could hear the clink of glasses, the clatter of cutlery, the music playing softly, voices chattering in a language I was not familiar with, the laughter of women, the baritone of men, the swish of silks, the patter of footsteps. This was a ballroom that had happy memories seeped into its walls, into the beams that held it up. I looked up to see a huge chandelier looming overhead, the crystal tinkling every time a soft gust of breeze blew in from the windows Victor had opened to get rid of the musty smell that had become overpowering, the smell of disuse.

'It is beautiful,' I said, mildly shocked by the extravagance that was now mine. What would I do with such largesse, I who only needed a room to myself and my thoughts? Maa could come and stay with me, I thought. 'It's huge. Too huge. How will I live here?'

'As you can see there are too many rooms for one person to live in peace,' he laughed after we had peered through all the rooms in the right wing.

'You will be staying here too, won't you? When you visit? Six months of a year.'

He shrugged. 'I don't know. Things are rather complicated now, wouldn't you agree? There's no way I can bring Leah here.

And there's no way I can keep visiting without her wanting to accompany me. Unless....'

I grabbed at that unfinished sentence with all my hope. 'Unless....' I repeated, hoping he would conclude the sentence with what I wanted to hear.

'Unless we end this thing between us and never mention it again.'

I stopped mid-step, my hand suspended mid-air, at the balustrade going towards the left upper wing of the house. This was where I'd seen the woman going, this was where, in my dream, I'd been sucked into a vortex with a million blazing eyes in the darkness. This was where it began and ended.

'We end this thing between us and never mention it again,' I repeated, testing the words on my lips, tasting them for finality. Nihar whispered into my ear, from his perch on my shoulder, 'Lotusface....' I heard him. I didn't. I closed my eyes. He whispered again. 'You're mine. Always were. Always will be.'

A shudder ran up my spine. I opened my eyes, Victor was looking at me, expectantly.

'Okay,' I said. 'It's over. It never was. Unless. We let this thing continue and never mention it to Leah.' Nihar caressed my spine with fingers of ice and fire.

Victor shook his head, a brief change of expression that could have been anything from a smile to a grimace to the beginning of a scowl.

'That would be wrong.'

'I don't care,' I replied. 'I'm not asking you to leave her. I'm only asking you to be with me when you're here, is that too much?'

A strange expression crossed his face, of longing mixed with a certain self-inflicted righteousness that would forbid him from doing what I wanted him to. He struggled with it for a moment, raised my hand to his lips, and kissed it.

'No. It is over. It was stupidity, I wasn't thinking.... I should have known better....'

He stopped. I should have known better too. But how would I know that the body would have a mind of its own. And a heart that should have been in mourning would fall in love again with someone who didn't want that love. Perhaps the imbalance in loving and being loved is what makes for the curious tug of war that the human heart faces when trying to keep itself on an even keel. I had never experienced this, this utter willingness to obliterate my ego for another, this hunger to be with him that made everything around inconsequential. It was humbling, the knowledge that a man I had barely met a few weeks ago could have me willing to change all I knew about myself.

'What's on this side of the house upstairs? I don't see anyone going there too often.'

'It's normally shut given it's not in use and it doesn't make sense to keep maintaining so huge a space.'

'I'd like to see it.'

The stairs were a different shade from the stairs on the opposite side of the house. These were darker, blackened in patches, like something burning had been dragged up or down. We went up, the passageway outside the rooms was spotlessly clean. Lucenzia was to be commended, her housekeeping was immaculate or was it the fear of Kamini's wrath that made it so? Would the standards slip now that I was in charge? Was I in charge and, more importantly, did I want to be in charge? I looked at our hands. Perhaps the decision had already been taken for me and it was a fait accomplis in the manner that most fait accomplis are and all I had to do was to go with the flow.

Like on the other wing, there were four doors on this side of the house on the first floor, a common passageway outside all of them reaching down to the almost circular balustrade that went down to the ground floor. The doors to all of them were locked, the contents within those rooms unknown.

'Do we have the keys to these?' I asked. Da Costa who was hovering at a discreet distance came over bearing a bunch of keys, and opened the first door. The cobwebs hung low and trailed over everything with the languidness that their making had bestowed upon them, the right of those undisturbed over time. A lizard scuttled across the wall on the far side, disturbed suddenly from his reverie. There was light in the room, and dark, a dark that came from sunlight never quite entering the place thanks to the closed windows. Something scuttled in the shadows in the corner, a shade, a presence, the rustling of leaves through the closed windows. I started. Something cold trickled down my back. On my shoulder, the weight increased, bearing on me. The weight of my dead husband I now carried with me everywhere I went. It flitted off my shoulder and clung to the ceiling. I could feel his eyes boring into the back of my head. I didn't dare look up.

'What was that?'

'What was what?'

'Something moved in the corner.'

'Probably a shadow from the trees outside.' Perhaps a shadow from my soul. Perhaps a shadow from another soul lurking around. 'You have an overactive imagination,' said Victor, narrowing his eyes as he looked at me. 'What did you think it was?'

'Nothing. I don't know.'

I took in the general state of disuse of these rooms. 'Why is this side of the house kept locked and boarded?'

He laughed, a half snort that was a multitude of things, including an escape from answering the question directly. 'I have no clue, but it has been locked for years. I'd assumed it was because caring for such a large space was difficult for your aunt given her limited mobility over the past few years.'

'What about the room at the end of the corridor?'

'No one goes there.'

Da Costa had spoken up from the shadows of the passage where he waited to take us around. I turned to look at him.

'Why is that?'

He shrugged, non-committal.

'Don't know why.' He pursed his lips. 'The master got it closed, and it has remained closed.'

'I want to open it,' I said, raising my chin imperiously, realising as an afterthought that this is exactly how Kamini would have said it. There was a bit of her in me I could not deny ever. They both looked at me, their expressions varying. Da Costa suspicious, Victor eager.

'Don't have key,' said Da Costa.

'Go get it made, or we can break the door down, can't we?'

Victor shrugged a shoulder so solid, I could imagine it tunnelling through miles of rock with no resistance. 'Get me a good axe from the shed,' he said. Da Costa hesitated. 'Do as you're told, and don't overthink. I think this was long overdue. I've often wondered why we never bothered to get that door open, and somehow never got around to doing so. Kamini never allowed it, nor did my dad. Do you think there's something stashed there? Skeletons rattling away in the cupboards?'

His eyes gleamed, a gleam that was just a glint away from toppling over into the darkness of the manic.

Da Costa trotted off to fetch an axe or a hammer, and we walked out of the room. The tiling down this part was blackened, burnt. The walls were scorched, soot tinged the edges of where they met the ceiling rafters. At the end of the passage, the door stood boarded up and ominous. This room had never been restored after a fire, that much was evident. The passage with the balustrade looked into the central part of the house, I looked down. It all seemed strange, yet familiar. I had seen this before, this vantage point, although I was sure I had never been to this part of the house ever. Déjà vu. Seen again. This was seen again. But when had I seen this before? A sparking, a misfiring of neurons within the brain, a kind of epilepsy, this déjà vu, firing through familiar neural pathways I had never walked down before physically. Or had I?

It was then that I saw her, standing at the end of the corridor, or was it her? In a dress that reached her knees, an indeterminate shade between slate and grey, or was it a dull brown that the shadows had claimed for their own. She smiled at me from a face I could not distinguish the features from and then faded into nothingness. It was bright noon, the sun high in the sky, and nothing that would spook anyone in front of me, except a door with boards nailed across it, boards we were going to pull down now to investigate the room that lay beyond.

I had seen her before, in a hospital room, wearing a nurse's uniform. Dragging herself, step by step, up this stairway, in the dark of night. Behind me, Victor was running down the stairs to bring something to prise out the nails that boarded the door up to the room that had never been opened. A room that I knew I had to open because somewhere within its forbidden recesses was the reason why I had made the journey all the way from my home in the mountains, then to the barsati in Delhi and from there to the tiny one-bedroom apartment in Bombay. This is what had been waiting for me all these years, coiled, slithery, ready to take me for its own.

⚬⚬⚬

NINETEEN

HERE, NOW, PAST MIDNIGHT

I had woken with a start from a deep sleep, gasping for breath. It was that same dream again. I was running through a labyrinth with Nihar just ahead of me and turning a corner as I was reaching him, within touching distance, turning to smoke in my grasp. The labyrinth we ran through was the same in all the dreams. I had no ball of wool to find my way out of the labyrinth, the monster I was chasing was not one I wanted to kill, but one that I wanted to let go, I was my own Ariadne. Seeking and not finding, chasing and not being able to grasp, the frustration building up within me, hot, heavy and dissolving me into tears that spilled over in my dreams and made damp patches on my pillow. And then, just when I'd given up, he'd turned and reached out to me.

He was Nihar and not Nihar. The man I'd loved. The man I'd hated. A monster. His eyes two pinpricks of a glowing red flame behind the darkness of an indistinct face. I turned swiftly to flee, running on feet which did not touch the ground but ran through air, suspended above the slick, rocky floor of the labyrinth, drawing on every ounce of my willpower to make them move.

I could hear his footsteps clattering behind me, heavy and hard. 'Lotusface,' he called, the familiar voice I had so loved. 'Kamie, stop....' I almost did, slowing down, wondering why my feet were not on the floor, and the only footsteps I heard were his when I felt his breath hot at my back, almost singeing the flesh off of me, and the walls of the labyrinth began closing in on me as I ran back towards a turn that would take me, perhaps, closer to the exit, or further from it. The darkness pressed on me and the air was hot, humid and sulphurous with the stench of a fire that blazed somewhere within the recesses. 'Kamie... please...stop,' he called, his voice pleading. I could never resist that tone he used. I stopped and turned around. He stood before me, eyes level with mine and the depths of torment in them, red and blazing.

'Why?' I stood still and closed my eyes. Is there a greater sadness than to know that what one once yearned for is not what one wants anymore, is that the fate of us humans, to be constantly renegotiating the boundaries of wants, needs, desires and, most important of them all, love?

The walls closed in on us, now almost touching our heads. I gasped, I couldn't breathe, there was no air left to breathe. His face was almost next to mine, the darkness we were enclosed in was luminescent, a faint unearthly glow from the rocky walls enclosing us, lighting it up. In the distance, the sounds of hounds howling, an unearthly sound that made me shiver in dread. I put a hand up to touch his face. I touched nothing. I put my arms around him. I grasped nothing.

I closed my eyes, this was not real, this was a dream and I would wake up, I knew. I had to wake up. Wake up, I told myself, speaking out loud, hearing my voice echo back at me, a million times over, wake up, run away.

He put his hand on my wrist, I screamed. The next thing I knew, I was awake, in bed, gasping for air. There was the smell of burnt flesh in the air. My hand was on fire, burning with a crackling flame that extinguished itself before my terrified eyes as I slowly came back to wakefulness. My wrist was in agony from the flames I could not see. I ran to the bathroom and doused my wrist under the tepid water that did nothing to alleviate the burning. A raw red burn remained, a bracelet of burnt flesh around my wrist.

It was that part of the night that hung awkwardly between the witching hour and pre-dawn. The wind rustled the leaves of the mango tree gently. The fragrance from the rose bushes that bordered the porch wafted in gently through the windows, heavy, indolent. Through the netting to keep the mosquitoes at bay, the gibbous moon outside the window was foggy and indistinct, ragged at the edges, like a giant piece of cheese an invisible rodent had nibbled away at.

I was alone tonight. Victor had stayed away. I hadn't gone to seek him out either. He'd gone out in the evening to meet some old friends, and hadn't returned by bedtime. I'd eaten dinner half-heartedly and taken myself to my room and my Kindle. Somewhere between midnight and the witching hour, I'd fallen asleep, sprawled awkwardly across the bed. It wasn't sound sleep though. I switched on the bedside lamp. The night was velvety dark outside, a darkness that had a band of stars streak down the centre of the sky in an arc. The vault of the heavens. Balls of helium, hydrogen and other gases burning up, imploding, celestial fireworks, universes beyond our ken, sentient and waiting. Life forms we were searching for, proof of intelligence other than the earth. The heavens above, the hells below and all of us who lived in the worlds between the two of them. I'd never felt as alone as I did at this moment.

I hadn't checked the clock. I needed ice. I went down to the kitchen in the hope that the antiquated refrigerator would have some ice, or at least a frozen pack of something I could hold across the wrist until the burning lessened. There was the faint light coming in from the moon outside that let me navigate the stairs. The banister was cool against my hand, a coolness that was reassuring of me being alive and in this world where pain was felt, and was essential proof that one lived. The wrist of my other hand burned in unmentionable agony. I had brought it upon myself. The dead deserved to be left alone, I should have known that.

A startled lizard scurried behind a shelf as I switched the light on. I found a pack of shelled peas and held it against my wrist, the iciness reducing the burning. Someone moved in the corner of the room. A rat, probably. These old houses were teeming with them. There were rat traps on the floor and one on the kitchen platform. Something moved again, just behind my line of sight. I turned quickly. I could hear the startled squeaks, perhaps complaining peevishly to each other about this human who had infringed on their foraging time.

'Lucy', I called out. No one responded. Someone walked briskly in the passageway outside. I stepped out, the passageway was clear. The kitchen was right at the back of the house, hung with drying knots of onions and sausages, a strange aroma infusing the room from a combination of the day's cooking, the spices stored within and the victuals hanging from the beams across the kitchen, salted and dried for a rainy day. Against one wall was the grinding stone with its pestle cleaned and dried for the next day's work. The red cement floor had been wiped clean for the night, the rag used to mop it was drying on the sill of the window. It all looked normal, regular, but there was a hint of a menace to the entire scene, the bats fluttering outside the window, in the fruit trees, making sibilant sounds to move around, the wind blowing through the wooden slats of the closed windows, the soft sighs of the trees outside shifting their weight as the breeze blew.

The packet of peas was losing its chill. I needed ice cubes. I looked in the freezer again, coming up with nothing but some more frozen things. My wrist was still on fire. To the naked eye it looked just like a discoloration, a fresh burn, like red hot metal had been wrapped around my wrist.

Something moved in the darkness beyond the door, a quick shifting of a shadow. The humidity pressed down on me. The darkness moved again. Then nothing, stillness. I switched the light off and went out through the narrow passage that would open into the central area leading off to the dining room, the parlour, the formal living room, the studio and the master bedroom, and from there to the stairways leading upstairs, impassive in their solidity and curve, like the pillars outside, running the length of the porch on either side, solid and immutable. There was darkness, except for whatever light filtered in from the moon outside the windows.

There was a movement just beyond what I could see clearly, someone or something was running across the floor, through the passage, through the door leading to the hall. Running with soundless footsteps, something small, a little head bobbing, a child. There was no child in this house! There hadn't been children in this house since Victor was a child.

'Who is it?' I called, running after the shape. It ran swiftly ahead of me and reached the banisters where it paused and turned back. I couldn't make out the features, but it was definitely a child, a little boy, he couldn't have been more than five. His expression was indecipherable in the darkness, but an overwhelming sadness descended upon me.

'What is it, why are you here, where is your home?'

He stared at me for one long moment, shook his head from side to side and then ran up the stairs, up the other side of the house, and then I couldn't see him anymore in the darkness that swallowed him up. I went off to the back of the house where Lucy and Jacinta slept, knocking at their door. Lucy opened the door, her hair tied off her face in a tight bun from which no tendrils dared escape even though she must have been asleep at that hour, her skin slick with the application of a cream that sat on the surface like a patina of white—a luminescence of hope handed across by a Gulf-returned niece that would erase not just the wrinkles, but also the heartbreaks that brought each into being.

'Whathappent MissyKamla?'

'Is there a child staying in the house?'

She looked at me strangely. 'No chillun. Only big people. You go to sleep. Why you come down, just press bell, no? I give you what you want, don't come down in dark night. Don't come out of room in dark night. All lizards and things in dark, no, sometimes snakes is also coming inside, no, one foot on them and will bite, no?'

Jacinta peered over her aunt's shoulder. I noticed her features perhaps for the first time in the dim light of the night lamp. She might have once been beautiful, ten years ago, with the first flush of adolescence, with her olive skin, patched by the sun into unevenness, sharp dark eyes and brows that arched over a face that was sturdily fetching. Hers was a solidness of youthful beauty that had gone to waste in the service of a house in the middle of nowhere. I had never really looked at her before, she had always been someone around, a slim, lithe figure in a floral dress stitched to the same pattern as her aunt's, which while it emphasized the decay of middle age in her aunt, underlined the youthfulness of her own body, yet to sink into the dereliction of tyres and varicose veins.

'Don't worry,' she said. 'He won't do anything. He just runs around and goes back to his room.'

'Who is he?'

Her aunt hissed at her in their native tongue, Jacinta drew back and went out of my line of sight. 'Stupid she is. Imagining things. Should have married Peter when he proposed, but was acting too hoity-toity. He went to the Gulf and then all the village girls were after him. His wife, Miranda, comes now once a year to meet her parents, fat like a cow and wearing gold from her fingers to her elbows. Stupid girl. Spends all her life mourning Peter. Like he's mourning for her, made four children with that cow.'

I had no clue how the conversation had suddenly turned towards Jacinta's bad luck in the matrimonial stakes and Peter's virility, but it didn't answer my question.

'Who is he, Lucy?' I caught her by the shoulders. They were sturdy under my fingers, shoulders that were bred to work hard. She looked at me in the eye, unflinching.

'Go to sleep, MissyKamla. I will tell you when you are ready. You shouldn't have had that door opened. Now you are still learning about the house.' Her eye went to my wrist, the burn still black red and raw despite the icing.

'Ohjezuz, whathappent to your hand? How it got burnt?'

I had no answer. She took it and examined it, and then flinched. 'Who did this to you, MissyKamla?'

'No one did. I burnt myself with the....' I didn't know what I could say I had burnt myself with, a burn so deep that the skin had blackened all around.

She put her finger on her lips. 'I may be old lady in village but I know the devil's mark when I see it. Take this....' She fumbled on the dresser next to the door and pulled out a much-thumbed rosary, handing it to me with a furtiveness that seemed out of place given there were only three of us here.

'Don't be silly,' I interrupted, 'I'm fine, but if it makes you feel any better, I will keep this with me. Although I don't really have much faith in all this.'

'Wear it,' she said, and did so herself, murmuring a prayer while she did so. 'I call Father Dominic tomorrow morning to bless the house, should have called him today when you and Vicky baba decided to open that room.'

The light from the lamp dangling in the centre of the room was casting strange shadows on her face, her face morphed from the familiar to the darkness of the featureless as it swayed lightly with the breeze.

'I'll be fine.' I looked her in the eye. She nodded, there was a wariness in her nod that got me thinking. I wasn't scared of the little boy, or the woman I saw on the opposite side of the house. I was terrified of the one who came into my dreams and dragged me through subterranean landscapes.

'Okay. Close your door. Lock it. And don't open it for anyone until sunrise.' No locks would keep him out. No rosaries wrapped around my wrist. The dead did not fear what the living did, their rules were different.

I went back to my room, out of sorts, closing the door behind me, not locking it. There was hope yet—Victor would return, tap on the door, push it open and come to me, his body sliding in next to mine, hard and planed where I was soft and sinuous. I tossed and turned in my bed, feeling the never-ending burning on my wrist, then jumping up, switching the lights on, and rummaging through my things for a salve I could apply. I always travelled with half a pharmacy in my bag. I found some aloe vera gel and applied it. But it did not help much; the burn was beyond redemption and burned incessantly.

The crossing had almost happened. I was lucky to have woken up. How would I live out my life afraid to fall asleep? Who could I talk to about this, who would understand? Would they take me to an institute again and fill my bloodstream with medications that made raising my hand to take a spoon of food from my plate to my mouth a challenge of willpower over chemicals?

I stayed till the night began falling away. There was no tap on the door. There was no Victor. I thought about the strangeness of the day that had passed yesterday. Days passed here, on this estuarine island with the sluggishness of swimming underwater—everything heightened, dappled with intermittent refracted light and requiring all the resistance one could summon to merely get through them. Susegad, as they said here, taking life easy.

It had been the strangest of days yesterday, when we'd finally managed to get the boards across the door at the end of the passage break open. The room's original blue plaster wash, that was typical of the Portuguese, was peeling off, the walls dusty with aeons of disuse sitting upon them, the cobwebs hanging down from the ceilings, festooning the fringes of the room in an oddly gay celebration of neglect. The room was devoid of any furniture, strangely bare in a home that was filled with things. Perhaps everything within had been removed when they decided to board it up. The Azulezos, the typical Goan painted tiles, with their beautiful patterns, were burnt in patches and not replaced. The blackened patches seemed like burning feet had stood on them, walked through from the outside to the inside, and from there, paced all corners of the room. There was a curious tinge of sulphuric acridity in the air, of something still burning somewhere, though the room was clear. The room was cold. Nothing was ever cold in these homes, baked as they were with the tropical sun all through the day. A chill had run up my spine.

Sunlight had filtered in through the chinks between the boards on the window.

'Let's open these windows, shall we?' Victor had said, looking like he could rip them off with his bare hands, his beautiful square solid hands which I could still feel on my body, cupping my butt, squeezing my breasts, kneading out the knots in my spine, caressing the nape of my neck with his fingers, prising open that place between my legs that pulsed and yearned with those very fingers bringing me to waves on waves of bliss.

The strong young lad Da Costa had brought along with him from the carpenter's workshop wrenched out the nails off the boards and opened the windows. Fresh air entered the room warily, along with strong beams of sunlight, dissipating the chill. As I stepped in, something clattered above us on the roof.

'Monkeys on the roof,' Da Costa said as I started.

There was something in this room. I knew it, I could feel it.

'Why was this room boarded up?' I asked again, searching for an answer that no one had, or if they did, refused to give it to me.

'Don't know,' Da Costa replied, his face shuttered in. 'We should not have opened it.'

'Why not?'

'Was closed for some reason, should have left it closed.' There was disapproval in his voice, a disapproval that seeped through his every pore, tempered with a strange wariness.

Victor snorted, 'Perfectly good waste of space, let's get this cleaned up and some extra furniture moved in. I guess we could make it a bedroom?' He was enthusiastic about putting the house to work as a homestay. It wasn't something I thought I could handle, but he had been slowly warming me up to the idea of putting the property right eventually, slicking on a coat of paint, fitting in some spanking new bathroom fittings and putting it up on Airbnb.

'This would make it four bedrooms and one master suite,' he said, looking around, checking for dampness on the walls, noting where seepage had taken over, noting that the branches of the trees outside, unpruned, prevented the windows from being completely opened. The room was strange. The walls were mossy in big patches, sunlight hadn't streamed in for quite a long while, months, years, lending a strange stillness to it.

'This room will take some work to become presentable again. I wonder what this is,' I said, sitting down on my haunches, looking at the burnt tiles closely.

'No clue,' Victor replied, 'But I'm sure we could find replicas of the tiles to replace the tiling as close to the original as possible.'

'What is the story of the house?' I asked.

'I've never really bothered to find out. It was built by a Portuguese nobleman. His family lived here for a couple of generations and then the house was passed on to the Braganza family. That family moved to Portugal when Goa became part of India, and it was uninhabited for quite a while, and after that it came to my father.'

'He bought it?'

'At an auction. Three of them were found dead in their beds one morning. The grandmother, two children. The rest of the family moved to Portugal. The house wasn't lived in for ten years until my father came to Goa on a holiday, saw it and unearthed the trail back to the bank that now held it for lack of legal heirs. He bought it for a song, then set about restoring it. It was a work in progress all through my childhood, in fact I think it still is.'

'Did they ever find out how they died?'

'There were whispers, of course. But I grew up here, the first ten years of my life. People were careful about what they said about the house in front of me. There were rumours of it being haunted, though personally I never experienced anything. My mom, in fact, was very uncomfortable living here, but Pa would not move out. Perhaps that was one of the reasons their marriage ended.'

We were out of the room, walking down the passageway to the curving stairway that led out to the ground floor, the main entrance hallway and the massive door and the porch that surrounded the house. Da Costa was hovering behind us at a distance. 'Shall I lock the room again and put the boards across?'

'Not at all,' I replied. 'Get it cleaned up and let's get it painted.'

Victor smiled. 'I can see you are coming around to my plan of making this a nice little homestay.'

I took his hand, uncaring of the disapproving Da Costa, uncaring of the looming shadow of Leah, a smiling face in his gallery of images in a phone now lying somewhere in the bed of the Arabian sea off the coast of Goa. 'I am only going to do that if you are in it with me. Completely. I can't manage it on my own.'

He nodded, tightened his grip on my hand. The chill that had crawled up my spine and sent gooseflesh into my arms dissipated as the warmth of the post-noon sun crept past the open main door, through the porch and touched my limbs. Everything would be alright. Perhaps this is what it was meant to be, this is what Kamini had in mind for me when she called me here and set into motion her little plan to will me this house jointly with Victor. This was a strategy if ever there was one. Perhaps all would be well, the room, now opened, would free the spirits into leaving, now that they realised we weren't about to give them their own space. Spirits often were just confused. All they needed was to be told it was time to go. All would be well. I would see to it tomorrow, I'd told myself yesterday. I'd told Victor I would stay there for as long as it took to get the house functioning as a homestay.

I was bound to this place, something that had crept into my soul and rooted it here, to this house, set in this grove of mango, peepul and banana trees, in this overgrown, unkempt lawn that tickled one's ankles as one walked through it, with the dogs roaming the grounds and coming up to nuzzle one—little security for the residents against any thieves who might want to take their chances on the antiques that packed the rooms. Perhaps this was where I was meant to come to. This was the restlessness that drew me away from Delhi. This was where I would find closure and solace, and the tranquillity I was searching for. Or this was where it would all end, if I slept the sleep that would take me to where Nihar was, and I didn't wake up in time to escape the labyrinth of burning stone that closed in on us.

Heavy footsteps passed my door, closed and unlocked as it was. I sat up straight in my bed. The footsteps halted then came back. Whatever it was outside was standing right outside my door. The hair on my hands and the nape of my neck stood on edge. I could hear heavy breathing outside and then a muffled groan. Something tapped against the panes of the window on the other side of the room, I looked at it, there was nothing to be seen, except the branches of the mango tree swaying in the night breeze. I sat up, grabbed the rosary Lucy had given me, put it around my neck, clutching it with the death grip that fear brings.

'Who is it?' I called, my voice thin and scared, regretting my decision not to lock the door. But if what I was dreading was on the other side of the door, a lock would not stop him. Or it. What could I call what I'd seen of Nihar?

There was a rap on the door in response. Then silence. I lifted myself out of the bed. Another rap and then the sound of something heavy falling to the ground. I ran to the door and stood against it, breathing heavily, wondering whether I should open it. The monsoon wind took the decision away from me, blowing into the room in a heavy gust, pushing the unlocked door open where it jammed on something, someone that lay on the ground, slumped awkwardly. I switched the light on, wrapping my arms around myself closer as I moved to check who it was. Victor. Slumped low, against the door jamb. And on his thin cotton shirt a dark stain blooming, spreading as I watched. Blood, thick, sticky, black in the dark. On his hands where he had clutched it. On my hands as I touched him. I screamed. Lights went on, footsteps came running up. They found me kneeling next to him, my hands bloodied, screaming, screaming, until my voice went out.

TWENTY

HERE, NOW

He lay on his bed, in a deep medicated sleep, while I sat at the head of his bed, stroking his head. His lips moved, speaking without sound. He was in conversation with something, someone, and I was not part of the conversation. I moved the footstool I was seated on so I faced him. If he opened his eyes, I wanted to be in his line of vision. I clutched Victor's hand tightly, knowing I needed him right now more than he needed me.

'He will sleep for hours.' Lucy was standing by the door. 'You go to sleep, na, MissyKamla? I will wake you when he wakes up.'

'No, I want to be here.'

She shook her head disapprovingly. 'Doctor said not to disturb him.' I was not disturbing him at all, I told her.

'Good doctor came home, otherwise we would have to take to hospital, it would become police case. And so much tension then.'

Victor's skin was pale and clammy, his lips were cracked dry. I dropped a few drops of water into his mouth. He gulped them down greedily in his sleep.

I remember peeling off his shirt and attempting to staunch the bleeding with it, feeling the blood bloom under the pressure I applied, thick and metallic, an insidious black stain spreading in the darkness, across his torso, dripping onto the floor. The audience of three that had come scampering out of their rooms on hearing my screams, Lucy, Jacinta and Da Costa, Da Costa bringing out his phone and dialling Dr Pinto, hanging out of the window on the landing in order to get better reception. Lucy being sensible and bringing antiseptic and gauze bandages, applying pressure and making a rough tourniquet from scraps of cloth. Us, lifting him with great difficulty to his bed in the next room. The never-ending wait for Dr Pinto to arrive on his wheezing asthmatic scooter, the buttons on his hastily pulled-on shirt askew, his hair not brilliantined to perfection as it was through the day, the dogs barking their heads off with the excitement. My overwhelming urge to throw up my dinner as Dr Pinto carefully cleaned, cauterized and then sutured up the gash. The sense of heaviness hanging over the room, the air, the dim moonlight straggling in through the window as the crescent moon lowered itself unkemptly over the distant undulations which led down to the river and the sea beyond it. The faintly fecund smell of the damp earth from the slight drizzle that had passed came in through the windows, mingled with the tang of the salty air. The salt, it hung in the air, it settled on your lips, your sweat, your tears, all tinged with the salt, of the ocean from where one came, from where one would eventually return.

It was a stab wound, he told us, that luckily hadn't penetrated too deep to cause any major damage. He'd dressed the wound, sutured it together, given Victor a mega dose of painkillers and advised us to let him rest. He would send a nurse to clean the wound and change the dressing in a couple of days. What had happened, how it had happened, we knew nothing. Until he emerged from the sleep he was in, I would have to hold the questions that bubbled over in my head, spilling out through my ears. When I woke, he was stirring. His fingers were in my hair and my head was on the bed next to him.

'Kamla,' he said in the accent that made my very ordinary name exotic because it just sounded so different from the run of the mill. 'Were you here all this while?'

'Where would I go?' I laughed, plain happy to see his lips move with words that made sense.

The clock on the wall said two. The sun was mellow outside. Dark clouds were drifting past, a grey pall hung over the sky, hushed, in anticipation of the drops which would finally give up their resistance to the earth. The wind was suddenly brisk and business-like, blowing in rain drops from the outside, confused visitors bringing disorder into the neatened order of my room, blowing my hair across my face. I pushed the hair out of my eyes, my mouth was fuzzy.

'How are you feeling now?'

'Alive.' He laughed, a wry laugh that ended up being a grimace.

'How did this happen?'

He laughed again, his eyes faded with pain, the whiteness of his skin pale beneath the bits that were now sunburnt, his nose, his forehead.

'A supplier,' he replied, wincing slightly, struggling to lift himself to an upright position. 'I probably stirred some nests. An acquaintance led me to people who knew something about how your husband died. It was a hit job, ordered by someone really powerful. I don't have a name, but the man wanted Nihar dead within a day. They killed Nihar and made it look like an overdose, your aunt got the postmortem report changed to heart attack....'

I didn't want to hear more. I didn't want to know more. I'd just about started layering over the wounds of losing Nihar, this was opening it, picking out the encrusted scab and letting the blood flow again.

'They suddenly decided to knife me. Luckily, a police van drove up just as they began on their hit job. They left me for dead. Luckily, I could drag myself up to the road and hire a taxi to get me to the ferry. Bosco from the ferry got me home on his bike.'

'You could have called. Gone to the hospital.'

'And had a police case out of it, and enquiries about what I was doing hanging out with these disreputable sorts? What could you have done from here? And I'm fine, it's nothing serious, just a scratch. But we know now Nihar's death was definitely murder, not an overdose, not a heart attack. Don't you want to know who did it and why? What do you want to do now?'

I put a finger to his lips. It didn't matter anymore. 'Nothing. It's over. Nihar is gone. I can't get him back. I can't risk losing you too.' I stroked his forehead and laid my head on his chest. The weight on my shoulder disappeared, followed by the faint hiss of something moving through the air straight up to the ceiling. I raised my head. Nihar was up, looking down at us, his eyes pools of hate that sucked my soul towards his. I shut my eyes.

Victor's eyes followed my gaze. 'What's there?'

'Nothing,' I replied. 'I thought I heard something on the roof.'

I looked up again, there was nothing there, not even the diminishing shadow of something receding into another dimension.

The thin shirt he had on clung damply to his torso. The fan whirring overhead did little to dispel the sultriness of the air. Lucy came in, on footsteps that had learnt to become soundless after all these years of being obsequious. She coughed, and we moved apart. She brought a glass of water with the medicine he was supposed to take. 'Doctor said to give this to Baba three times in the day.' Antibiotics. Painkillers. He struggled to sit up and swallowed obediently. 'Doctor will come to change the dressing in the evening. No bath. No water.'

'What'll you eat?' she asked him. 'It's afternoon now. Both of you people have not eaten. Lunch is ready. I made dal khichdi for you.' She looked at Victor pointedly. 'Only light food, doctor said. I'll get it up.'

'Do bring some food for me too,' I requested her. She nodded, cracking a smile. 'You can leave him alone, you know. Nothing will happen to him, no one will carry him away.'

I was torn between being sharp with her, and laughing at her impertinence. I settled for the latter. 'I'd like to see someone carry him away. That would need some bicep strength.' She squinted at me suspiciously and left the room, perhaps the word bicep confused her, threatening to come back with food which we were not to waste under any circumstances given how expensive everything was. This statement was accompanied by a dire accusatory look at me, given I'd barely played with the food on my plate at my last meal and then abandoned all attempts at eating it. She'd taken it personally as an affront to her culinary skills. I needed to reassure her it was simply the result of the digestive system not being the same ever since I'd ingested more than the requisite amount of salt water after my toss into the ocean.

Victor sat up gingerly, examining the bandage on his torso with some curiosity. His hair tumbled to his shoulders, catching the morning light streaming in through the windows, framing his head in a golden nimbus. He made me catch my breath, his beauty that was so rough-edged and unaware of itself. He was unkempt, his jaw bristly with a couple of days of stubble on it, his torso bare, his body sweaty from the humidity.

'How bad is the cut?'

'Not too bad, it needed a little needlework,' I replied, lying through my back teeth. 'Should be healed in a few days.'

'It feels like hell. And there's the hangover to add to my misery.'

'Why would you want to find out?'

'I thought it would help you, give you closure.'

'I have my closure, I don't want to know. What will I get by finding out? I can't get him back. I don't want to know, you should have just let it be.'

'You mean to say I almost got my lung punctured for nothing.'
I laughed.

'You shouldn't have bothered. There's nothing I want to know about Nihar's death,' I told him. There was a shower to be taken, a bathroom visit to be made, and my night dress was still stained with the blood from his wound. I wasn't at my best, I was sure of that. But there was a strange comfort with Victor that made it irrelevant. He'd already pulled me out of the sea, and seen me puking my lungs out. Nothing could be more unappealing.

The water was warm in the taps and the sputtering shower was tepid and strangely relaxing. Through the slats in the bathroom I could see Da Costa working on the car as he always did, the two dogs moving around the grounds, barking at random things, a bird, a car driving down the road, the boys playing football in the ground around the corner. When I emerged, Victor wasn't in my bed, he'd moved to his own room. The house was perched on a little hill, a slight elevation from sea level, I could see the gentle river curving its way past from the little balcony the room opened out into, stately and measured in its undulating progress, a matronly restraint in her movements.

I went out there on the balcony after I'd showered. The cool breeze blew into me, a collision I welcomed. Before me, broad strokes of green and blue, as the sky and the trees strained against each other. In the distance the approaching grey wall of a monsoon cloud formation could be seen, marching onwards like an approaching army. I knew there would be a storm today.

A moth flew into the room and settled on the wall. The eyes on its wings glared at me malevolently. It was a strange time of day for a moth to come in, in the morning, with the sun out. Bad omens, Maa used to say, and they always sought her out, fluttering in from the cold and the fog, their wings beating frantically until they found a spot where they could stay put undisturbed. Next to her, next to me, we were of another world, both Maa and me, and they sensed that.

The band of burnt flesh around my wrist still stung. I applied some aloe vera gel on it. The gel evaporated from the heat my wrist gave off. There were no flames but my wrist was still on fire.

Lucenzia came into the room, knocking politely at first, then discarding all pretence to politeness and pushing the door open without waiting for a response. 'Coming down to hall room? Fadder's come to meet you.'

I splashed some water on my face and tied my hair off my face. It had grown down to my waist now, straight and thick. I went down the stairs to the parlour or what she termed the hall room. I noticed the cobwebs beginning to accumulate in the high corners near the ceiling.

There was a man with her, a priest by the looks of it, by the air of authority he exuded. He was in civvies. A neatly pressed pair of trousers, shiny where the fabric had worn out from overuse, with a shirt bleached yellow by overzealous administration of whitening agents. This was Father Dominic, I guessed, the priest of the small parish of a couple of kilometres and a village that had as many families as you could count on the fingers of both hands.

'Kamlababy,' Lucenzia said, altering what she called me to suit the tide. I felt nothing like a baby and had no idea why she would feel comfortable infantilizing me like this. 'Dis is Fadder Domnick. He wants to aks you about wot you saw that day in the morning in the graveyard.' It felt like a lifetime ago, what I'd seen in the graveyard. I hadn't gone running since, I realised.

He rose from his seat, came forward and shook hands efficiently.

'Good morning, Father,' I said, gesturing for him to be seated on the settee that was part of the room, with the two single chairs adjoining them. 'How can I help you?'

He was a thickset man with a face on which the strains of mercy from the heavens had descended rather heavily and had pulled it down to the earth. His expression was one of perpetual anguish. He pulled out a handkerchief and dabbed at his face meticulously.

'So sorry for disturbing you. And my deepest condolences on your aunt's demise. She was a wonderful lady, so full of life.'

I shuddered for the faithful parishioners condemned to bear his eloquence at the Sunday mass. 'Yes, indeed,' I replied, 'she is dead, and there's nothing to be done about it.' There was another man with him. He wore the oiliness that came from a life in public service for self-service. 'Meet our local corporator, Jayvant Naik.' Mr Naik smiled and joined his palms together politely, his hands were chubby and encrusted with thick gold rings. His teeth revealed a gutka habit.

'Pleased to meet you, madam. Nice house, your aunty left for you.'

As far as opening lines went, this one was guaranteed to raise hackles. I joined my palms in return, not bothering to reply.

He continued undaunted. He was not, it would seem, a man who waited for answers. 'I have an investor who wants to buy these old properties. He's willing to pay good money, more than market value. I can bring him here tomorrow and finalise the deal.'

Father Dominic put a hand out. 'Now is not the time, Jayvant. This is a condolence visit.'

There was no condolence I needed from people I did not know. They resumed their seats, the ones they had stood up from when I entered the room. Father Dominic drew a deep troubled breath. 'I believe you were the first one to see that something had been done in the graveyard.'

I nodded. 'I didn't see anything happening, I must confess. When I reached all the graves had already been broken into, the crosses broken. There was no one around.'

He drew another of those troubled breaths and stared at the
floor, trying to find the words that he wanted to say. This was
going to be one of those conversations, I guessed, punctuated
by pauses that stretched on until one wanted to scream.

'That's what is surprising. First three graves were vandalised,
then yesterday five, the remains missing. In the earlier times,
people were buried with jewellery depending on the wishes of
the family. But male graves have also been desecrated and the
remains would have had nothing more than a wedding ring on
them. Most surprising. This has to be the work of outsiders, no
one from the village would do such a thing to their own people.'

He rubbed another weary hand across his brow and shook
his head sadly apropos of nothing.

'I can assure you I wasn't out digging up graves. It's not my
idea of a fun recreational activity,' I said.

He looked at me solemnly. Perhaps he had considered it.

'No, no, no, madam, I'm not saying you did it. I'm
wondering why people would desecrate the graves. The police
are investigating. But I thought I should talk to you and ask you
if you saw anything that day.'

Had I seen anything, I wondered. I had noticed nothing until
Buddy ran into the cemetery through the gap in the wall. And
then there was that odd feeling of being watched as I ran away,
a feeling that still lingered, of someone watching me.

'I really wish I could help you, but all I remember is that it
was around 5.45 a.m., just before sunrise, and for a moment I
did think someone was hiding in the copse of trees just beyond
the other side of the graveyard, where the hill begins sloping
downwards.'

'Did you see anyone? Was it one person or many?' he asked,
sitting up straight, sudden excitement invading his voice.

'I really couldn't make out,' I shrugged, 'There was not enough
light. And then it was a graveyard, it was before sunrise, there

are several things that flit in graveyards in the dark.'

He shook his head trying to collect his thoughts as he spoke.

'A haunting? Hauntings wouldn't bother about digging up the graves, they can go right into the graves you know, if they want to, with no trouble. There is nothing to hide behind there, just one thin line of trees and then a drop down. Just a straight cliff and then a thin beach. And some caves. No one goes there. Rumour has it that the caves are haunted. Most likely though that rumour was probably started to keep inquisitive villagers out from prying around. The caves were once used by gold smugglers. A lot of illegal stuff happens all around. All I can do is try and keep my flock clean and god-fearing. Which is why I hoped you had seen someone, anyone I could track down and speak with. You probably wouldn't recognise anyone, but perhaps you could describe them to me.'

I shook my head to indicate a negative. 'Alas, no, I couldn't see anything or anyone, it was dark in that part of the ground and covered with trees. Also, Buddy began behaving really strangely, pulling me away from there. So after I informed the baker's boy that the graves were dug up, I came back home. And of course, I heard about the desecrations from the house help the next day but had just thought them to be the work of miscreants. Grave thieves.'

Lucy brought in tea and biscuits. It made for an effective lull in the conversation.

'Does the smuggling still happen?' I asked, 'What kind of caves are there?'

Were these the caves of my dreams, I wondered. A small hole on the surface of the earth which led deeper and deeper into a realm that only existed in my dreams.

He shrugged. 'Caves. The river goes in for a bit in a thin stream. Then it is rock, and goes down deep. It used to be the perfect landing spot for illegal activities. Now it has stopped.

The authorities have become strict. But still....' He opened his palms upwards and spread his hands out in supplication. The man next to him snorted in derision.

We continued a desultory conversation that even the vagaries of the weather failed to enliven. After a few well-thought-out reminiscences about Kamini, it was clear that there was absolutely nothing we could chat about anymore. Lucy told the Father in rapid-fire Konkani about the need for the house to have a cleansing. He nodded gravely and promised to come back the next day with whatever he needed to do so, and get it done.

'This is not a Christian-owned house anymore,' he explained to me, but Lucy and Dom were members of the parish so he would do this for them. I was grateful, I said. He asked about Victor. Lucy replied he was asleep, had been out all night. The good Father shook his head solemnly from side to side. 'These boys....'

He turned back to me, the condolence visit seemed to be at a close.

'Thank you, madam. I look forward to meeting you again, I believe you are going to be staying here permanently now?'

A sudden hand of panic clenched my heart. Was I going to be living here permanently now? I didn't know. What was permanent anyway, except where temporary stopped, and weren't we all just temporary in our residence on this planet, in this dimension, anyway?

'I'm not sure right now, I still have commitments elsewhere. I might come and go as required. But for the moment I'm here for a while.' A sudden sense of ownership filled me, right now, at this moment, this house was mine to do as I pleased.

For a man of the cloth, he had all my hackles on high alert. But then what was religion, and the men who peddled it to us, but a bureaucracy between us and God, as a wiser person had once said. He shook my hand and stumbled out on feet, I noticed with a faint surprise, that were ridiculously small for someone his size. It was almost as if the creator had replaced his feet with a child's, and I wondered for a long while how those tiny feet bore the weight of the rather weighty torso he possessed without their bones crumbling to dust. I stood at the window of the parlour, looking out as he walked out towards the main gate, his steps mincing and delicate for all the corpulence he bore. Jayvant walked beside him, his gait all-encompassing with the benevolence that power brings. I knew these men. I had dealt with them once. They came in useful if only you could lay your hands on their secrets, secrets that could destroy them. Jayvant would have some secrets too, I know. Secrets he would do anything, even kill, to keep from being revealed.

I went to Victor's room. He was lying down on his back in bed, his hands behind his head, his hair spread over the pillow, damp skeins of gold catching the stray straggling rays of the evening sun as it entered through the windows that ran the breath of the wall facing the verandah. A gentle breeze blew through, rustling the light curtains.

Victor sat up when he saw me. The movement took effort, the strain showed on his face. Infirmity, even if temporary, is difficult to deal with when one has always been vigorous and healthy. Had Victor always been strong and energetic? Had he been sickly as a child and worked himself into this muscled specimen of manliness in reaction to being constantly bullied, or did it come naturally, his father's genes giving him the height and span of his bulk and his discipline adding the muscles sculpted onto this torso and his limbs. I knew nothing about him. He was a tabula rasa that I coloured up with whatever shades I chose, making him a creature of my imaginations.

'You look refreshed,' he said, 'which is more than what can be said for me.'

His face was washed and the pallor showed.

'Are you feeling any better?' I asked.

'Alive, and that's what is important, I guess.' He smiled, wan and drawn, his face all planes and angles, square jaw and straight nose, strained with the pain.

He reached out, I flinched and moved back, more a reflex action. He stared at me quizzically, took my hand and kissed my wrist, where the burn still blazed, a pain that I had now become inured to. 'Why are you so fragile? Why do I get the feeling that you will shatter if a loud voice comes at you?'

I smiled. 'I'm definitely not going to shatter, don't worry. Try the loudest you can. Nothing you say can shatter me.'

He kissed my wrist again, his voice went soft, very soft. 'Now how did this happen?' I felt a churning begin in my stomach and my mouth drying up in panic.

'I can't explain it, it just did.'

He stared at me quizzically and the thoughts came into his eyes before they came to his lips. I knew I would crumble into motes of dust as the words hit my eardrum.

'You do know I'm going back to London, this has to end,' he said, 'as soon as this wound heals and I get the repair work on the house contracted out.' He paused, looking down, reluctant to meet my eyes, and continued, 'What about you, are you staying on or going back?'

The knife stuck itself into my entrails and twisted around, ripping out vital organs.

'I don't know. I think I'll stay back for a while. There's nothing in Bombay or back home that needs my time or attention. When will you be back?' The question trembled on my lips, the weight of indecision they carried tipping me over the brink with the uncertainty.

'I don't know.'

Hearing him say it was a swift blow to my jaw.

All I could ask was 'Why?'

All he replied was a soft, 'Because Leah's there.'

'Can't you be with both of us?'

He shook his head slowly from side to side, a rejection that was more damning than a push away. I rose and walked out of the room. Perhaps there was nothing to be said, and there was nothing to be heard. Perhaps all we were destined to be were moths to the flame, burn ourselves out in the pursuit of the next light we saw. This light had burnt me out. And all I could do was wait till I rose, phoenix-like, only to be burnt again.

TWENTY-ONE

HERE, NOW

Five Months later

Victor flew back to London as he had promised. Months after he said he would. We slipped into an easy routine, that of a couple, without the permanence of being one. I could deal with it. It was what he was comfortable with. If there was any resentment I felt towards Leah it evaporated when I realised I had taken him away from her for months, and she had not protested. She remained on the horizon of my conscience, lurking. A ghost I ignored. The ghost on my shoulder had gone away. We could love, I realised, without the promise of exclusivity that one had been raised on. And there was no shame or guilt in that, it was just the way the human heart was, four-chambered, with an infinite capacity to contain others, more than it could contain itself.

The house took him in while he was here... the meetings with the architects, drawing up plans, finalising suppliers. The homestay would open in time for the next tourist season, he had decided. I laughed gently at his ambition and nodded along. The interiors were almost done, old furniture had been polished to a gleam, hinges refitted, blackened mirrors replaced, the plumbing changed. The rooms made self-contained with bathrooms and sit-outs. The kitchen was being modernised, with a hob on a central island, and work counters in sleek chrome and granite fringing the room. It drove Lucy crazy, the new obstacle in the middle of the room. The asthmatic fridge was replaced by one that opened down the centre and could fit in a couple of dead bodies. If the house had any protests about being shifted from an indolent private residence to a place that welcomed complete strangers into its confines over and over again, it did not let us know, nor had we asked it for its opinion.

I wasn't very delighted about the influx of people we would have to handle. He was astoundingly confident about our abilities to get this off the ground and make a success of it, ambitious given neither of us had any experience in hospitality. I was carried along by his optimism. Or perhaps I was carried along by him. It is dangerous to be carried along by a person. People change.

He would be back after a couple of months, he just needed to settle a few things so he could focus on this for the next year, he said. The internet kept us connected, conversations that bordered on the perfunctory and focused on the renovation, the lurking shadow of Leah making me circumspect about what I said. If, in some remote pocket of my heart, I hoped for him to break our self-imposed formality, I was disappointed. He remained exceedingly proper online. I sought evidence of affection beyond the commonplace in small signs, a smile, a wink, a 'take care' thrown across casually, but found none. I scavenged in the remnants of the plain, spoken words of our conversations over Skype to find some longing, some missing, and found none. I was practical, a convenience to have there to oversee the work being done in his absence.

'We can run it together,' he said, completely confident in my abilities to be a hotelier, given I had no such confidence in myself. I was a business proposition for him. I knew that. He was fond of me, I knew but it was nothing compared with the overarching obsession I had with him. I appreciated his honesty though, I would settle for fond over disinterest. Like scraps one threw for the dogs from the dinner table, I scrimmaged for words from him that would reveal more than an affection that went beyond the mundane. I didn't find them. I was being needy, clingy, I could see it when I looked at myself. I was also helpless to change what I felt and how I behaved. I hated being not even a second preference, but just a momentary dalliance.

A month before Victor left, Lucy had called in someone she knew who dealt with the afterlife from across the river, from her village. 'I trust him,' she said, when Da Costa questioned this choice over the services of the good priest. The man did a tour of the house, every room. We followed him as he did so, stopping for a much longer time in the room with the blackened tiles. The air in the room was still muggy, thick, like a transparent soup one had to struggle through, lending a strange weariness to one that dissipated the moment one stepped out. He was a tall man, thin like a rail, his skin a deep brown with the sun and the sea, his face that kind of indeterminate which never let one know a person's age. He could be anything between his mid-thirties to his sixties. Mathew, for that is what he was called, was gentle with me, asking me to pray in whatever manner I knew for the peace of the restless souls in the house. I did so, standing in the room with tiles on the floor scorched with unknown hellfire, my body tingling with the sensation of something electric passing through me. He prayed too, words unfamiliar to my ears. I felt the air in the room begin to sift a bit, to lighten. When it was done, he led us out, blessed the room and closed the door. He gave Lucy a jar of salt and instructed her to sprinkle it in every room.

'We might have to give a mass for the souls of the deceased, Lucy will help you speak with the priest for that,' he said. 'If the disturbances continue, do let me know. Lucy, will you call me after a week and let me know if anything has happened again? These are just souls stuck in purgatory who need to be released, there's been no harm to anyone all these years. If this doesn't help, you might want to call in priests to do a proper blessing of the house. There's no need for an exorcism, this isn't demonic activity.'

I thought of the burn on my wrist, my other hand went involuntarily to it. Victor noticed it and took my hand, smiling down at me.

'What if there was harm?' I held up my hand. The faint stripe of a burn scar, newly healed, curled around the wrist, the imprint of a hand not from this dimension.

Mathew took my hand gently and looked at the burn carefully. 'This is worrying. How did this happen?' I told him the story. He touched the burnt area and recoiled.

'You have been marked.'

Lucy crossed herself again. 'I told you,' she said to me, victoriously. 'You didn't believe me.'

'What does that mean?' I asked.

He looked away into the distance, took a long deep breath. His voice, when he spoke, was soft. 'You have been touched by a spirit who wants to take you. Think of it like being possessed, from the outside though, not within you. You have this spirit with you wherever you go, it will find you, and either make you kill yourself. Or....'

His voice trailed off. 'Or what?' Victor asked, putting a hand on my shoulder.

Mathew smiled. It was a smile that was sweet and sad all at once.

'Let it not come to that.'

Victor tightened his grip on my shoulder. 'Are you saying there's a risk to her life?'

'I'm saying she needs to be careful.'

My intestines knotted up in Gordian knots. 'What could happen to me?'

He looked up and straight at me. His eyes bored into mine, searching for something he couldn't find. 'You have invited this

on yourself without understanding the consequences. Only you
can set it right. The next time it shows itself, tell it clearly to go
away. It draws its power from your fear or your need.'

'That's my husband, not an "it".'

'Your husband. Yes, your dead husband.'

Mathew left, pressing a scapular into my hand, asking me
to tie it around my neck. 'I know you follow a different faith,
but this is what my faith has for protection.'

We had the *taveez* that Daadi would reluctantly tie on us
after bouts of severe illnesses, on Behra's insistence. We would
get better, fling them off, only to go back to the tenuous hope
they offered the next time we fell ill again. I tied this one on.
There was faith that defied rationality.

I was always dreaming of finding him in caves, perhaps I
would find him there, I thought. I set out the next afternoon,
slipping out of the house when Victor had blazed out on his hired
Enfield to get into town. It was post lunch, the sun was mottled
and blurred by indifferent clouds that quibbled about whether
they should rain down on the small island or pass it by and reserve
their fury for the mainland. The clouds cast sifting shadows on
the road, in light that dimmed to grey and then lightened to a
pale egg yolk yellow. I walked down the narrow, asphalted road
until I reached the fence that demarcated the graveyard from
the rest of the church grounds, and the narrow gap between the
fence and the wall where Buddy had slipped through the other
day. I went in. The graveyard at noon was not as forbidding as
it had been in the hazy light of the pre-dawn. The graves that
had been desecrated stared on at me, questioning my presence
there at the height of noon. Some of the undesecrated ones had
flowers on them, roses, wildflowers, garlands of marigold. It was
a Monday morning. The flowers must have made an appearance
after Sunday mass. Residual evidence of lives not forgotten, the
guilt of the living spilling over to intrude upon the sleep of the

dead. At the edge of the graveyard, the slight slope of the land leading down and then the steep drop down of the cliff. Below, the faint ribbon of a thin beach, the silica in the sand glinting hard in the harshness of the overhead sun.

The caves were exactly the way I'd dreamt them. A small steep path leading down from the other side of the cemetery, away from the copse of trees, down steps carved into the bare rock face, a string rope fence thoughtfully hammered into the stone of the hill. I'd descended carefully, my heart in my mouth, aware that a single misstep could send me careening down to certain death. The steps curved around and ended on a narrow strip of sand, a beach so clean and white, it glowed, a bay that curved inwards and led on to a yawning maw where the river and the sea merged their offerings and flowed into a nether-worldly darkness.

There was nobody here save the feeling of being watched by a million eyes. Going deeper and deeper into blackness. I had been here before, I was sure of that. The floor was slick with water that came and went with the surge of the tides, and then a sudden shift and the path bent downwards, deeper and deeper, where the sun's rays couldn't bend and turn around rock and stone, walls that were hollowed out from erosion of a kind that the elements had carved into them over aeons. Phosphorescence from life lit up the walls, a dim glow that pulsed, the beat of life. With each step I took, I knew. This was the labyrinth of my dreams, this was why I had come here, this was the pathway to There. I would find him here, this I was sure of. I called his name. Somewhere in the distance, through layers of stone and rock, I could hear the hounds guarding the exits to this dimension, growling, low, deep, menacing growls that chilled me to the bone. I stepped back in fear. Was I prepared to deal with what I might find? I called again, his name echoed off the walls, the sound twisting on itself, sounding alien, unfamiliar. I sat and waited. He would come, I was sure of that. The darkness weighed on me, tiredness overwhelmed me. I felt him before I saw him, standing at the end of the tunnel, just where it bent off. A shadow that shimmered as it swayed, flickering like a hologram that projected itself into my mind. Tears blurred my vision. I had loved him so.

Memories are nothing other than ghosts of our past selves that haunt us. Ghosts are nothing more than memories trying to get our attention. I wrapped my arms around him, and held onto him tightly, afraid that if I let go, if I opened my eyes, he would be gone forever, and he would not hear what I needed to say. I opened my eyes. I held air, fetid, stale air. 'I miss you,' I said, with the earnestness of one who did. What else could one say to a man one thought one would live out one's life with? He stood before me, shimmering, flickering, the walls of the cave visible through him. I had loved him. I had hated him. Somewhere between love and hate was where it had all begun and ended. The fights, the controlling, the gas-lighting, the slow and steady way he had begun cutting me off from the world. And then the physical abuse, the beatings, carefully done so the face didn't show any bruises, and the final blow, the kick in my stomach when I was in my first trimester and leaving me to almost bleed to death alone in a locked house.

The call to inform me that he had been done away with came much before Mohit had called. Almost a day before. I knew it hadn't been a heart attack or a drug overdose or a suicide or an auto-erotic asphyxiation gone wrong. It was a hit job ordered by someone who owed me a major favour from my crime reporting days. No questions asked. I thought I was finally free. What I didn't know was that he wouldn't let me live my life even after he was dead. Here he was, a wraith, standing before me, his arms outstretched, unwilling to let me go on with my life.

'Let me go. Isn't it enough that you made me miserable while you were alive, why won't you leave me alone when you're dead?'

'You know why, Lotusface.'

He began dissolving into dust even as I looked on. The hounds stopped barking in the distance. I felt myself sag to the floor of the caves, my knees buckling under me. When they found me, I'm told, I was sleeping soundly on the patch of sand a little beyond the entrance. It was late in the evening, the stray dogs had been sniffing around me.

'You were in deep sleep, had to put water on your face to wake you up,' Da Costa said. 'Why you went there without telling anyone?'

They were infamous, it was where the dinghies landed, with their contraband of drugs, gold, arms and heaven knows what all. It was why this island was slowly being bought over, it was a convenient landing spot, out of the radar of the coastal patrol. They had worried I would have been in the wrong place at the wrong time when a consignment came in. It was a side of the small state I had only heard about. I never went down to the caves again.

They had also unravelled the mystery of the grave desecrations when they came down to find me, after one of the helpers at the church found it curious enough to mention he spotted me crossing the graveyard at noon. There were heavy implements wrapped and hidden in the corner of one of the caves. The markings on one had led back to a construction site, and a man who had been sacked from his job. It led back to a group and a sordid story of radicalization and the plan to foment communal disharmony for the benefit of the local political heavyweights. And of course, petty thievery, robbing the corpses of the jewellery they had been buried with. I was rather sorry to find there were no black magic practitioners involved. Nor demented individuals trying to free trapped souls, like souls could be contained in graves no matter if they had marbled tombstones.

More desecrations had followed in graveyards across the state in the months to come. Police were still conducting their enquiries. It was us, the alive, who wouldn't let the dead rest in peace.

The weight on my shoulder disappeared after that visit to the caves, I realised later. Nihar had stopped coming to me, both in my dreams and in my wakefulness. It was the scapular, I thought, now wrapped around my wrist. It had sent him away. Perhaps it is best for the dead to remain dead and the living to live out their lives. Something had changed, sifted. I wore my skin independently now, nothing sifted beneath it, waiting to take me over.

Vikram came to visit, sometime in the thick of the monsoon. He arrived one afternoon with a single duffel bag and mussed-up hair, drenched to the bone. It had been quite a journey for him. He'd messaged, and I'd told him I was on an island in Goa, and named it. He'd tracked me down. I wasn't hard to find, I guessed. It was strange, sharing the house with two men who were my lovers. He stayed for days, strange days where all we did was chat with each other. It was too rainy to move out of the house, so we stayed within, with the garden creatures that slithered in seeking refuge from the wetness, snails, earthworms, little grass snakes. We sat on the porch and watched the raindrops hit the elephant leaves hard, the grounds converted into rivulets of squelchy red earth. He tried hard to convince me to go back with him to Delhi. 'Not now,' I told him. 'Not yet.'

'When?' he asked, his face concerned.

'I don't know, but not yet. I'm not ready for Delhi yet, I need to be away.'

'Whenever you want to come back, let me know. Come straight to my place. There's no bother if you have no place to go.'

I had a home, tenants lived there now, the rent got credited into my account every month, it left me with nothing to do to earn a living.

I had no place I wanted to go to, I told him. I was happy here. He didn't understand. Nor did Victor.

'How can you be happy staying here in the middle of nowhere? Is there someone else?' It didn't even cross his mind that I could be in some way involved with Victor, even though I'd introduced them.

'No,' I said. It was the truth. There was no relationship with Victor. Just as there was none with Vikram. He left, taking with him his bag and his earnestness, as well as his offer to take me with him. The sky, clouded over with darkness, split with lightning as Da Costa drove him out to the ferry. I watched him go, wondering whether I would ever take him up on his offer, whether it would be sensible to do so.

Was it possible to love someone even though the person didn't love you back? Was this love I felt for Victor, in the strange disjointed way that I knew how to love, warily, handing across bits and pieces of myself, watching how he handled them before entrusting him with more of me. Some he dropped, some he flung away, but for the most, he had gathered most bits of me to him and tried to make me whole.

'What have you decided?' I had asked Victor one morning over breakfast. It had been four months since we had both come here, three and a half months since Kamini's death. He would leave three months later, but that morning was when I'd realised things had changed irrefutably.

'Nothing yet. What about you?'

I shook my head. I needed to get back to Bombay, to the flat with the locked front door and the sunlight streaming in through the leaves of the tree just outside the window. It was tempting to fall off the planet and continue living here like this, waiting for one day to segue into the next. I had spent four months here on the island, after Kamini had died. Four months of falling off the grid.

We were sitting at the table for two by the window in the little parlour. It looked out onto the curve of the road, and the gush of the river that flowed beyond the gentle drop down to the flat lands that led to the marshes. When the wind changed direction it brought the smell of the river with it. I was pushing around an omelette with a slice of soft pao, wondering why I was so constantly nauseated. It was the skanky smell of the river and the marshes, I told myself. I moved my chair. I had no appetite.

'Why aren't you eating?' he asked.

'I can't seem to keep anything down,' I replied, rushing to the washbasin to throw up yet again. The breakfast on my plate went untouched. The smell of food being cooked wafting in from the kitchen was unbearable. 'It's probably this constant smell of paint and varnish, it's making me nauseous.' We were living in a swarm of ladders and paints, carpenters and sawdust, masons and stone sheets piled discreetly against walls. Kamini's works had been shifted to a safe storage space.

'I should take you to Dr Pinto, perhaps you're coming down with some bug.'

I nodded distractedly, counting back in my head, days and months and the blooming of red between my thighs, a horrible realisation dawning on me. It couldn't be. How silly and irresponsible could I be. I needed to visit a chemist.

I had the car taken out that evening ostensibly to visit Panjim to stock up on essentials and rushed to the chemist along the promenade. A bigger city, a bigger chemist, someone I didn't know, wouldn't visit too often. It was early evening. The cruise boats gleamed, decorated with fairy lights and enlivened with live bands playing local Goan folk songs, and girls in local folk costumes danced to them, while tourists went down the Mandovi for a couple of hours of empathetic jollity. The river rolled against the banks going out to the maw of the sea, sedate and matronly. The world went about its business, uncaring of the churn within me.

The chemist handed over the pregnancy test kit to me with no expression on his face. I picked up some other stuff I didn't need. Creams. Sunblock. Aspirins. Anti-depressants. Sleeping pills. Never know when they would come in handy.

I returned home and sat in the bathroom, waiting for the second line to change colour as I knew it would. I watched it form before my eyes. Chemical proof of life in my uterus. There was enough and more contraception available to ensure that sperm and egg didn't meet, from prophylactics, to pills, to morning-after pills. I knew when it had happened. He'd forgotten to pull on a condom, as he always did, spare the first time when neither of us had factored sex into our itineraries. I had pulled him deeper into me as he came. I remembered the night, dark and moonless, the burn still fresh on my wrist. There's always a reason why, I told myself. There had been no morning-after pill. Not the next morning. Not the morning after that. I hadn't forgotten, I had tempted fate.

I came out of the bathroom, keeping the test strip on the dressing table next to the bed, and went out into the balcony. Night had fallen outside, the birds were flying back in formation to the nests they had abandoned in the morning. The evening crickets had begun their chorus. On the distant horizon, a tinge of orange heralded the lingering sunlight, still sinking clumsily into the waters. I clutched my belly. I imagined a beat, a thudding, a vociferous shout of life pulsing through my palms.

I didn't hear him come into the room. He moved pretty soundlessly for a man his size. I smelled him before I heard him, the faint muskiness of his sweat mingled with his aftershave, a muskiness that always made me want to pull him into me, hard, thrusting. But now, at this moment, there was only a yearning to be held and soothed. I turned around and looked at him. His eyes were cold and angry, pinpoints of steel.

'Is it mine?' he asked.

I slapped him across the face with all the might I could summon.

'How dare you even ask? Don't you know I've been here with you for these past four months?'

He rubbed his cheek. 'Do you want to have the baby?' There was nothing I wanted more in my life. I nodded.

'I'm having this baby.' I didn't know why, but I knew I would go through with this pregnancy, this birth.

He tilted my face up to him and stared at me. Ice blue, the pupils pinpricks in an ocean of blue. I fell into them, floating, buoyed. I closed my eyes. 'Look at me,' he said. His voice was tense. 'Do you want us to get married? I can do that. We can get married if we agree to get divorced after a couple of years. I don't want any child of mine to be born a bastard.'

His voice got tauter, his accent clipped, losing the lilt of India it had acquired over the past few weeks. I could see the scar on his chest, now shining pink with new skin under his half-opened shirt that billowed in the gentle breeze that came in through the open balcony doors.

I shook my head. 'That doesn't matter to me. It won't matter to my child.'

'Are you sure?' I nodded. I didn't want marriage. I wanted him. But for that he had to want me. I was prepared to wait till he did. There was a dignity in waiting, that reaching out and grasping did not bring. The relief came off him in waves. I could feel a tear beginning its journey from the corner of my right eye, trickling down my cheek, and the next one from the left. Then they were a drizzle, and a torrent coursing down my checks, splashing onto my chest, leaving little droplet stains on the cotton fabric.

'Don't cry,' he gathered me to him, laughing, saying, 'What are we going to do?'

I pulled back. 'You are going to do nothing. I am going to

have this baby, with or without you.'

'You're not doing this alone. I'm here', he said, pulling me back to him. I nestled against him, hearing his heart beat against my ears. Stolid, strong, reassuring. He was here. He said he would be here. And now he wasn't. But I was here. He would be back, sometime, and I would be waiting. Outside, the winter sun was breaking the sky into bands of shimmering yellow and gold.

'When are you going back to Bombay? When are you coming home?' Maa would ask when she called.

'I don't know', I would reply. Honestly, I didn't know. I felt tied to this house. Home was no longer home, nor the home up in the mountain town, not the home in the city down on the banks of a meandering river where the pollution had citizens wear masks in order to breathe. This was home now, this mouldering villa, with its high ceilings, and green grounds, its balcony, and the monkeys running riot through them. I felt beholden to it, a home given to one when one was still finding oneself was an imposition, an imprisonment. I felt compelled to stay here, there was a trust reposed in me by Kamini that I could not betray. But was it what I really wanted? To live out my days here, the rest of my life, on this island, measuring the passing of time not with days but by the seasons and the shift of light from the sun's rays coming into my room.

I instinctively put my hand to my stomach. I was not showing yet, or at least not in the loose sundresses I had adopted since I'd decided to settle here. Whom did I trust? No one. Did Victor know? What had he found out about the day Nihar died? Had he asked too many questions of men who were quick with knives, had my name come up? Why couldn't he leave well enough alone, why did he need to dig up, to try to find me closure when the only closure I needed was to deal with the guilt. Victor's absence was like a disembowelment. Luckily, I was writing again. But the words were flowing sporadically, a tap that had been choked up and was suddenly spurting water. They came to me at the oddest moments—while I was sitting on the edge of the hill, looking down to where the slope gently curved into the river bank, when taking long walks in the morning, past the little houses, the lives within unspooling day by day, as mine was, only to reach a point where they would end, as I would.

I had a routine now. I would wake up, go for a short walk until I felt breathless and come back, Buddy with me, refusing to be leashed as always, barking when cars came around a bend. I would return to the house, bathe, have breakfast that I hoped would stay down. Once the first trimester was done, I was ravenous. I was eating for two or three or four, the stomach was perennially gurgling with the demand to be fed. The afternoon would be spent at my desk in my room, at the window, the upper edge of the laptop the delineator beyond which my patch of island unfolded to my view. I wrote, or tried to write. The manuscript was submitted, the edits were being done, chapter by chapter. On some days I sat and looked out of the window, seeing and unseeing. Ideas floated in my head, ideas I needed to pin down to words, sentences, paragraphs, chapters. The burst of a parrot escaping the green of a mango tree in the garden was a story by itself, the gathering of the storm clouds on the distant horizon, roiling and prescient in the damage they could inflict, an epic in the retelling.

The retreating monsoon was on us, ferocious in its last burst. The dampness seeped through everything. The smell of the marshes came floating in on the breeze and poked its tendrils into corners of the house. The ferry didn't cross on some days when it poured too much and the tide came in. Those days were spent huddled indoors, wrapped in clothes to keep the chill away. There was a chill that came from water that seeped in through the skin and dissolved bone. Creatures from the damp earth emerged from their homes in the ground, slithering away on the damp overgrown grass, onto the stairs, the patio and squirming their way into the house. Survival, it was, risking being squashed underfoot over being drowned in their homes. Earthworms, snails, small snakes, insects. Life survived seasons and inundations, and poured itself out onto higher ground. The islanders watched the flood marks carefully on the bridge when it rained and the tides came in. There was always the church to run to if the water threatened to rush in, there was solace in the divine. I didn't believe in religion anymore. All I had was a wary belief that there were more things in heaven and earth, as the Bard said, that one could explain. And perhaps we were not meant to explain these, perhaps we were only meant to experience these, live through them, and emerge, bearing on our bodies and our souls the carbuncles of the lived experience, now fastened onto our selves.

It wasn't something I'd bargained on, getting pregnant. And there was Leah, unaware, on the other side of a long-haul flight across oceans, mountains, continents, cultures. Victor would go away and be back, I knew, there was too much at stake here and I was a caretaker he hadn't factored in. I was waiting.

'I have to tell her in person,' he'd said. 'I'll be back soon,' he promised. Words that went into my ears and emerged out from the other side of my head without being processed. He would be back. He would keep me docile and placid, and in love with him until it suited him, then perhaps he would try to get rid of me, buy my stake out, or worse. Falling in love with him was an inconvenience, an iron ball around my ankle. Perhaps, to him, I was an inconvenience too. I'd surpassed my utility. Pregnant. With child. Encumbered. Heavy footed, as they said in Hindi. *Barefoot and Pregnant,* as went the title of one of my favourite books. I could feel the stretch within me, a ticking in my uterus, a time bomb biding its time to become flesh and blood and human. The womb contained what I'd never thought I would carry to fruition. Not this. Not like this. A moment of lust spinning itself out into a lifetime in the flesh.

The size of a little dark spot on the ultrasound, a blob of rapidly dividing flesh and cells in my uterus, a zygote, a morula, a blastocyst, an embryo and, soon, a foetus. Within a few months, a baby, kicking and straining against the walls of my uterus, eager to be released into this world. My stomach swelled up, a protuberance that leached the flesh off my bones, the energy into itself. And one day, a quiet morning as I lay down after a light breakfast, a slight kick, then a flurry of little punches to the wall of my abdomen. I put my hand there, soothing my baby.

It's okay, I said, to ears which were yet to form completely, which could hear me through layers of skin, fat, uterine wall, and amniotic fluid. 'I'm here, I will take care of you.' It was a boy in my womb, I knew that. A boy with Victor's blue eyes and square jaw, and my peachy skin. He would run around this house, barefoot, climb the trees in the grounds like his father had done before him. He would grow up and have his skin kissed by the sun into gold. The salt of the ocean would flow in his blood and he would know nothing of the darkness of the caves below the earth his mother had wandered within. I could feel the rush of relief flooding me. I was finally free.

And then it happened. A flurry of punches to the side of my abdomen. His voice in my head calling me. 'Lotusface....' The beating inside my womb, a heart. Tiny. Insistent. I am. I am. The sudden rapid thudding of my own with the realisation. We are. We are.

ACKNOWLEDGEMENTS

This book is a special one in many ways. It is a book that has clawed itself out of me, a story that wanted to be told. Like *The Face at the Window*, and *Missing, Presumed Dead*, this too has hacked away chunks of me, and smelted it down into the words that appear in it.

There are many people I am grateful to for this book, and indeed my entire writing journey. It would be remiss of me to not thank them, for all that they bring to my life, and the invaluable support and courage they provide me.

My family. My husband, Kirit, gratitude for never providing me feedback on my books. He knows I won't take it seriously.

My son, Krish, for the wisdom he brings to all his sixteen years. I draw on it often when I sit to plot and keep throwing options and plot twists at him.

My mother, Shama Sheikh, for making sure I had enough books to read through a childhood where I went through one book a day, which was a demonic pace for a young child in the age of no Kindle and instant downloads. The Bandra in this book is dedicated to her, a true blue Pereira from Bandra.

My mother-in-law, Leela Manral, for making sure the house runs on autopilot when I sit to write. This writing would not have been possible if the drudgery of the day-to-day kept intruding and I owe her immensely. Also, in this book, the mountains I write about, and in my previous books, *The Face at the Window* and *Missing, Presumed Dead*, I owe to her talking to me about life there over the years.

My sisters-in-law, Pramila, Chanda and Tara, for all they pamper and indulge me.

My wonderful editor, Rashmi Menon at Amaryllis, who has been such a champion of my writing, and who has consistently made me feel cherished and loved as both a person and an author. I will always come to you with my books from the heart, the ones I write from my blood and dreams. To Bidisha Ganguly, for going through this one with a fine-toothed gaze. To Mishta Roy of Drawater. For yet another haunting, evocative cover.

To Vikas Rakheja and Manoj Kulkarni at Amaryllis. For the unstinting support for my writing that refuses to neatly box itself into convenient genres. These are challenges for publishers to take, and I am so thankful to you for taking them.

I would also be remiss if I didn't thank Priyanka Chaturvedi, Parul Sharma and Ashwin Sanghi. Priyanka and Parul for getting me started on this journey. And Ashwin for insisting that I continue writing when I had all but given up after my first.

To all those who read my books, thank you. For believing in my stories. What else does a writer want but someone to listen to them, to read their words, and to believe in the stories they tell.

www.ingramcontent.com/pod-product-compliance
Lightning Source LLC
Chambersburg PA
CBHW022350020726
47500CB00002B/204